MEMOIRS AND MEMEMORMEES

To Mum, Dad and Alison

MEMOIRS AND MEMEMORMEES

KEITH MORTON

M&N PUBLISHING
HUDDERSFIELD

© Copyright 1996
Keith Morton

The right of Keith Morton to be identified as the author of this work has been asserted by him in accordance with the Copyright, Designs and Patents Act 1988.

All rights reserved. No reproduction, copy or transmission of this publication may be made without written permission. No paragraph of this publication may be reproduced, copied or transmitted save with the written permission or in accordance with the provisions of the Copyright Act 1956 (as amended). Any person who does any unauthorised act in relation to this publication may be liable to criminal prosecution and civil claims for damages.

First published in 1996 by M & N Publishing Co. Ltd
3 Lion Chambers, John William Street, Huddersfield HD1 1ES

Bound and Printed in Great Britain by
Edgar Woffenden Printers, Birkby, Huddersfield

Designed by Ian Chatterton
975 Leeds Road, Deighton, Huddersfield HD2 1UP

Paperback   ISBN 1 899865 21 7

Keith Morton

Chapter One

Every day I disappoint myself, without fail my commitments conspire to prostitute my creativity. Come clean, I know more about selling myself short and my image long than actually making anything of that self. In short, I know more, infinitely more about prostitution than creativity: my venality serves as a prophylactic against my going soppy and striving to embody any true worth, or any of that existentialist hokum. I'm a victim and, like it or not, I'm good at it. Now we're talking.

I am, as a rule, ruled by my base thoughts: the lower these sink the higher my star, though I am ever mindful that an excess of this brutally simplistic credo, no matter how crassly efficacious, is malpractice. It doesn't always do to think it's so smart to seem so stupid. No, I disappoint myself because I don't fuck every girl – fuck it, *everything* – I meet. Around these inauspicious, indeed wretched mundanities I would beg your indulgence as I strive to fashion a morality tale. Fuck that! My kind of audience. Let me make it quite, quite plain: I seek to pervert rather than convert because, by the looks of you, given that head start, the former will be easier. Besides, it's more fun this way. Who am I to pervert you? Tell that to the rest. I'm you, that's who I am. You. Just you. Only you. Only more so.

The given name is David. Dave to my parents. Perverse. Crucial to this tale, perversity. Fairbrother's the surname. It's not my dad's fault, he was a nice bastard. He was though, in both, um, recognised senses of the word. I'm his son alright. Born out of wedlock, in the once so prurient they've now turned blind, eyes of the law. If plod weren't so blinkered and strait-jacketed by duplicitous strait-laced connivances he'd know how to insult me with impunity, adding inevitable injury for good measure, he'd see my sin and hate this left-field, outright sinner. Free as a jailbird in flight, that's me, singing songs of freedom, informing on my fellow incarceratees. No, not that kind of informing. What do I do? It's not immoral, no, but it's not moral either. Definitely more not moral than not immoral. Luckily I'm amoral. So that's it then, a lucky bastard, a no good made good, an adman's dream. No, not quite.

I am an Oxford graduate. Got sent to this posh finishing school for being *primus inter pares*, top of the class in deriding authority of those environmentally challenged chums I can just about now bring myself to term my coevals. A smart bastard. Funny that, the toffs treasuring a brat like me. Benevolent? Enlightened self interest? No, merely stupid. Reminded them of their own blessed issue, I wouldn't doubt. Stupidity. Crucial to this tale, stupidity. Me, I'm still cocking a snook at authority. I'll leave you to judge which of us is more stupid. I *need* you to judge which of us is the more stupid.

My business, crudely and appropriately, is exploitation. Mainly of women, most would say. That's put it bluntly and, to put it more bluntly I would love, no, I would welcome the chance to put it more bluntly. What's my line? Not the type to admit to, let alone on to normal TV (increasingly the oxygen of moronity, of course), that's what. Pornography, that's my line, my main line. Not the soft focus, peach fuzz *ersatz* Victoriana your average mug punter can legally, if ever furtively purchase in this despairing council estate of a country, but the *echt* goods, the Scando-Latin-Saxon deep breath of fresh air that so characterises and motivates most of us this post permissive age, if we would but admit it. Mind you, it's still bowdlerised. I'm no patriot (Dr Johnson, if a scoundrel, was right, and I'm Scottish on my distaff side: my mother loved her country so dearly she left it on gaining the ability to walk) but I fully understand *The Sun* combining tits and union jackass shorts. And that's just the lads. That said, that's not my thing. My primary objection to such chauvinistic love of the mother country is that she, she of the tits, should be sucking an Italian stallion off to the caption 'The European in Me', if the greatest of our great national scandal sheets could stomach such scandal, such *lèse majesté*. If that strikes one as the exploitative trivialisation of a serious issue, *mea culpa*, my country's son for sure.

In my eyes my prosilient sin would seem to be that I personalise my beliefs, superstitions, hates, loves. Where most are satisfied to hold them dearly and fearfully at arm's length, to employ the photoset patois of my trade, if I'm a wanker they are self-molestors. I live with the lady I love, love with the lady I live. Used to be her pimp, after a fashion. Used to be? After a fashion? Hypocritical, both. Used to be, yes, after a fashion, still am. Thankfully she decided to give it up. I would never presume to presume upon another that way, not even one so close, so close at hand. Suzi, with an 'i', she's insisted ever since a photographer's insistence (and who am I to tell her it should be without an 'e'), that's the wife. Not a graduate, not a better class of person than I. A better person, though.

So, I'm biased, but you'll come to agree, of that there can be no doubt. Suzi is, ah, everything a pornographer could wish for in a wife. But to me she's more, much, much more. She is poetry at repose, and I don't mean 'in bed'. In bed, well, when she whispers in my ear "time to get up" she awakens the poet in me. Up to work, I mean. Disgusted? That someone in my insidious line should recognise poetry in his cool, cold, calculating heart? Is it better to have cold feet? Can an innocent man write poetry? Still uncomfortable? That the love of my life inspires me, her keep to acquire, to degrade others not entirely dissimilar to her less good self? That's life and increasingly these days, that's love. Love it or leave it, live it or fake it. Like I said, I'm you, only more so.

Suzi is mine, I'm hers. The rest – you – are merely on the bedazzled periphery of our lifestyle, you are the penumbra that blindly defines, delineates, describes our star. I expect you feel the same about me, about us, about us all. Only natural: we are of less import to each other, oh!, we autarkical souls, than are our consumer endurables, our communities have developed a built in obsolescence that would fix a smile on the ferocious beast about to become the wallet of the Chief Executive of the *Consolidated Edison* company, light-bulb division. Indeed, self-vindication has so become insouciant invidiousness it is a matter of some marvel that the inevitable dinosaur that was ever the Soviet bloc survived so long beyond its sell-by, its selflessly appointed extinction date. The catchpenny triumph of the west wasn't so much a victory over totalitarian censorship – for its own censorship, that over the imagination of the majority of its citizens, blinkered so that, high days and holidays aside, they never need see past the end of their noses, has finally proved more efficient – as a throwing in of the towel by an avaricious manager on behalf of the punch-drunk exponent of the noble art of community: if these poor schleppers were to take such a beating at least grant them professional status, the better to compete and, vitally, the better to reap. I am part and parcel of, participant in that world. My sin, as personally perceived, is just that admission; as perceived by *my* society, by the company I am disallowed from keeping, it is that I am the 'prime purveyor all that is degrading and disgusting in this world', as one of my detractors put it recently in a national tabloid that surely knows about these things. Would that they were right! Ever! For instance, if they had but told the truth in this instance I would be the richest man in the world. Well, as rich as their proprietor, the credible cretins' incredible Croesus. And if, as they propagandise, the tabloids told the truth about most everything they would be financially bankrupt. Moreover, were this easily influenced sphere of influence we call our world a vat of veracity, intoxicating its imbibers in the manner of a drink or sink truth drug, we'd all be teetotal. Heady stuff, truth. Too heady. Would certainly bankrupt me. Alas, it's no good dreaming, not now.

Suzi and I live in the demi-detached-monde that is the metropolis's foremost *fauborg*. Essex, of course. Where else for the likes of us? Vegas? Not crass enough. There the houses are business concerns catering for transient populations whose singularly uniform, yet wholly indecorous taste, while benighted, is perceived as conservative, tactful, almost cultured in the light of the surrounding leisure complex pyrotechnics. You can't be anyone in Vegas, the place trains so may spotlights on itself that those peopling it take on a doe-eyed acquiescence at the next approaching show-stopping knockout blow to the senses. I am not the man to put the virtu into virtual reality, but, then, who is? No, I like to be in charge of my environment and any pyrotechnics in the vicinity of my star, my status.

In my adopted part of the world – and the adoption is mutual: 'Essex welcomes flash bastards' ought to be the county motto – you've really got to get to know that the Joneses are arriviste swankers with more cars in their garages than cells in their brains; this knowledge is crucial to out-performing them in the little, yet all important matters of the new status rituals. It takes time and its latest upstart neoligism, plenty K, to outgross and *ersatz* Georgian rococo (wrong George, but who's counting *that*) mansion detached from reality, set in landscaped grounds, laagered by topiary apparently in homage to *Disney* characters which would give that yet to be anthropomorphised fabulous beast, the honest estate agent, his version of the casuist's nightmare that is pause for genuine evaluation. Yes, the place, my place, like Essex, my county, takes the breath away. Like a kick in the solar plexus. Speaking of which: where else in the world can one enjoy 10 lagers, 10 *English* lagers, a fight, a curry ordered in that aggro argot that is a hellish teratosis of *lingua franca* and patois adopted by all self-regarding smart bastards; namely, parochialism, provincialism, nationalism crossing the border on xenophobia, and still get subservience? Further, get served breakfast in bed by the legitimately wary yet undeniably glamorous missus one beat up and spectacularly, gallantly, manfully failed to rape the night before? No, that's where you would be wrong: the Islamic states which tolerate alcohol have more reverence for their womenfolk. Not that one indulges in all of the aforesaid. Not every night. I freely admit to being a tyrant in boardroom and bedroom. I'd be a tyrant in the broom closet too if that would get me anywhere. Simply put, I fully accept the challenge our society obliges its denizens to face. No, I accept it with one reservation; I dreamily reject its necessity while never dreaming to deny its existence. Any metaphysician metaphorists out there who see in that a cry for help which, through the vicissitudes of life working above, beneath and beyond this person, has manifested itself in hysterical delirium — can — can congratulate themselves on doing their sums.

We've got all the mod cons, of course. And, yes, I am keenly aware that the pejorative interpretation of that phrase justly predominates. In spite of being so readily spouse led and suckered by the market, the homestead isn't quite the monstrosity alluded to as the bide-a-wee to put the wind up the Joneses (though I don't doubt it and they exist, and somewhere nearby). Rather, I'd like to think of it as a fastidious monument to the sharp practice of Thatcherite opulence: something in the way of a homage, in fact. Besides the business it was, like all my dwellings past and present, substantially funded by property deals. Not counting the weekend château in Provence (strictly between thee and me, neither does the taxman), this is my eighth *pied-à-terre* in the 13 years since I started getting it right. That was in '82. That's where I wish to commence the story of my life. Skip the formative years, the schooling, the university life; life begins at the 40 plus hour week. What now follows will be relayed in the third person, the better to disassociate myself from getting too personal and, who knows, who knows, breaking down on you.

Chapter Two

The stairs presented a threatening series of gradients which could only possibly be negotiated individually with singular care and alertness. A number of precipices, each, with dizzyingly mounting paradox, succeeding in degrees of jeopardy their loftier predecessor, declined seemingly *ad infinitum*. His mother bellowed from the bowels of the scullery like some hostess from a game show shot in Hades, incidentally peopled by an invited audience of nightmare relatives, in case there could be any doubt as to the location.

"Come on down, love, I've made you a fry up."

Oh Lord, he didn't know what did for him most, his mother's heart attack special sizzling furiously, or last night's bubbly, his first ever. No contest; he was planning on getting used to the champagne.

"Your auntie Ida's just discovered a half-empty (aha!) bottle of Moat and Chanson," shouted his father. Not yet.

Last night David Fairbrother had come home to kith, kin and Barnsley for the first time in six months. Clutching the banister he would sail down as an innocent a lot less than a lifetime ago, he vowed that, on somehow lowering his corpus down these drops, this Schröder's staircase, resurrected he would take the upwardly mobile flight of no return. The reason behind this valedictory visitation to haunts long since disavowed, if not quite yet disowned, was as necessary as it was symbolic. The necessity? He had just graduated from Oxford – *2:2* in politics and history – and his parents, while denied an invite to the graduation ceremony proper, had all but demanded to see him. Parents, you can't choose 'em, he shrugged. Lose them, yes: that, he fully intended to do, just as soon as he had done with this, his last duty as a dutiful son. The symbolism? Well, they didn't quite get to Oxford. This was beyond symbolism, this was recrudescent schism, albeit one they weren't as yet aware of. He was going to make them so proud of him, of that he was sure. Just as sure as he was of the inescapable fact that *he* could never be proud of *them*, of *this*.

The family dog bounded up the stairs, a barking, mad thing, infinitely more enthusiastic than its old master at this seemingly miraculous reunion. Subsequently, the family dog descended the stairs even quicker, its fall courtesy of a boot into gravity, to the accompaniment of its own directionlessly crazed crescendo of despair, now almost infinitely sadder than its erstwhile master at this disastrous reunion. Or so one might have thought. But no. No sooner had it touched rock bottom than it flew, tail wagging assent and ascent, back up the stairs full of life, full of faith in its master: a shot off a shovel, like the great Bloom. Dave patted it sadly. Mangy old brute. Never were much of a looker were you, Towser. And you should have set upon your owners for dumping you with such a hackneyed pre-soiled, shat on name, the canine equivalent to John in the East End, Jimmy in Glasgow, — Dave on a visit home. Sorry Towser, old chum, but this boy is not taking any mutt bearing that moniker for a walk, let alone walkies. Neither one of your type, you flea-bitten, toothless guard of this ramshackle hospice for the long term hapless.

"Towser, brekkie-wekkies!" yelled his mother. Both their mothers, reflected the practically uterine brothers, conditioned so to respond. Aptly enough, the old cur responded to this Pavlovian charivari as hopelessly as lesser sailors than Odysseus to the sirens' songs. Probably not even hungry, smirked Dave. Then, reminded of the greasy gourmand's delight that lurked in the larder in lardy wait for him, his physiognomy reverted to its more naturally downcast configuration.

"Dave, lad, get your arse down the kitchen afore your grub congeals," barked his father, ever the enticing sergeant-major commandeering what passed muster for preferment in the naffest of NAAFIs.

"Coming, dad," burped the prodigal, breaking his silence in time honoured and temporarily propitious fashion in this fast rifting household.

He sidled delicately downstairs and into the inferno of the kitchen. Though the welcome was warm to stifling he felt a chill run his spine as his auntie Ida spoke the fearsome words.

"T'aint it grand, back in the bosom of his family."

"Kiss your auntie Ida, love," goaded her sister horrendously. Extraordinarily, he achieved the thankless status of the first man to fulfil this function practically voluntarily. Sober, too. Deathly sober. The deathly sober that is seriously hungover. Well, neither of them would shut up if he didn't. He smiled, quietly satisfied at his being *sui generis* in these particular fields: kissing Ida without comment from her or her sister. The smile subsided in a creeping disgust at the things he did for this family.

"You alright, love?" asked auntie Ida presciently as he came grotesquely to embody the now revealed horror of what he had just done. He nodded. To answer truthfully would only encourage their prattling midwifery to bring forth a stillborn valetudinarianism, much mourned, with a life of its own but none here. To answer with words at all could only serve to encourage them. It was a stupid question.

"So," probed auntie Ida, ever, forever, armed with a slingshot of supplementaries that slayed by volume, acoustic and numeric, "you're going to become a teacher, love?" He shrugged.

"Don't bloody shrug your auntie Ida," censured father, misreading the gesture as personal and threatening towards the blessed aunt when, in fact, it was aimed, if a shrug can be aimed, at him, at them all, at the whole world; more *urbi et orbi* than *ad hominem*: he toyed with bestowing upon those gathered here benighted the benefice of this so backhanded as to be, at best, baffling benediction. No. Most of all it was an implosive gesture none can shake off.

Just off the milk round, he had been offered a post as a history teacher by his old school. Oh! they would be honoured to welcome back an old boy, was what his ex-headmaster wrote on confirming the job offer. There was no problem with that, David liked the old bastard, he had been the catalyst to kill off any meanderings on an average future for the boy. Hoist by his own petard, though. David had ideas above this kindly old pedant. Besides, it was all the other folk who would be honoured to the point of aesthetically truant, contagiously second rate subservience, that really nagged at David, his imagination serving to warn of its imminent demise as it dulled at the thought of such sterling service, such homage to roots so mundane as to detract from growth in any other direction. This boy was excelsior off the old block. No, such *noblesse oblige* could only be returned with increasing haplessness as it was received with increasing gratitude: less a life, less a combined force for the good upon young lives than a marriage of convenience whose secret only one party was in on and which, for convenience's sake, neither could subsequently get out of. Just as their gratefulness at his remaining true to type would see its destiny as a sort of *Saturnia regna*, only gradually hinting at a determinedly recondite self-loathing each succeeding sundown, so he saw plain the price to be paid in sponsoring a fool's golden age. No, he wasn't stopping around here. He'd met people, real people. Not the exaggeratedly real people like these here museum exhibits of tomorrow, these theme park cast members of today, these pridian dwellers, but people whose people funded, if not founded those very museums. He intended to take a position in the City, a position tentatively offered him by a university friend, or rather by the father of a university friend. Initially David was bedazzled, "that amount of money for that kind of shit and he hasn't even met me," he protested, but his dissent was of the in-house, keep it in the family type designed to fall exclusively on deaf ears, not to be taken at all seriously. David learned, there and then never to look a gift-horse in the mouth again. In truth, he had never countenanced such a gift-horse as this and consequently resolved to see many more of this sort of beast, leaving well aside the talking variety which have so bewildered the Irish and other mug punters to those who, while scarcely able to afford losing, seemed pathologically disposed to being losers. He was going to do it the proper way. Ask no questions, educe no lies. Politics? Oh, he had had them before he was old enough to exercise their rights. Since coming of age his apathy towards them had incremented as his former antipathy had declined; increasingly, prodigiously, he ceased to struggle to see the point. Indeed, the point seemed quite, quite simple: those who complained of them most had most reason, those who didn't didn't, and any politician worth his or her status wouldn't dare tamper with the loaded logic of his or her existence by enquiring into abstracts like equanimity. No, David decided on embarking for Oxford, that was a logic which couldn't be changed. Derided: certainly. Utilised: absolutely. Changed: no, never.

Oxford provided a means to an as yet undecided, yet decidedly determined end. Bustling with the best minds this nation's stultifying education system somehow manages to throw up, like a gourmet gourmandising his fare in a fit of excessive self-promotion, David (henceforth known to all bar family and intimates as Fairbrother) was scintillatingly aware of his potential. An outsider from oop narf, as they say dahn sarf, as they say oop norf, *ad nauseam*, he refused to pay even the whinyest lip-service to such petty tribal litanies to a Utopia much like all the others: one that none would give an inch, let alone give up land to found. Quite clearly and clinically, he recognised the opportunity there presented to him. If he, from a piss-poor compo – 'hilarious' Oxford (sixth year repeat *ad nauseam*) argot for a comprehensive school – in a depressed region, could come this far against all the odds, what, in such an invidiously governed state, was there to stop him going further than anyone was ever meant to have a right to dream?

Conscience? He didn't have one. Not to speak of. Well, not to be able not to boast of. Disgusted by an upbringing offering little but rhetorical communal redemption, Fairbrother was acutely, almost guiltily aware of cutting free from his roots. And, as chance, and not a little dogmatism would have it, on his coming of age, free really did mean free. Personal expiation wasn't in it either. He hadn't even begun sinning.

It was the almost pathogenetic voicing of such mercenary characteristics that saw him successively expelled from an executive post in the Labour Party Youth, voted off the Positive Discrimination Committee of the National Union of Students (11 females, 10 males, 11 ethnics, 10 indigenes, he, being cited in the motion, wasn't allowed a vote: whichever way one cut it though, *nemine dissentiente* is fairly decisive), and requested to vacate the top table of the Federation of Conservative Students dining club cum pre-parliamentary cabal. In all cases he was too, well, too *too*. To the once great party of the left he brought a too revolutionary zeal – in itself an extreme distinction, out of sorts of sorts, in 1982 – which all took too seriously bar himself. The final showdown came over an arch, understandably misconstrued motion he put to the AGM that *The Guardian* wasn't a proper forum for cartoons. The counter motion, a compromise in caricature, '*The Guardian* isn't the proper forum for Steve Bell' won the day. To the great wine and cheese party of conscience's protracted final fling he brought his uneducated, dare one say uncivilised and intuitive doubts which none but he dared design to entertain. To the party of no longer polite misrule he brought a mirror, as functional as it was unflattering, plain in its surrounds, squalid on reflection. Here the showdown had as its catalyst no less calamitous a presence than the then unenobled Mr Tebbit. The then, and surely immortally titled Chingford skinhead, attending the AGM in an *ex officio*, bordering on *ex cathedra* capacity by invite from his loyal bent backwards foot soldiers – the tyro-chiropractors and chiropodists of the FCS – found himself being heckled from the very Berchtesgaden heights of the platform upon which he sat, a hitherto magesterial presence, Dauphin to the corporeally absent, yet ever lurking presence of his Marie Antoinette.

"On yer bike, Tebbit!" came the voice that must haunt such semi house trained fat cats at such gatherings: the stench of refuse aired in public rises, and that's not just the stage manager shitting himself: a spectral miasma of misdeeds soliciting concessionary indeeds as the full horror of being answerable to an audience more venal, more power crazed, more covetous, more capable of pronouncing *autos-da-fé*, less principled than oneself hits home. All good knockabout stuff to the great man, of course, though not so to his precocious praetorian guard. The heckling from the platform continued.

"Say what you mean. Make it logical or don't make a proposition at all. Repatriate the benighted devils, deny Social Security to all that won't work for it, reinstitute conscription, if it moves privatise it, if it doesn't move consign it to the scrapheap of history: where there is discord let there be riches, where there is gruel let them eat gruel."

This was too much even for Stormin' Norman's inchoate incendiary tendency of double fire damaged mortagagor-abees: "Hold those views at your convenience, indemnify with our connivance," motto of these agents of the estate. It is doubtful that even the generaless in messianic 'Rejoice! Rejoice!' mode would have remained on the same platform as such a leprously clanging endorser. Had she and her like fully examined the face they were presenting to the world they would have been as petrified as the most endangered of their charges. As it is, such, um, conviction politicians don't only appear to be stone-faced professional non-apologists, but it is closer study, brinking on mad-eyed certitude into the ways of the world, and not the caprices of their own psyches, that best achieves this expedient transmutation. They will by turn scare, inspire, appal, goad their terribly subjected denizens, yet their personal drive is merely a crude dynamic derived from their wider manifesto. Personal integrity is *infra dignitatem*: they are right about the world. And, yes, they are right in that the politics they espouse are mirrored in the characteristics they embody, but as in any walk of life, indeed more so than in most, such bare-faced cheek, such nakedness of ambition would be better masked. Further, while naked ambition can be a self-perpetuating condition in free marketeering politicians, such honesty, if taken to the breach far sooner than history yet far later than yesterday comes to resemble a heinous and unnecessary admission of guilt, evil intent, madcap veracity, *und so weiter*. In short, it is the *hubris* that finally kills them off, but until then these players on the public stage, who know a thing or two about blood from a stone heart, can easily work similar alchemy on their public face to produce surprisingly human tears. Usually more adept at producing tears of cruel laughter than yet tears of rage, let alone tears of sorrow, it was an at least fish-eyed polecat who turned to the speaker of those words in amazingly silent amazement.

On exiting the Federation of Conservative Students Fairbrother promised himself an apolitical career, satisfying himself that, at 23 years of age he had tried all shades of political opinion and found all wanting; wanting a little less grey, perhaps. Whether such an adept polemicist could steer clear of the political was another matter, but Fairbrother definitely ruled out a parliamentary career, just as the feelers – from the Liberals and the SDP, funnily enough – were encroaching. As already mentioned, on graduating he also turned down a teaching job back home. An Oxford colleague, born to be more than capable of charity, inevitably sooner disposed to ill-bred trumpery, afforded him a helping hand. Shallow though it was, this friendship was important in confirming Fairbrother's upwardly mobile status. He was now officially beyond the state subsidies and/or familial handouts so necessary to every growing up, and like most young men and women eager to make their way in the world, the parts played in his life by state and family diminished drastically. These partings took the forms of less than fond, ungracious even, farewells which evinced an ambition to be well rid of such outmoded constraints on a stand alone personality all set to become a someone. Definitely, defiantly beyond handouts, heading for backhanders, golden hellos and golden handshakes, he had grown up fast and his ultra-conventional ambitions were exaggerated to a degree by the brightness of his prospects in no more nor less marked a manner than in that fellow oxymoron, the average Oxbridge graduate.

On assuming the position of Senior Assistant Commodities Broker, Fairbrother entered upon a world as divorced from Oxford as was Oxford from the glum and grim and glued to roots character of a northern childhood. Sure, there had been hedonistic excesses at Oxford too, but this bright new world was even more wonderful in that one never felt honour bound to think *about* them or *them*. Indeed. To dream them was sufficient; invariably they came true for they existed in no other context than that they could and should exist. Fun was fun and this was it.

Fairbrother soon revelled in the bespoke cut and thrust of single issue excellence that substantially comprised his 'chosen' vacation, and was soon rewarded beyond the dreams of the most catholic imagination by almost instantaneous access into *la dolce vita*. Verily this was the world of privilege his gifts had trained him at.

His starting salary as a Senior Assistant Commodities Broker (and it wasn't merely the initial oxymoron which forced a brief reflexive smile upon his otherwise earnestly set features) was £11,000 per annum. Not bad for '82, more, for instance than his father – retired 1985 – ever earned from April Fool day (wage rise granted) to the succeeding April Fool eve (living standard same or worse, owing to inflation) in any of his 52 given – given? taken! – years (factories and mines, of course). But Fairbrother wasn't to be satisfied in merely beating his father as the latter had browbeat his wife. Such lifestyle comparisons were odious to him. Besides, 'twere nowt to write home about. Yet. No, if he were to obtain a decree absolute from what seemed already to be a badly moulded *déclassé* lumping of prematurely mouldering ne'er-do-wells, he would have to succeed in multiplying the minor factor of their wages by an exponent substantial enough to result in a number way out of the limited field of their lowly calculations and over the head held merely high horizon of their very limited comprehension. And that exponent (which some term incentive, and yet others call trade, which in this case would more accurately be described as the closed shop of cupidity) was purpose built into his new job, no, position, in the potentially spectacular form of commission. Commission, there and then, in that world, in that the City was no reflex perquisite such as is surrendered by all but the drunkest of drunks to all but the most obnoxious of taxi drivers; neither was it the insult to injury his father and other manual labourers knew only too well as piece-work; no, in the City of the early '80s, commission was more or less akin to the lookout man's cut, or the bent security guard's hush money on the successful conclusion of (irony of ironies) a bank heist. In that climate of clandestine collaboration it was assumed, – and generally correctly – that those who could pull off the big deals had transgressed the law somewhat in so doing. And, thick as thieves, regulating bodies and transgressors would provide mutually supportive alibis which amounted to no less than traded character references in lieu of any shared morality. As yet another irregularity escaped their notice, the officials at the DTI and SFO would grumble at being overworked and, what's more, trapped within labyrinthine procedures which, apropos the old chestnut of the trees obscuring the wood, would make most other public servants seem as free and straightforward as lumberjacks. Similarly, the transgressors would cite overwork leading to oversight and laws so complex as bound to baffle

Sherlock Holmes, let alone jumped up little barrow boys made good, your honour. Yes, there were many pleas of 'your honour' among these thieves, but the greatest bonding agent was that on being cooperatives in an environment deliberately kept secret by a government intent on misdirecting its powers of scrutiny on more honest, if politically challenging areas of activity.

While the government of the day committed itself to a curiously doctrinaire policy whereby it laid into as well as laid off vast wastes of the workforce, the nation's economy was largely entrusted to its entrepreneurs and, more specifically, their errand boys, the nation's gilded parasites patriotically transferring a diseased ideology into the body of the realm, calling the shots at the flip-flip of a two-headed coin. And the alibis overtook the regulators all unseen until, in the light of revelation all could proclaim, beyond mitigation, past redemption to obsequious acclaim, a balance sheet so healthy any true liver of life would surely see its divine intervention as alien to further probing; a final theft, a stealing of the limelight from the searchlight. Alas, there were fewer true livers of life beyond the charmed confines of self-worship's temple, wherein dwelled what used to be termed the moneyed classes, and what remained of the agitating infiltrators tended to meet the ends logical to their lack of individualist zeal; that is, they became sacrificial lambs by dint of occupying, however briefly, the same cage as these monstrously lionised capitalists.

Within six months of going to work in the City, Fairbrother was so highly prized by his employers and, more importantly, by his clients, that his annual salary had hiked to 15K (note the semiotic change, no smaller than the pronounced monetary one), with anything between a cool 20K and an obscene 100K commission for the asking. It was in those first six months that the nascent entrepreneur placed his first significant investment. 'Placed' is the verb, but there the resemblance to the mug's doubles, jailbreak trebles and pissing in the wind hailing Mary accumulators so beloved of his father's cronies concludes. This was an altogether surer thing, a different human race entirely.

A colleague put him 'in touch' with an estate agent friend of his (the colleague's) wife, who (the estate agent) was to be involved in 'the project' next. Though outwardly resembling a John le Carré plot, the whole operation emanated a miasma of too sweet, sickeningly too sweet, inevitability which tends to surround transactions conducted by the stinking rich. Fairbrother wasn't in that class yet but he was sharply cognisant that acting the part was the quintessential prerequisite for accelerated entry therein, merely the practice necessary for gaining the *perfecto mundo, la dolce vita*. Many may, many did applaud this radical alteration in the nation's polity, when, at last, it mattered not whence one came, though such admiration for the dawning of long derived common sense may be tempered somewhat by the reactionary corollary that it seemed to matter even less how one arrived at one's self-appointed destiny. No 'glad confident morning' then. At that point in time Fairbrother's immediate destiny was entrusted to Xara, the aforewarned estate agent, like him entirely untrained for her vocation which, along with the times, conspired to choose her, too. So convinced was he of her professional competence (and of his own ability to earn vast piles by the hour, it has to be said) that he didn't even stoop to visiting the imminent homestead. How could he lose with another of the chosen ones, the contacts, on his side?

The interior was decorated by his colleague's wife, Briony, in a style that could best be rendered the injustice it begged as 'showhouse saleable'. Briony's concept of design was straight out of *Habitat*, which was precisely whence it came. No matter that she charged Fairbrother 1K commission for two shopping trips ('hugely rewarding': she wasn't kidding) to a pretentious warehouse in which everything looks the same – made by convicts paroled halfway through; short stay convicts at that; the ones who failed, no, never took woodwork –, at prices more criminal than samey; it was expected of him, of those with such a lifestyle, to share the good fortune with those others seemingly predestined to make good their fortune. That it was a house aspiring to become a commodity, namely the as yet unknown, as yet unknowing next buyer's ideal home, was crucial to all the plans. The 1K which he tossed the high class furniture juggler notwithstanding, he had all the finances worked out to the *lira*, and not just in case a Turk or an Italian showed an interest. And even Briony's sting was not, he would have felt, entirely wasted. In fact it proved to be something of an investment as so much apparently idle money changing so often proves to be; for these transactions are so deviously deceptive that what looks like charity is rarely given lightly, seldom dispensed without, as it were, the accompanying trumpery of its own advertisement. At last Fairbrother felt comfortable. He was his own man and it was in his nature, moving freely from far off worship to self-centred contempt, that assimilation was to be merely his opening gambit.

After a year in the City and five months in his new house Fairbrother decided a change was called for. Clearly this was no economic casuist; indeed, if he had a conscience it could only be disturbed by a discovery that it had barred the way to the best possible deal for him, his company and its scandalous partners in crime. The ordering of priorities set out in the preceding sentence should not lead one to suppose that matters of conscience did arise all that often in the conduct of Fairbrother's early working life. They were all, individuals all in this together. Indeed, while recognisable acts of penitence are as rare in the boardroom as in the dictator's command bunker, the truly conscience free are those in whom individualism has usurped the *esprit de corps* of the most tightly closed ranks; those who through expert, usually innate understanding of the collectively corrupt fancy themselves as star performers in those most dangerous and rewarding of games. This is not to imply that Fairbrother was in any way unique; quite the contrary, his career took to a typical trajectory for such a high-flying time and place, one, if not openly admitted to, certainly envisaged, fashioned and covertly encouraged by his employers. There would be others even more ruthlessly ambitious to take his place when inevitably he moved on. And when they moved on? They too would then have proved themselves worthy, for excessive company loyalty was evidence of failure, the death-watch beetle whose relentless ticking kept golden hellos, handshakes, maybe even carriage clocks effectively outwith earshot. Temporal measurements of contracts had so contracted that were one unprepared to move and shake in that dervish paced world of golden hellos and funny business handshakes, one was not likely to be considered worthy of wasting one tick of precious time on.

As corporate life moved on apace so naturally did the private lives of corporate employees. The thought of working 12 hours a day, seven days a week may appal all but junior doctors, hard men enslaved to menial piece-work and unemancipated housewives, yet somehow all enervation just dissipates like sleep from the eyes as they stare at a cold shower when the thought of earning more money than fast fading dream land ever offered hoves into view. So, an eighteen hour day it was – 12 hours work, solid; four hours socialising, ditto; two hours preparation, dressing, travelling, crucial; six hours sleep, reluctantly taken, all week, every week. As a matter of routine those four hours of precious time per day were not wasted, one was forever bumping into actual and potential clients at cocktail parties, restaurants, wine bars, media launches and so on. That these meetings were no more arbitrary than those of the averagely contented husband and wife never served to diminish that power which theatricality wields in the business community at work and play: thus would a 'delighted to see you, old boy' lend an air of smokescreen conviviality, feigned kismet with which to preface then shroud acts of too real collusive skulduggery. Almost all of these small talk to big deal scenarios were most peculiar in their orthodoxy, aping as they did a colonial past where the can't do otherwise viceroy meets the will do colonel prepared in turn to sacrifice the must do privates whose big, tragic scene, while yet to come, mustn't be allowed to reflect negatively upon the glory of those exalted to sit in judgement, however ill-considered and ill-advised that judgement be.

This orthodoxy, which served up a heady cocktail of cloying obsequiousness laced with dashings of ambition sufficient to desire to be on its receiving end, indeed served to render any society but its own contemptible; and, *natürlich*, it had a place for women, a place in the kitchen where drinks could be spiked but not drunk. Rarely were these exquisite creatures of contemplation and plunder elevated to the cabals of their bank robbing sugar daddies; cabals which would admit to no real wrongdoing in these respects; the exquisite ones may not be allowed in on the planning and executing stages, but for them were these masterpieces of trickery devised.

Fairbrother escorted many such inspirations to plunder in his first year on the self-styled 'corporate circuit' which, while conspiring to produce social intercourse more mundane, offensively conventional, insular and workaday than that held at the average sales convention, never yet failed to inspire its participants who, to a man, looked numinously upon these ludicrously contrived evenings out in the penthouse suite a floor up, until, finally, the summits achieved, the finer things in life redefined, one could afford to indulge oneself in something a little bit out of what here passed for ordinary by superseding the 'You don't have to be mad to work here, but it helps!' truism of the paperweight weighing heavily on a bursting to insane in-tray with a tranquil photograph of the spouse and issue inscribed with the immortal words of the poet Browning (or rather those words of the poet Browning which instil in one that great oxymoron of the age, temporary immortality), 'Ah, but a man's reach should exceed his grasp, Or what's a heaven for?', ostensibly as a homage to the angel one married, actually a naughtily chosen mnemonic to and on behalf of the mistress. The first of these potential *demi-mondaine* elevated to a world of far from exclusive partnerships to be taken at all seriously by Fairbrother – i.e., out more than once – was an accounts clerkess from his firm, Julie, whose invites to such gatherings clearly were not earned by the position she held in the company, rather gained by the company she was prepared to keep and the positions she was expected to adopt while both in and out of it: nigh literally out of it, for there was a storm of cocaine snorted at each of these soirée, not least by the already nauseated 'entertainment'. Not having noticed her at work, Fairbrother quite literally stumbled upon the poor creature at one of these nights out.

She was crying at the foot of some bloody stairs to some bloodied bedroom where some bloody executives had taken some bloody liberties (perky!) with some stupid bloody cow about to avenge herself partly by informing some stupefied, cowed cows of bloody wives. Plainly this girl needed to get a few things straight and not the beautiful thing that she was even more twisted.

"Your first time on the corporate circuit?" opened Fairbrother to the tearful wretch reddened with rage, whitened with disgust manifesting itself as a fearfully resipiscent purity, as she sat shivering feverishly at the foot of his friend and colleague's stairs.

"What!?" she counter ejaculated, startled by the thought of another predatory male, further appalled by the redefining of rape as a casual episode, an introductory gambit on the 'corporate circuit'.

"First time on coke?" pressed Fairbrother, feeling something akin to pity for the benighted creature, though never quite waiving the birthright of such men as he over such vulnerable waifs as she, a birthright which allowed, almost demanded her exploitation.

"Yes," she hung her head, "but it's not that." Fairbrother made to enquire further but on engaging those eyes was met with a blank despair in its own way too horribly eloquent to be met with an offer of more drugs.

"I was raped," she finally sobbed, the culminating word almost choking her, frail womanhood and all. Here we go again, thought Fairbrother, another headless chick on a new drug, afraid to let herself go, hyper-aware of her position in these circles as a harlot or nothing, feeling sorry for herself and inventing stories Vladimir Nabokov would have been ashamed to put in a signally psychotic protagonist's diary. However, two could play that game, the proffering of a shoulder to cry on being the best foreplay he knew.

"Oh, when?" he prodded with all the sincerity of a tabloid journalist probing the latest anonymous crazy claiming to have slept with Elvis.

"What?!" came the startled reply.

"When?"

"Does it fucking matter?" she shrieked.

"Looking good, Dave," joshed an innocent passer-by whose reading of his walk-on-walk-off part in this melodrama was, while mischievous, essentially *pour encourager les autres*. Romantic was not the language which sped his departure because, in truth, there were to be no more innocent passers-by in this girl's life.

"Fuck off!" she screamed as he did.

"Easy, easy," soothed Fairbrother, "I know this nose candy can evoke the bad times, but you've just got to forget them. It'll go. Next time it'll be better."

It was then that Fairbrother was involved in what the politically correct, poetically challenged may choose to render as cross-gender violence (though why such serious matters should suffer mitigation at the hands of smooth talking semanticians is a strongly stressed absurdity, or, between you and I, a fucking nonsense). To be fair to him, he didn't retaliate. That would come later. In fact the poor sap apologised, as all men must do on having provoked an unasked for response from a female. Gobsmacked, he half asked half confessed, "I'm sorry?" This unrehearsed response of bewilderment mixed with intense interest seemed to soothe her. A bit.

"'Forget them.' 'Next time it'll be better'. Fuck you!" Well, she didn't hit him with anything other than violently inappropriate quotes. 'When?' she recommenced the condemnation, "I don't know, I wasn't looking at my fucking watch."

"Your watch?" gaped Fairbrother, and slowly, belatedly the date clicked. "You mean you've been ——— raped?" he gulped gawpily.

"What the fuck do you think I was saying," she cried.

"Tonight?" he sighed sickly, as if delivered of a kick in the balls. "By whom?"

'*Whom!*' Rapists don't introduce themselves. Not in the formal manner," she spat. Somehow this breach of etiquette served to reveal the full horror of the violation to the acting *cavaliere servente*.

"I'll kill him!" he rose in improbably heroic mode.

"Whom?" she sobbed bitterly.

"The bastard!"

"Which one?" she implored caustically.

"You mean —?" he gaped.

"You going to take the four of them, huh? This little girl managed it," she struggled.

"But — but — you must know them," he followed suit.

"Biblically, yes, but as I said, we weren't otherwise introduced."

"You must recognise them," he insisted.

"How good is *your* eyesight through cataracts of tears on a drug that's making the darkened room spin through a blindfold?" she countered.

"Oh," he ohed.

"For all I know it could have been you," she shivered. Fairbrother was horrified.

"How could you?!?!" he exploded.

"What?"

"Accuse me?" he moaned softly.

"Don't worry, nobody's going to be accused. I know my place here now as well as you've always known it."

"Which is?" he probed honourably.

"Don't get cute," she hissed.

But cute is what he got. She got. They got. Fairbrother escorted Julie to many similar, fortunately less unfortunate nights during the next six months: he believing he was providing a much needed sensitive ear for her understandable wailings: she understanding that with him she wouldn't get raped at these functions, still so valuable to her career; more so now that she had seen, she had been, what goes on.

They were happy with each other, as most couples are until one or other attempts literally to marry their respective forces of attraction, as often as not winding up too close for comfort, horns locked in the would be immortal combat lovers declare themselves fair game for with each succeedingly extramundane, impossible dream disembodiments of each other. One night after yet another party, or socially imperative gathering, at which Fairbrother perceived Julie to be having her best time in his company, mostly out of his company, oh, far too good a time for a real rape victim, on arriving home (which we men know to be home ground advantage in the eyes of the law should any argument get out of hand) she was confronted.

"Julie?" he begged as she was nodding off.

"Not tonight, David, I'm tired."

"I shouldn't wonder," he harrumphed.

His tone woke her as sure as an intruder in the house hoping to come and go unnoticed but prepared to demand booty and, who knows, beyond with menaces if it wasn't readily identifiable. She felt this stranger had to be confronted.

"What do you mean?" she urged explanation, sitting up in an automatic posture of attention to, not least of all her own vulnerability.

"All that dancing."

"So?" she shrugged, disgusted and fearful in equal measure.

"The night we met ——," he began, immediately sensing her terrible mood. Her hackles rose as she experienced an intromit cowing, insult to injury, sickening her further.

"Yes?" she offered, aptly feeling accused as the woman who wouldn't say no. Then he hit her with it.

"Are you sure you were raped?" It was stupid, brutal and, at a heart-rending stroke it undid all the hitherto well meaning good work he had put in in counselling her rehabilitation. She didn't answer. Of course, the question didn't deserve such dignifying, but the bitter truth was that she couldn't. Tears drowned her response as she looked away from this fool who needed confirmation of her distress and his right to exploit it.

"How do you know there were four of them? I mean, if you were blindfolded."

"How long have you mulled that one over?" she asked the only question that could now have any bearing on her future. The relationship was over. She needed only to know how long ago it ought to have drawn to its sorry conclusion, as at once veiled and revealed through tears she set out on the wrong goodbye. He confirmed her worst, saddest fears; it ought never to have commenced.

"The first night," he confessed, in her eyes going from green to red. If his envy had been an injudicious product of a fevered imagination, his shame was surely designed to give his mind even less by way of a treat. This was no act. "Are you going?" he offered, chivalrous at last. She nodded three times, slowly through the dumbstruck automaton eyes of one of those crying dolls of her long gone, just buried childhood; like the doll she now embodied as if shaken for a known, an as advertised reaction by one empowered so to do.

"For good?"

"Definitely," she confirmed. He nodded. He didn't say. At least he knew he had trespassed beyond redemption.

A week after Julie moved out the flat had been sold. She left the firm, too, and ought never to have been seen again; an unrightable wronged Fairbrother could, possibly should, have devoted the remains of his life apologising to. However, Fairbrother vowed never to get emotionally attached to house or co-householder again. He moved onwards and upwards, turning an 80% profit on his flat and purchasing a 'four bedroom former maisonette (sic), twice the price in twice the area, let that be your *raison d'être*' (assonance misplaced for assholes) as his ever loyal, this time twice as costly, coincidentally, estate agent, Xara, remarked. Again, Briony did the interiors, exhibiting, as was her wont, the ego of a brain surgeon taking the oath to put the life of a blissfully ignorant pools winner right because, since the skiing accident, he wasn't legally fit to dictate a will. There to take by the hand on coming round. You know the scene. Thus, Fairbrother, from environs where failure to have three flying ducks on flock wallpaper bestowed upon one a degree of sophistication too blatant to be worth the candle (in *ersatz* stately home candelabrum, of course), entered, as if to the manner born that other extreme, a dwelling of tasteless opulence sufficient to reduce Lloyd Grossman to silence, or elevate him to English, and the celebrity contestants on *Through the Keyhole* to just the type of banal generalisations which invariably identify the inhabitant. You know, with the pinpoint accuracy of an astrological chart, they will get their man:

"Something in showbiz?" (Applause) "Something in music?" (Invariable applause: they all sing, no, make records). "Does he/she make people laugh?" (Ditto). Hardly be a street cleaner's house, would it? All that junk would be bagged and ready to go, for a start. Fairbrother was no showbiz celeb, but with money to indulge who wouldn't ape the famous, particularly in their televised incarnations? From Hilda's ducks to South Fork's acres of patio: in the first case by not having it at all, even if it means trashing the beloved 'muriel' behind anaglypta, in the second by breaking fast in the glorified window box that is the veranda, originally designed it seems by a miniaturist architect for the purpose of airing dolls' clothes. Fairbrother had the money, therefore he needed to go shopping for the trappings, pretensions and indulgences; otherwise who would know he had the wherewithal? He had it the easy way round the great money-go-round. This way one paid another and one pretended to what the other advised one ought. The other way, the no way, the flying in the face of fashion, the way of most, one pays dear for the non-fulfilment of one's dreams, *specifically* for the non-fulfilment of one's dreams.

Suffice it to say – or perhaps needless to say is better – the house was done up like a creation specifically designed for, nay, built around one of those sex 'n' shopping coffee table writers, as if the *mise en scène* for a docudrama of the money making machine, wrongly designated 'the author', dreaming of inenarrable riches to come. This isn't one of those, though Fairbrother's coffee table boasted not a few of those brick built, plot boiling monstrosities.

Professional Fairbrother took his services elsewhere, too. Still in the City and enticed as much by the golden hello (20K and index-linked to the amount by which he could, ahem, inflate his clients' coffers) as he was repulsed by the thought of working in the same company Julie once kept. Repulsed is not the right word. Apprehensive perhaps is, but repulsed he would be soon enough, just as soon as she attached her understandably vaunted, yet so far from lucky charms to another.

Chapter Three

The news in the City was good, if not in further flung places. It was with a sense of irony all but emblematic of his life then, June '83, that Fairbrother found himself in a wine bar called the *Free Falklander* celebrating the re-election of a repeat term Tory administration. Furthermore, irony rarely stopped at recognition with Fairbrother. Where most (who could discriminate its gentle nudgings towards self-knowing poignancy from its more demotic provocations of cruel sarcasm) would stop that stranger in its tracks and subsequently adjust their degree of guardedness on whether it proved friend or foe, Fairbrother would merely laugh at its declaration – as if once ironical, never to be taken seriously –, look the other way, thus inadvertently ushering in many more unchallenged paradoxes to be faced later when corruption had eroded their charm and left them betraying nothing but the bitterest, most eschatological of contradictions. That he hadn't voted Tory was another irony Fairbrother preferred to let pass. From his much maligned class betrayal to his much mocked pretence at being a natural Tory, Fairbrother worried little over such things, was incapable of guilt or shame abstracted to the edifying perception of others. Sure, some accused him of turning his back, and he freely admitted to this, but, then, he never felt he belonged. Sure, some could level charges of opportunism at him now and then, but he would experience no remorse for he never felt opportunism to be a crime; in fact, its lack more often than not turned a person to crime. Like Levin in *Anna Karenin* – not a connection he would then make – he set out to believe in the sole motivator of self-interest. As it was for Levin, his quest wasn't to be that simple. Alike in both there was a paucity of hypocrisy in this pursuit: Fairbrother was individualistic, if only through its literally representing non-conformity: if he could be said to have been with the times it was more in spite of them than because of himself. Initially, at least.

The other ironies, those lost to others, he accepted readily. Chief amongst these that election night was the celebration of a government unelected and unloved outwith the narrow-minded concerns of this peculiarly pecuniary fulfilled class, but then few genuinely trouble themselves with the casuistry of their own success, no matter how blatant the evidence of its having been gained to the direct detriment of those not so blessed in this most inhumane of human races. Such quiddities are only elevated towards the essential when they rise to pose a threat, but here in a bouncer protected parlour, in the market protectorate of the square mile, politics promised to the point of allowing no rhetorical questions, let alone genuinely challenging and threatening polemics. Here seated and sated were the new officer class, a class to which all the foot soldiers were to aspire rather than respect and, Lord knows, the excluded mutineers were still revolting to themselves up north, way up north, blended into the bleak landscape of Blackpool, decanted into the false atmosphere of its Winter Gardens, wherein with internecine bonhomie, rather than conference, or, heaven forbid, congress, coming closest to conjuring up the mood, they would unite in pouring boiling scorn upon one and other as if as a method of livening-up their workaday more ambrosian than, Hyperborean cheerleading, their chillingly under-privileged little (belittled) existence.

Fairbrother's new boss – one of the old school; some things rarely change – was toasting the health of the re-returned Prime Minister in the quasi-enlightened mode most male chauvinist careerists felt it necessary to deploy in those days.

"To Maggie. Best bloody man in the cabinet," he proposed, ostensibly swallowing manly pride (aided by a not insignificant gargle of the Dutch courage), actually speaking to a truth common to himself and Herself herself. True, she had discomfited the traditional massed geriatrics who before her reign had expertly, naturally, genteelly buffered the Tory Party as was from the gentlest of contacts with the quotidian world, yet in her inability or refusal to view any other class – i.e., non-officer material and women – as other than a hot water bed of perverted revolutionaries, mutants hatched in the '60s, that most 'second rate of decades', she would never countenance any social change inimical to her quite brilliant power grab. Indeed, her vision of civilian life was becoming incessantly militaristic in its configuration. And while those who went from Sandhurst to bath chairs via the natural attrition of the years were always as thin on the ground as they would become on top, many more, many, many more were prepared to join up to an apparent ordering of a none too apparent society that promised prosperity in flagrant breach of the Trades Description Act, let alone manifesto pledges or, ironically, given its standard bearer's benignly distorted mirror image, common sense. It was a triumph of marketing over any real market, of decency bewildered by the intrinsic power advertising held in such a theatrical market, much in the manner pioneered by the genius of form over content who dreamed up the 'Join the Army – See the World' recruitment campaign. Just as that clever clogs hadn't bothered to focus his rose-tinted vision on the six counties and their environs, so Madison Avenue 'values' had culminated in creating a UK plc in the late '70s which the Tory Party presented to the populace not so much as a place to launch a manifesto, but a place to look up in next year's travel brochures. More so than in the tyro-Thatcher years (i.e., prior to the coining of that cheap, nasty, brutalist, abjectly accurate adjective, 'Thatcherite') of the late '70s, in 1983 the Tory Party were willing and able to offer themselves to the electorate as holiday reps purveying certain flights of one's own fancy as being determined mainly by two factors: *1*, how far one was determined to take it: *2*, how far one was prepared to countenance being patronised to have a nice day while being patronised by a tour rep as one's spiritual, societal guide, as one's very *raison d'état*.

Fairbrother returned his boss's toast.

"Absolutely," he smiled as his thoughts flitted to another woman, *the* other woman, his secretary. His boss's, that is. Oh, he had his own, of course, had had his own, of course, but now he desired, no, felt he deserved something better, of course. And, of course, his boss's *would* be better, wouldn't she? That such women, any women, each and every woman might see fit to refuse such crass and corrupt advances never occurred to Fairbrother any more than do the cries of the victim to the average rapist. The *average* rapist? Yes, Fairbrother could envisage such a beast back then had he but the introspection to admit it. Other men? That's for them to decide, dependant on the development of such introspection. Then, Fairbrother was all front, all mouth and trousers, kinetically hyper as any in Whitehall farce, and in the circumstances the women he came into contact with could only button this wide boy up with *ingénue's* disregard for their career prospects in a foolish but entirely in keeping squandering of natural assets. It is an axiom that women's liberation never penetrated to the soul of the average man, for, average as he was, though necessarily not as he perceived and was perceived, he still was able and willing to avail himself of the iniquitous opportunities that lay before him in the workplace; taking advantage of his particular status soon negated any generalised advance in the status of women; the women who were built to resist or return his favours with the contempt they – the favours, not the 'favoured' – deserved were not of this world, the world of conventional practice, rather they were the barren, frustrated (and not a little frustrating) assistant librarians of the chattering classes, extrapolating strap-a-dick-to-me theories of heterophobia, perversely asexual creations of self: the women inhabiting his world were gaudier creatures, their variety fair game for his own matchless variety of self-esteem rationalised as ambition and compartmentalised as a means to dirty deeds filed away for future reference. Of course, it didn't do to involve oneself more than very occasionally with one's own secretary – too much like marriage: "never mix grief with work", his boss had advised, half jokingly – but those of others were far fairer game. In this blatant imbalance a curious equality was easily realised if one was but blinkered enough to view only the pivot on the scales of justice. Indeed, conventional wisdom has it that what holds justice together is the crucial, no, the only legitimate, aspect of justice.

Mr Nosworthy – Fairbrother's boss thrice removed – had a secretary whose pivot was only too distracting: appended to which were the wild imbalances, the most of which at least were all of her own making. She walked into a boardroom as if into a bedroom, seducing the big boys merely by a venal acceptance of their invitation to make the coffee. Fairbrother and his colleagues knew she was there for the making alright, indeed his boss could be expected to confer favours upon the liquidly lunching Lotharios, who in turn would be almost duty bound to confer favours upon his grateful mendicant. The making of such a match would be in everybody's interest, however much the priesthood of women's liberation would bemoan in their inimical, unnatural fashion, like some neutered charivari of latter day Cassandras declaiming prophesies whose sell-by date had long since been realised by their far more fastidious targets. At one remove the boss would deliver himself from temptation too close to home; one of his 'lads' would be delivered into taintless ecstasy for a duration and a price of his choosing. And the lady? That was no lady that was someone's secretary, someone's right. Besides, no one was forcing her, right? Not in the sense understood by any of the parties involved, no, the whole operation being founded on mutual coercion, but as those self same practitioners would point out, would continually point out with their nauseatingly threatening tactic amalgamating the wider view and painfully realised self-awareness, there is mutual and there is mutual. This contract between one's vulnerability and it's necessary counter brutality was known to all participants in such scenes, and this damning document, this indictment of being was naturally deemed strictly confidential – something we all have over others and others have over us – and filed to forget.

"Some truths are like that," was Fairbrother's justification for keeping his unprincipled sides of the bargain. What he was to find out was that he was only partly right, almost wholly wrong. Mere subjective truths are bound to reveal themselves as lies, as home truths, and sooner rather than later. Most other truths are alike, though more circuitously home-hitting; all truths are potential home truths or they are nothing, for all truths, save perhaps one, are ultimately subjective. From the squatters who greet one on return from an over-indulgent business trip cum holiday, to the heavy breathing caller one suspects isn't entirely anonymous to the piece of rigid flesh occupying one side of the bed only, looming large like an incubus in the past of that wicked way with all other flesh never to be trusted again: these are all potential scenes in which we could be victim or offender, often victim *and* offender. Like most of us, Fairbrother knew only of himself as potential victim, thus unleashing the unprincipled antagonist with nary a second thought. Oh yes, he would soon prove to others, if not immediately to himself, how wrong the worst case scenario was. Him! A victim! Not any more, but, once bitten twice as virulent.

In league with Fairbrother's disgusting disregard for the female of the species sat a curious alliance of orthodoxy and devil may care daring. As with all, it began in childhood, specifically in relation to the dreams hatched therein. Yet where most believed these reveries of the hitherto acknowledged best years of their lives to be the birthplace of fantastic flights, young David at once instantaneously and eternally saw them for the nest egg they could be. He realised then what it takes most a lifetime to realise; the literal meaning of childhood ambition. More precisely, that to fail to realise these otherwise foolish indulgences is a curse which marks one for life. He didn't disown his dreams, merely never saw them as just that, as dreams. Rather, he pursued them relentlessly in their only pragmatic and realisable form: he was going to make money, to make dreams come true at all costs. Not for him the saddening pauses that punctuated the *curricula vitae* and punctured the pretensions of the caricatured thought bubbles of the would be footballers and film stars who only got to be (oh, conspiring fate!) assistant groundsmen and couch potatoes; he saw soon that the preponderant tragedy in life, in any life, was to spend it doing other than that which one wished upon a star for as a child. Clearly comprehending the limits placed upon wishes by the very word's 'hope for the best, expect the worst' connotations, he consciously downplayed them until they resembled nothing more, nothing less than potentially highly rewarding obligations. With this brutal approach to the quasi-magical world, always seemingly just beyond our grasp, young David entered into an always honest if almost as constantly unprincipled relationship with his potentialities; from there sanctimony was the inevitable attitude towards his fellow man, those idle dreamers striving vainly to recreate themselves in an image which never quite got beyond the most primitive form of creation; that form which, were God really to be portrayed by a man, would have the world peopled by pacific perfectionists whose whole existence sought only culmination in a frenzied internecine sycophancy towards their creator (devout enough to put the two legged lapdogs in the Royal household to shame) by composing a threnody to a self sadly realised and, by implication at least, badly defined.

In a nutshell, Fairbrother was prepared from an early age to be contemptuous of all but himself. With the supreme, if untried confidence of the autodidact he confided in no one his schemes; but that confidence betrayed many secrets, chief among them this: the self-taught are merely the self learned and, even as they erase the environmental factors from the equation which adds up to their positive self-image, they lose not a little of themselves: in zealously craving individuality they emigrate outwith the community which serves to make individuality a tolerable constituent of the equation; without that factor the individual just doesn't add up:

"Too many lives are needed to make just one" and "— the gesture of a life that is not another, but itself" are two quotations from Euginio Montale's *Occasioni* which seem rather apt, if a trifle formulaically called. Pretentious? And I was going to cite them in the Italian just to flatter you. Arrogant? No, I'm serious. Are you? Good, we have sorted the wheat from the chaff, the men from the boys, the clichéd classes from the clique of cliché turners.

Inspired by the polarisation clinched by the 1983 election result, Fairbrother's life came increasingly to resemble that of one then born to rule, that rare and worshipped thing, true Thatcherite success. Moreover, his undoubted business talents were in constant demand, as much at play as at work. He mined such a lucrative sideline with off the record briefings to clients past that it became increasingly likely they would soon become associates. In October '83, at 24 years of age, he left *Nosworthy de Klerk* , the firm of investment bankers in whose employ he had quadrupled his accountable salary within two years (in the early '80s it was thought quite proper to have salaries ordered in exact reverse to the way the Queen orders her birthdays: one official and accountable, the other unofficial – cf. public schooling – and far more pompous) and, spurning more golden hellos, he resolved to strike out on his own. Or, rather, while invariably that is the term used, almost as invariably there are others involved, each with the same, not quite the self same, individualistic perspective. In this case there were three proud entities striking out 'alone': Fairbrother, replete with 'monster reputation' – his words – for seeing a quick buck where lesser lights foresaw murk (nothing intrinsically remarkable in this 'talent', it being but a Pavlovian study of human behaviour in which the ability to see deals was precisely this: the talent to recognise those desperate, brave enough to, erm, overstep one of the desultory borders which existed – not very noticeably – to contain the money making money merchants from taking, erm, journeys into the unethical): Tristan Edmond, an old Oxford chum, at 26 a rising young star in the fast booming new addition to the pantheon of crucial establishment professions, the protean discipline of corporate law: finally, Garvey Saddler, a curiously named, spuriously claimed Texarkanan American son who, lacking the grades and/or athleticism to attend even an Arkansas college, did the best thing next and took a position in an advertising agency, where his copywriting skills soon aided in landing the company several large accounts at the crasser end of the market. That no one, particularly in advertising, went broke underestimating the taste of the public is as inarguable today as ever it was. The proof that there is a crasser end of the, well, marketing market may keep the jury out rather longer.

Styling themselves *Boom Bros* – the registered company name was the more conservative *Fairbrother, Edmond & Saddler, Investment Portfolios* – they were rapidly known throughout the City for their bold advertising campaigns and, well, being known throughout the City for —— their bold advertising campaigns. There was little chance of old style Conservative values being espoused by any of these three thrusting

Thatcherite trustees. Combined, in association, such quaint prospects dimmed like final, irrevocable nightfall on empire, spooking these, the torch bearers of the new Olympian individualism, into emerging more for battle than mere competition. As for that old canard of the spirit of competition, these three would no sooner recognise that than would they own to bending the rules themselves. Such was their expedient approach to their business: emphasize its brutal nature but never admit to deploying this yourself. Not in the presence of someone else's lawyer, anyway. *Primus inter pares*, or near as damn it in these dog eat dog worlds of high finance and the high class hawking of Madison Avenue was that mutant species of human pit-bull which wouldn't stop at masticating your mutt to oblivion, it'd have the children, too. *Sui generis* of this almost wholly pre-Darwinian phenomenon was Garvey, at 23 years old Madison Avenue's *wunderkind* of '82 who just last fall had generated enough publicity, controversy and subsequent litigation (advertising campaigns so exaggerated as to be seen through by Americans, honesty via come-uppance!) to have the accountants and lawyers drooling at one and other's earning powers for a change. This grotesque spectacle amused Garvey greatly – 'like seeing leeches sucking their own', he told the *Wall Street Journal* in his valedictory press statement in which he announced his 'hop over the pond' to 'where a guy can really be on the make'. A fan of Mrs Thatcher in much the same degree as a British bookie could be said to admire the boxing promoter, cum accessory to manslaughter, who pits another pitifully bloated Brit gross-weight against some sure-blade of a Chicagoan street mugger, Garvey made all intentions clear before the off – 'Ah'm gonna git ma ass over to li'l ole Inglun an' make me unaccountably rich, maybe make me a Countess or a Duchess, too.' Or *hubris* to that effect. Yep, this good ole boy from the Texarkanan mire was whooping it up good style, but while no one's worth the kind of money he was then commanding, the brash country boy exterior was concocted to mask a brasher, unsurprisingly smart operator underneath. It was to be the perfect match: brash, grossly exaggerated American meets trite little England, all distorted image and none the wiser: just like in the movies, or, better, the trailers. But he really did have a knack for parting the punters from their hard earned. Forget coals to Newcastle, this dude could peddle the *Encyclopædia Britannica* to footballers, even to football managers, bikinis to Teheran, even condoms to the lesbian mothers' support group on the grounds that they would keep the old fellow out of harm's way.

After six months at *Nosworthy de Klerk*, Garvey hadn't yet achieved talk of the town status. Indeed, so stultified felt he by the inherently Conservative – large C, as in C19th – working philosophy of *Nosworthy de Klerk* that he was on the verge of leaving. Not for another Brit outfit, for *N de K* was typical to the point of being quintessentially Limey, but back to the US when, lo, the kind of future Mrs Thatcher simultaneously threatened and promised with every spasm of her formidable repertoire suddenly appeared as more than a mad witch's dream, revealed, no less as a personalised vision. Bats in the belfry or not, perhaps merely piecework campanologists tolling for thee, it matters little, Garvey had seen the future and, at last it was he, he was it. He and his new partners, that is. Fairbrother and Tristan also were poised to 'rescue their talents' from the 'dragging influence' of *N de K* and, intent on freer flight than most, they served notice on their employers in the most spectacular fashion, announcing their departure at the shareholders' AGM, at which both had been billed with a droll joviality, even nearer the knuckle than intended, as the 'Artful Dodgers who will make your retirement as interesting as it is comfortable'. An interesting evening was had by all that AGM.

As the tenebrous cigar clouds threatened the first fully indemnified passive smoking fatality with a guaranteed six figure pay out, *Nosworthy de Klerk*'s Chairman, a preposterous mutation of atavistic protectionism and proxy sponsor of juvenile criminals, entitled Sir Gawain Godolphin Chippendale (and, indeed, he is entitled), rose saint like to cure the impatient coughs demanding only his presence. Meanwhile, behind the scenes two of this longeval Santa's erstwhile little helpers were preparing a surprise package for all the little boys come to participate in the simple ritual of self-aggrandizement. Rapt in attention the assembled shareholders eyed the Chairman's prefatory falderal with the childlike anticipation of the chosen soon to be delivered of their due. They wheezed as he teased, for, as sure as obscene profits hail phoney prophets, revelations as subtle as a flasher's would soon ensue. At this stag market night, where the only women in attendance were waitresses and bar girls, i.e., only women in attendance, all the celebrants were at least as richly created as the pudding and about to be sated further.

On announcing an average profit per share of 50%, the third

successive year such a handsome dividend had been delivered, Sir Gawain Godolphin Chippendale clearly had his ever hungry shareholders tamely eating out of his hand, like pigeons in Trafalgar Square, uncaged as nature intended, yet more unafraid than one feels she would deem it in their best interests to be. Unafraid to defecate on the hand that fed them, one felt sure, but such acrimony seemed less than likely to impinge upon this sweetest, most agreeably unanimous of nights. Tonight would see the shareholders exhibiting all the servility they saw fit to display, for tonight they were to feed at their masters' tables; an invitation none could refuse, yet one in whose terms the tone and magnitude of attendance was demanded by an atypically low-key and secondary afterthought.

Sir Gawain (nicknamed 'God' by his half-jesting underlings), seemingly hell-bent on climaxing, rose again to beg no more thanks, as one who can easily eke out more than enough, thank you very much. Cajoling by signal appreciation the last defiant spasms of sycophantic approbation, he gestured for, and readily received contemplative silence from his hitherto frenzied audience. To an outsider unsure as to the nature of this gathering, its *modus operandi* would at least appear to comprise a significant element of worship: in applause there was a ravished, in repose a post-ravished, hue on these fully focused and fascinated faces, a phenomenon all the more noticeable and remarkable for the singularity with which that focus was directed upon the discomfitingly uncharismatic, disarmingly nice, suspiciously dull figure of Sir Gawain. And the uninitiated guest would not have guessed far wrong in believing this lavishly bedecored, slavishly attended gathering place to be a house of great repute, such was the messianic ambience exuded therein. That the only god possibly contemplated on these premises, on this particular gathering's premise, was the great cash dispenser, Mammon, clearly suggests such uncritical attentiveness to be more tangible, if less than truly touching, in these predominantly secular days when worship was (and still is) expected to provide its own reward more along the lines of index-linked plus and capital transfer tax avoidance in an untraceable overseas haven than in the abstracted gaining of an idyllic place among the transmigrated souls in an even more mysterious heaven. That these very worshippers were themselves the gurus of the short-term approach to economic management perhaps suggests further that here was a case of quasi-religion founded on expedient nostrums, as much designed to serve as canards against the infidels of the left who, unopposed, unsullied would surely attempt to outlaw such practice as zealously as, well, such practice should attempt to outlaw them. Loins girded agin the would-be arch emasculators of positive discrimination and would-be wielders of communely reclaimed ploughshares plundered from the burgeoning heritage museum industries, these times of legitimised piracy were publicly justified in the most swashbuckling of terms; entrepreneurs led from the front, vaunt-couriers facing the gangplank, sharks to be thrown to the sharks, shareholders led the baying mob, while employees existed to man the crow's-nest, spying lands to be pillaged and so elevating their status to the mob of shareholders enjoying the privilege of being chief amongst the sycophants; failing to spy such land resulting in a keelhauling through the murky shark infested depths lurking 'neath the not so good ship, HM The Economy. That night, God blessed all who sailed in her, not in spite, but because she was charting a course which could most charitably be rendered as close to the wind. These were times of great derring-do, and in this age of creeping democracy and electronic disinformation, news of such mundane matters as the economy and her performance had better be dramatised – better melodramatised – where once they had been suppressed or deemed too complex and involved to convey. Far from news reaching the little people via great lumbering steamships, it now hit the presses too instantly and constantly to truly be taken in, let alone as gospel, hit the ground running its own publicity campaign, faster than you could say unattributable. With all this freedom abounding, campaigns of disinformation were a piece of cake, if brilliantly managed by governments and their acolytes, roughly comprising all those in their employ and or under the spell of those neo press barons, the multi-media moguls. It would have been surprising, nay, inconceivable to imagine a modern democracy founded on British prejudice and peculiarities to respond to the '80s any differently. History, ancient (read: exhumed without permission) and modern (read: buried beneath contempt) had set the stage for this battle royal between the quasi-republicans with the temerity to bemoan the tragedies that succeeded the storming of the Bastille, and the curators of brattling Britannia plc; a battle long since, by mutual consent, too long since postponed by extraneous considerations such as empire building, disenchanted colonials, disenfranchised citizens, empire surrendering, world wars and the like. But now, hip-hip-alack, the time was ripe for the so long oxymoronically titled United Kingdom (or Great Britain and Northern Ireland; you pays your taxes, you take your choice) to go to war on itself.

Sir Gawain Godolphin Chippendale was coming to the conclusion of his peroration, and like any performer worth his stage, he had saved his best to last. Theatrically teasing the assembled gawps, he instilled a definite air of pantomime into the grand hotel's glorious Queen Elizabeth II function suite. Only the children were missing. In truth, they were not missed. No one was present to shout 'Oh yes he will'. No one doubted that he would. Reveal all, deliver all one could honestly as for, that is.

"And now," the great balance sheet prestidigitator bated the baying scrum of barely behaving celebrants, "a little matter of money!" How they laughed and cheered, and in the case of those under thirty, whooped and exchanged high-fives. Their Chairman was an excellent Master of Ceremonies, receiving applause merely by confirming that the star act had arrived. If the secret of good comedy is timing, the tricks of the trade in addressing shareholders are less likely to overly delay their revelation; there is only one secret to this act, and an open, artless one at that. The timing has to be right in but two respects: the pencilling in of 'AGM' to diaries, and the rate at which the economy is ticking over. The rest is as inevitable as a mugging; you don't have to be involved to know what's going on (cf. The Sermon on the Mound), but you do have to get involved to get *in on* what's going on. With that air of untitled certitude one wished were unique to titled Brits, Sir Gawain Godolphin Chippendale gave the sash a gentle yet authoritative tug and the plush blue velvet curtains parted, revealing to the eager hugger-mugger assembled their collective yet wholly detached window on the world. Would it be curtains for the much desired classier outlook and curtains for the wife, or would the coming year yield a change of habitation and two holidays or three? The doubts were almost entirely artificial – doubts in one's shares being, by extension, doubt in one's own judgement –, acquiring roughly the equivalent status in the make-up of the average shareholder as did the bleeding heart badge of honour for the heart on sleeve strain of liberal. If the thoughts of the assembly had been vocalised the preponderant sentiment may well have resembled a line, bizarrely optimistic, yet rehearsed with such zealous orthodoxy as to come true: 'It's curtains for the wife, too'.

Concealed by the ceremonial curtain had been the widely predicted annual return. What amused the assembly to an excess of their already high spirits was the method of its presentation. The revealed financial wisdom took the form of pure wonder. No pound signs, no noughts, no commas, vulgar figures and even more vulgar fractions, just the simple legend 'Double Your Money!' embossed in laméd gold on a luridly offset Union flag. The *chutzpah* of the phrase greeted the gathering as an overly flattering self-portrait; one knew that there was more here than met they eye, but the truth was all in the concealment. Incongruously, these types with more front than Buck House were faintly embarrassed by their prodigious ability to make money make yet more money. A small price to pay for those proud of their venality and corruptibility, but a lurking presence nonetheless. Right now the reward was all, and as a *reductio ad absurdum* of all socialistic arguments as to the impossibility of running an economy purely by surrendering its more societal functions to market forces, this blasé at birth display of an economic miracle as a game show benefiting an entire community of deserving pools winning players who would spend, spend, spend for Britain was about as convincing as rough-house, rednecking, fingerlicking politicking gets. With these determinedly antagonistic gestures to all malcontents not in on this particular scam scheme, the shareholders of *Nosworthy de Klerk* were knowingly setting out their stall and, more than a whelk stall or no, it would be minded by the praetorian guard charged with enshrining the rapidly establishing new heterodoxy in the Tory Party. In just four years the *arrivistes* had bucked the establishment to such a violent extent that they were, if not entirely distinguishable in character and indistinguishable in power from its erstwhile representatives, at least plainly the grouping with the whip hand in driving it from its near terminal intromit atrophy to an extrovert crusade wielding goads for the dubious benefit of 'go for it' converts. Non converts? Well, the freedom of the market being relative even in an early '80s Britain gung-ho for such radicalism saw that those not fully cognisant of, or able to partake of these selective fruits of economic liberalism could either quite happily survive on the dregs of despair and their own bitter tears or, trying that for a trying period, theoretically at least, seek out a richer, sweeter diet. It was as representatives of that new polarised Britain representing more brightness and bleakness, wherein the *demi-monde* of single motherhood and the like had been eclipsed, rubbished as benighted and lurking without the intermediary caveat or future promise of a penumbra, as representatives to this men in buckram world, the cold hearted, warm dressed world of the City, that Fairbrother and Edmond were introduced into the proceedings. As the wage slave waitresses wheeled out trolleys unimaginable in their neighbourhood supermarkets, of sumptuous cheeses, ditto, to the seated sated, double ditto, the indigestible *coup de foie gras* was being acted out on stage.

"And now our joint nominees for Young Executive of the Year, David Fairbrother and Tristan Edmond, distinctly formidable, combined a veritable quintessence of this company's and this country's future, who will give a presentation of this great company's and this great country's future."

Debauched hoots and hearty applause greeted this announcement. Again, our hypothetical visitor from another planet or equally abstract council estate, our descendant from ancient bastard tribes with no conception of primogeniture, could be excused for sensing tribal loyalties about to be exposed and battle joined. That such ingenuous gatecrashers would have been quite right in their interpretation lies less in their understandable misreading of the signs of well jollied rugger club joviality as hostility to an enemy in the midst, than to the existence and imminent entrance of a Trojan horse so mysteriously absent hitherto as to appear worthy of the alien status generally only bestowed upon the butler in an Agatha Christie *dénouement*.

Fairbrother and Tristan commenced their address conventionally enough. But then, imperceptibly at first, the converted were spared yet more feelgood worship, whence the sales pitch, ostensibly a paean to their just paid off (and singing all the way to the bank) loyalties, began to bear signs of betrayal. Initially, this corporate *lèse-majesté* seemed nothing more than robust cabaret, high-rolling high-spirits, expected by and from almost any large, predominantly male, well off, well on gathering, but the jokes soon wore as thin as the calefacted *After Eights*, muckily spreading on astounded paws, halted halfway to agape mouths. To a man, if not as one, the assembled guests took offence at these invited gatecrashers. Fairbrother had started it, jesting that *Nosworthy de Klerk* was still such a bastion of old fogeydom that the company's future clearly lay in taking over all the law practices required to deal with the imminent upsurge in shareholders' last wills and testaments. Unsurprisingly, the youngsters – i.e., those under 35 – and those who considered themselves youngsters – i.e., those whose other interests weren't sufficiently remunerative to afford them the luxury of yet dismissing their holding/position in *Nosworthy de Klerk* as peripheral to their ambitions – enjoyed being on the right side of the barb. Even they were less than vocal in their support for the next routine, however.

A funereal hush descended upon the great hall as Fairbrother and Edmond joked about the economic consequences of the recently returned Tory administration. On this topic the City remained sufficiently old fashioned to testify – again, mouths agape, simultaneously conveying mute incomprehension and the loudest condemnation – that the inenarrable was indeed the unpardonable. The joke was this: by the time the Tories managed to galvanize this nation's ne'er-do-wells into establishing small businesses the country would be all but the property of foreign multinationals. In the early '60s this would be been the stuff of *TW3* : in the early '70s these two young chaps might have been permitted, even encouraged to venture off the rails for a while on an injudicious sabbatical to the land of *Oz*, appalling, desultory housing, ditto hygiene and fashion; nothing to take too seriously lest if blew away mama's delicate immunity to valium addiction. But this *lèse-majesté* struck home in the early '80s, particularly because these were times when extravagant, not to mention nasty claims were being lodged on behalf of our great nationhood. That the 'slope-heads' and 'slanty-eyed devils' would soon be buying the place up didn't bear thinking about at such gratuitous a celebration precisely because these were acknowledged to be critical times; such eventualities could be faced tomorrow, always tomorrow. One could sense the contentment rush out of the till then bloated assembly, as, lacerated by those with the wit to point out that the one miasma sure to overpower dirty deeds is that of one shitting oneself in ironic homage at their revelation and, furthermore, that one's scent, the heady scent of gas even more noxious than hot air, was being picked up. Being the early '80s, toilet jokes were as, ahem, indispensable polarising agents as were anti-establishment quips in the late '60s, but what offended the mainly sober suited and still predominantly middle-aged audience more than crudities and profanities was the profoundly pertinent nature of the message: no amount of sheep rescuing triumphalism could lead our homegrown flock out of the economic bondage and ultimate slaughter into which they were heading. *Nosworthy de Klerk* 's 'Double Your Money!' pledge was, announced Fairbrother, "a short-term gain for those with the economic attention span of a game show contestant daydreaming that she is the hostess. And, should her implausible dreams come true she gets to power dress, but only once a week for two times 11 minutes either side of *echt* campaigns for real, mostly imported products. This isn't a rallying call to nationalism; you can no sooner protect jobs and markets with that than you can with state socialism. No, this is a call to you to get off your fat, complacent, conservative backsides, repair the Brit devised remote control and hop channels to the real world, *viz*, the European market. If we – as a people representing a government seemingly hell-bent on misrepresenting or neglecting a substantial number of *the* people – don't urgently grasp the point of making other things besides money we are dishonestly brokering an inevitably soon to be remaindered economy."

To occasional boos and frequent other vocal protestations along the lines of 'neither the time nor the place' Tristan announced that he, Fairbrother and Garvey Saddler – the very three prodigious young executives further nominated for 'Young Business Team of the Year' – were departing *N de K*'s "highly remunerative but ultimately inefficient operation," to set themselves up as the 'Boom Brothers', part ad agency, part investment consultants, part hands on investors in the real world of manufacturing. "*Nosworthy de Klerk*," scoffed Tristan, "threatened itself with extinction so long as it esteemed its shareholders higher than its employees, its balance sheet before innovation. Sure, profits are nice. That is why we fully intend to make them every year." To a highly charged good riddance the whiz kids departed the scene knowing little of the details of their future, but clearly sensing the fun they were bound to have.

Chapter Four

The *Boom Bros* office was abuzz with happenings. Not the type accompanied by sitar tuning stress therapy soundtracks, incense and more efficacious noxious odours. No, this was the kind of happening that was, well, happening in any early '80s business worth its reputation for financial chicanery. Thus were the thaumaturges with visitors' permits to Threadneedle Street characterised. They made things happen. More prestidigitation, without a doubt, but illusion was still paramount in a nation belatedly coming to terms with the fact that it had long been far less than a fairytale existence. No matter that the remedies being proposed were bound to be more appealing to a barrow-boy than an economist, drastic changes were being actioned by the default of a *laissez-faire* administration sociologically, governmentally unfettered from the twin evils of punitive taxes on top earners and gratuitously rewarded by the excesses of a largely discredited and dramatically outmoded union movement; ambition's path had never cleaved this clear since the glory days prior to the sacking of the dark Satanic mills. Soon would see the catharsis of the Miners' Strike that would symbolise and culminate the paradox that was government policy, but in 1983 that battle royal, while widely acknowledged as inevitable, was still some way off. The election had concluded as successfully as had the Falklands War. In keeping with the times a seemingly pointless, almost wageless war waged throughout the land: in its own long postponed civil war the opposition's efforts to effect its own defeat were supreme. The least said concerning Galtieri's conscripted *kanonfutter* the better, but as for that other nominal opposition, from the moment they elected a paraffin lamp their leader (lovely and endearingly eccentric though he was), even Labour's *Grand Guignol* internecine strife became secondary to the electorate. To paraphrase a catchphrase from that era, they could not be serious. Notwithstanding the ease of the right's victory, complacency on policy matters was not to prove a characteristic of its performance in office. While it could casually neglect whole swathes of society in extending smooth preferment to its chosen, with its mind clearly made up, this was not a government overly beset by thought, let alone doubt as to the correctness or violability of its actions; such introspection that may have led lesser administrations to admit the word reappraisal into their lexicons was anathema to the frantically thrusting dogma that held the day to such an extent that even complacency was driven. As with the government, so with the people, its people. The paradox of a government led by a woman which together went a long way to replacing unmanly with ungentlemanly in the pantheon of English vices is one that has not been overlooked. Suffice it to say, here and now, for what it's worth, and many other conservative clichés by which, by and large, we still conduct/filibust public debate in this country, that it is in the author's opinion that such a revolt could not have been so exigently staged were a man, specifically a gentleman, at its head.

Fairbrother was perched on his functional, minimalist, bordering on hair shirt of a seat. In his left hand he held a businesslike piece of headed notepaper, in his right he held a pen. In the no longer clearly delineated crevice between chin and clavicle he lodged the telephone, the entire telephone. In spite of being in a fully wired office – his, their office – he preferred to communicate with the wider world, and specifically those watching, through his mobile cordless. Well, even secretaries can sense status and, while not necessarily aspiring to it, they could come in handy for temporarily conferring it when the desire to take one took one. Martha, she of descriptions commencing 'she of', was gazing at the epitome of thrusting young manhood she is privileged to call boss, thought Fairbrother as he suffered the costly and tacky indignity of muzak on hold. As Beethoven or Bach or A. N. Other of them long dead kraut bastards suffered the dual bastardisation of synthesised reproduction and the less than amphitheatrical acoustics of a telephone earpiece seemingly designed first and foremost to pick up interference, Fairbrother thought of asking Marsha out. She could hardly refuse him, could she? Let's see the poor cow try, Fairbrother smirked to himself as Marsha smiled for her boss. It was the smile of an innocent child over eager to please, of a baffled *ingénue* desperate to convey that the joke had been well and truly got. It was a smile that bearded a grimace.

"Ah, Mr Smart," Fairbrother broke his silence along with the eye contact which, on inevitable resumption, would soon threaten to promise Marsha more than she could bear, or rather dare to resist. Thus dismissed from his thoughts the hitherto transfixed Marsha got on with something useful. Not exactly her life, she worked for this bastard, after all. Not exactly useful either, doing the bidding of these frighteningly plausible conmen. She knew precisely what was going on in that mind of this. She didn't like it, but she could handle it. Not surprisingly, she liked that.

"I hear where you're coming from, Barry," enthused Fairbrother to the now familiarised Mr Smart. "Can do, will do," he summarised the conversation and removed the phone by lifting his head, catching it (the phone) as it fell into his left hand. Mundanity given the bravura treatment, sighed Marsha as she eyed him contemptuously. Her voice, however, betrayed no such perceptions as she requested of the object of loathing that, perhaps, he was ready to give her her orders. "Best coffee, best biscuits, conference room *numero uno*, 14:00 hours, this day. Four guests, *et moi*, " he duly instructed, deploying that mishmash of military precision and ludicrously unbecoming grandeur she found particularly loathsome in a man, especially in a boss.

"Yes, sir," she simpered.

"Will do, can do," he implored.

"Will do, can do," she incanted the official mantra, applied routinely to the simplest of tasks in an almost entirely unsuccessful venture at instilling self esteem. "Fucking evangelist of the fucking obvious," she thought. This time she smiled at him. It was all she could manage in the maintenance of her dignity, and the sustenance of his, to stop at a smile.

"Believe you. Believe in you," he sickeningly responded. Thankfully, Marsha wasn't required to respond in kind. Yet.

The Mr Smart, Mr Barry Smart, to whom Fairbrother had imparted by telephone that he had heard where he was coming from, had arrived. In the *Boom Bros* conference room *Numero Uno (really)* the visitor and his entourage admired the proudly functional surrounds as an Athenian may have eyed a Spartan's dwelling in days of antiquity. Different, but of great interest, precisely because the great and the good, never to neglect the greedy at *Smart Investments*, deemed these upstart *Boom Bros* worthy of time, consideration and motion.

'Know thy enemy rather than know him through envy,' one of the many maxims comprising the *Smart Investments* training manual was aired by the Smart one himself. In true *Boom Bros* David versus Goliath style, the four impeccably besuited representatives were to be faced with but one *prima facie* unbusinesslike protagonist. Marsha sashayed in with coffee and sweetmeats as keenly aware of the eyes begging her on to burlesque as she was that such was life: these bastards paid the wages, the wages of sin. Keenly aware and deeply disgusted, she fulfilled the terms and conditions of her employment to a practically parodical degree. Trouble was, once established, a prejudice could only be parodied in the eyes of those able to recognise it as such. Here it was just very much established.

"Marsha, do the business," Fairbrother half commanded, half announced in the manner of an MC of a sleazy strip joint rather than that of a man requesting refreshments. The audience snickered. Marsha was always paraded before these dills. "It pays to be friendly to and, if necessary *with* the customers," her terms and conditions gushed, reminding Marsha of nothing so much as the vacuity of the old Baldwin by Kipling on press barons, man made maxim on power without responsibility. Today she was 'privileged to know' (their words, not hers, but then they could make a dummy a ventriloquist and make it believe it had a voice, she smiled woodenly) Justin Oakes, a twice privileged, doubly execrable upper middle-class oik who, even had Marsha fallen for that fabled woman's intuition bit, still wouldn't bear thinking about. But Marsha wasn't what these men with the most imagined most women to be, though with their equally fabled, wholly genuine lack of insight they could not see the revulsion they stirred in that fabled woman's breast. If of romantic bent they may have seen in there the mother's milk of the marrying kind, though not the milk of human kindness (these suckers are the products of some bad nursemaiding, she smiled), if of the more typical, the married kind, they definitely saw in there a passion that was more than a match for any revulsion the late 20th Century may have hinted lay in wait for them there. Today she was 'honoured also to know' Cal Whipsnade, a slightly less chinless variation on the themeless theme that was Justin. At least Cal knows more than one reason why he's an arrogant bastard, Marsha noted in a muted mental shorthand comprehensible only to the female of the species: Justin thinks I should want him just because he's a successful businessman, Cal thinks he's sexy besides. Nice try, Cal, but my type need a degree more backbone to support their individualism than that. No, Cal was thrice damned, a spineless wonder who believed that the obsequiousness he was prepared to dispense towards his superiors could only be exceeded by the gratitude he was prepared to accept from the chicks. Today, oh lucky day, she was further 'privileged to make the acquaintance of' Horace Balsam, a prematurely bloated thirty something accountant with the look of a bouncer gone to seed on too many unwarranted entries to too many old pals' act nights out. Always mistaken for one or the other at stag nights, yet never actually groom nor best man, she smiled inwardly, wickedly, as if deliberately concealing an orgasm. Horrible Horace noticed this conceit and thought, correctly, though more by accident of girth than birth making designs, "I bet I could put more than a smile on that face". Caught between grimace and hilarity, Marsha smiled sweetly. Lastly, she "fulfilled 'every woman's long held ambition'" to meet Sir Barrington Smart, as was, now Barry Smart again, widely famed entrepreneur who, while born into serious piles of old money, had made good better in financial terms, coincidentally finding favour in the eyes of the '80s administration by being reborn (1979) as what even his own mother would be forced to admit was a proud and utter bastard.

"And I wish I had known of my yearning to meet you before 'twas so swiftly shot down in glorious flames; flames which once were a spark, yet now, alas, would threaten to engulf my marriage," he blazed mock clutching his heart, a gorillagram declaiming *Sonnet 18* to the wrong recipient on the Friday the 13th adumbrating St Valentine's Day. On that melodramatic entrance Marsha was ushered out, sweet enough to dispense the popcorn, too 'innocent' to view the movie.

"Thank you for your attendance, Sir Barrington, Mr Oakes, Mr Whipsnade, Mr Balsam," Fairbrother ceremoniously acknowledged his guests. The desired result was instantaneous, the victory so visible.

"Don't stand on ceremony, David, we've all got Christian names, even if one of us is a Yid," barked Barry to unchristian roars of approval, not least from Balsam, the butt of his master's humour, of which, in the latter half of this century, only a northern club comic turn (*pace* his audience), because immutably thick or similarly venal, should justifiably be proud. Or perhaps not.

"Reet then, down to brass tacks," continued Barry in a garbled giving of a working class accent, the likes of which only the decidedly non non U can still get away with. That Barry came close spoke volumes, sorry, sed loadz, for his failure to assimilate barrow-boy status. The people who counted counted him as one of theirs, though, whatever guise they bad him wear.

"What can you do to raise the profile of *Smart Investments plc* significantly above that of our rivals? And cut the crap," Barry urged, his encouragement not quite sure it was not profoundly misplaced.

"Right, Barry," rose Fairbrother to the challenge, "no crap, no visual aids. This is not the vicar's slide-show." Murmurs of appreciation at what this was not rose from the seated suits as fears deserting, shackles lapsing. "We will raise your profile by the simple expedient of highlighting the success of the competition." Intrigued, Barry Smart begged him continue. Unorthodoxy was the in thing, after all, a little more extremity was bound to follow. "In that very act we shall draw attention to the untapped, well nigh limitless potential of *Smart Investments*."

"Slogans, boy, slogans," commanded Smart, thumping the table with urgency and determination which conveyed to Fairbrother that, with one half-decent, half-indecent pun or feebly poetic alliteration, the potentate of the hostile takeover was his to toy with.

"How about ——?" began Fairbrother.

"You tell me," boomed Smart, finger pointing, Kitchener style.

"He needs me," smiled Fairbrother. "Here's one —— 'If we are so smart how come you've never heard of us?'"

"*And?*" sneered Balsam.

"That's it," smiled Fairbrother.

"What kind of —?" Balsam began blustering but was blown out by his boss.

"No, wait. I kinda liked that. Why *do* I kinda like that?" he challenged Fairbrother.

"Very simple. *Smart Investments* is a new offshoot for you Barry, right?" Barry nodded as enthusiastically as a rear window puppy doll. "Your name is well know, to put it mildly," Fairbrother continued in an orgy of almost orgasmic, mercifully muted mind-jerking assent. "You are one of the highest profile corporate raiders in the nation." At this observation all nodding ceased. The silence slipped from mute wonder to muted threat. Twenty seconds of glances between the three Smart representatives and the Smart man himself finally fixed four-square on Fairbrother. "No crap," he smiled, gesturing quotation marks in the rather clouded air hanging threateningly above. Clearly Smart saw the intention as if in a revelation.

"And we should use that to attract investors?"

"Entice," admonished Fairbrother.

"*Eh?*" queried Sir Barrington, so unaccustomed to being refined, he took it as being contradicted.

"Entice investors. If we are to take this account we take it on our terms."

"And those are?" sniped Whipsnade.

"Total integrity," smiled Fairbrother.

"I've never heard the like," jeered Justin. "Integrity in advertising," he guffawed his incredulity at this bumptious, ingenuous upstart.

"OK, we change it," complied Fairbrother. "Say we portray your total integrity in business matters." The atmosphere was turning oppressive again. Barry lifted the gloom.

"Of course, of course, you'll call a spade a spade —"

"A bastard a bastard," chirped Fairbrother.

"Quite. Quite, A whatever a whatever, and —"

"*You* are rewarded for our honesty."

"And *our* honesty?" fired Balsam, shifting on his seat as if were he to feel more uncomfortable he would shortly spring from it like a confidently agitated boxer at the sound of the first bell.

"And you are rewarded for your dishonesty," Fairbrother responded to the challenge, refraining from adding "as always" as being too obvious for even this company to take no offence.

Sir Barrington threw in the towel at this. Well, it had 'hotel' written all over it and he wasn't averse to paying his man to take a dive.

"But, 'corporate raider' —?" he pleaded for leniency.

"*Total* integrity. Pride in being a bastard. Profits will soar," insisted Fairbrother. Smart stared into those cocksure eyes.

"Yes, he's honest enough to do my lying for me," he noted to his own satisfaction. "I like this boy," he then announced. "Boys?" he enquired, his lurking grandeur so simply summoned.

"Yes, sir," echoed Whipsnade and Oakes exuding a eagerness a chat show host talking to and on behalf of royalty could barely have matched.

"Yes, sir, Sir Barrington, sir," cooed Balsam and more than did.

The professional partnership between *Boom Bros* and *Smart Investments* was an immediate success. Full page advertisements were placed in the qualities, advertisements which soon saw the copywriters sharing star billing with the client. In mock make-up of movie posters from Hollywood's golden age, the legend ever commenced '*Boom Bros* announce —'. The initial identifier was to be writ ever larger as the campaign took off. The first in a sequence soon to be withdrawn from the qualities and placed in the pops (when even the plebs have disposable income to invest the time is indeed ripe for a democracy of shareholders) bore the legend '*Boom Bros* announce *Smart Investments* in your name.' Nothing else. The intrigue generated by such an enigmatic use of unequivocally serious money was enough in itself to drive the message home. A week later the readers of those qualities were enlightened less by the full page disclaimer '*Boom Bros* announce on behalf of *Smart Investments* that they and their aforesaid clients would wish to disassociate themselves from any inference that last week's advertisement (placed in this paper, on this very page) was designed to infuriate, annoy or in any way play on one's nerves. In short, we deny that it was placed by and on behalf of Smart Alecks. But then we would, wouldn't we?' This did the trick. By the following Thursday, when the next ad in the sequence – '*Boom Bros* announce *Smart Investments* are not inappropriately named *NB*, we'd like also to announce that we told you so.' – was placed, the cat was out of the bag. In that week following the 'disclaimer' the three *Boom Bros* had appeared in such features, interviews and photo-opportunities the like of which any politician in the throes of a close campaign would all but kill for. The phrase 'Smart Alecks' and rather more robust variations thereon were soon synonymous with the three *Boom Bros*.

From practical obscurity outwith the necessarily cloistered environs of the City they became instant celebrities. Within two weeks of the first advert they were featuring, almost to saturation point in the great organs of the establishment. Vapid articles focusing invariably on the 'rapid rise of —' had rarely seemed so apt, for these very features featured their subjects to such an extent that collectively they were clearly the major partners in 'this remarkable story'. That *Boom Bros*, in their copywriting guise, and *Smart Investments*, in their infamy as Sir Barrington's latest questionable shot at borderline legitimacy, were able to grab such free and partial publicity owed less to the skill of the advertising campaign *per se* and more to its astuteness in recognising that the social and marketing conditions existed for such apparently benign exploitation to turn such a handsome profit. In short, 'money well spent is money risked' seemed to be the precipitate and proud of it recommendation of the government as well as the then predominant dictum of the market. 'Venture capital' were the swashbuckling words on the respectively well-licked and lickspittle lips of the captains of industry and the practical hordes, of the great and the grotty. From the Chancellor of the Exchequer to the newly knighted and benighted Mr and Mrs Average, as were, now Lord and Lady Shareholder of the Shires, or roads to, mouths uttered, "More! More! I want! I want! More!

More!" in the manner of spoilt brats acting, truly acting the part of Oliver Twist in heartless unknowing parody.

In consequence of this heist of a campaign, *Smart Investments* grew like a hard-on on an humungous men video on fast-forward. Uninterfered with by the *BBFC*, of course, *Boom Bros*, too, were an Instamatic hit, popular with the public and, in the particular of their personal lives, with the ladies. Their meteoric rise to fame inevitably reached the tabloids: just as water finds its own level, so news finds its own definition of balance. Again, just as their introduction to the public at large was largely fuelled by self-generated hyperbole, so their elevation to, or rather descent into that curious domain that is public curiosity was achieved with an apparent effortlessness that would have rendered any Jezebel deb greener than Vivien Leigh's creeping peepers in Pascal and Shaw's *Caesar and Cleopatra*. Their celebrity was assured with a few variations on the once shocking, long since tried and trusted tactic of courting controversy. Be it in their work, their utterances to the press, their behaviour at all the right parties, the word which sprung to mind was, still is, *arriviste*. It was with more luck than judgement that they, as it were, arrived when the word had lost so may of its pejorative connotations: it was with laboriously minute calculation that this opportunity, once copied, was fully and frankly exploited. With notoriety so readily bestowed, money making was easy. Put simply, they cashed in on their luck and, as interest gained in it, so they were able to judge assiduously how best to do so. Luck bestowing expertise may seem a curious method of running an economy, but that was about as deep as the doctrine of the time ran: except that those two strange bedfellows were given the titles of risk and just reward in official circles. The newly cemented special relationship with the USA served to further endorse this epic view of the mundane and the grubby. It was as if the economy were a film which all would pay dearly to see, but in which only the chosen few could act, let alone participate, let alone identify themselves. The rest could dream.

Chapter Five

The *Boom Bros*, attending all the best parties, attending to all the best parties, offending all the seasons' lost causes, were rarely out of the tabloids. As their star shone ever brighter and the big accounts reflected their new found status so these three narcissists found their self-adoration fully and richly requited. Never without a pretty girl, be she a gum chewing bubblehead of a secretary whose talent to annoy was only superseded by the, uh, soothing compensations of her mute willingness to be extravagantly contemplated, or a nightmare helper who was an even more glaring example of the marriage between the heaven that is a woman for the taking and the hell that is a woman for the talking. The type favoured, *nem con.*, by the *Boom Bros* were the type who could be innocently guilty of provocation rather than mere evocation; the type that wouldn't merely stay hit but would come back begging for more like masochistic rag dolls from some spoilt and cantankerous child's dream. Not that much hitting went on. When one had that kind of power, violence was evidence of a denial, a negation of that kind of power. Yobs hit women until it hurt all concerned. Nobs allowed their women to hit on them, but never until it hurt.

Around this period, mid '85, 18 months after their launch, *Boom Bros* initiated a collective professional concern (and individual personal interest) in a rock and roll singer, a kind of shore leave Madonna for vengeful sailors with AIDS. Going by the name of Syreenah!, the subtlest aspect of this lady was the exclamation mark following, no, climaxing her name. No superstar with the wider public as yet, Syreenah! made her money performing sub-Marilyn burlesque routines to all male executive audiences only distinguishable to the pouting performer from a stag night of sozzled stud-U-like adult channel couch potato sub-humans by the regularity of her appearances before them. Like a streetwalker encountering the beak, Syreenah! came to know well the whims and fancies of these her big lunch judges and potential lynch mob members. Every weekday lunch-time they would come in in their threes and fours and fives and more, never company, always crowding, at first eating and talking as seriously as only businessman can, settling their arguments and their bills with a bravado that betrayed not so much a lack of seriousness as, well, a lack of comprehension. These things, the male bonding, the loudest laddest camaraderie, the blithely dismissed bills which Syreenah!, in a previous incarnation as Sheril, waitress, knew to be way beyond blithe dismissal, they were all in evidence of a performance every bit as hollow, crass and self-degrading as the little theatre of shame she was truly sorry to put herself through in their presence. Almost immediately the audience of lunch-time lads-di-da, and particularly the *Boom Bros* entourage of twelve or so paradigmatic pricks, started showing an interest in both the making of this cunt and the making of a cult. Predating karaoke's assault on these isles by some five years, Syreenah! encapsulated the very same triumph as travesty as did these, her first and most devoted fans. Soon she would be miming and grinding her way through alternative venues and TV studios like some ill-fated auditionee to opportunity's knocking shop.

With that combination of the juvenile and the patrician that forever will suggest petulance, the *Boom Bros* crowd beckoned Syreenah! to table. "We may be childish enough to like your show but we're also plenty men enough and rich enough to buy and sell it, to sell you, more times than even you could imagine," quoth Carter Wainwright, copywriter extraordinaire, as he held out what was plainly crafted to be her chair. Of course she wasn't joining only him, she was joining the club, running the gauntlet: hurdling the initiation curve by dint of her highfalutin, never really much more than tartish beauty, she was invited into what she was expected to perceive as an intimate circle. Straight away she saw it was no such thing, of course; there was no more genuine intimacy here than could be found in a gang rape. To be fair, she wasn't gang raped. Well, not then and there, not all at once. All ten there present were to have her at one time or another. These liaisons were at times pathetic, brutal, frightening, enjoyably vague, hard to stomach and finally promising if not ultimately fulfilling. All ten had her but she had one. But one she had so bad; the potential revenge exactable on that one soul could have more than compensated for the pummelling her personality had been well, though never adequately recompensed to undergo. But then, just as she was about to unmask the poor *klutz* for his pathetic worth, a funny thing happened. She reciprocated his love. Truly, fully his infatuation had chanced upon her exhibitionism and, bingo!, a match was made. That it was to prove a match more akin to those made by boxing promoters than registrars and clerics should come as no surprise given the erstwhile protagonistic/deuteragonistic approaches of those joined to those joined. Yet, for a while at least, it was a love match.

Chapter Six

It had been a particularly rewarding morning. Garvey had produced an idea of as yet uncapped brilliance. Fairbrother and Tristan had been in receipt of a fax informing them that a long sought after client 'most definitely in the financial sector' was all but theirs for the taking. It was with a jaunty step that the *Boom Bros* and their charges hotfooted it to *À propos de rien*, the bar cum private members' club where Syreenah! was then strutting her lunch-time bump 'n' grind; the lads wended their way down the club, an anthropomorphised snake forming a chain of command. At its business end the boys who put the bite in *Boom Bros,* right down to, bringing up the rear, the flagellant, the factotum, the baby of the business, as happy as a tolerated irritant with a rattle, content to subcontract himself as the arse end of the pantomime thoroughbred while his long-term role of understudy continued. The malevolent conga paused imperceptibly at the door, immediately regaining its rhythm and increasing its tempo as it gained its natural environment. To throbbing beat and lights more appropriate to the witching hour than the lunching hour, they made their entrance much as a boxer's menacingly exuberant retinue does to the *Eye of the Tiger*. Hi 5s were exchanged as fellow diners rose in celebration of, well, ten men lunching. Whoops of recognition echoed back and forth as entrance was greeted and welcome reciprocated in a display of enthusiasm bound to puzzle all but the most contemporary of that season's social anthropologists. An unmistakable sexual charge rent the air, though one could be mistaken in one's identification of the object of desire. Almost exclusively populated by clean-cut, exquisitely groomed young men, one's primary impression would have been of a multiple gay wedding or some such revolutionary ritual in progress. But progress and revolution would not be *le mots justes* here. Ritual, certainly, but ritual as recalcitrant fashion. Chief amongst these paradoxical fashions stood the role of women within the club. All members were male, all visible, presentable staff, female. To the strains of a ditty which the Oslo jury on *Eurovision* duty would no doubt award 12 points, were they not disallowed by nationality, service made its all singing, all entrancing entrance. More cheerleaders than waitresses, more burlesque wenches than girls next door, they would appear to our much bemused anthropologist, aka the common man, to be dancing with food to the crazed choreography of a gourmand cum anthropophagous major-domo. Of course, no gourmand worth his salt could be satisfied with the miniature portions concocted by *nouvelle cuisine*, no cannibal sated by such sparsely, if exquisitely proportioned long pig, but taken as a whole the resultant effect upon the spectator was overwhelming. Even the food looked good enough to eat. Indeed, to spectate here would result in being overwhelmed. So loud came the parade, one instinctively, or rather reactively joined in very much in the manner of a neurotic busybody screaming at a sado-masochistic, with a seemingly gratuitous pneumatic drill, to explain himself, or one simply suffered. All in all, a greedy, raucous exaggeration of society at large and, each to their own, perhaps a bit much of a lunch-time.

As if in homage to the national hypocrisy towards the still unsettled woman question, Syreenah! slunk on stage to the strains of *The Police's* 'Roxanne'. 'You don't have to sell your body to the night' blared out as the woman's rep endowed and equipped with the diverse freedom to be a wage slave on less than the then EEC's recommended minimum wage, or a sex slave on significantly more, but precious little in between, was revealed to Fairbrother, as if by imprimatur, as the permissible, unmissable object for his as yet unpenned *billets-doux*. Through a song overwroughtly concerning itself with the rescue of a damsel from the *demi-monde*, Fairbrother was galvanised into whatever degree of romanticism can pass in such circumstances, in such an age of vicarious symbolism. He had been in bed plenty before, but never knowingly in love. Her story, he suspected almost correctly, would be similar. Furthermore, she had been in beds of stranger bods; bent double for troubled couplings in backs of cars, burnt for sins atop hair-shirt textured office carpets and such with, *inter alios, über alles*, most of his present company.

As insubstantially clad, similarly remunerated service danced attendance, lunch was truly launched. Pushing the boat out as conspicuously as possible was this particular season's corporate and governmental policy, the status afforded by conspicuous consumption far and away outweighing any costs, any 'expenses' incurred.

"Syreenah!, Syreenah!, honey," rasped Jasper and Carter, phagocytes and acolytes, fast becoming parasites, gadflies on Fairbrother's gourd.

"How about granting a request just for *moi*?" commanded Jasper, not for much longer Fairbrother's favoured assistant.

"Anything for you, sir," she acceded, concurrently simpering with a vulnerability close to habit, even closer to her terms and conditions of employment, and simmering with a likewise venal sexuality. That's just the trouble with these things, mused Fairbrother as his inspiration flirted with the other, more noticeably attentive company, thereby granting requests left, right and centre. I'll bet she's had more pricks than Cupid's arrows, Fairbrother concluded limply, prematurely. As Syreenah! concentrated her undoubted, undoubtedly disingenuous affections on the task in hand, utilising admirable, if mercenary assiduity, Fairbrother lost himself in that warm ruminative world which his present shit-hot-to-trot lifestyle avowedly precluded. If his colleagues could see him now. But, of course, they couldn't, what with having other things on their then more than ever one track minds. As Fairbrother drifted wistfully to a past that he at last realised had never been given a chance to be a future, he thought of girls with less of Syreenah!'s glamorous artifice, girls who kept their given names and only surrendered their surnames when love bid them productive union. Carol, 'his' girl in the 5th and 6th forms, was contrasted in mind's eye, heartfelt replay with Syreenah!, herself very much in the flesh. Whatever she had done with her life, Carol surely had produced a prouder mother than Syreenah!: just as the male child is the father of the man, so is the female child mother of the woman. More, the daughter is the mother's mother: more so, what in this day and age a girl would need to revert to! Strait-jacketed and whaleboned prudery to make her mother believe in her! Though Fairbrother was well aware that this bout of maudlin atavism would earn the wholly justified scorn of even his father, he couldn't help viewing the female of the species as a whole, and Syreenah! in particular, in every sublimated particular, as respectively potential victims only rescuable by a Chris-de-Burgh song and cloying devotion to one clinging man, or as an actual victim since corrupted by contagion many a devoted man could too readily fall prey to. The first type, that was Carol and, for all the fond memories, thanks for those, but no more. Syreenah! was the second type, of course, in execrable excess, yes, but in sanctifiable *excelsis*, too. Such apotheosis must be definable if his entreaties to Carol could ever have been adjudged worthy of the name, well, of love. Bless her, probably wedded to a good and honest artisan; to win her he'd have to be good, to desire to do so he'd have to be honest, to come clean. This, too, was going to be a challenge. Did he, neither good nor honest, take Syreenah!, evidently deserving of neither

qualities in a mate, nor apparently desiring such a creature, to be his —
—? He was getting carried away with himself. Luckily, as tears threatened to cloud his countenance (much overdue as a purgative though they were) he was brought abruptly back to a reality which for once asked of him no dissembly. As he snapped back to the present there wasn't a dry eye at the table.

"David's trying not to laugh, but I can see the tears," Tristan gibed and they all guffawed anew.

"Maybe he thinks we were being sexist," roared Carter to the pre-Darwinian, fuck it, prehistoric, fuck it again, post-Darwinian accompaniment.

"Maybe he thinks we went a little too far," and again laughter rattled. Knowing nothing of the cause of this uproar and consequently understanding all by a process with misapplied an analytical, fuck it, fuck *you*, gestalt on the group and an emotional eye on the particular, Fairbrother grunted.

"Assent or dissent? Aye or nay? Consent or incest?" sneered Jasper. Whatever the merits and demerits of the proposition, it produced a response that in its sorry and cyclically trapped, not quite conclusive syllogistic state provided a metaphor for what we men – consenting adults, remember – laughingly term the female condition. Syreenah! (hereinafter shorn of exclamation mark) returned his gaze, at once begging his intervention and begging it off. Clearly she was upset in more ways than one. First, at having been the butt of a joke that mercilessly targeted her self-esteem; second, at having had recourse to cry for help, for she didn't like pretending to like this sort of thing, the performance didn't extend that far; third, at having to cry off that cry and try to regain that composure so recently routed as absolutely as manufacturers' claims on run-proof mascara when faced with more than cosmetic emotions. Clearly it was all too much for her. As tears scarred her brave put on face her full saddened self came out as if in sympathy, the effect being as dramatic as taking the piss and applying to it litmus paper. These perennial sixth formers had got her the wrong kind of hot. They had gone too far, that much was clear to Fairbrother. She appeared before him increasingly beautiful as, for the first time in his life he saw what the emotional woman was all about: not given to emotion *per se*, rather one given too many emotions. Hitherto he had experienced only, no, perceived but these emotions served up red-hot and passionate or ice-cold and vengeful; that is, too extremely to evaluate as desiring anything but a like response. But ——— this girl was more complicated. In truth she revealed that they all were.

"What's the matter, Syreenah?" Fairbrother begged enlightenment and introduction in equal measure. She could have been forgiven for suspecting he was further taking a rise, but something in the eyes precluded this being a liaison conducted by taunt from havens afar, from which entrenched positions each side retreats further as much for inexplicably zealous belief in his or her sanctity as out of any fear that it is the safety of his or her good repute that is in any respect under attack. Their eyes met, their tears pooled, and in those solemn depths, he felt, they took the plunge, across that crowded room they came together, not waving but drowning, determined to perfect that kiss of death as kiss of life.

"You don't have to listen to these morons, Syreenah," Fairbrother offered.

"Why not, we have to listen to her," interrupted Saddler. It was an uncalled for remark, they, we! paid to listen to her. Syreenah smiled the gentle smile of angels: thank you for believing in me, it said, even as it transcended that belief into awe. Dumbstruck, Fairbrother deployed the ostensible fail safe of man through the ages, seeking not to woo but win woman. Like most tried and trusted theories, its relationship to the truth was subjective enough to be none, so convinced was it of its right to be downright deservedly wronged. In hitting Saddler, Fairbrother finally found his voice. Neither eloquent nor inspired, it was on the side of the angels nonetheless, low on evolution, horse high on chivalry.

"You – we! – pay to listen to – her!" he brawled at his prostrate and bloodied colleague. But still, as if assailed by a dampening chorus from the pits, his *con brio* was modified from a position of no great, yet cruelly replenished strength. "Listen to her!" screamed our incredible stridulator, manifesting a degree of messianism that would soon transfix his own poor soul, cruelly spotlighting the onset of bathos bound rapidly to engulf the man who, without knowing what he himself really stood for, would stand up for a woman, knee-jerked and wrong kind of dated, as if for any woman, every, each and every woman. With the possible exception of his mother there wasn't any woman on earth more idealised in Fairbrother's eyes, so to say he was prepared to defend her honour belongs in the same league of understatement as the contention that the great British judiciary are a bit behind the times, *in re, inter alios*, no, *inter alia* the woman question.

"Listen to her!" screamed Garvey, sensing in Fairbrother's audible and physical paralysis these past five seconds that his own was now so much the upper-hand that there would be no need to raise it, let alone the remains of his body. Indeed, to ensure the erstwhile aggressor's crippling discomfiture would take on all the elements necessary to inducing a doomed comeback ending in hubristic collapse, he gauged it best to stay put. "I never even listened to her when I fucked her. Neither did any of the lads round here. Right, lads?"

"Right!" they screamed assent in a union as yet exaggerated in number, yet still able to serve as a legitimate progenitor of paranoia in any poor bastard foolish enough to face its way in anything approaching an adversarial manner.

"Put the music on way up loud – not *her* music," spat Saddler, chin extruded, commanding no one in the particular of his text, many with the general thrust of his menacing mien. "I'd never want to listen to *that*," he spat again, this time the appearance portraying a man not far short of summoning up the quarantinable drool of the truly maddened.

As Saddler's standing had grown in inverse proportion to his physical position in the post *tête-à-tête*, so now did Fairbrother's apparent superiority of motive shrink and shrivel until, casting a pleading, shriven glance his angel's way, its blithe return from a still imaginable high withered him to the pits the more. He did it for her! How ludicrous! They were all laughing now, even Syreenah, made up no doubt to escape being the butt for once. To a man his colleagues, his erstwhile chums, had done it to her when he had so burned to do it for her! He now saw fit to indulge in a little winner takes all ringcraft, rustier, more full of holes and shit than that practised by Gerald Ratner.

Syreenah! (all appellations were being cried out in exclamatory mode) giggled nervously as Fairbrother, now fallen to pathetic prayer to the ground that wouldn't swallow him, gazed up with a look of supplication, Matthew 27:46 in apostatical charade, beetling his brow so severely that his eyes appeared cavernously noctivagous, as if searching for a way out of this situation, that head. Appropriately enough he felt drained of that most basic constituent of *élan*, adrenaline, get up and go, the lack of which, on bad days barely distinguishes most of us from the cadavers we are to become. Yet when, in a position of indignity, having been sent sprawling in a manner so undignified as to best be politely ignored, he was shown signs of life. Syreenah! held out her fair hand. Twitching back to being he accepted her help and, seeing her smile beatifically, he decided to make a final sacrifice. Throwing Attic salt on the wound, he began laughing like a corpsed comedian with a staged foresight rarely sustainable either side of the punchline's delivery. He sized up that making a fool of himself might just pay beautiful dividends, if pursued with the requisite if grossly dissembled deliberation.

"Only joking," he joked as she gallantly helped him regain his posture, if not his stature or backbone. In his desperation to appear embarrassed at the whole affair he merely increased the momentum of that first named quality until its unintentionally scene stealing manifestation as an unlikely agitant ruled out any corollary between his original intention and its perception; it was an increasingly dangerous act.

Like a self-fulfilling soothsaying with a paranoid streak, his every attempt at conveying the fact that, yes!, he too had found his behaviour funny, that, yes!!, of course he was embarrassed, came out all wrong. He was in no fit way for engaging in knockabout bouts of self-deprecation; one seldom is immediately on the back of excelling extemporaneously in it, right in it, for the seemingly exclusive benefit of all but self. And so the recognition of one's propensity to farce readily exacerbates one's tragedy. We can all laugh at ourselves alone. What we can't all quite manage as intended is being laughed at excessively, to the point of the audience pleading 'too much', baying for 'no more!'. As Lincoln never quite said, 'You cannot be the fool of all of the people all of the time.'

And how they were laughing! His "Whozzahmattuh?" conveyed to its targeted audience a risible solemnity similar to a pantomime dame's 'Oh yes he is!' to his/her/its. The indeterminate, nay, protean mating roles taken up and discarded like the window dressing of 'Top That!' sale signs adorning decreasingly attired mannequins in a recession, made this scene all the funnier. From defending the honour of a lady (machismo) he knew little of (chivalry), evidently less than those he challenged (naïf, Naff!), to being brought down to the floor by his own shame (real catholic guilt, proxy contrition, misplaced), to admitting he was looking a bit foolish (make 'em laugh!)! As understated as such an admission was it could never hope to disguise the magnitude of the gross caricatures of sexual orthodoxy he had just enacted. His predicament had presented three parallax views whose viewers, as if in imitation of caged tigers, paraded round its confines in order to view it face to face: *1*, his friends', *2*, hers, *3*, last, but by no means not least, his.

1a: he defends the honour of a lady he alone would appear not to have had the honour of, *1b*: he hits a friend and colleague out of an inexplicably oviparous infatuation, *1c*: he then retires to the floor in the all shunning manner of an acid head circa '67, seriously enamoured of the madcap's Floyd, making with the foetal position, *1d*: he then claims to have been *only* joking! God help us, he does!

2a: he defends *my* honour, *2b*: he proposes to defend *my* honour to the death! *Whose?!*, *2c*: he looks like death, *2d*: he denies acts *2a* to *2c* inclusive.

3a: he defends a maiden's honour, *3b*: he slays her a dragon, *3c*: she was no maiden, *3d*: there are no dragons.

The lunch, begun in the then everyday spirit of entrepreneurial triumphalism, threatened by *hubris* , delivered by farce, bundled in *Armani* , would be long remembered as a classic of its kind. As power lunches go it had the lot: the show of strength, of fiscal muscle, of new money power dressing: the female element as crucial to the play as the stimulant stiletto to a doolally rape case judge: fisticuffs betwixt friends: the unmasking of the strumpet as unworthy: the laughter at the expense of others. Fairbrother paid the bill and left alone.

Chapter Seven

It had been a hard day. A wasted day, it seemed. Ribbed mercilessly by eternal sixthformers for being a repeat year retard who had never kissed a girl properly, he ought not to have minded. After all, he could buy and sell most of his employees, could as easily pick and choose working and sleeping partners (and to be fair to the thankless bastards, most of the ribbing had come from thankless bastards of rival firms). He was in that half state which, given the inch, becomes the mile, which overwhelms even as it is recognised as silly: he was worried about being worried. Was he so vain that a trifling loss of faith threatened the erasure of his personality? Indeed, did he have one worth speaking of?

As is so often the case, loss of face forced him to face his self. Not exactly a daily occurrence thus far, this was an alarming experience *per se*. In a bound of inverse faith akin to an inbred backwoodsman seeking psychotherapy, he was forced to admit the grotesquerie of process and revelation both. In a catechism as unsatisfactory and one-sided as most, he became a man staring, then toppling, into a vortex, then begging "Why did I do it?", then "Why, in that way?", then "Why didn't I conclude it more firmly?", then "Why did I do it?". Shot out of this compass-boxed maelstrom of giddy self-analysis like the refuse of a much maligned digestive system, fast food, fast shits, tasteless at both ends, he could now beg only "Why am I asking myself this?" At this parlous juncture, where hypochondria feebly seeks justification in botched quietus, the telephone tolled. Really. Not for him the Mickey Mouse *bbirrringg-bbirrringg;*, the afore-mentioned animistic object, while bearing approximate resemblance to the afore-named anthropomorphised vermin, tolled (surprise! surprise!) as sure as Big Ben does on News at Ten. He wasn't about to answer it. Oh, no, he was engaged in conversation with himself, he muttered to himself, aptly preoccupied, troubled, alone. Besides, the answering machine would — —!

"Hi, it's Syreenah," purred the unimaginably disembodied voice. Heart bounding beats instinctively he grasped the phone as a dying man does a pardonable lifestyle.

"Hello!" he hallelujahed his fate.

"I need to see you."

"That'll be nice," he responded with nice understatement.

"I'm hoping so." It wasn't one of the world's greatest conversations, but that, besides being beside the point, was the point. This was the kind of girl one arranged to meet with an exigence born of desperation to be in her presence, no, to be in her, and an obviously founded dumbstruck disbelief in such luck. This would set the seal on a relationship which would never really rise above the unsatisfactory form of a series of meetings with the realisation implicit at the outset that the succession was directed to its own end as surely as life is to death. In many ways it would be a typical love affair, for love is nothing if it doesn't begin and end with mutual suspension of previously held beliefs, not to dwell upon disbeliefs. In the beginning its serendipitous nature is thankfully, greedily, accepted before being suspected, in the end its fate is bemoaned. But he was not yet in altogether idyllic reverie. First he had to ask her out.

"Hello?" said her mouthpiece to his earpiece. Disembodied, yes, unimaginable, never. Unimaginable!

"So. You believe in Catholicism?"

"What's that?"

"You wear the cross. You tell me."

"I like you," she sighed sweetly.

"I'm a bastard."

"I'm attracted to bastards." Christ, what a Madonna. She had struck him as the type to save that for the parting shot. You know, the maddeningly illogical scene that is too often love's too apt anagnorisis:

"You're the nicest guy I've ever known."

"But —"

"I'm going out with your best friend."

"But he's a bastard."

"He's *your* best friend. Anyway, I'm attracted to bastards." At this hypothetical point Fairbrother knew the Rubicon of his tolerance would be crossed. At that point, woman or no lady, he would hit her. Might even win her back, what with her fondness for bastards and all. But, Christ, here she was, up front, inviting it, begging for it.

Now, for the time being it is the beginning. Now, for the first time in four or more years he felt a twinge of ideological conscience and, to his delighted surprise his normally abnormally power-crazed self begged no anaesthetic; there was a woman who, because requesting this abuse, commanded his respect. He was in love, on a rescue mission to liberate this wench, too beautiful to be a contemporary suffragette, too vulnerable to be even herself, too too to be one. He would take her on. Thus he delivered himself of an absurdly smug *sine qua non*: to wit, she would amount to nothing without him. One (he reflected some years on as he cast back on the adumbrating folly of getting into bed with such strange bedfellows) at least the hypocritical, inaccurate and wildly implausible par of the electorate charging the Labour Party with the heinous double-whammy rabbit punches of daring to change and daring to resurrect Red Robbo. Fairbrother would groan as he recalled the turgid irreconcilability of that old *bête noire*, but that obvious double-whammy conceals the real sucker-punch: that the electorate was allowed, empowered, bought to deliver. Deliver itself from what? From itself, that's what, from *sine qua non* to begrudged footnote. Deliver itself from itself? The question itself was meaningless, not because it was blatantly contradictory, but because it was a non question. The question, in short was but rabble-rousing rhetoric, deliberately undermining itself and any real debate in the process. Such shenanigans were evidence of a nation's keepers protesting too much, something to behold and behold again in Conservatives and conservatives. They knew, we knew the Labour Party had changed (They knew, she knew we all ought to have changed, did he?): the rejoinder ought to have been, "How dare they ask?" Sadly, the only answer to that is the hoariest of political axioms; they dare because they are empowered, practically obliged to do so. The question then is not one of principles compromised but of hypocrisy justified, of taking compromise, particularly of others, as a for granted personal principle. And, however many leaders of the Labour Party have been and are yet to come, they carry but one card, one vote at a time; we, the voters, the vengeful, outnumber them hideously, ambuscading them, all politicians but particularly them, from the unattainable hinterland screened by paparazzi swarms. In such gloomy light we see revealed occasionally that Lincoln's famous saw has come to read: "You can't be honest with some of the people all of the time, and all of the people some of the time, so it pays to be dishonest with all of the people all of the time." Fairbrother was duty-bound to lie to Syreenah. To them all, but to her above all.

He was to meet her on a territory of her choosing. There is rarely anything more crucially revealing to a first date than its venue, be it chosen as compromise or proposed and conceded by manners, it will always turn out to seem a strange meeting place. Of course, in meeting as strangers with a definite view to becoming something else, something, anything more, the venue, not yet the world, takes on a whole different aspect, its most innocent ambience portentously analysed, as if being there is insufficient, one has to feel it is there for one, staged for one. Well, two. The compromise venue will tend to effect each participant in its unwitting dramas in one of two ways: *1*, well, it wouldn't be my choice, of course, but if it's OK for him/her, *2*, *O tempora! O mores!*, I'm not coming here again, going *anywhere* again with *that*! While avoiding the potentially infuriating former product of 'you first' politeness leading on to biting through the bonds to a sorely tried hitherto tied tongue, the latter risk is, of course, multiplied when the liaison is the exclusive choice of one or the other. Thus was it dodgy ground Fairbrother and Syreenah were destined for.

   He had insisted she choose (still the greatest oxymoron of the age), grateful that introductions were one area of inter-gender relationships still to uphold the rights of the chivalrous. Where one went from there was ever the problem, but a chap was generally best to force the pace gently (same oxymoron), and not a little surreptitiously, by insisting he was at her service. And while the modern girl may be fooled into reading something beyond mere commonplaces into these introductory protocols (something sinister, decidedly not an engagement ring), so violable is still her state at such points in her life she would even less likely dream of dispensing with them altogether. Part fear of the unknown, part romantic dreams of same that would find the best in a beast, guides our little lady to her suborned rendezvous with fate. The approach of her would be mate is similarly a bizarre amalgam of trepidation and abandon: logic is out the window, but witnesses can and will be found to retell the manner of its going. Her patch, then.

   At least as ready as he had ever been, he set off. She wished to meet at some club, *The Golden Saddle Bags*, where her brother sang. Probably a bit like the *Pizza on the Park*, he mused, with an urbane young wit – her brother, he was meeting the family already – tinkling out tragi-comic tales of treachery as the waitress, not her, classier, no!, older, no, not her, thank God, the wise old waitress took the orders and read the fates.

   Leaving the Merc in the garage he decided on the Tube. Normally he would take a taxi but tonight he had the bravado of the adventurer in him. Besides, an overdose of anticipation had put him a speed-freak's step or two ahead of schedule.

Vowing never again to convey himself from A to B (let alone A to Z) by a method transportation which imprisoned one in the unremitting company of a bewitching number of hellish sociopaths, Fairbrother met the overground running into a sense of life reclaimed, soon to develop into a sense of adventure resurrected. Acting as if begrudging a busker a gratuity were in the dragon slaying class, he strode confidently to his destiny; others had paid variously hush-money, had given even more reluctantly under nascent menaces, whereas he had given nothing, given in to nothing, met the mendicant supercilious eye to all but miraculous configuration of downcast eye in painfully raised head, the whole tilted as if gazing at a low horizoned heaven, the heaven that was a potential donor. As if, indeed!

He felt good. Denuded without his wheels, he had expected to find perambulation perilous but, no, it was with a swagger that he emerged from these brushes with those fate had failed, these oddly bewildering couplings twixt he and that constituency his success had so long obliged him to take for granted. Everywhere his eye met with endorsements of his superiority, all that he beheld indulged him further in his aloofness. As he sauntered along the surprisingly filthy streets he waged imagined war on its people. At a distance somewhere between mendacity and mendicity a not so gentle youth of the road, no the streets, confronted him.

"Spare a copper for a cup of tea, guv," he begged, in tone and content Dickensian to the point of beggaring belief.

"Pardon?" Fairbrother begged back.

"Spare a copper for a cup of tea, guv," echoed forth the hollow mantra *da capo*.

"How do I know you won't drink it?" volleyed back the somewhat baffling rejoinder.

"How do you know I won't mug you, you smug bastard?"

Thus did the Great Bratish arch-capitalist and his logical conclusion, his *doppelgänger* cum *reductio ad absurdum*, apprehend each other fully in that greatest of *lingue franche* which served to span the great divide between even such entirely coincidental coevals: *videlicet*, money talks. Fairbrother hadn't bargained on such hostility. To one grown so accustomed to the luxuries of life, a cardboard box was a receptacle for the purpose of packaging items other than (and obviously of more worth than) human bodies. To those not so blessed by the deceptive distance that so becomes the blind-side of connivance, the humble cardboard box had attained an almost religious symbolism as a modern day shroud, a coffin wherein the living dead discards waited out their pathetically ineluctable destiny. Even as cultures clashed beyond his control off the beaten track, Fairbrother expected the constabulary to effect an heroic rescue of this one minimally peace breached victim. That he held such expectations serves to emphasise just how casually success in excess can serve a smug divorce on reality.

For fully ten seconds they stared into each other's eyes, face to face, eyeball to eyeball, no quarter given, no more superciliary or primeval posturing. Then, in a manner of speaking, a quarter was given.

"Will you take a cheque?" enquired Fairbrother.

"What the fuck would I do with a cheque?" spewed forth the ungrateful gamin. Fairbrother was truly baffled this time.

"Why, cash it?" he offered, unsure that he was responding to a serious enquiry.

"Where? How?"

"At your bank — ah!" The word had served as a trigger to sensibilities long since in aestivation. Of course!, the penny drops!, head, if not heart, returns from holiday!, there are people without bank accounts! But now was neither the time nor the place to congratulate oneself on spotting an example of this rare species in the raw; its expectations had been raised, hackle wise, and, with that, one's own survival instincts. Sheltered naïveté was not sufficient to see off this storm. It was as if the car window had been wound down in the safari-park, the better to convey a banana to a cheeky chappie of a chimpanzee, only to receive in return for this quaintly ingenuous attempt at communion with the animal kingdom, the unforeseen, never again foreshortened perspective of a murderous gorilla whose satisfaction point would appear far to exceed the satiation point procurable by these herbivorous offerings in particular, indeed any diet less than gluttonously pantophagous in general. One drove on. No wheels now, though. Cursing his fate (such is luck born out of negligence), Fairbrother compounded the chances of his chances fracturing.

"Give me your address and I'll send you, say, £20? That should buy all the tea in China," he babbled maniacally. The paraffin lamp was more exercised than one would have thought any lazybones ne'er-do-well had any right, inkling or talent to be.

"You taking the piss!" This was not a question.

"No." This was not an answer. Divested of £20 taxi money (this being the only logistically justifiable carrying cash, earning, as the pennies dropped replaced the meter's click, subvented by the elimination of the breathtakingly long-drawn out sharp intake of breath accompanying the cheque scribing ritual, a nice little bonus from becoming mired in an interchange between one who could otherwise afford not to carry the filthy lucre and one who could not afford to declare its receipt; some of the finest international bankers – offshore – must have started out as upfront cashiers of such conveyances), Fairbrother, confidence shot, sought refuge and Dutch courage in equal measure in the nearest hostelry.

On being ejected – "You taking the piss!?", that phrase again – after commencing a cheque, before touching a drop, while flashing credit cards to no personal credit and much derision, he found himself on the streets again. He was learning fast. He took out his calculator/notebook gizmo and keyed in:

"Investigate the reasons why cheque books and credit cards not universally acceptable."

On the verge of becoming genuinely scared off by this foreboding start to the evening and lightened of demeaning wherewithal, he did what any contemporary alienated soul would. Thirsty to the point of incipient dipsomania, he scoured the surrounds for an autobank, sighted one about 200 yards due, God knows where on the compass —— due him money. He scurried forth.

After four pints of 'best' bitter – the first beers he had quaffed in four years, for champagne and vintage wines had constituted his not inconsiderable alcoholic intake these post-graduation days until now, marooned in a bar with no wine, without meals and no reason to celebrate in champagne – he felt well enough to keep his rendezvous, unwell enough to extrude his libations in a manner orthodox only to bulimics and bizarre gourmands so force fed on the trappings of celebrity that every second lunch-time is eaten up with trying to gain entry to the *Guinness Book of Records* for most pickled eggs gobbled while farting the Marseillaise.

On achieving the rendezvous point, *The Horseshoe Bar* in *The Golden*

Saddle Bags (roughly translated as *The Horseshoe Bar* in *The Golden Saddle Bags*), Fairbrother was strangely reassured to find himself alone. Not in company, that is. Not that he required more time to work up greater Dutch courage, but something nebulously traceable to his make-up informed him that this was right, that things were going to order: her tardiness was an obligation conveying its own compensation. It was with a feeling of mounting intoxication that he envisaged a pouting, pomaded, preening, perfumed playmate putting it all on for him and him alone. It was as if on a whiff of her perfume he had slung it down his throat, so heady was this reverie of this, his dizzying blonde proving. It was with a hard on more *urbi et orbi* than *ad hominem*, that is, more pornographic than poetic, that he summoned the waitress. No Syreenah, of course, on the gross side, but, boy, was he horny. Flirting dutifully she took his order. Curiously, no wine was on offer, only beer and spirits. Again. Luckily it was American beer, mere wino's mouthwash. Stranger still, the configuration of the bar was in no way inspired by the expected, the advertised horseshoe shape. Neither was the waitress a genuine American cowgal, though cow and gal, though not necessarily in that order, she certainly was. On an estrade got up like a down-home porch a cowboy announced himself in an accent as implausibly Glaswegian as was his singing voice to prove, whether accurate or not, bizarrely Kentuckian. The cowpuncher phrasing of this announcement added the further surreal touch which had the mind's eye conjuring up a vision comprising John Wayne, a Saturday night brawl and Sauchiehall Street.

"Hull, yawl. Mason Dickson" (poster festooning the walls revealed this strange spelling) "here. Wurr gonnae git doon 'n' kick some ess, if yawl know whur ah'm cummin' fae." Not at all sure of this, indeed rapidly relinquishing any grasp of his purpose in attending such an inbred backwater, Fairbrother seriously entertained the option of bailing out, but just as the prospect approached likelihood, to the bizarre soundtrack of the bizarre Mason Dickson bizarrely twanging *Stand by your Man* fate bizarrely intervened.

"David," she responded properly. "Sorry I'm late," she smiled half-truthfully.

"This place is — is — is bizarre," he noted. The observation was to prove something of an understatement.

Over several tongue loosening, ideally leg opening Buds, Syreenah would reveal much concerning the character of the *Horseshoe* and, by extension, that of her own. In epitome, the *Horseshoe* was a gay bar as in, bent as a horseshoe, the waitresses were a particularly confusing crossbreed of tomboy cowgirl transvestites, Mason Dickson was a cowgal and *Syreenah?!!?*

"Relax, I'm all woman."

"But?"

"Why am I here?" Indeed, metaphysics was clearer than this. Fairbrother gawped that the question, if not yet the answer, had lodged.

"Because. Because I'm all woman —" Fairbrother struggled yet with adequate response. It was all happening too fast. First, the succession of shocks then the too enticing cut to the chase.

"Because?" Fairbrother gawped, too much on his mind to render speechlessness the speedfreak's reflex garrulity. Syreenah understood. These things were relative. Poor lad, must have come as quite a shock, being brought here. Almost on the point of revelation, of apprehending just about why she had done this for/to him, he was denied the consolation of accusation by her prompt, literally pre-emptive counter denial.

"Can't you see, I don't get bothered here." She was playing it, her part, particularly him, beautifully.

"Oh, I see!" he sighed in an oxymoronic exhalation of delirious relief, declaring himself, at the precise moment of total blindness, to be 20/20. The cat and mouse game that would initially characterise, finally stigmatise their relationship, had commenced. She had found her fool, he his muse. However, one may have noted, we are not about to culminate a century greatly noted for its lyric poetry; fools tend more towards the cynically philistine these days, just as muses tend towards the manipulative faculties clearly recognisable in inspiration. That night passed harmfully: she took him to bed, of course.

Chapter Eight

Naturally, on this his intended's day of days (did that imply she intended to be some others' intended, also?) Fairbrother's thoughts were uniquely concentrated on this one woman. Strangely, this fidelity wasn't to his betrothed but to his mother. Did she think of him on her day of days? Most certainly! Technically he hadn't quite yet made an appearance back then, but certainly the bastard to be produced a simulacrum of a glimmer in the eyes of the bride to be, his lurking presence barely betraying more the strains of morning sickness that attesting to the often anyhow paradoxical manifestation that is a young woman's joy of joys. What were her dreams for him, or, more apposite to those days of greater innocence no, greater faith in ignorance, when bastards had better be blessed as consciously produced evidence from the lucky dip of dreams against any accusations of guilt, what did she fear for him? Did she want a he? If so, was it he she wanted? If no, ah, fuck it. He really should have told her, today of all days, just what his life, her gift meant to him. And awkwardness needn't have got in the way – the symbolism of the day would have served as sufficiently eloquent to smooth over the previously insurmountable depressions in the rifts of separation. But it wasn't to be. Was their estrangement so final, the bond so stretched beyond repair, the mother and child reunion too difficult to promote? Yes, today of all days would confirm that it was too late.

To the inaudible but definitely ethereal strains of 'Get me to the church on time', the day commenced as over rehearsed thus trepidatory panic incarnate, and continued thus but for one hour's extemporaneous calm reflection. As his body hurtled from shabby repose to ostentatiously spruced and laundered uprightness in a comically accelerated period entirely at odds with the leisurely pace at which he defended with a straight bat the vicious attacks of any other rarely granted, richly cherished non working day, Fairbrother soon found himself pampered and carnationed well ahead of the pomp and circumstance to come. In reflective mood he sat down, confronting his mirror image for fully an hour. Garvey, the best man (winning that honour in the tried, not quite trusted City fashion by trumping Fairbrother's other two partners at stud poker), wasn't due until noon. In spite of attending a stag night of staggeringly parodic excess the previous eve, Fairbrother found himself at least cosmetically bright-eyed and bushy-tailed with time to kill. No more preparation, this was it. All the clichéd anxieties presented themselves for inspection and, while not found wanting, they were heeded as foreboding only to those less equipped than he, David Anthony Fairbrother, successful way beyond birthright, to forestall. With money you can't afford to fail, he smiled as this no mystery train of reflex thought transported him to what by now almost amounted to preordained satisfaction. Should he have a mind to he could retire and live comfortably ever after the honeymoon. At 26 years of age! By what quirk of fate, what freak of circumstance could this boy fail! It was then this train of little thought was stopped abruptly in its tracks by a seemingly oncoming rush of harsh enlightenment mercilessly directed at its own inconsideration. Motionless he stood, stock-still and staring down, yet still it came.

"If mother could see me now," spoke self to self in a doomed attempt to lend theatricality's ridicule to the task of debunking the melodrama that was playing his face like a spotlight suddenly projected onto the quondam trustingly anonymous features of the butler; suddenly revealed, he squirmed at the extraordinariness he had frankly divined within himself. Of course, mother wasn't present to answer back, having effectively, conveniently been passed away, if not quite into an unknowably eternal realm or pointedly final end, into the grim distinctly distant past. Confronted by the revenant of his own exile he froze for fully five minutes, his genuine grief exacerbated by the tiny droplets of salt water which gradually worked to excavate all smugness from his emotionally virgin features until his reflection, ineluctably, inexplicably metamorphosing into a facsimile of his mother to be on her wedding day, appropriated the hideously apposite mien of a weeping Madonna. Late to worship, too late, he was in greater need of a priest than a registrar as he confessed to the unpardonable sin of having lost a loved one through neglect. Something in him died as he accepted the ghastly fate to which he had consigned his long ago so beloved mother; what died was the invulnerablility he had hitherto supposed to be his by, no, not birthright, by career right. No sooner was this late, unlamented 'quality' consumed in a fiery passion to right its wrongs than that passion died, a scintillant squandering of estovers once thought *infra dig* to one so recently galaxies above such means testing. The story had met its end, by accident more than design, by culpable neglect more than accident, its final pages would not be written, its unsatisfactory conclusion rudely interrupted mid-chapter by the eruption of a blood stained rubric obscuring any sense, any sanguine feelings once contained in that artificial, suicidal end.

The front door bell rang. Fairbrother took his face off, this being distinct from the putting on of a face, via the application of cosmetics favoured by the female of the species (being applied concurrently by *the* currently favoured female of the species), by consisting in the removal of the tell-tale signs of an emotional creature lurking therein. Daubing his cheeks with the ceremonial handkerchief could not entirely disguise the recent outpourings from the now arid well spring of his emotions, and so it was an apparently be-rouged groom to be who greeted a more than apparently harassed best man.

"A fucking nightmare!" were the first words of the best man. On the very day he would be called upon to recite a politely risqué paean to love's young dream this did not augur well. Nevertheless, relieved to concentrate on another's pains, Fairbrother invited his friend in to unburden his soul, as it were, such as it was. Typically, the trauma proved trivial and clichéd, no more than a parking ticket, no less than a commonplace superstition risen to portentousness on this most remarkably nerve-racking of days. And he was just the hoop carrier, Fairbrother grinned, offered his frothy friend the first of that day's many inevitable toasts, joining in willing a fairy tale ending, to the day at least. The first drink did the trick, easing Garvey's anxieties as its purposeful content toppled down the thropple, its deceptive warmth presaging its warm reception in the eagerly awaiting to be deceived brain. Not a drinker, succeeding tipples would that very day lead him down less benign paths of character alchemy until, in characteristic American businesslike fashion, on the following morn's rude awakening, he would asininely abjure the noxious depressant once and for all, for good and for better, from valetudinarian sickness into rude good hypochondria. But if the rest of the day's intake were to inspire such debate and capitulation, the first drink most definitely agreed with him.

As the first cheer furnished the two imbibers with distinctly motivated but equally desired rushes to the head, the race was on again, schedule once more the master of ceremonies which this very day would propose to host the rest of one of their lives.

The journey to the registry office was uneventful: indeed, it was as if the sedate pace of London's traffic was mocking the condemned man, its slow torture unimaginable in other, particularly Italian, cities. Thus it was, with the not entirely unattractive prospect of a quirk of fate intervening to interrupt its wider sweep, red lighted, stuck feebly in low gear, that the registry office was gained some 15 minutes late. Fate's last chance? No, round these parts, registrars of births, deaths and marriages are trained, practically ordained to pencil in those periods of delay caused primarily by the capricious *quo vadis* funeral flow of London's streets (there must be a better way!): even more frequent than two minded belated brides was the temporal highway robbery suffered by the vehicles conveying themselves and other halves to their teased out fates. Fate? As luck would have it Syreenah had enjoyed smoother passage and the registrar had those precious 15 minutes for a cup of tea; the reassurance required to overcome a given, like the London traffic, being far less than for a potentially more persecutionary commonplace such as the late or, heaven forfend, non arrival of the bride to be.

On entering the reception area to espy the first glimpse of the day of the woman he would be, should be seeing all but each and every henceforth till death did they — what the fuck is Mason Dickson — ? — in full — um —— cowboy — gal — regalia — doing — he —?

"Hi, honey," exhaled sweet Syreenah as if getting something, as in a modest discount, off her spectacularly voluptuous bosom, precariously panoplied within scant as it was battledress which would have been at odds with, let alone the day, any face less ferally warpainted.

"You know Mason, the singer —"

"Hu Huh."

"Surprise!, surprise!" she announced in the gut-wrenching, potentially heart-stopping manner of owr Siller reuniting two pacemakered makeshifts, two now very near ghosts to the respective sibling they had somehow both conspired to avoid these past 50 years. "Mason's my sister."

Recalling the location and circumstances of his initial encounter with this 'sister', Fairbrother instimaticly got the picture in its full frozen horror. The wrong picture, *natürlich*. How was he to know she would spring —? Syreenah was ahead of him.

"No, my real sister, silly," she soothed, getting the last word in and the right word out with a degree of accuracy made all the more unnerving for being entirely unsuspected. Cupid stood stupid, stuck, a silly-billy cruelly tricked by a mere girl. Not any mere girl at that; no less than his intended. Syreenah, soon to be unveiled, no, revealed as Sheril (phonetic orthography by illiterate parent, first confessed to during the marriage ceremony – "I didn't know if you'd want me with a name like Sheril!" – proposed and accepted for common usage hereafter within the solemn bond. In public, no, to her public, no again, same thing, she would still be known as Syreenah!) lent the occasion belated consistency: Mason Dickson, real name Cheryl (as it sounds; coined by easily impressed parent as the too good to waste suggestion of just such a functionary as was presiding over the present day's entertainment), was her one present relative on her day of days. In total the congregation, no, the gathering comprised Garvey, Tristan and Cal on the groom's side and Cheryl (ever the willing bridesmaid) on the bride's. The ceremony was, well, for those among you who have come through it, I would hate to cast it up again; for those of you as yet undecided upon, uninitiated in this ritual, I would hate to put you off. We all know the scene as if by heart, or at least second nature. Nothing more to report; the best man hadn't mislaid the ring, no one spoke up agin the union, the vows were exchanged with nary a slip, the muddled text rendered perfectly, the lean-to solecisms, inevitable in a ceremony by religion out of officialdom, sounding simultaneously trite and awe inspiring.

On regaining the street, photographs were taken, not seriously (by Cal and Tristan), with serious intent to bore (Cheryl: female, Garvey: American). In spite of the wealth there represented (male) and the debs gone Milano style decadent beauty of the females, no professional photographers had been engaged. The oddly antisocial, could have been a 'society' wedding must have been so convened to conceal something. Christ, look, the reception is an extempore affair; come as you are to the venue handiest. In the pub, *The North Pole*, one of London's would be charming little theme bars with no discernible bar, let alone theme (unless skimping on the brewery's fuelling costs and the warmth of welcome of their representatives on this outpost of planet earth can be seen as themes), the best man espied the watering down area beyond the inevitable scrum of would be wags, would be punters to the barmaids' extra-curricular activities, and got them in. To the uncalled for accompaniment of a jukebox peeping out music one just knew was awful if one could only hear it 'properly' (there are but but two volumes in pubs – inaudible, i.e., a member of the bar staff is on the phone to someone they know, and impossible, i.e., a member of the public, probably one, is screaming like a town crier at the phone to explain the point of its invention), an Australian soap opera of spectacular blandness pitched at a volume oh so histrionic, presumably as a *memento mori* to the hangdog mine host – serving, just – from his hardbitten wife, of people, real people, *stars*, ferkrissake, with *real* problems, and the beep, boop, boop, boop inambient punctuation of gaming machines attended by enthralled automatons, against these competing cacophonies, the order was improbably placed. Champagne for all, modified to a black velvet for Cheryl. The landlady (lady? – the beached whale of a consumer gawping in the melodramatic morsels on screen like so much plankton and krill) implored the admittedly noisy, though hardly surprisingly so, company to turn themselves down; life was going on on screen, marriage or no marriage, a death must soon be announced, for crying out loud. Amused apologies were proffered, and scorned for their providing further distraction, so it was in the style of Clifford, Ashley, Buckingham, Arlington and Lauderdale that the huddle toasted each other's health and for good measure added, within their otherwise polite company, screw the world, particularly this godforsaken end of the earth. Later they were understandably, if less than consciously thrown out.

The honeymoon owed more to convention than the marriage ceremony and subsequent poor reception had. In fact, it was positively hackneyed: conducted in Venice with team leader Fairbrother acting as bizarre amalgam of tourist guide, naïve American abroad, impossible interpreter. In learning a foreign language piecemeal one is always prey to the "I think I would eat a tomato," syndrome; i.e., stating the obvious ungrammatically as if in crass refutation of the concluding apophthegm to Wittgenstein's *Logisch-Philosophische Abhandlung*, *'Wovon man nicht sprechen kann, darüber muss man schweigen.'* (Literal translation: 'Whereof one not speak can, thereof must one silent be.') No one in their right mind speaks like that. Not in their native tongue. Even the insane can rarely attain such subliminal word wasting improvisational mouthings to a dubbed soundtrack supplied by a hitherto mute Svengali outside of Bergman films. Sheril loved it. They loved it. They weren't to know. Bliss it was. Bliss it would not remain. Ah, love! Not in this native's tongue. A foreign language indeed. One feels a tomato coming on.

On the last day, as Venice's quondam quaint odours had become the miasma only a practical, non sunblocked nose can fully appreciate, the happy couple became temporarily, yet ominously, two sad individuals.

Over an English breakfast of life threatening proportions (at home *au naturel*, they picked at continental breakfasts of life denying proportions), he with his paper – *The Sun*, "for a laugh" – she with her magazine – *Cosmo* in French ('O' level, C grade, insufficient for the captions, but the pictures spoke volumes in the *lingua franca* of hair-drier dwellers the world over) –, he was confronted with his misbehaviour of the previous evening. Apparently, for he had been drunk as a tourist on the wine, he had been making eyes at the Venetian verisimilitude of a Hollywood waitress. Worse, on return from the powder room, *Max Factor* externally, cocaine internally, she, Sheril, aka Syreenah!, had espied their enacting a clichéd but no less tragic version of Desdemona's kerchief kerfuffle; i.e., he was caught seemingly giving her a napkin. Explain that. And her a waitress too! To the symbolic stabbing of a tired looking sausage she launched their first noteworthy disagreement; the one luckier couples engaged in more blessed unions look back on with amused bewilderment, seeing the funny side and laughing: "How could we ever fall out over something so petty!" This was no such couple. Time would distance them alright, too far to remember, let alone with affection. For one of this couple at least the best part of breaking up was to be the making of money. Indeed, the breach had occurred at a meeting held a week before the wedding, finally to be revealed that morning after.

Chapter Nine

Then it hit him. More what the butler saw than revelation, admittedly, but miraculous for having been so successfully hidden thus far. Pornography! Better even than money making money, a field of human 'endeavour' which encapsulated taking liberties as a rapist does, gave fuck all back, took it all, the whole fucking world!

Garvey was addressing the partners, Tristan, Fairbrother and Cal Whipsnade, the last recently acquired in acrimonious, nay, litigious circumstances from *Smart Investments*. It was a week before the wedding. Before the groom to be, at least, had even dreamed of that day of days.

Boom Bros had had a good year. That was the problem. In the four years of their existence their profits had started obscenely in the first year, doubled the second, quadrupled the third. The fourth they rose a mere five-fold. Ever the pragmatic American dreamer, not in itself a contradiction, Garvey was first to see the writing on the wall in the slight levelling off of the rise on the company's profits. No matter that they had ridden spectacularly the nigh permanent recession that passes for post war British economic performance, he foresaw the end of their rise and thus the end of what he characteristically (and need it be said, unendearingly?) coined 'seriously serious money'. Brighter, brasher consultancies than *Boom Bros* had supplanted the original rebels as the City's loveable rogues. Garvey wanted out. Born into money, raised to make money, serious money, he couldn't disavow his lineage, his very nationality for the mediocrity of merely making a bloody good living.

"But," quarrelled Tristan, "the notoriety, the notoriety! Daddy would have a heart attack."

"I'll bet he will, the Limey bastard. And what a way to go. Don't you see, this is a country ripe for the pornographer."

"But we employ the strictest censorship in the whole fucking semi-civilised world," confessed Fairbrother somewhat shamefacedly, and not only for signally failing to evoke the spirit of Thomas Bowdler.

"Precisely: you Brits are so anally retentive and sexually repressed as to be incapable of distinguishing a fanny from a bush. Consequently you'll buy anything more risqué than a flake advert."

"But it's a sleazy business," wailed Fairbrother, to overenthusiastic, practically orgasmic nods of approval from Tristan and Cal. Garvey was unmoved.

"Second bonus point. You assholes like nothing better than denigrating success, legitimate success. But pornographers get off scot-free because you refuse to countenance their existence. They are your *infra dig* invisible earners. I wouldn't be surprised if the freaking tax man refused to sully his hands on their ill-gotten gains. Christ, in this country a pornographer doesn't have to shift his money offshore, the black stallion will take it, no questions, absolutely no questions asked. Wouldn't want to frighten the Exchequer, let alone the public, the stallion and the clerkess."

"But we have no need to resort to such underhand methods," bleated Tristan.

"We don't *need* to make as much money as possible, but somebody does. So why not us? What the hell is the shit with you shithead Limey bastards anyway, you commies, or what?" taunted Garvey, every bit the McCarthyite inquisitor.

"No," mulled Fairbrother, "we're not communists."

"The hell you're not!" shot back John Wayne's ghost, confirming that the old man's man never really did die in spirit, in spite of the (miraculously rare) occasions he failed to survive the tedium of his films. "Some scumsucker called me a commie and the mo'fucker'd be deader than a dodo's doo-doos, as you snivelling inbred shits would have it," Saddler loosed off.

"Garvey, can I ask you a personal question?" ventured forth a tentative Tristan.

"Sho, yo, go!" came the baffling riposte.

"Pardon?"

"What's yore problemmm!!! Axe yore fuckin' question, mother!" Thus tolerated, Tristan proceeded.

"Why, when the topic is money do you talk like a honky shit *Opportunity Knocks* auditionee, failed, doing a particularly misanthropic Richard Pryor impersonation on the stag night circuit?"

"Do I?" queried Garvey, shocked out of his very previous patois into something resembling English by this, because new, deeply disturbing perspective on his much cherished persona, in the tenure of which he was, as they say, something of a control freak.

"You do," nodded Tristan in the sage and colonial manner so characteristic of his upbringing. "Probably sponsored by subconscious liberal guilt or some such valetudinarian longing invented by your horrendous TV *vox pop* hosts, I shouldn't doubt," he sighed fastidiously.

"Let's get one thing straight, mite," responded Garvey, rendering 'mate' 'mite' in a might have been Cockney accent, *à la* Dick van Dyke with the annoying inaccuracy translated into easily comprehensible aggression, "one," he recommenced his point curiously numbering it, suggesting that there would be more than one thing to be laid flat, Tristan perhaps among their number, any man in the fucking room, mite, all non-American-comers, "one," he reiterated his folly defiantly gesticulating with his middle finger so as to register more than the count itself, "one," he re-repeated, "they're not my *vox pop* hosts, "two," the reverse Churchillian triumphing in unfavourability even over the previously favoured gesture, proving that he and his countrymen, when not crassly exporting their banal and brutal culture, were extremely adept at acquiring the vernacular vulgarities of other, lesser cultures, "two," he thrust ever onward, "we may have hang-ups and we may talk them to death, but, "three," abandoning 'two' as a soundbite that didn't sound right, "three," fingers now rearranged from neutral, neutered three-up on the one hand to left hand reverse Winston, right hand in a display of native 'intelligence', middle digit upwards, skywards, up yours, God, "three," the reconfiguration of the perceivable form taking a toll on its mover, "three," the crowed thrice "we aren't as fucked up as you fuck-ups!"

"Four," two *echt* Churchills, or masochistic signals, boomed Tristan, "without your lot we wouldn't have won the war." This instantly eased the tension, though Garvey, now laughing, was still on his soapbox.

"That's what I'm saying, assholes, and I mean that affectionately. One," here we go again. Thankfully, having seen, having *been* the joke, Garvey was in wittingly self-parodic mode, quite an achievement for an American, "one," no bodily accompaniment, "we won the war together, two, in the name of capitalism and free enterprise, three, you boy scout fuckers are so emotionally retarded pornography'll be easier to peddle than hooch in a speakeasy, than stockings during war time. You mothers are still in separate beds." Seeming to have made some kind of hideous sense, definitely creating an impression, this was greeted in true emotional retard sense by silence. The Queen Mother would have been proud of our boys. "And here's the clincher, me laddies," Garvey slapped his thighs in parodic pantomimic piratical fashion, all of which, being foreign to him, he carried off woefully, i.e., wonderfully (Mike

Tyson standing in for our Frank and 'acting' Brian Blessed – blessed be! – off stage). "We have just the girl to front for us," the word 'front' accompanied by a suggestive hand-cupping gesture that didn't so much play to the gallery as scoop them up like the willing participants, the putty in his hands they were fast becoming.

"Eh?" queried all three in anticipation guising poorly as disdain.

"Syreenah!" announced Garvey, proud as any father of the bride.

"Mmm?" mmmed Tristan and Cal.

"But — but ——," rebutted Fairbrother. "But I'm going to marry that girl!"

"You are?" moaned a frankly disappointed Cal.

"When?" enquired a frankly delighted Tristan.

"Perfect!" pronounced a frankly frank Garvey.

"I am," replied a conciliatory yet firm Fairbrother. "Next Friday," revealed a proudly fraternal Fairbrother. "What?" enquired a frankly puzzled Fairbrother, seeking extrapolation upon Garvey's fairer than fair comment, while verging upon having his raised hackles heckled.

"Perfect!" came the imperfect iteration, frankly more now than a minor irritation.

"What the fuck do you mean by this?!" challenged Fairbrother, arms outstretched, uncharacteristically emotional, as if he carried the raped and mutilated carcass of his intended in his arms (*à la* Atlas, world on shoulders) towards the prime suspect of such foul doings.

"She can be the editor, star model and, in this ever respectable isle, publisher's wife. She's got it all: no pretence at editorial control, no '0' level writing, I wouldn't doubt, no mean pair of jugs, no principles worth mentioning, and the logical, exploitable sum of all these things, a rich old man who happens to peddle porn."

"Hold your horses," beseeched Fairbrother.

"No bestiality, strictly soft-focus. Wouldn't want to frighten the humans," joshed the motion's mover.

"No way, no fucking way is my wife, my betrothed, fuck her, *it*, fuck it, *her!*, my intended, getting involved in that low-life business! No fucking way!"

"And you?" smirked Garvey.

"Tell me more," sighed Fairbrother.

There then followed several discourses sooner suited to the stag night than the boardroom. *In fine*, Garvey outlined his plans for *Boom Bros* to maintain their "legitimate interests" without Fairbrother on the board of directors. He would still receive his quarter of the board's not inconsiderable wedge, but it was, Garvey proposed, imperative that any official links with the parent company be severed. In return for this act of corporate sacrifice Fairbrother would be charged with developing a new company, *Gloss Bros*, having beforehand publicly announced an amicable rift in the *Boom Bros* boardroom. The schism would need to be promulgated as amicable so as not to frighten off the shareholders, yet must also be made known as irrevocable. The remaining board members would issue a counter statement, in effect a glowing testimonial to their quondam "brother in Boom", while politely distancing themselves from his new 'ill-advised' venture. All wonderful, because free publicity for both sets of *Bros*, of course. Behind this smokescreen the two companies would run as one, their outward configurations purely cosmetic, such boardroom shenanigans a tried, tested and, incredibly, trusted method many times used on the animals of the financial press corps, not to mention those other dumb brutes, the faithful shareholders. And once you have *them* foxed, once *they* buy it, the animals comprising the great British public will ravenously pay dearly for the privilege to be in any way associated with any such enterprise so obviously, so officially sanctioned as kosher. Or, at least not rubbished as *trayf*.

"A public that'll not only watch Grand Prix racing, but purchase primarily the cigarettes liveried liberally on the winning car without demanding that the number one driver drive in the 28th car, vice versa, *und so weiter*, let alone acknowledge endorsement of the product (too life threatening!), that public knows the price of everything and the value of nothing. This is where your very own brash American comes in: he's gonna set your people free, guys!" promised Garvey

"How so?" quibbled Fairbrother.

"Mrs Thatcher's blazed the trail for you, right?"

"Right. But not for pornographers."

"If your money's good enough – no, if your credit's good enough, that's plenty good enough for the old girl, The New Lady of Threadneedle Street."

"OK, but we don't tolerate the cruder end of the market: male genitalia standing to attention and the like," cavilled Fairbrother, speaking both from the heart and into his chest, cleaving the decent from the indecent on behalf, he felt, of both sexes.

"*We* don't or *they* don't?" teased Garvey.

"Both," conceded Fairbrother.

"Cool, cool. No, I wasn't thinking in terms of real hardcore, more a backdrop of American images, themes playing on the special relationship: girls accessoried by bullet-shaped cars, cuddling six foot Mickeys 'n' Minnies ever so suggestively, blow-jobbing the classic *Coke* bottle, tonguing liberty cone ices —"

At this point Fairbrother chose to call a halt to this orgy of naffly applied *echt* Americana, the lump in the throat an unvocalised, slightly sickening citation to his bride to be.

"So you aim to appeal to the *Playboy* reader, the *Penthouse* reader, you envisage a serious magazine containing coincidental soft-focus tits to take the readers' minds off —," off what we'll never know, for Fairbrother was interrupted by you know who.

"No, no, we'll be as risqué as your repressive laws will allow. Open cunt shots, shaved cunt shots, cunt licking cunt shots, the kinda stuff that your deprived 'n' depraved, yet somehow still discerning customer can really get into —,"

"Who do you see as the target audience?" the somehow still discerning Cal enquired.

"C2s down, of course. And the lame and the mad, naturally."

"Is there a difference?" drawled Tristan to the droll appreciation of all.

"Let's hope not," continued Garvey. "Besides, we have it from the deconstructionists: there is no good art and bad art: in fact there is no art, merely degrees of what they'd call definitively derivative statements, what we'd rather call marketable propositions, arising out of situations, good, bad, even indifferent. Thus have we identified the one unplugged gap in the market. If even the wily cold-hearted intellectuals can't raise an objection to the pornographic, the great British public will rise to the crudest bait at the crudest bidding. They're desperate for something to dominate, these poor bastards."

Tristan spoke to this tendentious proposition.

"Granted, our lower orders tend to achieve the same degree of sophistication and success in relation to the fairer sex as they just about muster *vis-à-vis* the school of hard knocks and its great graduating forum, life. And indubitably, their response to stimulants and depressants 'wot piss 'em arf' is brutal, primeval, disgusting and, given the derisory nature of their liquid capital, profligate and miraculous *in extremis*. But — sex, I'm not so sure about. Most of them would rather get pissed, too pissed to think about it," he concluded sniffily.

"That's where we come in," came in Garvey. "We're gonna get sex back in the public's eye, in the pubs, go-go girls, strippers, video shows, every weekend a stag night. And from the pubs, the natural habitat of these lonely, pitiful, yet solvent, therefore not at all pitiable creatures of the night, we can plaster our girls, our products, all over the walls. Might even put a bit of spark back into some marriages."

"More likely to give them ideas more akin to rape than love making," grumbled Fairbrother, adding gloomily "And where are we supposed to recruit these girls?" At this the other three laughed rather cruelly, unwitting devil's advocates all, protesting too loud to his blessed romantic. Garvey knew.

"It's a buyer's, seller's, above all a hirer's market, David. Has been since time immemorial. And right now in particular the economic climate is cherry ripe for plucking. We are talking prime young girls growing on, fuck it, falling off trees. They only need picking up, that's all."

"And where are we going to reap these rapists' visions, forgetting, always forgetting my wife?" spat Fairbrother.

"*Stringfellows, The Campden Palace*, nightclubs, Petticoat Lane fucking market. They're all over the place, there for the taking. You may be in love, David, and you may accuse me of denigrating women, but let *me* tell *you* this: it better becomes, it is to the greater glory that a girl becomes a whore at £1,000 a week than a checkout girl at £50 a week. It's just you Brits and you Victorian bloody hang ups — every other goddam culture has accepted being 'on the game' as a necessary constituent of commerce, it's only you half-dead motherfuckers see it as an unnecessary evil," declared Saddler.

"Wait a minute," interjected Fairbrother urgently, "nobody mentioned whores before —"

"No, and nobody mentioned 1K a week," teased Garvey, "of which a good, uh, hands-off manager could cut himself, oh, a 40% slice and still earn the respect of the girl — the *girls*."

"A manager? — A pimp!" ejaculated Fairbrother involuntarily.

"Whatever —— 400 sovs per girl at, say, a stable of 50 – hands-off approach; pays not to mix business with pleasure, I've always said that —— that's, let's see —— 20 K a week —— one million *per annum* —

— before incurring any running costs —— cards in local newsagents, pay-offs to other pimps, that sort of thing."

"But pimping is illegal," moaned Fairbrother feebly, incorrectly.

"So, we run escort agencies. Sauna and massage parlours. Nothing that goes on on the premises is openly admitted to, is as advertised. Pigs will comply. It's fucking wonderful; you have to be honest to break the law! Sticks and stones won't break the British bulldog's bones, in fact he'll fetch them to be cast again, but names will always hurt him.

"My wife doesn't fuck anyone," cavilled Fairbrother, seemingly exhausted at the mere thought. Amid supportive mutterings starkly belying the unspoken sentiment 'that's not what we heard!', Garvey provided reassurance.

"Of course not. Just fronts the magazine and —"

"And *nothing*!"

"Poses — for a few — harmless shots?"

"No!"

"Stills! Where's the harm in that?"

"Stills?"

"Stills."

"No moving."

"Only that necessary to get into position."

"What positions?"

"Positions of strength, Dave, my boy, positions of strength."

"Nothing dirty?"

"No, nothing like that."

"Solo shots?"

"Absolutely."

"Just her and the photographer?"

"Who is bound to be gay — you have my word."

"That he's gay?"

"— ! — well, — absolutely, no straight photographers need apply — – that'll be company policy, for what it's worth."

"More than you know. How many magazines are you hoping to sell?"

"Originally four, but —"

"No, no, circulation targets," chastised a now well inveigled Fairbrother on 'behalf' of an unknowingly mired wife to be.

"Oh. 100,000 of each, average, per month at £2.50 a scalp, that's a turnover of a ——"

"Million a month," drooled Cal.

Production costs?" queried Tristan.

"Negligible. It's not as if we are, uhm, mounting works of art here. This is a cheap and ——"

"Nasty business," croaked Fairbrother, looking quite unwell.

"*Lucrative* business," corrected Garvey, "that we will all do very nicely out of for a, pardon the pun, bare minimum of effort. *Boom Bros* goes on as before. This is merely all but undeclared income which will provide us with a bit of fun. Besides, we'll all get to know some hot and grateful dames. Not for me, of course, but anything to rouse you goddam quasi-commie faggots into paying the ladies their due attention."

"Pornography isn't the means by which to liberate we commie faggots and Edwardian spinsters from our chilled apartheid," chided Fairbrother.

"Can you think of a better way?" goaded Garvey confidently.

"Well, no —"

"Hell, then, try this — whaddya got to lose!"

"My wife," came the extirpated *de profundis* of a soul in treacherously low esteem.

Garvey either ignored the despairing tone or it didn't register. Either way it wasn't the type of thing to bother him into consideration. Along with his frequent citings of the 'never mix business with pleasure' maxim, he just as often declaimed the slightly more original, much more cynical, possibly empirical, 'never mix women with emotion' apophthegm. "Plenty more where she came from," was all he had to say.

The seduction over, Fairbrother submitted to the majority view to such an extent that all proposals were passed not merely *nemine contradicente* but *nemine dissentiente*. He couldn't even raise himself in abstinence. It wasn't quite the start to married life he had his heart set on but, then, he had been a bit worried about that —— about just what it was getting him into.

Chapter Ten

"I saw you give that cow your card. I know what you're up to. And on our honeymoon, too!" wailed Sheril, a special side-effect no doubt, still scaring all but the American tourists.

"It's not what you think," offered Fairbrother languidly, the legitimacy of this statement, while unquestionable, was not, however, quintessentially honourable.

"You should have thought I could think before this. It may be too late to save our marriage."

"But —". It was a moment for truth, no circumnavigation of it would lead him from the disastrous consequences of its prolonged avoidance. His marriage headed for the rocks directly from its launch; he set sail for them — they had to be survived. There were no guarantees that honesty would prove to be the best policy, but that it was now the only pursuable policy Fairbrother was in no doubt.

"Yes, I did give that young lady my phone number. But it was on my business card —"

"Charge it to the company! Am I supposed to feel better about that?!"

" — and a business proposition that I put to her."

"I know what kind of business her type is in," spat back Sheril, the firsthand experience somehow playing second fiddle to first-rate hypocrisy.

"And you'd be right," Fairbrother confessed. "Partly right," he retracted somewhat, though Sheril didn't reciprocate by retracting her claws noticeably.

"Well, what do you know! She's a halfway hooker, huh? A transvestite, perhaps?"

Fairbrother blushed at this insult to his very British manhood.

"No, no, nothing like that," he hastened.

"So. She's all woman. Come on dear little sweetheart, pray tell just what business could she have with you?"

"She's not a prostitute, if that's what you are implying."

"I won't even stoop to ask how you found that out. Besides, the British male's definition of a prostitute is not one he or she or I ought to be comfortable with. What do you call her as you whisper sweet nothings in her ear? A good time girl, a cigarettes and chocolate girl —— or don't you pay her at all, as such?"; this last speculation serving as an introspective *decrescendo* to seemingly unstoppable rising passion and voice.

"She's — she's to be offered a position in the company."

"Oh. Uh. Huh," came the punctuative invitation to proceed: fitly lacking eloquence, its subtext screamed on its behalf, "I'm at a loss for words! I'm all ears! Explain yourself!"

"Well, not in the company as such."

"Not as *such* !" inveighed Sheril witheringly, as one on a campaign for plain English might address a civil servant on his obfuscatory verbosities, his double dealing diplomacies, his misused, misspelled, deliberately mystifying Latinisms and accompanying show-off, shown up corrections *ad nauseum* (sic). "In a company adjunct, an offshoot, a branch, a scion, a separate venture, a —", the list of synonyms highlighting the chillingly logical similarities between official government and business modes of communication and our crises driven personal ones. When challenged, buying time seems to be the preferred option as we pay stammering windy, jammering lip-service to Roget, reeling off his seminal work as if rattling off a grapeshot idiot board blindfolded and untutored in Braille. Running out of the excuse for language that is the filibust, he came clean.

"I'm leaving *Boom Bros.*"

"What? Why?", all recent detached cynicism dissipated as Sheril was engulfed exigently in concern. He stood before her now, a species suddenly confronted with extinction, taking on the alarmingly decaying form of a previously banked on persuasive benefactor turned potential mendicant, just this minute fallen on hard times and come to call on favours long overdue, on promises now revealed as false. As, indeed, did she for he.

"Not exactly. Officially I'm leaving, though I'll still get my share of the profits."

Sheril's silence spoke to the urgency of further explanation. "It was Garvey's idea, really. At first I was having none of it but, well, you know how persuasive Garvey and his statistics can be." Sheril, her psychological calculations still centred on statistics even more poetic in most men's eyes than those calculated by mother nature, weighed this statement and begged its conclusion with a look which fast amounted to desperation. Fairbrother, recognising her peril, prevaricated no further.

"I'm going into, erm, publishing." This message was met with a degree of incredulity more normally associated with a comprehensively under-educated schoolkid's De Nero-ish response to being confronted with Shakespearian texts.

"What the fuck is this?"

"Publishing. Garvey wants me to front a publishing house."

"Publishing? What do you, — we, — for that matter, what does Garvey know about publishing?"

"He know — he knows how to make money — how to make it make money."

"Sure, if he's peddling porno-trash ——." The naughty schoolboy's look of a Halloween pumpkin that involuntarily lit her husband's face, allied to her recalling last night's waitress brought, by trick or by treat, even this so recently confused young bride horripilatingly to her senses.

"You're going to publish that insult to body, heart, mind and soul of women — and men?" It wasn't really a question, more an exordium, yet Fairbrother managed to interject a solitary, partly swallowed, half-baked "yes" before the torrent resumed.

"You've just got married and you're telling your wife, on your honeymoon, on *her* honeymoon!, you want to spend your life perving over tarts, because, because —— well you fucking tell me because — because that's not my idea of 'to honour and obey' — I won't stand for it, you hear!?!?! God, the thought makes my flesh creep —— say something, you bastard!!" she screamed, lachrymal cascades cleaving her cheeks, mocking, violating her laughter lines, the bluish-black-kohl streaming through the rouge like the very laceration of privacy which marks out a blush as pencilled in for the ridicule of its own spotlighting as surely as a cosmeticised bruise manifests itself as a cosmeticised bruise.

"It's alright, it's alright," he held her, her fists no longer pathetically pummelling his chest. Her face, so recently shamed was buried in that chest, emitting sob-sniff-sob-sniff-sob rhythmic reports, too fast for a lament, though precisely synchronised with the rapid palpitations of his hard-pressed heart.

"It's nothing dirty ——," he bowed, addressing the crown of her lovely head for the first time, the sickly sweet of her shampoo and holding agent not quite neutralised by the salt of his tears — "and — and — I want *you* to be my co-publisher."

Her face now gazed up at his lowered sights.

"What did you ——? —— say ——. What do you mean?"

"Just as I said, darling."

"But — you said 'no wife of mine will ever work for me at *Boom Bros*'."

"So I did. And I still say so. It's not *Boom Bros* and no one will be working for anyone. We'll work together. I want you to be my partner."

"But why leave Boom Bros?"

"Just a paper exercise. I'll be a *de facto* rather than a *de iure* boom brother."

"But why?"

"Garvey reckons —", she put her index finger to his lips to signify that whatever Garvey reckoned was inenarrable.

"I don't want to hear any more about what Garvey thinks." His nod signalled the withdrawal of this gentle instrument of censure. She bowed back, begging enlightenment.

"I —— we —— all think that it would be better to disassociate *Boom Bros* from anything, er, controversial."

"You mean sexual —, right?" On receiving no response she embarked upon a catch-as-catch-can catechism designed to give him voice again, to set free from bondage that suddenly shy, practically benighted former silvery devil.

"You never shied from controversy before, right?" No, his head agreed confusedly. "So why now?"

"I don't know," he dissembled. It had been a noble silence all the same. Sensing that the chosen approach needed depersonalising if it were to conclude satisfactorily, Sheril shifted tack from potential lifelong partner to future business partner, all the while pursuing the same line of questioning.

"*Boom Bros* have never lacked in profits, have they?" she stated, the final polite qualifier again serving to demand an honest answer of an Englishman.

"No," he responded, meeting the obligation magnificently.

"So they don't mind being associated with the controversial if it's lucrative, right?"

"I suppose not," he sighed, knowing full well where this was leading yet unable to halt its progress.

"But not this time?"

"No, not this time," he blushed brighter than ever had his bride.

"Because this time it's to do with ——?" she coaxed.

"To do with —," he reluctantly echoed.

"To do with — you know what," she teased.

"To do with you know what," he smirked.

"Say it, damn you!"

"Sex," he muttered shamefacedly (only after what the shrinks who reduce us all to, then wrap us all up in, clinical, nay, prophylactic obsessions would diagnose as an indecent pause for indecent thought), every bit the missionary position punter on being asked his preference.

"Say it as if you owned the shop, not as if you'd sidled in for some sleazy wares, you fool!" she screamed. Fairbrother raised his head to protest his unsuitability at granting such a request and noticed that she was smiling.

"Are you laughing — at — me?" he faltered.

"What do you think?" she laughed, the question soon becoming engulfed by her convulsions so that what was conveyed was a not inappropriate statement of exclamatory mockery akin to 'what do you look like!'

"You are! You are!" he wised up as embarrassment touched upon annoyance and bemusement, but briefly, before settling on relief. Relief that she could now stand as the accused, at least for a while.

"Of course I am!" she screeched, a minor admission of guilt followed by a devil-may-care release.

"What does this mean — that?" and off he went again.

"That I accept your offer."

"My offer to edit —"

"Co-publish."

"Co-publish —"

"And partner."

"And partner —"

"You."

"You."

"No, not me, you."

"You. No, not you, me." Me Jane! she thought but kept this to herself.

"In this venture."

"In this venture."

"For better for worse."

"For better for worse."

"For richer for ——"

"You're taking the piss!" sparked Fairbrother, and soon the honeymoon couple were rolling round the bed to the accompaniment of tickle inspired girlish giggles from the Mrs and mild-mannered affectionate epithets from the slap-happy Mr.

Chapter Eleven

That Sheril had been on the game when the debased vision that was her public persona first hoved itself into her future husband's view was, is, will be forever irrefutable. To all but her future husband, that is, was, forever?, who at one point looked set fair to swear blind to the maggots one day to invade his *Totenraum* that she was as pure and lasting an epiphany as the lovestruck dare see. Oh, and to herself, for, for Sheril —— being on the game was a game in itself, informed in her case by a derring-do as uncharacteristically masculine in its aggression as is the average 'good time' girl's almost pathetically defensive in its knowingly vulnerable femininity. Having chosen such a career, then, she could no more lay claim to appreciate the deprivations that drove almost all of her colleagues thus than could their collective clientele. But, having chosen such a career (this point cannot be emphasised too much, so out of the ordinary was she in this respect), we must admit her motivation to be strange enough for us to give her the benefit of the doubt, if not yet the perquisites of our intrigue.

Sheril and sister Cheryl had upbringings both different and interesting enough to attract the undivided attention of that exploitation/porno movie director manqué (schizoporno may be the *genre's* given name) which lurks in all little boys. We get to fuck them in the end, of course, but only when they are irredeemably fucked up by what, in our whenceforth expedient absence from the many scenes of many too many crimes, we deem casually to be their own hands.

At one week old, abandoned balefully by a mother, once seen, to but never attended to, by a father, these two swaddled wards of court were separated, the one to scrumptious surrounds, the other to scum in slums: Suffolk, upper middle, older, childless couple: Port Glasgow, lower, lower sinking childhood sweethearts/divorcees, respectively. As of then, the then that never had a future, in Simpson's Maternity Hospital, Edinburgh, it was the opinion of the nursing and midwifery staff that only those who could tear them apart could tell them apart. Their mother, their birth mother as the — for heaven's sake!! — their *mother*, considered by those in the know, those that matter, to be unworthy (not least herself, alas poor lass, not least herself) of these two identically ill-starred heartbreakers, was unceremoniously and, fair's fair in love and war, uncomplainingly relieved of her cursed issue before she could know what they might become, before she could become what they might know. Her one parting wish was that they kept the names she gave them, lest she be forgotten. She needn't have worried.

Such was the lottery of life in 1963 for two farmed out wards of court, its inequities almost matching those of, oh say, present day dossers at Victoria and the mocking face on their rare coinage and rarer notes of the realm of the first family descended as if from another planet just up the road. Pronounced identical, raised not just separately but gulfed, the two sisters met by chance, by fate's full and fickle circle, some 20 years later. As if to emphasise that recognising a kinship can be inescapable even in the furthest flung families, the two strangers immediately knew they were sisters. Oh, not twins, and not even those type of sisters, but sisters under the, no, of, *of* the skin. Embarking on a love affair at first sight, Cheryl – then (1984) known as Willie Half & Half Nelson, and singing in the 'Alternative' C&W band (everything, even C&W was impossibly alternative in them days) *No Blokes, Fast Strokes & Cowpokes* at the *Nowt as Queer as Folk Club* in Campden Town – and Sheril, then known as Sheril, not so wet as ticklish behind the ears: postgraduate (Oxford 1:1 in Media Studies and Politics) – were two uncharacteristically narcissistic dykes literally in love with their own mirror images. While heterosexuals tend to epitomise at least the expedient view of love as a twin backed beast into which opposites attract, what Sheril and Cheryl lost out in the plain Jane stakes – i.e., what the rest of us lost out in them being in love with each other, truly in love with themselves – couldn't disguise that their striking resemblance more than compensated for the atypicality of their striking good looks in making of them a true paradigm couple of the then lesbian scene. Chic – er, yes, chicker, no. Butch? Femme? Both, both.

Exclusively homosexual, Cheryl made the first move. Recognising not quite her kin, yet an ardently kindred spirit, she it was who was butch in the approach. The question "do you get asked if you come here often often?", with its sly undertones and *double entente* – encoded for outlaw consumption – served nicely by way of an introduction. And in all the time they were lovers – one year, felt like two months, tallied – they never once suspected the terrible truth. Terrible? More terrible than being rent asunder from each other and mother as from their very after birth? Well, no, society does have a problem or two with its taboos, not to mention its foibles, concluded but these two of its happier go luckier experiments, quite justly according it no thanks, little more thought than it had they. Having come out, on being found out (nothing sinister: mutual friends innocently pieced together the fragments of their past: quite simple, a jigsaw sky with lots of clouds on the horizon) they determined not to tell no one. That is, they would never deny they were truly twinned to anyone who asked and who they *knew* could be trusted. That that sentence reads wrong should be taken as right. For a while their love lust blossomed in the light of the potential inquisitorial scrutiny they were courting, but after a while even young illegals can tire of flouting the law and flaunting desire for the mere taunting's sake. Parting better friends than most siblings and parting couples could dream of, even in combining to sentimentalise their former fellow feelings, the two taboo twins vowed never to lose sight of each other again: the odd couple, keenly aware that what they were, if anything, was oddly part of us all, continued their long since divergent – if truly love letter bridged – ways; Cheryl, in a succession of rather good, if more than rather too raw-boned 'n' raunchy to get closer than flirtation with popular/populist acclaim, all girl C&W bands; Sheril, while working as, yes, a copywriter at the lucratively remunerating *Nosworthy de Klerk* (joining nine months after the departure of the then already notorious *Boom Bros*), pursued a secondary career as a nightclub hostess cum burlesque female impersonator's female impersonator. It was in this latter guise that the *Boom Bros* crowd chanced upon her shapely form in *À propos de rien,* as we have chronicled elsewhere. And she upon them? Chanced upon them as the Assyrian coming down like the wolf on the fold, as one who was, appositely enough, once adjudged to be mad, bad and dangerous to know once observed.

On graduating, Sheril had high hopes of embarking upon what used quaintly to be known as a civic minded career. Of course, the Janus faced cynicism of the electorate being long since halfway justified, such a designation had just as long since lost its last deposits of resonance. Young, gifted and idealistic (Tory), Sheril was almost destined for a life of growing up fast in the fast lane, managing her own exploitation and autarky, the sum of which aims were protective, the result of which stance was, rightly or wrongly perceived as aggressive. Perceived rightly or wrongly, such a seemingly devil take the hindmost stance was widely championed in the early '80s. Her Filofax entries for those halcyon days of conspicuously exuded nasty bad taste (one word:

spritzers!!), to this day betray a young lady very much in step with the times. While not exactly a goose-step (though somewhat less gentle of tread than one moved by jerk of knee), many facets of '80s British manifest destiny gradually began to strike young Sheril as paying mutated homage to ugly precedents. The discordant Falklands triumphalism was all the more ethically problematic for idealistic young women to take, if only for its being primarily orchestrated by one at least biologically as they. What finally shook Sheril's faith in the powers that be, and her, till then, empathy with their ideology was her almost entirely happy relationship with Cheryl. Up until that point, that life redefining moment, that first impression forever lodged, Sheril had been exclusively heterosexual: that is, like a good Young Tory, she had always fantasised about the thrusting young male members of the Federation of Conservative Students when shamefacedly frigging. One day her prince would surely come in the guise of a future knight of the shires. Until Cheryl. Meeting Cheryl was sheer serendipitous bliss. Well, not exactly. Unknown to Sheril, her FCS colleagues had expediently happenstanced – *à la* the Third Reich and the Final Solution – upon *The Nowt as Queer as Folk* club in Campden Town, intent on proving there was nowt as righteous as bashing them kind of folk. Subsequently, to those poor, oh so benighted devils ever taking the hindmost, Sheril would, let's just say would not vehemently disagree with anyone violently in disagreement with them, until then her 'us'. Politicised and reclaimed in one (the birth mother naturally, geographically, economically, environmentally and emotionally closer to the Port Glasgow surrogates of Cheryl's – social workers, subsequently in need of colleagues to help on the very antisocial occasion of their divorce – than to the Lowestoft gentlefolk of her own), Sheril sought to put her obvious talents to their newly revealed, therefore more exigent use.

Taking up a position at *Nosworthy de Klerk*, she was comfortably off; comfortably enough off to ought to have known beyond a measure of a doubt that she was at least comfortably off. But, reinvigorated by love and rediscovery, though lately, amicably split from her sister, she couldn't be comfortable with this as any more than a holding position. Ending each day double effete-ish (adspeak for worn out by childishness?), she would shed the power, all but cross-dressing of the nation's prime executive suites for the power, almost tacky as cross-dressing of the nation's prime fantasies.

As if in revolt against a system which patronised – with the uncredited designation – 'her kind', Sheril's first fully consummated heterosexual encounter was also a highly commercialised exchange. Working by day on an advertising campaign for a ludicrous product, chocolate vanilla scented shampoo, she increasingly apprehended all involved to be prostituted at the altar of imbecility, to be paying daily and dearly the price which such crazed worship exacts. All involved, *naturellement*, involved all: the quite ravishing post-ravished *gamine* pouting Sheril's filthy doodlings on the margins of an otherwise bimbo bleached blank page ('Now I smell good enough to eat': Your *hair!*), the manufacturers of the product and the makers of its marketing, the cretinous dupes who comprised the credulous members of the public to buy this autopilot sales pitch without revolting against it, let alone purchasing the product, and last, alas most, herself. After hard days grafting on to this tacky frivolity the manufactured crucial importance that is of crucial importance to manufacture product placement, she sought to unwind in a world more literal, less venally suggestive. The *frisson* of a double life was all that got her through those days, the duping of those supposedly in the know became the knowledge on which her delayed rite of passage to full womanhood was predicated. Realising it was not at all clever to think oneself clever merely because one could simply pull the wool over the eyes of stupider sheep by but turning one's back, Sheril needed something more dangerous, albeit with her holding the whip hand, than a career in deception, mass and self. The far from negligible comforts afforded colleagues best placed to appreciate the '80s – youngish, in self advertising, verily the ghost copywriters of the acquisitive society – were quite literally lost on Sheril. Seeking herself in the shadows that so become the creatures of the night, she shunned the bright as a button office culture, preferring to rendezvous with far less assured, assuredly far more 'interesting', inarguably sadder, equally inarguably wiser studies in humanity. Finding employment in a massage parlour, quite literally at the drop of a hat – from the proprietor's 'works every time' honoured interview ploy – hatstand missed: 'Miss!' – which got her bending down, the foreplay to giving serious, expensive headgear back, to his seeming *obiter dictum* — 'Nice ass! When can you start?' – Sheril was to prove an 'enthusiastic and popular employee'; the limited adspeak that is pimpspeak for docile in respect of employer, co-operative in 'exchanges' with clients. For a year this double life consumed Sheril's every waking hour. Her other hours were, as the Freudians would say, consuming her too.

" At *Nosworthy de Klerk* the 'legit' Sheril could see that her brilliance as a copywriter threatened to be as big a drag on her beliefs as did her sex, particularly her particularly attractive configuration thereof. Like many gauche teenagers who grew up late she had compensated by doing so extraordinarily quickly. Disinterest in the pinstriped yahoos at the office and contempt for their readily condescended secretaries – all as gorgeous and gormless as they were undeniably female – vied with a growing desire to 'out' the enigma that was her after hours persona. Increasingly she felt that the evening wear and tear she subjected herself to, while gruesome, was closer to the true Sheril, to the true woman, to her true, until now preconditioned position in society. Literally tiring of the entropy which threatened to burn out many '80s whiz-kids, she decided to make a clean break from both ways of living. In future she would advertise nothing but herself. As befitted a disillusioned consumer she considered herself no longer for sale.

Reincarnating as Syreenah!, she disappeared overnight from the lives of her previous circles, leaving no forwarding address and precious few clues. Now unrecognisable to former *N de K* employees and business lunch admirers (though her erstwhile night-time workmates and clients would recognise her), Syreenah! accentuated her femaleness to such an extent that many who caught her act swore 'hers' to be a drag act. At the very least she appeared to be a transsexual: the six inch patent leather stilettoes didn't hinder. Indeed, for a while she teased many a gay club audience into her illusion. Miming to pop standards, she was gainfully employed in a bewilderingly dull variety of nightclubs. Her act was certainly burlesque but, perhaps to keep up the mystique of keeping up, if minimally and lewdly, her gender, her private parts, her *naturalia* naturally became her talking points among what was readily becoming her 'public'. And, in spite of there being no smokescreen without fire, there was nothing there to talk about. Ah, but out of the ordinary – sex – comes the extraordinary – sex!

An icon on the gay scene within a year of this new career's commencement, a curious thing occurred to this object of much curiosity. The lady started doing business lunches again: as an act.

Yes, consumption was so conspicuous then that even lunch had to portray itself as decadent. Hired to strut her stuff at *À propos de rien*, she rendezvoused with pigtailed little boy big lunchers, among them some previous colleagues oblivious to the person behind her charms. She even slept with some previous colleagues; such was the change in her that they suspected nothing, save perhaps that originally she had been a man. None, but none there gathered knew anything of her pre-Syreenah! life.

While making *après* lunch dates Syreenah! took no money for surrendering her favours to what, after all, were a series of pimply youths and jumped up little office boys. Presents, bribes, you name it, but no base metal.

When she met Fairbrother she was genuinely attracted to him. Oh, she knew chivalry to be a tired and not to be trusted try on, but there was something in him and his inept attempts to protect her that told her, this is his first time —— it's not a line —— it's the real thing with this one. Of course, just as the ineffable fact of Sheril's glamour acted as both spur and barrier to Fairbrother, his gaucheness, allied to his undoubted wealth – they were all wealthy in *À propos de rien* – acted as a spur and spur to Sheril.

Chapter Twelve

"I move we four put it to a vote," snarled Garvey in a Texas patrician manner LBJ addressing a constituency of ever willing cheerleaders to scream 'All the way with LBJ!' and mean it, heart, soul and flesh, would have been hard-pressed to beat.

"But she's my co-director, we can't exclude her," countered Fairbrother, the personal pronoun and its accusative case (not possessive, 'her majesty's thighs' is possessive) respectively, though less than respectfully referring to, well, the wife. The lady kept her counsel against these twin assaults of generalised misogyny and that which she appeared to inspire within the evidently cloying confines of the marital state. She glanced sweetly at her sickeningly reciprocating husband.

"But —— but, today's agenda is not a woman's business," moved Garvey.

"Bollocks!" roused the husband, mindful of emasculation. Perhaps subconsciously, he continued, "If Mrs Thatcher could hear you now!"

"She would never contradict me," wailed Garvey, ingenuously revealing the deluded reciprocal worship most idolaters truly believe they inspire in their chosen ones.

"That's not the point, and you know it, both of you," countermanded Tristan.

"Pray continue," mocked the genuinely wounded Texarkanan from the Grantham school of hard knocks, common sense and parvenu megalomania.

"I remember you argued against 'elevating' a woman —— Joyce —"

"Allardyce, if I'm not mistaken," prompted Cal.

"Allardyce, if he's not mistaken," proceeded Tristan, not at all sure.

"What of her?" snapped Garvey.

"Well, your objection then was, if I'm not mistaken, that as so many of our customers – in insurance, merchandising *et aliae* – were women, we would be mixing business with pleasure at our peril in making Joyce a board member with particular remit for women's markets; that is, we knew where we were with men because, well, we were, uhm, we are men, and it follows we know where we are with women because, well, we are men and they know where they stand with us."

"Yes?" enquired Garvey wearily.

"Cal argued against Joyce — our most qualified member of staff and, as I recall, you concurred —"

"Indeed I did. Still do," said Garvey tetchily, clearly a man who, having seen the point, was prepared to put it about bluntly that it was little or none, even if, as in this case, he had been its original illustrator.

"So, women are only inferior insomuch as we are unable to relate to them in positions of power with us, as our equals?"

"No, Tristan, no it's not just us. It's a societal thing. Our customers weren't ready for it. We were, we are a buddy movie type operation. And I would remind you that I am on record as stating that Joyce was a deserving candidate for a directorship."

"One whom you and Cal blackballed." Ignoring the unworldly, Utopian, unworthy gibe, Garvey proceeded.

"But she, Syreenah! is —"

"My wife, whom you proposed as the editor of, correct me if I'm wrong, *Gali Guzzlers*."

"Yes, yes, but that would be just a front."

"As is the entire operation."

"Well, as far as the taxman need be concerned, yes."

"Well then, have the balls to recognise that she can bring a completely uncontaminated vision to these enterprises —" Fairbrother's honourable defence of his wife's honour was rudely and inevitably interrupted.

"What!?" exploded Garvey. "She's going to be getting her jugs out, poking her fanny and her, uhm, bush, fuck it, in men's faces, women's faces, fuck it!" To the divisions of a common language it must have seemed that at best this man was making her out to be a contortionist swingumajig while, at best again, this speaker was making of himself a complete arse, cunt, what you will, head, heart and soul wise.

"I haven't agreed to anything yet," she demurred, demurely enough to elicit an apology.

"I'm sorry, Syreenah (always Syreenah, no exclamation mark offstage and outside the marital abode), but you make my point. We're going to be talking dirty, real, real dirty here today. I just don't think that, as a lady you, as David's wife, should have to hear it," proposed the gallant Garvey.

"Some of this talk will be about me, right?" suggested Syreenah.

"Well, not specifically," tarried Garvey, blushing.

"About women?" she pressed.

"Well, no — not specifically. Gals".

"And these 'gals', and, specifically or not, *I* will be asked to appear in *Gal Guzzlers*?"

"Asked, yes. And you will be well rewarded for it."

"Maybe I ought to stick around and decide upon that."

"Oh no, you're not their union rep," moaned Garvey. Being no great fans of unions, or indeed of sisters in any collective sense other than in orgy staged for him as voyeur or star participant (he didn't mind), Garvey naturally had the rest of the board on his side.

"No, that's not on," grumbled Cal, personally, professionally and sexually slighted. He spoke for them all, heads nodding in some displaced mute knee-jerk of fraternity.

"I don't care what the other little bitches get," spat Syreenah endearingly. She had their ears. "Not at all. But either I'm a full board member, like my husband, or I leave him to play with his own company and his bored member." To schoolboy giggling, Fairbrother ran to teacher.

"You can't mean that," he begged. To no avail. Syreenah had won the lads round. True, it was at the expense of marital dignity but it proved she was not one of those dread wimmin creatures. Indeed, she was one of them, by which is meant us. To all assembled, not least to Fairbrother.

"So, you think you can offer this enterprise a —," began Garvey.

"Completely uncontaminated vision. Absolutely. She is the product. What can be a purer sale than that?" replied Fairbrother on her behalf.

"And we —," proceeded Garvey, but again Fairbrother was hot to display his *bona fides*.

"We are the consumers —,"

"Not us," interjected Cal, "but those —"

"Seedy little men who need taking to the cleaners," finished Fairbrother, cleanly rounding off this little vignette on the art of storytelling as an art form superseded only by that of passing the buck. How they laughed! On getting back down to business, Fairbrother felt it incumbent on himself as spouse and, well, natural spokesman for the lads, to forewarn his wife. "We'll be discussing some strange things. In some dirty words," he adumbrated to appreciative male 'hear hear's all round.

"And I'll be doing these things, and I'll be miming those words," shot back Syreenah to inappreciative male coughs and a "Quite, let's get on," from her spouse.

And on they got. Off, too. On and on they discussed the off-colour, arriving more often than not at a hue of blue somewhat grittier than aquamarine. The minutes of the meeting – taken by Syreenah for reasons of tradition, secrecy, nudge, nudge and propriety, whoop, whoop – tell tale of a gathering in which inhibitions were variously discarded, found out to be falsely assumed, mourned in others, treated with the suspicion they deserved, more than the suspicion they deserved, the suspicions they aroused. Exactly the same goes for the lack of inhibition. The minutes read thus:

'Private and confidential minutes of extraordinary *BBB* meeting, somewhere, sometime, with some attendants — *C, T, G, & D* (members) *Sy* (sec)

1.1 Apologies for absence: no one.

1.2 *G* (chair?) commenced this extraordinary meeting by stating at the outset that the secretary, "having consented to minute what promised, or threatened "(joke)" to be a 'colourful'" (spelt) "exchange of views, should not feel consequently obliged to minute all 'Anglo-Saxonisms verbatim.'" (in Latin?), what with her being new to the job, no shorthand and all.

1.2.1 The *sec* replied, thanking *G* graciously for his gallant concern, differing only in conveying that this wasn't only the first, but the last time she would fulfil this function, so content was she on a "career as as big a fucking bastard" (Anglo-Saxonism: minuted) "as you, *G*".

1.3 Thereupon *G* welcomed formally *(sec) Sy* to this, her first – and last – such meeting.

1.4 *G* continued, forwarding the following proposal:

"That this nation is so sexually inhibited as to house an almost unnaturally untapped market for the entertainment of adults." When challenged, by *(sec) Sy*, to elaborate, *G* conceded, "alright, alright already, fucking porn, if you must get smutty". This quodlibet over terminology aside, the meeting was in broad agreement with *A*: the proposal and *B*: the possible financial benefits it promised. *G* gained consent from the rest of the quorum to toss a few idea(l)s about. All agreed he should toss away forthwith.

2.1 The "vision thing", according to *G*. "Henceforth no porn, only eroticism." Agreed *nem. diss.*

2.1.1 The explicit was out of the question. When asked to be more specific, more explicit, *G* refused to be so, "not in front of a lady" (his words). Ignoring comments ending "that's the wife", the *(sec) Sy* forced

G to concede that by deploying the euphemism 'explicit', he, G, meant to cover up the "disgusting", such as the "sexual act in all its forms bar glam gal on glam gal", depicted in any way that could accurately or inaccurately be deemed/recalled/imagined by any judge in the land to be "graphic". When challenged by *T* what this left, *G* cited the aforementioned *GG* on *GG*, solo gal, gal with loofah, solo gal with banana, solo gal with guy in voyeur's role and, if nude (gal), in "decent posture", solo gal outdoors, indoors, in water, out of water (just), in nude (rarely), in "gear" (all other times), in leather (specialist market, own mag). On getting gist, *sec (Sy)* was invited by *G* to concede that women's bodies were more beautiful than men's This she did readily – neglecting to add "minds, too" –, eliciting plaintive but futile gainsaying from *D*, who failed to extract from *(sec) Sy* the promise not to appear in any *GG* on *GG* shots.

G continued, first dealing with "first things first":

2.2 "First things first": Magazines.

Before continuing on this topic, *G* added the observation/caveat that though he had no objection to "muscling in on the video market" he had always found stills photography to be more in his line, to be more his strength. When asked if a stills image was thought preferable because easier to infiltrate and dominate, *à la* Errol Flynn crashing *tableaux vivants* of vestigial virgins got up as the unoriginal Madonna, he assumed an almost criminally low profile in declining to comment. Further reluctance ensued, to much good natured joshing. Reluctant to relent, and on inviting the meeting to draw its own "filthy conclusions", he was met with the question: "Would he really like his caricatures/cartoons animated or in moving strip form", *(T)*.

2.3 "First things first": (reprise)

G proposed the following titles for magazines in the, mmm, stills photography *sans* perspective genre:

Gal Guzzlers, a paean to the manifold wondrous and natural methods by which a car could accommodate a centrefold and naturally, vice versa.

Les femmes, for its combination of the exotic and the perverse (yet so easily understandable!). When it was mooted that this was less than an original title, the challenger, *D*, was himself challenged to, um, come up with the evidence behind such an assertion. "Precisely," (*G*) This wasn't "an area of our culture in which self-publicising litigants would do open battle over the sanctity" (sniggers: unisex), "originality or very thought of an idea" (*G* again). Accordingly, *Les femmes* was endorsed.

Go-go girls go for it!, accepted *nem. con.* as comprising the benefits of alliteration, never to be sniffed at, climaxing, as it were, in the sixth form suggestiveness (dear to all potential customers) of the exclamation mark. The British, it was remarked *(G)*, like it plain and simple, preferably obvious to the point of simply smirking over the topic in hand (smirks: male): they being perhaps the last surviving people (men only) to believe in the omniscience and omnipotence of the missionary position; indeed, only they could market *it* as a naughty sideshow to the vicar's slideshow (off camera, off colour, but never off the mind), an attitude befitting a people embarrassed by sex but peculiarly, very peculiarly, conspicuously not by their consequent embarrassing treatment of same.

Automatrons, thought to contain a nice pun combining the grace and power of the machine with the just so domination begged for by the multitude of perennial schoolboys inhabiting these isles. *G* favoured it for the cars and bikes ("Brit and American only") it would parade in its feature spreads, the better to feature in its advertising pages, but was disabused of the notion of launching this publication as a "semi-serious" rival to *Mechanics Monthly* and the ilk. Such a strategy could prove seriously counter-productive, opined. *T.* Car mechanics, continued *T*, are "worthless little oiks" who would much rather spend their spare cash (if any) and time (no ifs) gazing on oiled pneumatic blondes than greasy pistons (just), and, while conceding the corollary, the judgement of the consumer should be trusted. Again, the nature of the market, as, indeed, the beast – "ready formed and simple" – was cited. *G* concurred, concluding that "fuck-ups should not be unnecessarily fucked about with."

Rock Tease: was accepted for its obvious lewd connotations, fortuitously providing a format in which to 'dress' young women as the age's other great icons, *viz*, rock 'n' roll groupies. The level of suggestiveness that could be enabled by this format was generally agreed to be as limitlessly climactic as that subliminally offered by the otherwise comically vacuous backing vocals of the 'bop-sha-rah-rah' school. However, it was proposed the title be emended from *Rock Tease* to *Rock Teasers*, the feeling *(nem. diss.)* being that the former (!) was too passive (!!) for the subject matter (!!!); i.e., likely to prove too much like hard work for the consumer.

Sun Sea & Sluts ("no comma – it looks like a sperm", *G*) was accepted into the already tumescent canon as satisfying the already (simply) identified consumers' pathos steeped desire for the exotic, the erotic and, in short, a sex life (coincidentally, the ampersand was welcomed whenever called upon as a semiotically sexier surrogate for "and"). Acceptance was provisional, the following caveat being issued (by *D*) and heeded (*nem. diss.*): 'Not a fucking naturist magazine. No nudes, however shapely. And stilettos must always be worn, even on sand.' This last stricture was granted, the bonus being that this presented great opportunities for some 'extremely compromising positions' (*G*).

Virgin Soldiers: it was felt this title combined neatly to offer an ideal platform on which to parade the quintessential eroticism of women in uniform, lesbian love and young (though post paedomorphic statured) maidens inviting deflowering. For obvious reasons this magazine would not offer its consumers the voyeuristic voyage of discovery that is the "open piss flap shot" (*C*). Quite.

Advertisements were to be particularly welcomed from customers for the following products (all markets to be closely monitored with an eye on the chance of moving in as manufacturers/wholesalers/retailers): single girl videos, dual and multi-girl videos – four at most; more could confuse they eye, "lead to premature blindness" *(sec) Sy* – sex chat lines, pre-recorded and 'live', sexual aids, the sensitive side of S&M (S? M? &?) – such last named traits to be catered for in strictly specialist publications/videos/product lines. Blow up dolls, it was felt represented the unacceptable end of the market; likely to give eroticism a bad name, providing, it was agreed by all, pornography's (that word) only link to rape likely to, ahem, stand up in court. Paedophilia was out in all forms: thought by all to be too controversial, and by all but *C* to be too disgusting for words. *C*'s comment, "if it happens, it happens; i.e., it can't be ignored" was noted as hard to ignore. Its sentiment though was rejected. Reviled even.

'No poofdahs!' was the rallying cry endorsed by all but *(sec) Sy*. Nothing funny, untoward, twisted, gender bending, TVs, TSs. Penises? Penii? Penes. "Trust you to know", *D* (once you've seen one). Alas, definitely no erect whatevers, if that's the word, in, gulp, shot. Singular, flaccid, untouched and unretouched, friendless, just as the law allows. 'Nothing too adventurous for the average couple.' (*D!* & *nem. diss.*)'

Chapter Thirteen

That night Fairbrother had a dream, the first he felt duty-bound to recall in years. Hence was he seated the following lunch-time in the Harley Street surgery of one Dr Henrik Travolta, social acquaintance and trick cyclist of the charismatic school. Styling himself a 'motivational therapist and stress consultant' to cover all the angles, he had too little Latin to achieve even the relatively humble status of GP, and his grasp of psychoanalysis would appear to be all Greek to genuine practitioners of that much derided art. From his improbable name, even more improbably given, through his upbringing – upper middle Jewish Italian Manhattanite – he appeared destined to do 'this' for a living. 'This' and not a little of that added up to quite a bit of a living. Entering England armed only with enough serious hand and wrist jewellery to tip off the less class conscious class of search and destroy machines that are customs men the world over, he proceeded first-class to inveigle his way into London's second street of shame *sans* reputation, *avec* more than sufficient moolah to demand one.

London's *beau monde,* and in particular the Harley Street set (definitely not the poor and poorly), were never likely to deny him his grand entrance to the flashy ante-room, in which ethics are as venal as a wino's plasma, beyond which complaisant wonderment rarely dares to pry. Within six months the young – still twenty something – charismatic had risen so high in his profession it would be no surprise to learn that his less spectacular fellow practitioners were able to keep going only by paying each other many visits and much money to have his meteoric rise explained. With no qualifications to speak of, save that from that greatest of '80s finishing schools, the university of life, this exotic young punk acquired instantaneous status as new kid on the block. Not generally the type of neighbourhood addition to strike terror in the hearts of the upper echelons of the highest salaried branch of the medical profession, the brash young *arriviste* nevertheless laid astonishing claim on the fuck-ups of the great and the good: a claim met with even more astonishing success and payments. Coming from a home in a district in a city in a country where it was not the done thing to keep an ego sized portion of one's expendable income from some fucked-up quack who would tell one how fucked-up one was, he would truly have had to be a genuine 'case' not to join the ranks of those who owned their own couchant potato heads. It being as simple and unavoidable as a schizophrenic's schism, he set up in Manhattan. Well, lawyers have to be real, at least to the point of graduating law school. For two years he thrived, buoyed by papa's bequest (the old man, big in prunes and, unremarkably, in meretricious Beverly Hills society, had helpfully pegged out on a widely syndicated chat show while attempting to display a corollary between the body cleansing properties of his product and the subsidiary necessity for all good and true Americans to purge themselves of original sin before the Lord: more specifically, before the AIDS virus, then looming like an avenging angel in the outlook of all all American lookouts 'came and took our kids away'; thus proving that the talking of shit can accurately and fully describe and, um, move a product) of $2m to two of his three sons: Hiram, the eldest, an obstetrician with a professional, personal, practically preordained predilection to the gynaecological; again, eerily apt for a woppish Yid: Heinrick, the youngest, was written out of the will, not so much for being a dancer ('Valentino could move. What an athlete,' the old man would say, getting his Rudolphs crossed in a manner so endearingly amateur theatrical that one had to suspect it of being deliberate) but for being a chorus line dancer; 'Showbiz 's' no biz for no kids I know' he harrumphed, recalling at once Tin Pan Alley and the once quaint, platitudinous Hollywood code of separate beds, nowadays again more likely to be 'honoured' in the observance than in the breach; same result, different insult, same, erm, ends, different, er, means.

    He really was a homophobe *par excellence*, which, though tough luck on Heinrick – Heini to his friends –, was fortuitous, case material and base material wise, for Henrik. Incidentally, it is this layman's contention that all one needs to practice as a top people's trickcyclist is an ability to quote Freud and Jung, just the names 'Freud' and 'Jung', a semi-honed, um, familiarity with the Oedipal myth and the balls to accuse each and every male client, or, if you like, patient, of latent homosexuality, and each and every female client of repressed nymphomania (in desperation only apply the uncontrolled appellations alkie and dipso: alas, these could prove to be accurate and lead to guilt ridden binges from which one's fees are irredeemable). Try it. Get a rich daddy, kill him off, rent some bricks in Harley Street and just try and keep the cocksuckers from battering the door down with a phallic axe-handle, anti-phallic head, before the paint is dry and the 'IA Quack, UA

Asshole' sign is well and truly hung up.

In New York, Henrik had styled himself successfully as 'performance guru to top people' and saw no reason, sane or more lucrative, to downplay such billing in a Britain that knew him not. Yet. A rich fuck-up is the barrow-boy's, corner-boy's dream in any culture, in any language, especially in the gobbledygook, more money than sense 'sense' of psychobabble. Why, then, did he leave his flourishing practice in Manhattan? Well, if there is one thing rich Yanks have expressed a preference for expressing a preference on it is the wish (even more so than employing a head case who will mirror their thoughts and snatch their stash while providing such thoroughly distracting distraction) to spend their disposable wherewithal by gambling at law. Hence, a weary client, a corporate lawyer, natch, had abused, ahem, professional, um, trust by taping their sessions, during which, natch, the man on the smart side of the couch informed the man on the dumb side of life of his incipient homosexuality. In itself this was not the stuff of litigation but, goaded by a honcho well-versed in making bankers hostile to his retainer cry all the way to and from the bank, he was tricked into a line of enquiry so charismatic as to render even the questionable ethics he just about possessed incontestably defunct. In short, he left the US under the threat of legal action from a corporate lawyer so rich he could afford New York State's most renowned libel lawyer: the action; 'Attempted seduction of a happily married professional by another posing as such'. The evidence? A mere twenty or so breathless incantations of the innocent – as a shot in the dark is innocent – and not a little baffling, hypothesis, "You want to suck my cock, don't you, motherfucker?'

The best Henrik could expect from the contesting of such a case would be his exposure as a charlatan charged with fleecing his patients by means of an approach so crudely antagonistic so as to fuck up, for the purpose of further stumping up, the theretofore serenest of persons. The worst? The double infamy that would result from the guaranteed massive publicity generated by such a case, and the equally undeniable massive tabloid terrors, explosive, failed boxers, ebony of torso, darker of soul, no necks and less headroom than a Dinky Toy, with desire, no, obligation to wholly accommodate his dreams. Not being homosexual, the nightmare proposition of a custodial sentence was hideously exacerbated by the special treatment he knew he would be subjected to therein.

But, happily or no, our trickcyclist had escaped that fate, that ignominy and so much more. These days his problems were more likely to involve balancing his obscenely rewarding money making practice with the freedoms it afforded. Some days he had to work, oh, four, five half-hour sessions to keep himself in the style to which he had become customised; to wit – 100K a year. *¿Qué?* Yes, the year was 1985, which makes it all the more offensive.

Already having worked two hours, Henrik was irritable at being detained beyond lunch-time; eager to meet the spouse of one of his 'referrals' – jealous husband, of course, who had no reason so to be until his psychiatrist began passionately probing his wife. He requested that the receptionist cum Teasmade cum secretary cum *nth* choice bedmate, consult his diary. She wiggled in.

"It's on your desk, Dr Travolta."

"I know," he grinned wickedly. This consultation over before it began, it was to a room of three surprised persons that Fairbrother arrived right on cue, as the diary would have told the then entire *dramatis personae*.

"Er, there was no one at reception," apologised Fairbrother, generally experiencing surprisingly little of the shame suffered by similar supplicants to a profession even older than the calling of a sad bastard a madder bastard.

"Quite, quite, Mr —," the good doctor scrutinised his diary with the fierce analytical look cultivated by RD Laing especially, it would seem at this blessed remove, to make long-term studies, *mementos mori*, out of haunted photographers.

"Fairbrother," he said knowingly. "That's all, Miss Fanshawe. No, yes, we will have that cup of coffee. Milk and sugar?"

"Yes. Please."

"How many?"

"Two milks, one sugar," gawped Fairbrother as Miss Fanshawe improbably squeezed her impossibly sweet perfumed jugs past the theoretically nigh impossible corridor of air betwixt his unbendingly stiff stance and a cold functional grey filing cabinet containing cases such as his. Every one in love with Miss Fanshawe, regardless of, and obsessed with, sex, he thought. Yep, he was in the right place.

"Quick Rorschach test then off to lunch," Travolta's amused glance offered an unspeakably smug diagnosis. Though acquainted, Fairbrother and Travolta weren't exactly bosom buddies. Yet. Fairbrother noted as much.

"Do you prefer, Mr Tit — Tit — Tit — Tttrrravoltaaahh!, to call me Mr Ff — Ff — Ff— Ffffairbrother," he lapsed into a quintessential Freudian slip, stuttering as he never had, adult or child, rather as he imagined he imagined one should in a psychiatrist's office.

"No, you be David and I'll be Henry. Had that stammer long?"

"R-r-r-r-r-r-r-w-w-weeon?"

"No, just enquiring out of personal interest."

"About 30 seconds." This served to ease the tension: Fairbrother's because he was able to make a conscious joke at his own expense to follow having made somewhat of a fool of himself: Henry's because he knew a man with a sense of humour was in need of no more psychiatric help than would be commensurate with his missing his lunch date. After the inevitable, "What, no couch?" rigmarole (which all trickcyclists now cunningly deploy, the unexpected informality ostensibly putting their patients at their ease, actually scaring the living shits out of them by inviting the follow up: "What, am I not good enough for his couch?", or "What kind of nut doctor has no couch?") David and Henry were set fair to commence.

"So, seriously, how long have you suffered from that stammer?"

"Just a minute or so. Never stuttered before in my life." Again they laughed: Fairbrother pleased that his joke continued to be adjudged funny now that the kid gloves were off: Henry rather disingenuously; this appeared to be a more serious case than he had heretofore bargained on. This called for some pyrotechnical second-guessing. The tabloids, one believes, call it astrology: Marvo the memory man, whom the people called a miracle, called it a living on Brighton Pier; similarly, this pervo the mammary man.

"Let's not beat about the bush. It's women — no, no," he closed his eyes, the better to represent the kind of vision, the deep, dark imaginings he was feigning, practically stabbing for his patient in the dark, "A woman — your wife?" As most psychiatric patients (i.e., those paying good money to be cured of being fucked-up, but first of all diagnosed as such: as if going to a psychiatrist were not diagnosis enough!), Fairbrother was like the innocent member of the audience cajoled on stage to be Marvo's foil and fool; before becoming the great po-faced's incredible straight man he was, of course, chief amongst the audience's sceptics. Tell that to the people who didn't come! Perhaps they had been right all along: from here Marvo's assistant looked like a plant both above and below the neck. As the routine settled down to matters more specific than blindfold diagnosis of an unsightly birthmark on a lifelong unsighted, the session, to the great and the good's doctor's chagrin, began to build up its own characteristics and hence its own lunch threatening dynamic. This wasn't Dr Travolta's territory at all.

"Yes, but back to your wife. She's fucking around. Am I right?" tempted the doc.

"No, no, it's not her, it's me," issued back the stubborn response.

"But she made you what you are," teased the doctor.

"No, no that was my mother."

"Are you familiar with the story of Oedipus?" fished the doctor, close to despair yet closer still to the hackneyed line of *ersatz* scientific enquiry which had earned his profession the bloated and fearful reputation it so richly enjoyed. But no, dammit, this was no mere awkward customer. A serious head case, a fuck-up who wasn't parting with vast wads solely to salve some remnant of conscience. Oh no, this one would swear there was a soul secreted about its person. His wife didn't understand him, in that he was a textbook case. But who can blame her?, poor cow, mused Travolta as he suffered in silence. No, the undetected placebo, which was about as close as his type were both required and able to get to a cure, the subliminal double Mickey Finn of auto-suggestion and catchphrases, analysis as deep as a game show host's on current affairs, all the old standbys, useless. Maddening! Fairbrother was giving him it straight. Speaking of his first encounter with Sheril he recalled his first few impressions and threw in his surmise of hers for good measure. The doctor tolerated this tedium, for if there is one thing head doctors enjoy better than mouthing platitudinous *non sequiturs* to agape patients it is to try a little role reversal in this respect. At least he's doing my job for me, Henry thought, as Fairbrother analysed himself. Meanwhile, the good doctor could dream of lunch with the galloping major's fourth wife (both high on horses, low on horse-sense), the latest dashing young filly to supplant the previous knackered old mare.

"So, when I first met my wife there were eight thoughts going through my mind, and in such rapid succession as to be practically simultaneous," babbled the fast learning layman. "It's as close as I have come to love at first sight —." Recognising this old saw as his cue to at least pretend to be earning his money, Travolta attempted a smooth and professional take up.

"That's interesting —," was the inevitable opening gambit. And, indeed his interlocutor must have concurred for he continued unabated and apace.

"And they weren't – only my thoughts! Hers too!" Fairbrother announced, boggle eyed, every bit the caricature mnemonist himself now. "Primarily, she thought, he wants to fuck me. Secondarily, she thought, who the fuck does he think he is? Thirdly, she thought, what the fuck does he think I am? Fourthly, she concluded, I want to fuck him!" This boy knows his onions and other vegetables, sighed the doc, almost weeping, in two minds whether to listen further – for this one may need a shot of real convincing jargon – or to think of a real convincing excuse for missing lunch (oh, the truth wouldn't do!). An interesting patient: she knew him better by far than he knew or intended knowing any of his patients and, what's more, he knew she knew. As if on cue the case put itself.

"And me?" shrugged Fairbrother, exuding the type of flamboyant bodily rhetoric rarely seen outside a football penalty area, a cricketer's appeal or an amateur's amateur dramatic society in Sicily. "What do you think I'm thinking?" he asked, at once charismatic, enigmatic, bemused and self-assured, very much the pot calling the kettle black. The doctor shrugged, more wearily than patiently now, closer to despair than intrigue. It couldn't be reasoned away, lunch had gone.

"I'll tell you. Primarily, I thought, fuck me, I want to fuck that. Secondarily, I thought, fuck me, I want to fuck her. Thirdly, I thought, I want to make love to her. Finally, I thought, fuck me, she wants to fuck me! All this within an *Augenblick*, mind you," he enthused, employing a smattering of the Great Men's native tongue to put his evidently fretful analyst more at ease, less at angst. At last the latter spoke.

"Perfectly natural. What's unnatural, if I can deploy such a term, is that it so bothers you. That's why I'm here and, may I venture to suggest, why you are here," counselled the doctor as humorously as his position allowed.

"Good. Good, so I've got a problem," smiled Fairbrother. The doc nodded. His patient's reassurance was to be complete, there was a cure.

"Before going into your marriage in any great detail I'd like to scrutinise these first impressions. Take yours first." Fairbrother nodded grimly. "First you thought, and feel free to correct me if I'm wrong," droned the quack, knowing at least that if the 'feel free' wasn't quite the master stroke, the 'correct me if I'm wrong' supplied the *coup de grâce*, "'fuck me, I want to fuck her'"

"'That,' 'that' —," protested Fairbrother with the maximum of hostility he felt able to vent in such self-incriminating circumstances and likewise surrounds.

"Quite. Now that 'fuck me'; just a dysphemism for 'holy cow', perhaps?"

"Yes."

"Sure?"

"Yes! What are you getting at?"

"The truth. Your words, Mr Fairbrother, my expertise," retorted the doctor officiously.

"OK."

"'That'. What did you mean by 'that'?"

"Just 'that' — just an ill-chosen pronoun," shrugged Fairbrother.

"Really, Mr Fairbrother, this is intolerable," harrumphed Henrik in an intimidatingly sinister display, eerily recalling the Latin histrionics of his father and the martinet temperament of his mother as only a charlatan psyquack can.

"Sorry," Fairbrother duly apologised. "'That'? Depersonalised, I suppose. From my working class upbringing, I suppose. Ought to have grown out of it, I suppose," came the half-hearted, second-handed, shorthanded apologia. The result was necessarily some way short of expiation.

"From your upbringing?"

"I suppose so. Yes," Fairbrother conceded hesitantly, on the *qui vive* as one responding to a query put the same unacceptable way the second time around is duty bound to be.

"Not relevant to your current way of thinking, your current lifestyle, then?"

God, *no!*" laughed Fairbrother, colouring at the thought. Coincidental to the blush was the patient's warming to the doctor's theme. Soon even his face would be sweating.

"You don't move in those circles?" ventured Travolta sceptically.

"What circles?" snapped Fairbrother, dizzily running from himself, as lost as ever.

"Ones in which men refer to women as 'that'?"

"Oh, that," smiled the patient, relieved to be off the hook. "No. Never. Not now," he answered honestly, proudly.

"Not even when talking to yourself?"

"I don't talk to myself," protested Fairbrother with a vehemence which would suggest the probability that he did, recently with an alarmingly increasing frequency, each succeeding time feeling just a little more ashamed.

"Then why are you here?"

"Not for talking to my fucking self," bristled the accused. Save that demotic adjective for later, Henrik said and smiled, all to himself.

"But you said 'primarily' —"

"*Said to you, thought to myself.* Let's get at least that straight," fought Fairbrother, aware that to concede the point would be to concede the honour.

"OK. It's just a way we, uh, professionals have of referring to one's thoughts."

"OK, then, cool. It's your job. You're the boss here. You're cool," simpered the patient, mopping his brow with a handkerchief. To his professional help and seeming opponent it might as well have been lingerie of questionable material and origin that he applied to his hot head. Like his glands, the man was on the run in this sudatorium of the emotions.

"Carry on," he gestured nervously. The doctor nodded benignly.

"Secondly, you thought — remind me,": invited Travolta disingenuously.

"I thought, 'fuck me, I want to fuck her'," confessed the by now thoroughly dispirited cripple who, having come with a whole life to lay bare was now more than a little miffed at these pedantic semantics over his admittedly ill-chosen thoughts and words.

"'Her' supplanting 'that'. Any significance?" smiled Henrik, struggling with remarkable success to check his physiognomy this side (the friendly, smiling, bedside manner of beside himself), the polite side, of a smirk.

"Invariably seeing the battle and inventing the result," Fairbrother snapped back.

"Which is?"

"It's obvious, isn't it," he iterated tersely.

"*Really*," carped the doc, his finger tapping the table impatiently.
"You want me to admit it, is that it?"
"Yes," bit back the doctor.
"And that's it?"
"It'll do to be going on with."
"Christ, this isn't psychoanalysis, it's — it's —"
"Talking to yourself?" prompted the pro.
"Yes!" announced Fairbrother, the disappointed tribune of false promise.
"At last we are getting somewhere."
"Yes," conceded the crestfallen patient, "'her' for 'that'," he proceeded gloomily, very much in the manner of a man conversing harshly with himself on a Friday night in. "OK, OK, I'm beginning to fall for her."
"Good. Good. We may arrive at a happy ending, after all you married the girl," reassured the doctor not at all reassuringly.
"Stick to my first impressions!" commanded Fairbrother in a tone so stentorian as more than to suggest a role reversal transported to *fin de siècle* Vienna. The doctor nodded his compliance. Fairbrother continued. "Thirdly, I said I *thought* I wanted to make love to her."
"Falling for her even further?" Fairbrother nodded. "No 'fuck me' this time. Getting to know her?"
"Hardly. We've not spoken yet."
"OK. Fourthly, you thought, 'fuck me, she wants to fuck me'. Two 'fuck me's. One still a 'holy cow'?"
"Yes, " nodded Fairbrother.
"'She wants to fuck me', you thought. Hmm, why not 'make love to me'?"
"I don't know," shrugged Fairbrother.
"May I suggest that, having envisaged making love to her, you had placed her on a metaphorical pedestal?"
"You may."
"But she was still a dream?"
"Was. Is."
"Good, good. Good to hear it. Not enough marriages survive these days. I like to think that is partly why I am here." The patient clearly charmed by this bedside manner, owing a little more than a little to the lullaby, the good doctor continued. "So, she wants to fuck you. Are you

surprised?"

"Yes. You should see her."

"Indeed, I *am* intrigued. However, you didn't think yourself worthy of her?"

"Guess not."

"And yet you think pretty highly of yourself."

"I don't know about that," blushed Fairbrother.

"Yes you do, and with good reason. If I were a woman I'd want to fuck you."

"Steady, doc, you'll be paying me next," reproached Fairbrother in a mildly suspicious humour.

"Why not? Successful, young, good looking. You'd be quite a catch."

"But I'm, *we're* supposed to catch her. Them. Still."

"We're coming to that."

"Oh."

"Her first thought. Did she reveal them to you?"

"What do you mean?"

"Did she tell you she had these thoughts?"

"No way. No way! She's not like that."

"But she had them."

"Oh yes."

"How do you know?"

"She's my wife."

"But you won't discuss her thoughts?"

"That's why I'm here."

"Touché. OK. Primarily. Standard. Agreed?"

"Agreed."

"Agreed. Secondarily, 'who the fuck does he think he is?' Standard?"

"Standard."

"Thirdly, 'who the fuck does he think I am?' Ditto?"

"Ditto."

"Fourthly, 'I want to fuck him'. Not always the conclusion, but not in any way perverse. Yes?"

"Yes," consented Fairbrother reluctantly.

"So there is no problem with her thoughts?"

"None that I can think of."

"And there are some with yours?"

"Nothing major."

"Nothing major. But the real problem is with your thoughts on her thoughts, if you follow me." Fairbrother nodded. "They're not unnatural."

"No," Fairbrother weakly affirmed, suppressing the 'but'.

"But," the doctor mischievously obliged, "they are peculiar in that they are thoughts. Why don't you discuss them with her?"

"No way!" She's my wife, not some little whore."

"And you'd know the difference?"

"Watch it, you bastard," censured Fairbrother, getting to his feet.

"No, seriously," said the doctor, maintaining a dignified calm effectively quietening the threatened revolt, "why would you not discuss such things with your wife and yet do so with a whore?"

"I've never paid for it in my life!" protested Fairbrother rather too revealingly. Quack or no, the doctor knew his man was cracking.

"But that's what you implied."

"Bugger implications, it's what you say that matters."

"And what you don't say —?"

"What you don't say —— you don't say —— out of kindness — and love."

"So you wouldn't dream of confronting your wife about her sexual desires?"

"Never."

"Not even when she's astride you?"

"That's different. Besides, I'm on top. Most of the time," coughed Fairbrother.

"Gesundheit ist besser als Krankheit. What about her past life?"

"What past life?" screeched Fairbrother, the private dick in him suddenly and shabbily revealed in this strange simulacrum of a public.

"Other lovers?"

"What other lovers?" screamed Fairbrother, verging on violence, unsure upon whom.

"Session over," announced Travolta. "Big lunch date. Business. You know how it is." Miss Fanshawe was summoned over the intercom, whereupon she led a dispirited and distrait man strangely oblivious now to her sexual charms. The doctor was always doing that to them, she thought. He'll be back, she thought. Never look at me the same way. They're all the same. Oh, yes, she thought, she thought.

Chapter Fourteen

The thronging traffic was suggestive of anything but a vacuum, yet that was precisely the sensation which visited Fairbrother secure in the confines of his plush new *BMW*. A moral vacuum. Behind him this, his!, satanic, phallic symbol trailed well and truly disturbed air.

Negotiating Hyde Park Corner and egressing into Park Lane, the sun, tired of pridian labours, greeted him obscurely, shining effetely on Marble Arch, bestowing upon it a jaundiced furze suggesting a rotted uprooted molar sold for sustenance by a now toothless old mendicant, a voluntary night watchman to a young world staying up late, who, wearied by embodiment, could no longer contain his disgust. Turning left at the archway between the improbable former sibling, now impossibly twinned parliamentary constituencies of Kensingtons South and North, the hulking great pride of the *Bayerische Motoren Werke* seemed to cut a dash through lesser lane rivals. Like the Bayrisch themselves, this car clearly meant business. The merest honk dispatched an immodestly fascinated yellow Escort hire purchaser with the ease of a goose corrupting a child's cartoon anthropomorphised expectations with an angry snap of its bill.

Gunning Portobello Road, the silver bullet drew glances of admiration as sincere as the envious glares attending to its pilot. A child, cynical beyond normal adolescence, skated up as the dream machine was temporarily held on red. Effortlessly sporting a ghettoblaster almost his equal in size, the hip-hop ragmop swanked towards the passenger door with the given grace of a tribeswoman under a hard week's washing negotiating a one in three gradient, at once ignoring and directing the camera's bewitched gaze. Luckily for we, bleeding heart liberals these 'our' people don't speak Swahili, nor, it seems receive the unexpurgated translations through the miracle of modern science that ushers into house and home a soft focus ephemeral *simpatico* portrait that pushes all the right feel good about feeling bad buttons for all we couch-potatoes out here in never, never again land. However, just like us, this kid could not be switched off.

"Yo! Man! Like, like yore metal in finah fettle!"

"Pardon?" retorted a genuinely baffled and scared Fairbrother, confused by portents of court cases to ensue from even this straightforward business enquiry from what nevertheless seemed to be

121

some Svengali's twisted, tortured catamite.

"Yo!, yore machine needs a sheen, man."

"Oh, you wish to valet my car," answered the relieved, suddenly released incumbent of the driving seat.

"No, no, yore colour's cool, man. I ain't here on no monkey business."

"No, I didn't say violet."

"No, you said violate. I hear you, man."

"No, I said valet. V-A-L-E-T, valet."

"I hear you, man, yeah, I hear you. Yeah, I wanna valley yore wheels. Name yore price and we can deal."

"One pound —— fifty?" ventured the great capitalist.

"You insult me, man. Doandoodoodoodatrounhere. Hear?"

"What do you suggest?" capitulated the capitalist, knowing damage imitation (if not literal translation) when the need arose.

"Ten'll get you out of here with air in yore tires and yore paintwork still beautiful," he menaced, producing a flick-knife with the sublime prestidigitation with which the fleet fisted Cassius Clay used to mug newly flat-footed and flat-faced opponents hitherto more familiar with the concept of happier predestination, than its sudden misshaping of them as big, black, blue and blitzkrieged. Fairbrother stumped up.

"Fine wheels. Nice 'n' clean," the hoodlum announced his parting shot, celebrating this home turf triumph by uncorking a glutinous greaseball on the windscreen just as the green for go-go get the hell out of here lit its arrow, better late than never, better any place than this.

Prior to being so rudely interrupted, Fairbrother was heading for *Swankers*, a chic new restaurant just far enough off the Portobello Road to be seemingly obliged to set charges so uncivilised as to effectively admit only the highly civilised. His particular cohorts of that breed were already seated at table as Fairbrother tipped the doorman another tenner for taking his camel hair greatcoat, presumably to offset any conceivable damages such as fire, theft and malicious retailoring which habitually accrue in such establishments. Having related the story of his intrigue *vis-à-vis*, hell no!, *tête-à-tête* the violent valet, altering only the facts till they told tale that no money changed hands, further, that the poxy little punk's ghettoblaster was rendered history under the wheels of steel, the diners settled down to some serious business. The *Boom Bros* board were here in full, the *Gloss Bros* equivalent were not, one spouse suspiciously missing. Her, um, other half was not wholeheartedly present either, that was as plain as the truth in the tale he had just glossed over.

After toasting the conquering hero in what was soon sure to be true *Swankers* style, serious drinks all round, concentrate on the gesture and bugger the expense, the cabal convened in a board meeting.

Fairbrother brought to the meeting the foreboding fruits of three weeks immersed in the dank underworld of pornographic publishing. There was, he announced in pure business speak, good news and not so good news. The good news: licence to publish was a cheesecake walk; as suspected, there stood no state imprimatur, therefore no clearly defined censorship as such on 'adult entertainment'. Pornography could only be deemed to be so when, if, retroactively seized by the Obscene Publications Squad. In short, you could publish what you wished until you were caught, at all times sidestepping damnation. If you were smart you would connive in getting caught regularly – tipping plod the wink, each time receiving a cleansed bill of health till filth got round to stickying your fingerprints again to the delectable deliquescent delinquents constituting the collective, the group orgy of the *corpus delicti* – the process at once proclaiming and discharging, washing its hands of one's, as it were, moral bankruptcy. No worries there, the asssembly's prior deliberations over what was fit and seeming in publications bearing the *Gloss Bros* livery coinciding, as if by clandestine rendezvous with the official view. All systems go, then.

The not so good news was so patently not so good it could have gone unannounced; it was painfully plain to detect in Fairbrother's corpse blue lidded eyes and bloated face. Marriage wasn't agreeing with him or, more particularly, with his latest line of work. Slaving over dummy runs of various magazines, he had witnessed a lot of fancy, some not so fancy, but always faithless female flesh. Not exactly conducive to marriage outside of polygamous societies maybe, but his problems lay elsewhere, closer to home. Married one month, he was already seeing too much of his wife, he felt. Literally; his heart missed missing a beat when lately he thought of her, instead choosing(?) to beat a capricious and desultory shamefaced retreat from the horrendous sightings which assailed him in his already battleworn mind's eye. She was with him every night, like the cold sweats, every day like the fierce flushes of adolescent solicitude for a former self seemingly back to haunt him. And already others (albeit wankers and professional photographers with openly declared, contractually confessed sexual proclivities less wife threatening than a *My Little Pony* hairbrush) were seeing too much of his beloved. Plainly, the man wanted out of the day to day running of the business, pleading desperately to be allowed to concentrate his talents on 'conceptualising shoots', commissioning articles, perhaps writing some himself. In short, he proposed becoming 'purely an ideas man' who didn't 'even want to see the trash we are peddling'. Tristan, while agreeing to the idea in principle, cavilled, pointing out that Fairbrother had been hired as ideas *and* tit man. Fairbrother, however, was adamant. He wanted out of all but a safely distanced editorial role.

When probed on the wife he bowed his head and wanly replied, "She can do what she wants."

"And you have no desire to oversee it?" enquired Garvey, striking a note of tenderness so alien as to be all the more remarkable for going unremarked. Fairbrother shook his head wearily. Handing each of his companions a black japanned valise to be opened "in the privacy of your own homes," he departed having gained the necessary concessions by way of sympathy from his colleagues. On arriving home he was not at all surprised to find no one there. Sheril, or was it Lynda (housewife with a mouse for a husband), or Cyndy (cheerleader making the most post play plays), or Ginny (horsewoman, all jodhpurs and jolly hockey sticks), or Valma & Velma (leathern sluts), or Venus (must always appear with a male organ close to hand: wordplay only), or Sharon, or Tracy (bimbo bints to out of work self-employed builders turned self-obsessed body-builders), whoever, she was out. He fixed himself a scotch of, for him, nigh suicidal proportions, washing down an unprescribed handful of valium (from a friend presently insider trading for *Hoffman la Roche,* soon to be in trouble for lacking the minimal nous to avoid the detection of the hitherto seriously, criminally, fraudulently, underachieving serious crimes and fraud squads, not to mention the Securities and Investments Board, that false witness of a watchdog unable to attract attention to the daylight robbery of its own teeth). Soon he was where increasingly he had to be these days, asleep on the couch, caressed into harsh oblivion by its cilician touch, knowing the wife couldn't disturb him when, if, she returned home tonight.

On arriving home each *Boom Bros* board member prepared themselves a drink, drew the curtains (each was alone this particular evening), turned the TV on for a simulacrum of company and, curiously, took their respective phones off their particular hooks (rather better, forced their respective ringing mechanisms to brute mute). Then, each comfortably arrayed on luxuriant sofas, automatically, naturally sussed the combinations on their cases – just like Fairbrother to remember birthdays – and unsheathed their presents. Five magazines shining with not to be revered, veneered, above all to be feared females lay within. Issues one all, the peeked out, penetrable all. Common to all magazines was an 'editorial' picture set starring no less than Mrs Sheril Fairbrother, lately lapsed of this parish, *née* a previous incarnation. A very previous incarnation. Arguably not the most beautiful of models in any of these jejune journals, nonetheless she was by far the most popular amongst this, her first preview group, groupies, gropers. Just as they only had eyes for her, so, she too, by dint of pornography's ability to reduce a Nobel Laureate to a blurb junkie with exclamatory points of interests to follow the gaze all over the room, she too for them.

There she was, the dominatrix, every member's dream (for Tristan and Cal, members of parliament and the judiciary were called upon as surrogates, for Garvey, members of the *beau monde* who could well afford return trips to the *demi-monde*), then the beach boy's bimbo, one girl merging into two drowning narcissi in the limpid pools beneath the eyes, then the schoolmistress, the nurse, on hand for promise of something worse, and finally the water-bed spread amidst the spinsterish antimacassars in the docudramatics of the Readers' Wives section (no readers as yet, one 'genuine' wife loosely attached to one definite non-reader: oh, how even the basest fantasy becomes the zenith of pornography). What our three friends and colleagues of the publishers did next we shall draw a veil over. Well, *they* did draw the curtains. As sure as man draws the salary and the caricature. Still. Nothing stirring it up but mice.

Chapter Fifteen

The *Boom Bros* boardroom was festooned with photosets more appropriate to a particularly sweaty locker room. On closer inspection – best undergone alone, Cal, as ever, was in first – presentation and presenter were one. In smart two-piece and pearls, in parody of an *M&S* catalogue cum S&M shoot, Sheril welcomed the convened company, all but one of whom couldn't take their eyes off the multifarious pictorial representations of her in various stages of undress. The one who alone couldn't take his eyes off the presenter in full corporate and corporeal glory was, naturally, her estranged.

Six months since launching *Gloss Bros*, Fairbrother, was not entirely incidentally, 20 weeks into a vicious therapy vortex, fast approaching personal vacuity, 187 days into a marriage, 2160 hours into a separation and instantly, forevermore back in love with this louse of a spouse who had in every sense outstripped his bare bones of a character and flesh of peach simplistic conception of her. She had excelled with the materials at her disposal, that could never be denied. Never had been. But this so much more nagged him as *crime passionnel* must a diligent jury, as a last ditch switch from hopeless innocence to a guilty but insane plea throws the case for the prosecution: the facts were plain to see, now the once never foreseen, the quotidian to pridian thick-skin had been shed, the thin-skin of the remarkable would have to be donned. Thus do we get what we bargained for by circuitous, tortuous routes: just as a caterpillar becomes a butterfly in a manner so dramatic as to render adolescent rites of passage the tritest of melodramas, so does sericulture become the customer; just as the grub of the deed disgusts so does its effect enthral.

Gloss Bros had 'cleared' £12 million in the first six months. An admiring, ostensibly unchauvinistic three-quarter round of applause greeted this, the plumpest of Sheril's revelations. Thus far, thought the member first to challenge the applause's probity with a stubborn silence. They could be patronising, dirty young, going on old men, mused her old man, soon to be good as dead old man. Sheril cast her angry schoolmistress on arrant pupil glaze at the boy who couldn't put his hands together, keep them to himself long enough to keep out of, oh, all kinds of mischief. Fairbrother buried his head as if immersed in the finer detail of the balance sheet, but these obscene figures represented nothing more nor less than testimony to her betrayal.

Estranged nigh three calendar months, Sheril, hideously revealed as not just a pretty face, more, much more than calendar girl, had recently filed for divorce. Coincidentally, while her husband's business head failed him (succeeded, if that anywise resembles *le mot juste*, by a head full of the impossible to grasp nobody's business of envy), her head for figures had further endeared her to the other *Boom Bros* who theretofore had but envisaged her as a figure designed, no, created for turning heads, if not tricks.

As the presentation continued to detail the success of *Gloss Bros*'s first ten titles, a husband was reduced to bystander, ineffectual bystander casting furtive glances at his wife's full figure flat out on the floor, on the beach, on the bed, on the *other woman*, on the razzle, always on the wall and on the make. Fairbrother found himself first disgusted, then aroused, repeat *ad nauseam,* in a dizzying carousel designed gradually to retard the discrimination of any one emotion from another until, as the ride halts, a sickly melancholy supplants all else. The approval of his colleagues displeased him – she was his wife, after all. Still. That thought aroused him. Eye contact presenting difficulties during divorce proceedings, his eyes shot in pop-gun-cork-on-elastic-mode to her defiled portraits. These disgusted him. These aroused him. This disgusted him. This aroused him. He excused himself from the room, visited the little boy's room. Came. Came back. No one noticed, least of all Fairbrother. Little did he know that they knew little of what he had been up to. So little did he know there was no doubt in his mind. They knew. Especially her. Always her. Always especially.

Melancholy's fuzz had settled into the crackpot's crackshot paranoia. Are all paranoids crackshots? Yes, notwithstanding their predilection for shooting their own feet – no half measures – because by the time the target realises its part in the tragi-farce the sights have long been set. But that is another story to stalk, one which may or may not so rudely interrupt this one. Right now the floor show was dedicated to other ends, targets legitimate and more than apprehended.

"When we decided to launch *Marquis*, our title for the weekend oblique occasional fetishist, little did we know how high we were aiming. Indeed, in the three months since its launch this magazine has alone been responsible for wellnigh 40% of our profits. That's a ballpark figure of, oh, £4 million."

"Profit or takings?" piped the meticulous Cal.

"Profit. Gross," she added almost apologetically.

"Quite," mumbled her spouse almost apoplectically. Spurning her spouse like a lover drowning out all romance in gross out self-engendered orgasm, or so he thought, she thrusted on.

"Our next biggest title has been *Les Femmes*, perhaps unsurprisingly," she commented, her nigh snide *obiter dictum* perhaps unnecessary for the comfort of her fellow, well, fellows. No, guys.

"Why 'unsurprisingly'?" It was her husband, rising to the bait, addressing his wife for the first time in over two months without recourse to the intermediary mercenaries of the inappropriately known legal profession.

"That's for me to know and for you to find out," she replied, sphinx like. The implication? These were women's things for sale: the men knew how to pimp but wouldn't know where to begin knowing how to really do it. The gauntlet, discarded, gripped the room. It couldn't be picked up. Continuing her presentation with all the of a boardroom veteran, she could never yet escape the burlesque in the minds of her audience. Yet it wasn't as if she were a victim of sexual discrimination – after all it was she who had hung her all on the wall. It wasn't as if. She was, but the agenda of discrimination was at least partly of her own making. It was this last surprising twist which most disconcerted her colleagues, three of whom plainly, no, nakedly preferred her as she appeared on the wall in the flashlit flesh (the fourth was thrust into flashback, of course,) than as she appeared now; in the flesh, yet not quite of the flesh. While she persisted in laying bare the facts, the four little fantasists at her beck and call couldn't help regretting the day they first let a woman in on their designs, their desires.

Her every pose, inescapable, now seemed knowingly to mimic the ideas they had bounced off these walls only six months since. And these mimetic mnemonics hurt precisely because they provided conclusive confirmation that these ideas, these requests by proxy, besides mirroring the fantasies of the sex starved masses, were a turn on for the feeble four now as potentially captivated as any of their unconsidered, suckered punters. Particularly haunting were the inane 'Suki sucks a mean XXXX' type blurbs which all five had so enjoyed concocting together. *Primus inter pares* in this bluster to blushes come-uppance cum metamorphosis was Fairbrother. One blurb blurtingly sprang to mind; that accompanying a photoset of his spouse in, briefly, and out, sharpish, the suit she now sported with such infuriatingly coy innocence. The one which created this, her alterego. He caught her haughty, fastidious eye when she deigned to look down, and he replayed every last horripilating word, every last joshing parody, every effete stillborn innuendo, magnificently, despicably trumped in the resipiscent uncalled for prophecy of a caricature come to life.

'Monika Caithness is a lady in a hurry. But first she desires you to take down some figures! Monika (no false moniker), former milk monitor at a swish Swiss finishing school, has a cutglass accent and a heart that definitely belongs to daddy. The rest is up for grabs! "He gave one the best possible start in life. And he didn't abuse me." Strange cove! Not to want to give one one! "I've always had this thing about older men." Mutual! "They've got the money and the needs. When the've had me I've got their money and no further need for them. My first husband was a Lithuanian merchant banker (really!) who was as tight as a nun's cunt until he met up with me. Finished him off with a heart attack on our wedding night, *before* he'd laid even a grubby little digit on me. The promise he was on broke his heart. Naturally, I inherited the company. My second matrimony was to a similarly well-endowed septuagenarian for whom sex too was, alas, a do and die thing. Dirty old bugger passed away inside me. Yes, I said bugger and meant it. Dirty and old, too. English, of course. Still, a mere muscle spasm ejected his vile member. Orgasm? Honeychild, he couldn't boil the liquid in that sea while he was, barely, alive! Left me a tidy sum. My third and current husband is a semi-retired porn publisher (still gets a semi when we retire and likes to picture me doing it with anything, and I mean any damn thing and every damn thing!!!), Charlie Caithness, late 60s, mean as an inner city nigger with, shall we say, an altogether different set of endowments. He's made me editor of this magazine" (*Les Femmes*) "and my four fabulous sisters, Corrine Johannsen" (Sheril in blonde wigs, outdoor settings and steamy saunas)", Donna Matrix (Sheril in mostly, mostly black, leather, often in Cleopatra and Morticia Addams wigs)", Kandy Kain (Sheril in hardcore poses, always with a penis to, tantalisingly never in, hand and a phallic substitute to, in lips; mineral, synthetic, vegetable, fruit, animalistic, abuse your imagination) "and Ginny Ramsbottom (Sheril in jodhpurs, society gowns, on horse, *sans jodhpurs*, society gowns, off horse)", respectively, though hardly respectably!, editors of *Scandolls, Marquis, Suck-excess* and *Thigh*

Society, all available at liberal minded newsagents and positively libertine minded specialist stockists near you now. And, if the old man should die, and he should, and soon, given my track record and proclivities, don't worry, all the little members of our buying public will be in my more than capable hands!'"

The meeting concluded with the three gentleman she wasn't getting out of bed with and suing for divorce singing Sheril's praises in tones pitched somewhere between astonishment and infatuation. Clearly, for them, Sheril was her alter egos all, especially Monika Caithness. The gentleman she was pursuing more (incidentally, Monika's Dr. Frankenstein) for his corporation than his corpus, alas, had long since taken his leave, apologising (sincerely) for feeling a little under the weather (a genuine, if rather psychosomatic and understated excuse me). On egressing he regained the lavatory, this time to be sick. One would dearly love to report that his vomit mingled with his spunk (as an expedient metaphor for love abandoned, turning to lust, jettisoning all fellow-feeling to hateful places, and finally having an emetic effect churning forth nausea or, if you prefer, lovesickness. But that would be too pat) as they dribbled down the porcelain, but he wasn't the type to leave that (first) kind of mess lying around fertile only for detection. Besides, he used the sink. On the second visit. Oh, alright, abuse your imagination again. Finished? Good. We can now wash our hands of this sorry chapter.

The sink mirror clean, Fairbrother left for one of the two rendezvous that were taking up so much of his incalculable time these days: if his time was money the same went for the, um, persons he was to rendezvous with. Tomorrow (Wednesday) and yesterday and Friday was the analyst. Today, Thursday, Saturday and – heaven forfend – Sunday (weekends were the worst) he would take what was fast becoming a routine walk on the wild side.

Chapter Sixteen

The man was demanding money, if not quite with menaces, he was exuding a lack of grace rarely spotted outside of a uniform in a rush hour (failed) railway carriage. Fairbrother sidled out of the half-light where a bulb on the blink lent his jaded figure's tired movements the not altogether deceptive appearance of a stroboscopic caricature somewhere between shadow and spectre. Jerking to the counter like the shadow of an enigmatically unseen cat, now on the ground, now on the wall, now on the ground, he was grateful for the subterfuge characterlessness granted him by the tenebrous character of this dingy little room. In front of him was a little man rendered grey from head to toe by poor lighting; grey, not just in this enclave for the unloved but in his lonely unpassionate comings and goings since achieving physical adulthood and, on *prima facie* evidence, little else besides. Here, the big wide world collapsed, revealing a half-life of desire, a kernel of waning resistance, it couldn't be called rage, against the dying of the light. The little grey man disposed of into his little grey world with his little brown paper bagged bundle further shrouded in a bring your own home spurned greying carrier, Fairbrother owned up and stumped up. Divesting his increasingly curious person of £75, he received in return (for his sins!) 15 hardcore porn magazines, none of which, he trusted(!), featured his wife.

"Goodnight, sir," were the first words addressed to him since entering 'Mr Alis (sic) Euro-Emporium for Adults Only'. It was as if one didn't exist, indeed, didn't wish one's existence acknowledged until one paid up and prepared one's escape from this den of desires defiled by disembodiment, dirty deeds all done. For now.

"Goodnight, Mr Ali," returned Fairbrother, obviously unworried at possibly being identified as a regular. In truth, once was enough: besides, no one else present was about to make any objections known any more than they wished to publicise their own presence.

Fairbrother was indeed a regular visitor to 'Mr Alis', a sleaze shop situated at that junction of King's Cross and hell. One needn't be more specific than that; no matter how you approach it King's Cross more than passingly resembles the road to some kind of damnation. Once a week he tended to come here, usually on a Thursday. Today being Tuesday, he would normally have sidled up the begrimed side-streets, guided only by the stiletto spoors, in search of some benighted young flesh, fast contaminating to drop-dead doped carrion through communion with the likes of him in particular and brutal commerce in general. On young girls aged between Margot in *Laughter in the Dark* and the egregious eponym whose wider infamy so unjustly dogged her selfsame creator, Fairbrother lavished money in lieu of affection. Single sex, missionary position, anal, threesome (two girls along for the ride, one driver), try some, tiresome, TVs and then some, anything that might serve to take a man's body off his mind. But tonight was different.

Shocked at seeing Sheril again (though he had known she was to be in attendance he couldn't have guessed in advance his reaction because, well, few then would admit to being so discomfited as to do so dance attendance) he felt phobic of flesh, not least of all of that which he was no longer particularly ardent to call his own. Indeed, tonight's haul may soon come to represent a triumph of hope over experience, or, put more prosaically, of a nascent, cleansed impotent over a practised wanker. Indeed, the drive home was less than delicious at all, resembling the disgusting far more. Where red lights would normally signal his impatient stop, acting at once as mnemonic stimulus and irritating break, tonight he obeyed their injunctions with the meek acceptance of one betraying no particular place to go. Where normally his illicit goods, or at least ill-gotten gains, accompanied him homeward like bundled up joy, tonight they lay featureless, the voyeur's grotesque of life therein for once never once springing to mind like forbidden fruit, contraband delight. On regaining the house he now shared with the ever increasing junk mail of porn shots and mags from lands afar, and, as if stolen from his heart, solicitors' missives from too close to home, he half-heartedly perused his package; his more personal, too personal plaything was accorded similar lacklustre attention. This was hardly surprising; it had to come to this eventually, these were only proxy *aide-mémoire*, after all. What he found shocking, all but intolerably disgusting, was this; on adopting his usual Thursday evening tactics, on this (admittedly) Tuesday evening (*viz*, the picturing of his estranged, beloved wife), these failed to arouse him sufficiently to even begin to get some of his money's worth. Exhausted and disgusted in equal measure, he fell to sleep betwixt sweaty sheets which threatened to be good enough for another couple of nights, at least for what and, perchance, any unlucky and unlikely who he had in mind.

The motes were crowding the beams, no longer their compliant reflective agents, rather the grit in the clam of this cluttered, sticky abode, glimpsed barely through the chink in the curtains announcing the light that, with a little husbandry can become a positive clean given in a life. They now took on a tendency to block, to censor, to drain, to suffuse, to subtract from the glory that once upon a day was, and forever and a day ought to be, a new morn. Thrashing about in unlaundered bedlinen with his single most embarrassing purchase from Mr Alis, Sheril, a bag of wind containing more potential flatulence than the lowest common denomination of spiced up spouse could ever serve up over 40 years steadily emitting that dying smell on a diet of fire beans and beer, this was a bad, dangerously routine start to a routine, dangerously bad day. Appearing to the naked eye of any desperately unlucky peeping Tom chancing by would be the cathartic sight of a man in the throes of an attack motivated heart, practising a curiously topsy-turvy form of mouth-to-mouth with a rather provocatively endowed first-aid doll. To any pupils looking in the message would be manifest: how not to do it, the teacher is sick, the doll, her legs jerked between lifeless recumbence and mind treat, hip-jerk victory, or fuck you salute, with every desperate thrust at revivification, the doll is no nurse, there is no cure; this, children, is doctors and nurses come full circle; from innocent probing that so became serendipitous discovery of self and others, to a form of guilt drenched premature extreme unction that plunders the life out of one very much in the manner of the collapse of the upstanding, even as it pathetically pants to erect a monument in latex to the overripened flesh of womanhood; but, alas, the customer (king, deposed) looking for bargains past their sell-by date will be ejected forcibly from the reputable stores and directed to the skip wherein flies gormandize on rottenly fertilised flora and fleas on the routinely rotting fauna of winos, themselves on a concessionary liquefying but nominally liquid-free lunch trip. Yes, as quickly as you could say 'that banana's off —— h'mmmm, I saw a programme where this got monkeys drunk as, well, monkeys —— I wonder?' we have arrived, through twists and tantrums, God knows where, rather than full circle, for a second chance at the foreboding fruit, to a sorry pass; sorrow's pass, where self-regard is exclusively pejorative, instilling just the right cocktail of bitter-sweet decay necessary to turn this attitude into self-fulfilling prophecy, which, when cut out as the euphemistic tumour brutal introspection will soon have it to be, leaves the vacuous husk of addiction; we have gained a nightmare journey's end, through fabulistic lands of monsters and maidens, to a reflex grasp for respectability's tiller, fatally surrendered to the night, finally to capitulate in bare daybreak cold sweats, etiolated, a ghostly, ghastly thing alone with no one and nothing to compromise, little left to corrupt, cultivate, sow.

Chapter Seventeen

The 1992 election came and went, the voters confounding the pollsters like so many bent insurance men in the night, so many perfectly camouflaged would be bank managers legging it to the crepuscular gloom before the even more treacherous false dawn. Fairbrother was not among their number. The reader will have noticed our story has moved on apace, but the author's task in ascribing to a character the furtive mien of a skid row wino is a particularly thankless one. One trusts that a period best, and blessedly nigh forgotten by his character is old coals not to be raked over lest they recombust in an act of not altogether unwilled self-immolation. And, should one seek documentary evidence of the fall of this one man, the newspapers, needless to report, tracked it with a ghoulish glee and a goading public. The back issues can be found somewhere, if you must. Too much cant for this one. Suffice it to say that, marriage having failed, therapy having failed (unless succeeding in preparing for succeeding therapies can be said to be a success), the great careerist rather careened through life, woes increasing exponentially like the fecund little fucking parasites they doubtlessly are.

Gaining the streets from *Boom Bros* and *Gloss Bros* in late '86 (dismissed for vaultingly eccentric behaviour, like flashing his feeble member to a febrile public on TV while ostensibly participating in a late night discussion show, "Marriage – worth the candle?", and partaking of rather too much of hospitality's finest with a delighted Irish priest, Father O'more: "That's my point!" the Father roared at the aforementioned display of his theretofore convivial interlocutor's vile organ, whose even viler organ orally accompanied the spectacle with a plaintive plea to his then recently divorced spouse, "You sucked it for them, suck it for me. Suck it! Fuck it!") he rapidly found the road to nowhere, that one way, wrong way *cul-de-sac* where the arms of Morpheus sweep one up rather as a kestrel does a baby vole, but only once, and forever, when rather too sufficient quantities of industrial alcohol have doled out one's cranium the chemical equivalent of repeated contact with a brick wall.

Within one month of the decree absolute, and three weeks of his unceremonious, frankly unmourned dismissal from gainful employ, he was homeless. Though ostracised from polite society, his was not immediately an impoverished position, though, as existences go, his was no longer on even nodding terms with that rather more vital society comprising his fellow man. His life, centred in that almost unbelievably contradictory coupling, a Billericay mansion, literally fell apart in a manner so dramatic it would have challenged even the poetic licence of that greatest chronicler of dynastic decay, one William of Stratford who, lest it be forgotten, could impart calamitous symbolism to a handkerchief. Mortgaged to the hilt, his golden handshake, given as lovingly as a returned token of betrothal by a betrayed ex, was soon gobbled up by wealth's greedy hangers on of lawyers, exes, bankers, businessmen, whose is now yours, recently privatised, continuingly monopolistic, therefore public utilities, cowboys, bill collectors, more lawyers' fees. *Channel 4* were suing him over his 'televisual exposure and accompanying use of gratuitous, if descriptive, obscenities calculated to cause offence.' The defence? You can throw a man out of a pub for being drunk but such scenes ought best to be played with a heavy heart and a redemptory RSVP. The verdict? He lost, and badly, the lawyers trousering much of his money, the case leaving little of his esteem. You name them, they claimed him. Abandoning the Sisyphean task of restoring his life, no less, claimed him: psychoanalysis had taught him a jargon with which he became instantly familiar (aren't all fuck-ups?) and everlastingly cynical. He was soon crushed by the avalanche of debt which his very public, highly practised cries for help quite naturally brought his way as so many flies to shit, so many rocks enclaving a hard place. The sale of the house, effectively conducted as a Dutch auction once his quite extraordinary, unadvertised, unadvertisable fees were extracted, was merely the beginning. The divorce settlement bore the same relation to amicable as do punters' losses to horsesense: *Channel 4*'s prickly pride demanded a golden penance. The lawyers, however, remained unpaid. Declaring himself a bankrupt as eminently preferable to sweating blood and tears and shedding innumerable other pounds to these licensed parasites, naturally he began to behave like one: 18 months gaol, officially for monies owing, officiously for offence given. Which explains, homeless and therefore unregistered, why he wasn't one of the aforementioned insurance brokers in the night who had bestowed upon the terrible Tories an incredible fourth term on April the 9th, 1992.

Like so many of us, Fairbrother won't forget that day in a hurry. It was quite literally his saviour's day. Not entirely coincidentally, it was on the evening of April the 9th, at the very witching hour of 10 pm, just as the horrible truth dawned on the nation like a hangover following an enforced night in, that his mother, Margaret Agnes Fairbrother, *née* Johnston, God bless her purity in retrospect, passed away just as television half-admitted to the evening's other shocking news. Dramatic licence demands that this poor, unloved factotum of a woman died primarily of figurative, secondarily, finally of literal, heartbreak, but the rather more mundane truth, as testified to by the certifying medic, was that the rather less romantic gnawing at her bosom which claimed her mortal soul was that of long-lodged breast cancer.

Embracing a fellow wino for warmth rather than ardour (though he and this tyro-hag did, incredibly, get it on once in a while – not necessarily a blue moon – or, rather, more or less credibly, according to taste, try to get it on), Fairbrother was to read of his mother's demise in the newspaper that served so well as his bedspread, *The Independent.* In a *feuilleton* – 'fiction, criticism, light literature, serial': how can you tell! – placed piece headlined, 'Disgraced Yuppie's mother dies in poverty' he was notified of his loss and belatedly reminded of his duties of a son.

He shrugged his companion off with the minimum of fuss and the maximum of effort. A dead weight drowsed in sorrows, no amount of fuss would likely have stirred her. Stubbornly she clung to his neck like a little girl to her favourite bed-mate, teddy, golly or whatever. The analogy is not entirely successful: Carol, whom he'd met as a prostitute and was about to leave as a wino and dopehead, was clinging on as if for dear life. It took a lot to get this girl this horizontal, a lot more than a few leg opener cocktails, a lot less than a good time. Lending credence to the much held – though far less held forth upon – view that prostitution is in equal parts a knowing and embittered parody of male desires, her story was the stuff of cliché and the stuff of truth. Like all of King's Cross's backstreet entertainers, she could relay a mean tale of sexual abuse (fathers, Uncle Willies, husbands, punters, in that order of unpopularity); like most, the tale was true; like most pros (horribly apt appellation) she was, in essence, honest by nurture, or, rather, lack of. These terrible tales, the stock-in-trade of these victims with dangerooous, sometimes murderous alibis, were liable to come bursting out at the first sign of tenderness from a relatively favoured punter, as if the human touch had become so disgustingly coarse that one caress could bring forth a reaction as childishly infectious as tickled out giggles. Then that punter may well become the favoured lying mate, the honorary gentleman in a life that wanted less, much less than sex from a relationship.

Fairbrother had been favoured with these confessions before, many times before. A gentle, broken soul, his consorts with courtesans were in the nature of a Sunday school picnic compared to what they usually had to do deals with. Eliciting pleas for forgiveness at a greater rate than the Pope visiting a Sicilian prison, pleas, furthermore addressed to one with no greater nor lesser calling to answer, he had spent the best part – quantity, not quality – of the last six years cohabiting in dingy bedsits with dreary dream girls whose unanimous intensely parodic idea(l) of domestic bliss was to have it off with a punter tried and trusted, hopefully tired enough to be so good as to fuck off immediately upon depositing his milk amongst the dust laden detritus of their lives.

Eventually, *corruptio optimi pessima*, after a fashion, he would do a little pimping for them then, finally, he would violently try to beat them, his fists a tremendous flurry of *delirium tremens* which only an epileptic with the reflexes of a master counter-puncher could hope to fend off; indeed, probably only such would want to fend off (to keep the eye in, so to speak), so ineffectual was his punching power, so wayward his aim. Ah, first we buy them things, then we buy them, then we sell them, and short, as things. Remorseful and resourceless, he would hit the streets, sooner than later, after blowing his fortnight's dole on one night's conspicuous consumption of a fortnight's booze; he'd stumble off down King's Cross, more accident waiting to happen than dangerous customer. There, gentle as a kid, as both Abraham's kid and ram, acting as nice as the ninepence he just about had, he'd while away the dead hours of the morning, bumming cigarettes, drinking coffee, and occasionally something stronger, with the girls he liked to call his saviours of the night. Sure, he had (tried to) beat a couple of them in the past, but the girls understood that kind of behaviour as normal; he found favour because he was abnormally unsuccessful in carrying out these assaults, as often as not leaving the tyro-relationship with a flea in the cauliflower of his ear, sporting shades for shame rather than, as he once long ago did, for celebrity.

Carol (different one: not her 'real' name) was his latest conquest in that nightclub of the doomed, where dress sense was at once flamboyant and come as you are. She had taken him in very much in the manner of a squatter kidnapping the former occupants' baby to give it a decent home. For a while it worked; the while she worked. Incapable of getting beyond incapable, he was, she recognised with maternal instinct manqué, in at least as severe a rut as she was. Eventually, as they all did, they found him employment by practically creating for him the position of pimp. No matter that he got them no trade, it would make him feel better to think he was vetting their customers, they reasoned. But they were kidding themselves; he accepted a position as a wino accepts 10p for a cup of tea; i.e., cunningly, lazily, with no more intention of honouring the contract than of crying over milk spilt by a wandering DTed paw reaching out for the sugar and spice an all things nice.

After running Carol's little operation with increasing ineptitude for three months, he at least achieved a subconscious ambition long held; he tore down the lean-to pillars of her ill-gotten gains, blew the roof off her cowering respectability. It was the least he could do. Unfortunately, but in large part subconsciously and therefore masochistically, he was at the time occupying a squalid moiety of that ever decreasing *lebensraum*.

From clearing £600 a week before she met him, to, three months later, clearing a couple of bottles of *Blackbush* and even more pills a day than the doctor ordered, she was, in the most perverse of ways, rescued from her immorality all to the betterment of poverty. One would be hard pushed to imagine the then head of the NVLA, granted fairy godmother status by Sir James Saville, having so profound an influence for the better on such a hitherto wicked life. But there you have it, deep in the soul of our man lies a censorious beast embarrassed by girls' talk, committed to the insanely jealous twin peaks of imagined deprivation and all too real depravity, who would not baulk at doing anything for his woman. Unfortunately, such a creature is so enamoured of his muse that he fails to realise, *A*, he's no poet and, *B*, she's no poem; no doubt about it, his mad ambition is the stifling factor as sure as the creator of Othello and Iago would have scared women shitless but for his genius in capturing the monsters in fictional guise.

Monstrously, Fairbrother thought nothing of substituting for the vital victuals of life, the mouldy incombustible leftover estovers of a wind sodden dark heart. Consequently, the only kindle-able aspect of his poetry was the paper it was written on; worth that and nothing more.

Like most tarts with hearts of gold, Carol (professional name, 'Candy'/whatever the customer/king decreed) fell for this not so much in a melodramatic swoon out of *Mills and Boon*, but out of a weariness at always having to stand up to these punch-drunk neither lovers nor fighters who, nevertheless by playing by a biased set of rules, seemed always to get the better of her. Here was someone different, yet not entirely alien, not at first sight. The difference between Fairbrother and her punters?: he didn't want to, couldn't afford to, couldn't afford to, couldn't possibly manage to fuck her in his fast fading state. The attraction? A still just recognisable gentleness which hinted at emotional rescue, if only in the highly mannerised manner of so many Sir Galahads who had theretofore gatecrashed many of her girlfriends' pay as you enter, come as you leave public parties bearing aloft the peace offering from the battle-zone of a little privacy in a relationship which, once established, offered never more than an evanescent truce, never less than a dream. How, then, did Fairbrother last so long; he who differed from other knights in shining armour in possessing no carapace of front, no aegis of angst with which to ward off the evils of a future otherwise unthinkable? In this respect precisely: those chancers were, erm, lancers, promising rescue and ultimately failing to deliver in their admittedly half-hearted, near-sighted and opportunistic attempts at playing Cupid, whereas Fairbrother, meek and mild, was too far down on his luck to appear as anything but an enigmatic introspective who, seeing himself for a trustworthy approximation of what he was, could accept the girls on their own terms, had no angels, no wounding slights to let loose. In short, in the already conventional sense, he didn't want her, she who had known only too well since the painful and final tender age of eight, that she was a little miss dynamite, had attempted her first, unprompted seduction at the toughened old boot age of 28, older, wiser, ever increasingly in need of the wherewithal on the person of an unignitable passion. Even as role reversals go, the desired result came about rather perversely; the seductress failed where she had never had to try before (too much practice making abject), and was herself seduced as she had never before been (too little practice making perfect, abstinence making the heart grow fonder).

 Having neglected to issue forth the mating call in the obvious, orthodox form, if not quite literally from the missionary position, he conducted their intercourse in what he perceived correctly to be the desired fashion; i.e. by a grotesque, inadvertent mimesis of the epithalamic genre. To be showered with poetry (bad though it certainly was) was immeasurably preferable to being showered with intermittent hail/shine violent lurches of abuse excused by subsequent generosity of perquisites, *ad usum*. From bad to verse, as Fairbrother may have had it. Indeed, would have had it. While altogether unrecognisable as the successful young businessman he had been once upon a time, some things you never lose, as the old saying goes, as the marketing men will always say. Unfortunately for this woeful chiaroscuro (or Clair-Obscure, as the girls might propend) of a former self, the hoary old homily saw him reclaiming a cruelly ironic, particularly benighted part of that former self. Never the most poetic of souls, Fairbrother had long been convinced of an innate ability to move hearts, minds and souls that would have made Milton, Homer, Jorgé Luis Borges, even Ray Charles, weep with envy at their own cursed lack of insight into the manipulation of those lying outwith the self. As he was convinced, others were conned, he was convinced the more, others conned the more.

English 'O' level (second attempt), the dubious tutelage of the university of life (albeit some at the Oxbridge branch), the school of mostly imagined hard knocks and final, at long last (read, if not overnight, sleazy weekend stay) success had combined to delude Fairbrother that he had more than the something to say with which the quiescently catastrophic, inartistically premature give vent to their enfeebled, aborted, feelings. Nothing he had achieved, and even more spectacularly surrendered, thus far gave him greater pleasure and professional pride than his brilliantly rewarded dabbles into the copywriters' profession.

At *Boom Bros* he had prided himself on beating back the feral competition (of two indolent, over-privileged, undereducated, somewhat gratuitously ambitious colleagues) to earn the respect of Garvey, that trade's then acknowledged master-craftsman. Together they would collude, collide, concoct and cohort over sentences like this one, sated with the cheap stuffing, the awful offal of repetition, cheap jokes and signposted (subliminal) alliteration(!), yet still grammatically too rich for the word starved, status hungry consumers out there to resist. None but the copywriter truly knows such frisson of fraud perpetrated under democratic state licence; few but these phrase challenged fripperers could claim to feed a family of not a few on a steady diet of sweetmeat gewgaws and still make their way ushering mocking hee-haws to the biggest bank account downtown: none, bar none, wield such influence formed on so little insight, are as apt to appropriate old saws and resurrect, through paraphrase and inscrutable parentheses (sic), old bores; never have so many been so fooled by so little as at a copywriters' conventions open to the laity (Ah, there is such a thing as society!). Fairbrother, possessing the insatiable curiosity of the consumer and the imagination of a dead plant laid to rest between unthumbed Biblical passages, was perfect for the trade, a direct entrant from the ranks the trade likes to think it reaches, wherein other trades can't reach. Intellectually hamstrung, his Odyssey was over the nugatory, niggardly territory of what rightly would be termed life's inconsequentialities had not money so long and so so made the world go round, bestowing upon this vacuous wasteland the self-aggrandizing, self-appointed characteristics of a war zone mined with potential killer titbits of infotainment pretending to informative status. The trick, as in real minefields, is in the detonation and just who to get to do it for you. As clear cut an enemy as any mine ever mock-heroically threw up to the gods, only to be surrendered immediately, everlastingly to the dirt, is the general public to the copywriter, whose (latter's) trade now cuts a vast swathe through the former's primary access points to the truth that is that sibling many-headed monster called the media, whose ever increasing battalions march on under the various united banners of tabloid journalism, film making, TV news editing, politics, user-friendly civil service, very much in simulacrum of their marketing. Their message? Why, don't shoot the messenger, of course. What better way to convince the public of a product's, a person's, a grouping's, an organisation's, a company's, a country's, always a product's worth than by insidious propaganda whereby the unheard of object becomes vaguely familiar through efficacious name-dropping unfortunately overheard, then desirable, then necessary, all by dint of the popularity its marketing acquires, first for itself, then for it itself, as the mind marketeers might have it. Wooooosssshhhh!!!!, suddenly the adverts aren't depicting one, one is aping them, condescending tone and all above one's head like a no longer signposted, no longer lampooned, lifetime guaranteed light-bulb characterised bright idea.

 She was his public now, the wretched muse for dreams a serial killer wouldn't reveal to a psychoanalyst for anything less than a 50/50 share in the movie rights; that normal abnormals wouldn't reveal unless he paid them. Yet, miracle of style over content, these crass confessions were received as if the quintessence of all man had in his gift to offer woman. Taking the more or less arbitrary form of a drunken slumber's mumbling, their reception stood in relation to their message in a somewhat similar incongruity as does the miracle of satellite TV to the beneath everyday man, woman and child pap which continually undermines its achievement even as it broadcasts its messages. This former storyboarder for the *Milk Tray Man*, or some such cultureless mulch, knew all there was to know, and more, and then some, *ad nauseam*, about the power, the sheer undiluted efficacy of cliché, the undeniable vice-like-hold which the cunningly dissembled stereotype could exercise on the readily fooled imagination. In genuinely treating his muse like a lady he earned that breathing space so often befouled by poets of honeyed tones, rancid thoughts and cockatrice vision. His first poem was two things. First, it was bad almost beyond veniality, second, it was redeemed because the first to reach its emotionally distanced recipient, arriving in her heart with the alacrity and slowly wounding effect of Cupid's arrow dipped in insidious toxins that so often characterise first love, no matter when it strikes one. That she was too well-versed in matters of the heart to fall for this kind of approach was an undeniable yet mixed blessing. The ambiguity of her situation served to cancel itself as one deceit too many, manifesting a straightforward desperation to be loved for what she felt she was; i.e., that special someone no one had hitherto deigned to designate her. That she felt herself someone special was more the by-product of last-ditch wish-fulfilment than belief. She was no more nor less than just what the doctor would have ordered for Fairbrother. But there was none.

That fabled first poem, written in commemoration of their first night together – yes, her place; she an anthropomorphised antimacassar contorted beyond her clients' strangest wildest requests; he, utterly wasted in the slumberland utterly wasted on him –, bore the inauspiciously blatant title of 'Lady and the Tramp'. In spite, or rather because of what her cohorts whiskered in her ear, she liked it, no, preferred it, plain and simple. It is reproduced here to, if you like, give it its day in court. Like evidence.

LADY AND THE TRAMP

Lady gets no chocolates brought her,
A bitter tasting bastard's daughter,
She walks the streets for ne'er-do-wells
To throw in their ha'porth called their selves.
One moonless night, a turning of the tide
Sees her taken for a taxi-ride
By a young man of slender means
Side by side with his own chagrin,

Who proposes nothing more nor less
To mean no when she says yes.
And so they gad about like Leon and Emma
Up and down the horns of a dilemma.
And her temptation he turns down
As unworthy and of ill-renown.
And they finally go home to her place
Where the red firelight penetrates the veil of lace,
For passers-by to pass comments, which
For monied fools are eminently rich:
From fine position they'd soon be parted
Pockets emptied and broken hearted
By the lady who ministers to the tramp
Turning her torch to a bedside lamp;
With all his heart, with all his soul
His repair needs repair to return to the fold,
And she shows him things that he always knew,
Just wouldn't admit that he wanted to do,
As his strength comes back he falls for her,
A lewd proposition to a *sacré coeur*.
But she knows beauty like only those who've lost it
And just this once she wasn't about to cost it.

It was love of this stamp which established their relationship on lazy, pseudo-romantic terms entirely of his proposing. Cutting her to the quick by mentally tortuous means, we had best quickly cut to the chase, or, in this respect, the escape.

Fairbrother yawned, stretched himself and surveyed a kingdom as foreign to long gone circumstances as a typical Englishman's home is to his castle. Beneath rainy skies, near sinking on badly irrigated land, one alfresco dosser descried his partner slumber, her position an inherited and doomed dam against the ever returning flow of street scum. If pneumonia doesn't get her, nor consumption consume her, he mused, museless, maybe she'll get lucky and get knifed (with a bottle, of course) *for good* over some low-life *sine qua non* like snout, or the utterly pathetic cupidity of a totalled pisshead envying her life with him. Poor cow, he winced, as more than the morning dew and more than her morning's due welled-up in the shop door front where she lay, an emotional rustic slowly going to rust, an innocent abroad closer in spirit to the sent to sleep creatures of the Somme than the sent to represent wide-eyed tourist in wonderland. As he pitied his partner he never once reproached himself. They were free spirits, after all, ever since Sheril had betrayed him this mantra like banality had become his *raison d'être*, increasingly resembling a *raison sans raison*. That his having to keep on the move down from high society, sinking to almost subterranean depths, had been a condition of his divorce was incontestable. Oh, not a legal condition, one set down in the stubbornness of conscience that has the grace not to challenge the verdict of defeat but lacks the backbone to learn by it. Legally, then, she was as nothing to him, and if she was on his conscience he would be the last to know. That is, no one would ever know.

Prior to taking a stroll to the 'Paki's' for some cooking sherry and Bombay mix to take down the reference library with its blessed warmth and aridity, conveniently sectioned off study booths and open arms to all and sundry bent upon the improvement of mind and the resting of soul, represented respectively by students and drunks, both of whom became mercifully or calculatedly reticent in close proximity to so many greater storytellers, Fairbrother, belated and feeble as ever these nigh eternal days, near as dammit made to give up his yesterday's *Independent* and this week's *Sunday Times* to his betrothed of last night (in a near calamitous ceremony he had given her his ring-pull from his *Tennents Extra* can, prompting a jealous co-bum to propose a few thankfully ill-considered ideas of his own) when the mother he had left as cruelly and irrevocably as his erstwhile wife had ex-ed him came back into his life, though tragically, no, sadly, never to come back into her own.

Shrugging her body off, he sat up transfixed by the terrible news. The dirty city rain mockingly lent his physiognomy the pathos his character craved. Rising in the manner of a marionette on one last string controlled by a sinister manipulator long since disinterested in this dull boy, curious yet distanced passers-by could espy a down and out wearily summoning up the strength to face the viciously ugly prospect of yet another day. In fact, just as beauty is in the eye of the beholder, so is its downside deceptive. What the mythical passers-by would have witnessed, what the genuine milkman did witness was a carcass reborn. And on the occasion of its mother's demise. Corny? Well, he *was* in advertising.

Abandoning Carol without a by your leave, he couldn't resist planting a prophetic kiss on her forehead in the returned favour manner of Christ and the unnamed, frankly unspecified 'sinner' – 'she loved much'! – mistakenly identified as Mary Magdalene (they've always all looked alike!), in all of whom we believe, had He not been such a foot fetishist and she (Carol) not been so on the nose. With remarkable alacrity for one so long so slovenly he departed the scene very much the lazy thief in the night, taking only her means and will to live (sadly, himself), transformed by necessity to make good and fast his escape.

Showered and shaved among King's Cross's lesser heeled trainspotters, he confronted his reflection with the increasing wonderment of a child striving to get in on the mysteriously fickle eye of perception behind the shiny foil window. Lord, it had been long since the world had seen him like this. And, by necessity, *vice versa*.

Gradually getting reacquainted with his look, not new, rehashed from many seasons back, he approached the ticket office, the disguise of anonymity being curiously stripped with every stride toward that first goal. By the time he had bought his ticket – first class return – with some money lent, no, donated by an emotional Garvey, whose generosity of spirit couldn't yet, after five years of unacquaintance, conceal an ego that paraded same shamelessly (quite a performance), Fairbrother was ready for anything. He had left a message explaining, confessing his straitened circumstances to the answering machine. An employee called(?) him back at the shelter, which kindly housed him one night in three, informing him to call back next midday, upon which a taped recording of his erstwhile partner's voice gleefully directed him, *à la* Hitchcock his cameo, to King's Cross where a man with a bowler hat, red carnation and *Financial Times* (!) would present him with a left luggage ticket which, upon redemption would lead him to the treasure he begged. The message concluded in an emotionally rendered jingle, "too busy to meet, never too busy to help" and, in spite of this condescension, Fairbrother felt someone for the first time in years. It isn't meant to suggest that the character can be cosmetically transformed, as management consultants so expensively advise the professional seminarians who presently hold an absurd charter to rule us by fair means and foul-ups. No, he wasn't a bank manager, though he near as dammit looked the part. He was, scrubbed, shampooed and sweet smelling, his poor mother's son. At long last he was about to come good. Whether one believes that or not depends upon one's attitude to those most evangelical of old saws: never too late, never say die. Suffice it to say, for Fairbrother these tried and until then never to be trusted old clichés appeared to embody some revelatory alter ego as close to deity as did his old rag discarded self now appear a hellish guise. Well, we've all gone through these transformations, though few I doubt of such Kafkaesque proportions. Well, maybe in the USA, but there routine is another world. He was merely returning to Barnsley, albeit in circumstances set to try Thomas Wolfe's aphoristic encapsulation of Proust's great trove. Could he go home again?

Fairbrother – who had once earned the curiously touching commendation of Mr Bachelor, his aptly named 3rd year English teacher, on the submission of an essay requested 'in the style' of Kafka's terrible fascination over the Samsa household, consisting in its entirety of: 'I was driving along the motorway and I turned into a lay-by' – was returning with recently revealed reverence for the plight of young Gregor and his unfortunate kin. Returning, not quite a six foot dung-beetle, but closer to that than the prodigal, such had been his initially very public decline, he nevertheless felt keenly that with his mother's death he had altered to an extent irrevocable in the Fairbrother family. While she was alive ——— but it was no good thinking such lazy, wishful thoughts; they were good for but the feeble humouring of an audience by an erroneously booked warm-up stand up for a stone cold tragedy.

As England's disappointingly grey-green meadows flashed by to the projector's rhythm of this man made projectile and God's good rain, he resolved to do his best by his family and, last but not quite yet least, by himself. Behind him London lay abandoned in his affections, and, as if cruelly mocked by nature, bastard human and Mother, Carol lay likewise from both his and its.

Barnsley proved to provide precisely the idea of a town that had been left behind, by himself in particular, by elsewhere, everywhere else in general. Not wishing to presume directly upon a presumably grief-stricken family – coming out of the blue in phoney mourning would lend injury to the insult he had already dealt them, he felt, not indelicately, though hardly too soon –, he sought out his sister, Harriet, fellow black sheep, who, true to type, was traceable exactly where last heard of some ten years previously.

Harriet, ever one of life's worthier souls, the one member of his immediate brood to constructively criticise his lifestyle when it commenced and continued its brutal upward thrust, worked as a lecturer at the Northern College, an old country seat with stables, lately an educational establishment for the inner city underprivileged and Trades Union representatives. Funded substantially by the Trades Union movement, here was a little piece of old England bought up by the proletariat, the scowling antithesis to smug Essex man, the piss-poor and proud of it real men hewn from pit faces long since shrouded by the exclusive mists of brutal times, who, one part incongruity, one part gentlemanly deference, gave a right Yorkshire welcome to the Nenehs and Silvers, the Winstons and Madhurs, the disappointed, disenfranchised and mostly plain different detritus from that highly suspicious, rarely rewarding Mecca called down South. Perhaps it was that recent years had them hopelessly witnessing the fatal haemorrhaging of their youth to this vampirish blood bank of lost heart, which saw the mask of insularity, as proudly worn by all Yorkshiremen as a pitman's grime or an ethnic's pigment, slip to reveal a come clean, honest understanding of the underprivileged's lot. Whatever one's politics, it was a genuinely heartening sight to see the recently vanquished pride of the coalfields, with their banners defiantly fluttering and flailing against the winds of change, in their officially extant, yet all but extinct King Arthur's sacked Camelot, find common cause with the single mothers and homosexual activists, aliens from an alien culture, but welcome as fellow sufferers at the hands of an alienating state. It was here amidst this attritionally societal detritus that Harriet Fairbrother found her vocation; amongst the live-in single mothers from Tottenham studying sociology and the role of women in the Trades Union movement; amongst the facility time union representatives come to hone their skills for the increasingly one-sided confrontation with management that scandalously passes for industrial relations in this country: here that, three days and nights after her mother's passing, on the eve of the old dear departed being spirited into that great urn on the mantelpiece, Harriet was to be found at work, carrying on, if not regardless, as if worried little for the regards of others not nominated in her terms and conditions of employment. How did Fairbrother know he could reacquaint himself with this little bit of family here this day? Simple.

Harriet, too, had fallen foul of familial favour when proud pursuance of her father's footsteps took her beyond the pale, past the well-meaning but all male picket at the gate of women's rights, straight into the arms of the wrong woman. In epitome, she cut her hair and then she was a he: still a walk a little too far on the wild side round these parts. Tacitly forgiven by her mother, reconciliation was impossible in the presence of a father who had made enemies of both women, mother and daughter, wife and freak, and, given more liberal times and environs, would have had a fair old bash at making lesbians of both.

The brother and sister reunion was awkwardly touching, both failing to quite better the other in the attempt to accept more than their moiety of the blame for the erstwhile schism, now definitely a healing wound, if not quite surgically sealed. When apologies finally failed both, the ante having been upped so that *hara-kiri* might have comprised the next anti-confrontational, desperately conversational gambit, their sorrows sought unity in an embrace which, if framed as representational, bore more than a passing resemblance to clinging on for dear life. Their mother gone, their love for her long neglected now burst forth in so many tears for too many yesteryears. In their embrace both imparted to the other the strength necessary, the once feuding, now fusing blood unity that would see them both tomorrow, safe, not quite sound, very sorry, the twin talking points of mother's third and final elemental day on this curiously concerned earth.

The crematorium seemed to be depressing the weather, framing it, very much the catalyst of decomposition. The chill swirling wind and driving rain seemed to suggest the deceased's revenge on the semi-professorial mourners who, while not paid to wail, wail for far more than they were ever worth to said departed. As the wind whipped the concern for appearances' sake into a frenzy of clutching at black straw hats, suggesting holiday boaters so often sported as to have tanned to an apt crisp, and the taxi-drivers extended sympathies preternaturally predicated upon perceived generosity of perquisites, genuine grief stirred among a little knot of family and friends rendered oblivious to the frankly quotidian elements by a far greater wind of change that had them huddled together, a certain brick missing, but with the warmth of human spirit generating an optimistic home from home on this seemingly preordainedly bleakest of days.

Attempting a breach of this close-knit family circle were two self-styled centrifugitives, recalled by memories hitherto neglected, asking not that these memories be respected, merely that they roughly correspond; positing not that their grief was in any way commensurate with the occasion and its chief bearers, but that it was a genuine, if far too late emissary from remorseful souls.

Brother and sister were rebuked by lack of welcome. In a country, more so, in a county where welcomes tend to be phlegmatic yet genuine, the brush off is unmistakably disdainful. Relegated to the row behind a family which conveniently refused to look them in the eye, or otherwise acknowledge their presence, Fairbrother and foul sister attended the ceremony with hopeless thoughts towards the worthiness of the dear deceased, yet in full knowledge that curiosity amid the far cheaper living would sooner rather than later effect a reconciliation. One thing about funerals, everyone knows why they are there and must subsequently prove it, so it is no surprise that this odd couple were fated to attract so much attention.

On returning to the family home for tea and sympathy, tipples and windbaggery, uninvited but tolerated, they were welcomed back into the fold by their father in a manner most curious to all but *aficionados* of the British working class putting on a bit of a do.

"Have a barmcake. Wouldn't want to upset mother." Thus was reconciliation achieved, thus did family ties bind with the proffering of crummy simulacra of mother's barmcakes, served as part peace-offering, part embodiment of the hostess as was.

Mother never had any taste, thought Fairbrother as he fondly eyed his surviving parent and barmcakes, both for the first time in ten years. Be it the magnificence of the ceremony or whatever, father hugged the two just paroled outlaws with all the magnanimity due the disappointment of deserving cause. At ceremony's end only the immediate family remained, as if gathered to conduct a post-mortem on the day.

"Smashing turn out. Smashing," opined dad.

"Aye, vicar't'said it were't best since the widow Hardaker," agreed Harley, Fairbrother's younger brother by two years, a recently qualified vet, well settled in the area.

"Folks were after her brass. Today they were paying homage to a gem," smiled dad.

"Aye, dad, you did her proud, she would have died happy —— if," attempted Jenny, youngest of brood cum clumsy local belle, currently dividing her time between the local *Ladbrokes*, where she worked, naturally, and the lads at the local pub with whom she supped in between breaking their hearts, ditto.

"She went happily, Jenny, love," reassured dad. "And I know what you were going to say," he added balmingly, "she would have died to see these two," he pontificated sagely, nodding likewise to the two prodigals reeled in by inevitability rather than skill. "Perhaps she died so that they could return," he added portentously. No one was around to chide him.

Chapter Eighteen

Though only domiciled in Barnsley for a week, Fairbrother renewed an astonishing number of long lapsed friendships. Dad wasn't one for going down the pub much these days – carry outs and especially home brew offering so much in the way of economies, which, in turn offered a convenient path down memory lane –, though the night the entire family went down the poignantly renamed *Ex Miners' Social Club*, he proudly led. In that one night it seemed to Fairbrother that he became reacquainted with half the town. Not knowing at least half of these forgiving old fellows, he took it on trust that they had once meant something to him. And if they hadn't before, the did now, for who would wish to meet then greet such an egregious snob cum flop as he but those of sweetest, most forgiving natures.

There they all were, the Freds and the Billys, the Mavises and the Ritas, the Brendans and the Brendas, each and every one small town characters *sans* character, *avec* caricature, provincial drabness personified in etiolated epitome. These were the very people Fairbrother had left to avoid becoming, but now they were just so becoming. Simple, happyish – which isn't at all simple, he reflected sadly – folks who seemed to have mated not only within social class but with class mates, they extended a welcome the like of which Fairbrother could not recall encountering. And not one mentioned his infamous decline, though, as avid tabloid takers all, they knew all about it as well as they knew anything.

While Fairbrother and Harriet faced the bar, its heavily subsidised prices not registering with the former, he being one of the 'lucky' many to have obtained cheaper alcohol in London these last few years, dad simply instructed all present that the past was the past. From this piece of definitively trite tautological folklore was gathered a tolerance and sympathy many a diplomatic historian could never discern in his subject, no matter his mastery of it. The past buried as sure as mother had been cremated, recently and irrevocably, if not as fondly remembered, the company revelled in the frankly dubious pleasures of bitter, bacardi and a bitterly bigoted comic turn whose ability to mine cheap laughs would have made the many Jews who peopled his jokes, as Hitler peopled Auschwitz, spittle mouthed with vengeance manifesting itself as greed and envy, the embodiment of his crudity. In spite of the constant charivari call of maniacal "Did you hear the one about the —?" *ad nauseam, and* response of manic laughter from even feebler, irresponsibly responsive minds, the lesbian harridan and the ex-cosmopolite felt at home because, all said and done, home is where they were.

That were a reet good night, that were, as they say up North, as it were. But life, its losing and its continuing battles, is not to be laughed off at the cattle-prod prompting of a club circuit comedian and the contrivance of reunion. Much remained to be sorted.

Withdrawn behind the lace curtains of the family home (ex-council, since purchased outright: redundancy money), father, Fairbrother and Harriet were in conference. Harriet was back in the family bosom for good, if not obviously for the better. Fairbrother, while begging greater questions of forgiveness, disownment surely being a greater 'sin' than unorthodox desire, had seen his past re-represented as a *tabula rasa*, expediently laid bare, like an alcoholic's blessedly blacked out memory, by the awkward emotional housekeeping of an awkwardly aged novitiate. On the other hand, Harriet knew that forgiveness was not to be hers, for, while that faculty can be born of little understanding, it, at the very least, requires thought of, not just displaced thoughts for, the perceived sinner, the latter quality on its lonesome provoking only pity, sympathy, anything but forgiveness. God forbid! God forgive! Father would ever feel sorry for her but would never even remotely be able to contemplate her case in sufficient detail to come to terms with it. Quite simply, the details disgusted him. Harriet half-apologised, pleading half-heartedly that she couldn't help what she was. Father greeted this piece of *arriviste* folk wisdom with a phlegmatic shrug of an inverse magnificence even a retired army Major faced with a *vox pop* of students discussing disarmament and the howitzering of Hiroshima couldn't have bettered, or better still, couldn't have shrugged off, even at his stiff upper lipped best. That unsaid, discussion, such as it was, turned to the prodigal and his imminent, some would say immanent, departure to whence he came.

As a feeble late afternoon spring sun failed miserably to pierce the crudely designed, definitely, defiantly! non-designer diaphane of the net curtains, Fairbrother rose to bathe the sitting-room in a greater light; as father harrumphed, ostensibly remotely, the disinterest as feigned as in an anonymous *communiqué* from a strange land, "What will you do down south?" in the fast fading gloom Fairbrother's thoughts turned yet again to estranged lands. But, far from making that remnant of mother surplus to heavenly flight turn in its, no, her urn, this was an enquiry to raise the spirits, its content's quiet sincerity gaining over its bluff-gruff tone in a battle royal of inverse proportions. Father's way, smiled Fairbrother and sister. Catching them at it, father grumbled, this time far from the pantomime villain, "It's no bloody laughing matter. You've got your whole life ahead of you. Again."

"I know, I know," smiled Fairbrother, betraying signs of thus far unimagined serenity. Then, in deference to the surviving parent's right to the recompense of a *mea culpa*, he all but readopted the long lost idiomatic characteristics of his home town dialect. Deciding that talking in tongues would be closer to home, stopping short of the accent as being too near mimicry in tone and miminy-piminy in substance, he revealed his future plans thus.

"I'm going back to London, back to what I know." Merely toying with the phrase, "ah knows" gave him that *frisson* which must accompany all performance. "It's starting from scratch, but I've got contacts. You never lose it, dad. Right's right and I've done wrong. But I'll be right. I've got skills, I'll get a job, forget my failures, my past, my divorce, I'm still young yet."

"Not getting any younger, our kid," commented Harriet, her concern but thinly disguised by her playful assumption of father's role.

"Ah'll thank thee not tit take piss, lass," chided father in a knowing send up of self, which immediately achieved the desired affect of relaxing the rather anxious gathering; the uncharacteristically demotic penultimate word being the particular giveaway.

"I got back in touch with one of my old partners before — after mother died. Truth be told, I had to borrow money — I know, I know," he signalled aside his father's imminent, telegraphed rendering of Polonious's advice to Laertes, ignorance of *fons et origo*, indeed text, more than compensated for by its harmless rehash as folk wisdom, "Never a borrower or lender be, but —". In spite of having his best line appropriated, father was determined the getting of the last line, the bottom line, would be his.

"How much do you want?"

"Nothing, dad. It's not about — Well, the train fare," he lied in particular though not in general. Dad was too honest to take any notice of such games.

"I thought as much. And what will you do when you get off the train, beg?" begged father, confident of his answer.

"Well, yes. A couple of hundred, maybe."

"That'll have done nicely when ah was a lad, lad, but you're not even a lad now, lad. Now, lad, grow up. How much?"

"OK. Enough to keep me going."

"Tha knows ah despise dishonesty with money. Name tha price."

"I'll pay it back."

"Ah know, lad, but let's not get ahead of thaself. Will £10,000 do?"

"No."

"£15,000?"

"No. £10,000's too much. Much too much."

"£10,000 it is then."

"I'll pay you back," came the crestfallen reply.

"Bloody right you will."

And on that note of laughter the prodigal departed once more.

Chapter Nineteen

Barnsley railway station had seen worse days, perhaps, but seldom can it have looked this bad. Huddled in an inadequately proportioned, too aptly named waiting room were some forty souls beaten into this rough hewn retreat by particularly elemental elements.

Playing dourly to type, that is against type, with a perversity matched only by the pained silence of enforced community, Fairbrother noted that there was no mention of the signal failure to conduct a rendition of *Abide With Me*. The train, right on cue, i.e. late (yes, signal failure), but not by enough to invite claims for recompense under the recently promised, already late for publication, *Passenger's Charter* (love that individual touch), was to transport Fairbrother from brief sojourn in the familial bosom to the by now confirmed more familiar territory of the nation's ailing, alienating capital. Harriet had wanted to come and see him off, but the manifest destiny of workplace duty won out over the differently rewarding sibling loyalties. Father refused to attend to such departures.

"What's the point? I might get a free taxi-ride to the station but I've still got to get home," he reasoned fixedly.

A baby cried in its mother's arms. Stood up in the sitting room, its mother smiled apologetically to all concerned and those who only seemed so. The swaddled yeller seemed at this, its first genuinely public appearance, to have acquired the requisite eloquence to presage a presence soon to provide more than a mere talking-point. Its cries seemed to well from the sudden ghastly apprehension that it had been thrust into a time and a place nigh bereft of promise; at least a hint of such dread reverberated, as if in echo to the morphically resonating pinball machinations of ostensibly maturer minds. As the battle hardened traveller rent the air, the youngest complainant to the aforesaid feebly fabled charter, Fairbrother chose to evacuate the cacophonous shelter and suffer rather the storm's vicissitudes than the *Donnerwetter!* of that near disastrous bundle of joy. In truth, he egressed the waiting room because he was about to shed a tear or two himself. For the baby he and Sheril never had, for the marriage he and Sheril no longer had, and had never really appreciated, for the mother, ditto, for the father, for the sister, last and least for the home town. The train drew up relieving him of his vigil, his tears mingling anonymously in just another windswept physiognomy. The return journey was by way of a rite of passage. At its end, as if, reborn, Fairbrother knew at last, in his gritty rather than glitzy way the way to grow up.

Among other things he found going through his mind as he journeyed to London were hatred, regret, shame and resolution. Oh, not the concepts in their abstracted forms, but each manifested in particular regard to his recent experiences. A Freudian daydream of sorts on the evening after the morning after the dream day before the dreamless night. Indeed, sharing his carriage were four companions closely embodying the direct objects of the wilder flights to which his fancies were now subjecting him.

Opposite, with *The Telegraph*, a quizzical brow knitted for the crossword and any politics to the sinister side of established privilege, was the type of fellow Fairbrother had come to despise. Like all in this slowly moving chamber of horrors, there was at least a little bit of Fairbrother in the tweedy old twit. These were self-recognitions not previously attempted without the benefit of a psychoanalyst. Happy at last, Fairbrother could afford a wry chuckle at his own past. Wonder who Travolta's doing now?, he smiled. To the old fraud's left sat his social and geographical antithesis, lacking only the whippet to cloth-cap it all as yesteryear's voice of reason silenced by now being greeted with a calamitous mix-n-match of incredulous cackling and incredible accusations. This man could have been his dad, thought Fairbrother, saddened by the aimless semblances toward stereotype to which the working classes casually surrendered any remnant of individuality. Like dad, he were't probably that peculiar mutation that is the dual unionist, Trades and the one presided, *lorded* over by the House of Windsor. It saddened Fairbrother that many too many of those best placed to call privilege's bluff, if little else, had a blind spot which saw them cleaned out every time it came to seeing the Royal Family's prestidigitatiously clean hands. It was this kind of muddle-headed subservience which allowed the tweedy twits to muscle in on all the juicy roles in the bizarre amalgam of soap opera and costume drama that British life was so fast becoming; something akin to Crossroads Motel meets a heritage park full of history's guardians, also known as stately home owners, in a maze of no direction, scripted by crossword compilers, peopled by the blind and dyslexic.

Seated by the window opposite old tweedy was a sharpsuited young exec attacking his laptop with all the verve an arcade urchin would apply to a pinball machine were he ever to know of such an anachronism. Sharp suit's every gesture spoke to making up for time lost on this godforsaken journey, his keystrokes betraying a certain DIY crudity that would have had tweedy crying out for a decent secretary. And not just tweedy: there was something indecent, at the very least not quite right, in this assault upon the keys to understanding, nominally representing civilised language, posed by this over-earnest-self-possessed little oik who could sooner ape sincerity than spell 'faithfuly' (sic). Glancing at the missive and its author, Fairbrother happily declined (to hell with two ls!) to point out the error of their ways. Trouble was, in all probability, its recipient would, likewise or otherwise, so decline. Fairbrother saw a former self and his stomach turned.

Last, but not least, sharing the carriage was, what else? but a man of the cloth. Sitting tall and dignified, reading *The Independent* as if inviting a thunderbolt, it was only the suffered presence of this slightly irreverent reverend that kept old tweedy in a civil attitude towards that nauseating little techno-freak now unnecessarily dictating (diction as bad as grammar) a letter to himself, his travelling companions, and lastly, legitimately, to a client, now phoning said last to vaingloriously say he was phoning to say he was, now quite unnecessarily, writing. No doubt, in tweedy's day it would all be settled over a couple of g&ts and luncheon at the golf club; not much more doubt, it was still settled in such a way. Wishing a plague on both their houses, Fairbrother contemplated the reverend; strong of jaw, blessed with a not altogether fortuitous resemblance to what's his name? in *The Thorn Birds* (the Lord giveth and the Lord taketh the piss), he was undoubtedly one of those modern vicars, for which, given the profession, read timewarped and God's gift-wrapped in some interminable early '70s *milieu* characterised by camp-fires and camp sermons, 'peopled' by nature loving, life loving fans of the late Cat Stevens (always dead for me; logically enough, utterly intolerable prior to becoming utterly intolerant); a regular Mr Tambourine Man, more evangelical on hedonism than Him, probably, christened Roger, his once good name now besmirched, with an innocence ballooning these last few years emblazoned with tabloid type mega point exclamation maculations towards a sublime reckoning. Still, a good man and true he undoubtedly was, a leader of flocks, a man of the people as well as of the cloth; an anachronism, yes: since Adam and Eve Christianity has had to be that, but in his risibly truncated stint as too fashionable for goodness's sake, or at least her public face, he had somehow outgrown as well as outlived the dull dudgeon of the Daily Dreadnought's dotards to look down with benign disappointment upon chronically succeeding generations of economic materialists, no closer now to attaining His heights than were ever their religious counterparts. The years may have rendered old Roj somewhat sill, and superfluous (competition brilliantly sponsored by government neglect), may have muffled his once clarion call to the charitable soul of the nation, like a bolt from blue comedians of so-called satire; cheap-shot cynicism and speculative scepticism may have reduced to ridicule the very act of sermonising to an amoral congregation, but nothing on this earth could invalidate the sincerity of mounting a surely doomed attempt upon familiarising the 'get thee ahead or get thee out of my way' degeneration of man with life's BIG MYSTERIES, no less. As the reverend enigmatically disembarked without a 'God bless you' (mind on other matters?) in reply to a God's gift of a sneeze out of Fairbrother, at some Lincolnshire town forever damned, one fears, as being a site forever haunted by the vagitus of the blasted Margaret (ascended to the real world – no further! – in refutation of Sir Isaac), who, being of the type who shall return, must have tested his faith awfully, Fairbrother found himself, for the first time in his life, contemplating his navel with nary a thought given to victuals. Maybe, just maybe there was a way — a way — (take these hyphens to represent tunnels, though don't hold the author to it) — a way — to — make — money —— morally ———!!!!!

Chapter Twenty

Upon his arrival in London Fairbrother wasted no time in seeking out old contacts. His first port of call was Garvey's Hampstead dwelling. Alighting at Golders Green tube station, he found the street through the *A to Z*, that most valued book to denizens and visitors alike. The house, however, was nowhere to be seen. On enquiring of a local, he was informed that he was standing on it. Flabbergasted, Fairbrother attempted to dismiss, escape from this obviously lost wino who, alas, clung on to confirm his improbable utterance. It was nearly enough to make the now resigned to be teetotal Fairbrother (no counselling, no worthy accounts of heroic struggle, he just decided to stop being so fucked-up) gibber for the grog.

"We call it the Alamo round here. That's where the Yank porn-baron lives. And belongs: down among the sewers. You from the Fraud Squad?"

"No — I — uh —"

"Only, they don't seem to know where to find him. We'd soon ferret his sort out." 'We' it transpired was the Hampstead Home and Heath Preservation League, a vigilant banding together of local dignitaries, long-standing residents and worthies all, hell-bent and heaven-sent to rescue their like 'minded' fellow denizens from the abnormals cavorting and contorting on the Heath, the new money Arabs, Philistines, classless spivs and, above all, most troubledly and troublingly, left-wing intellectuals who had been buying up the place with ill-gotten gains these past few years. Fairbrother learned all this while being eyed suspiciously by his old friend's less than friendly neighbour. Finally, the preamble of character establishment at last concluded, his interlocutor cut to the chase with an excess of brutality and lack of continuity that would have made Michael Winner wince.

"If you ain't the Fraud Squad what do you want with that — that — fraud?" he said, arriving through repetition at oxymoronic succinctness and simplicity, like a gunslinger with a twitch likely to prove just as uncontrollable and fatal as his much vaunted itch.

"I'm an old friend," admitted Fairbrother, "how do I get in, down there?" he asked, gesturing rather self-consciously at his feet.

"God only knows," spat the stranger, departing with a succession of distinctly non-neighbourly backward glances.

Eventually, Fairbrother espied a US style mail-box, the kind which stood approving sentinel over middle-class values, awaiting only long overdue good news in the final reel of those old Capra movies. All that was missing was the snow. Right then a Heraclean *Mercedes* screeched round the corner, performing its own ice-capades stunt on burning rubber and scorched tarmac. Fairbrother leapt on to the pavement to escape its breakneck momentum. As it turned towards the mail-box the road lifted, performing an Open Sesame to the den of iniquity. As the all black enigma cruised past, headed for a doubtless spectacular garaging, Fairbrother waved at his reflection in windows the like of which used to unadorn bookies and more recently, he recalled, certain sauna and massage parlours. Like a kid trying to peer within, and being rewarded only with his increasing curiosity thrown back in his face, he fought to catch the attention of the black bullet's occupant(s). Just as he was about to give up, expecting the car to disappear forever into the evanescent crevice of this controlled earthquake, it stopped (they stopped: car and earthquake), and out of the car's purdah, then out of the mouth of the earth's artificially wired jaws, from the ante-room to what was surely some private hell, emerged Garvey, his eyes attired in similar gangster chic, similar designer purdah (the *noli me tangere* of celebrity), as the blackened outlooks of his vehicle.

"David! — my man!" he gestured his lack of sincerity mirroring the lack of eye to eye scrutiny on offer.

"Garvey, thank you for the money. I'm here to pay it back."

"No need," waived the very hand which must have caused the earth to gape so astonishingly. "Don't need it. See this," he produced a remote control device which magicked the inverse concrete, that which had so recently granted his vehicle such mysterious ingress, to lower itself to the surrounding ground's gradient, granting the *Mercedes* now mysterious residence in that curious abode. Suddenly, as if previously as unaware of his surroundings as a mole by sunlight, Saddler glanced nervously, first left, then right down the length of the street, as if to cross. But no, he was preparing to beat his retreat.

"Let's get out of here," he whispered, as if the open air could be exited to, well, another world. Garvey Open Sesamed again and Fairbrother followed on foot the path so magnificently demonstrated by the *Mercedes*. Down a wino's dark alley of a passage, just wide enough for the big car and single file pedestrians, and curiously lit entirely by candles, he pursued Saddler, straggling in the wake of an evidently busy man.

"Gotta hurry," mumbled Saddler.

"Business?" queried his shadow.

"Pleasure. That's my business," came back the aptly cryptic reply. Some 100 yards into the tunnel's shallow descent a levelling then an almost imperceptible rise commenced. After another 100 or so yards the entire nightmare thoroughfare, illumed by candles, chosen it seemed as if to highlight the construction of a private, windless, rainless, sunless world, a crack, then a gradual room, graced to saturation by electric light, appeared to already suspended disbelief and maladjusted eyes.

As Fairbrother attained the conclusion of the incline he joined Saddler, gadget still in hand, in a boardroom presided over by a chandelier cradling candles of stunning inauthenticity and blinding, almost burning, wattage.

"This is the interrogation room. Where we test the sincerity of our applicants."

"Sorry?" smiled Fairbrother.

"Oh, you wouldn't know," explained Saddler, dimming the lights and lowering his own shades from nose to pocket.

"Apologies for the light. But that's what we're about."

"Sorry?" repeated Fairbrother, his smile waxing eloquent only as to his ineloquence.

"Sit down and I'll show you."

Following the directive in the precise direction of the gesture, Fairbrother found himself in a chair uncomfortable in inverse proportion to the rest of the surroundings. Except, that is, to the next seat. Incongruously arranged along the side of the large, splendid conference table was a wooden bench which wouldn't have been out of place at a non-league football ground.

"Sorry," offered his host, as if in explanation, "you and I will sit on this side."

On joining his friend, Fairbrother was treated to another trick of the multi-purpose gadget, whereupon a gigantic TV screen appeared on the wall behind. As the candles dimmed to achieve a scientific and whimsical half tenebrity, Saddler said, as if by way of explanation, "Been sleeping in the big newspapers, huh?" What followed was to change Fairbrothers' life as noticeably as had his soul been laid on by the hands of a faith healer.

Chapter Twenty-one

The surroundings were temporarily held on crepuscular. Suddenly, as if by *legerdemain*, it dawned on Fairbrother that all the mock candles had achieved tenebrescence's final state, and that such light as there was was emanating from the huge TV screen. Gradually brightening, it formed a ghostly image of what suspensefully revealed itself to be a human face (Caucasian, female, in photographic negative). All the while, music of a weirdness rarely heard complementing anything saner than a Derek Jarman film, or an attempt to make the *Guinness Book of Records* by presumably 76 trombone players at the bottom of a swimming pool, provided its for once apt accompaniment. As the low atonal moan suddenly achieved the frightening crescendo, the *diamant brut, diapason* abnormal of a mute virgin's genuine invitation to commune in orgasm, a bewildered Fairbrother started, to be restrained, if not relaxed, by the unseen hand of his host. Unknown to Fairbrother, subliminal images of religious iconography flitted across the screen, which would explain his then baffled state of heightening incomprehensibility, forming an unholy alliance with a dilatory and credulous joy. Just as the strangeness of it all threatened to force his surrender to imperceptibility's curiouser and curiouser terms and beg an explanation, the revelation came, right on cue, and surprising as it was welcome.

The cacophony of other worldly hints at the choir invisible cut in a calamitous screech, the whole process having the aural effect of a heart monitor's trace gone AWOL on ever keening, tear smarting sight. Then suddenly the ghost on the screen was revealed in all her angelic glory. Sheril! As the marginally more tuneful, yet no less meaningless, sounds of a heavy rock bank struck up, Sheril's lovely head raised its gaze. The camera somehow withdrew (we have the technology!) to reveal Fairbrother's ex-wife in full cowgal garb, surrounded by a combo of cowboys, revealing a lack of talent for song he could never have guessed she possessed. Singing a heavy metal/country version of *Climb Every Mountain,* backed by apparently hijacked, doubtlessly ever self-propelled, religiously insane indoctrinates who had somehow managed to jack-up its nausea factor, she had never looked so lovely. The sound was simultaneously shameful and shameless, but that mattered not a lot. What mattered was that she was almost with him, wholesome as a can of beans, confounding his dimmest expectations by remaining fully clothed throughout her excruciating routine. At the 'song's' conclusion, to the notational dyslexia of a steel guitar's numerous hashed rehearsals of *diminuendo*, Sheril approached Fairbrother (rather, the screen, rather, the camera) and uttered a word so uncharacteristic as to seem divinely inspired. "Hallelujah!" was the word. As the screen petered out, subliminal visions still flashing by, Fairbrother turned to his host.

"What was that all about?" he enquired of the unlit space immediately to his right. Receiving no answer, he followed up by asking of the void, '*qui vive?*' Same nil response. Preparing to fumble and bumble his way from this recently got up strange, dark bedroom, powerless since struck by the thunderbolt from the blue of his love's presence, he somehow made to rise. Just then a blinding light reimposed itself upon his ill-prepared cat's eye gaze, causing at the very least the temporary purblindness of scrunched eyes readjusting crudely to the 'natural' light by gradually, tortuously expelling the ghost of its shocking appearance. On regaining his ocular equilibrium he was still unable to believe his eyes. Afront the now retracted big screen sat Sheril, *sans* ten gallon hat, larger than love.

"Howdy," offered Fairbrother, ejaculating a nervous jocularity.

"Hello, David," she replied earnestly. "How have you been?"

"Fine," he lied.

"Good," she complied.

"And you?" he enquired.

"Great," she responded, topping him in degree and veracity.

On the verge of drumming the table top in counterpoint to long forgotten melody (yes, even the out of time tapped rhythms sang timelessly!), the two exes were relieved of having to keep each other exclusive company by the timely, probably staged, re-entry of Garvey.

"You kids know each other?" he joked to an unresponsive house. Soon Garvey effected a smooth reconciliation, however. As is always the way, as alcohol flowed so conversation followed, the polluted flotsam of a merry carnival float downstream. By the end of a wonderful evening's reacquainting, Fairbrother (back on the booze, but pleased enough with himself to maintain something like control this time) seemed to recall finding himself back in cahoots, business-wise, with Garvey and Sheril. Three questions kept nagging him as he attempted sleep's gradual strategic retreat from ebriety.

"Is Garvey really an evangelist?" And worse than that potential blasphemy, "Did she really marry him?" "And what about Him?"

Chapter Twenty-two

The telephone's harsh tones of enquiry started Fairbrother towards consciousness. Ill-equipped to subsist in this as yet alien state, he fumbled for the receiver and mumbled verifications of transmission, its call, his response.

"Huh. Nine o'clock sharp. Uh. The bunker. Uh. Huh. All the old crowd. Sure, I'll be ——," the dialling tone cut in, intolerant as ever when one had no one to call, when one didn't have its number. Peering in the half-light for some indicator of the exact chronology at which God had forsaken this hour, the recumbent drunk espied the horrendous digits *05:45* flashing each second, soundless yet screaming, as if produced by an invisible mockingbird perfecting a rooster's range and routine. Worse, not knowing where he was, he dared not retire again.

Needing a drink desperately or never again, he despatched his incipient werewolf with parlous ineptitude, producing enough 'fake' tomato catsup for at least a couple of snuff movie bloody marys. Repairing the nicks with a dexterity approaching an NHS ancillary promoted to surgeon in the name of (bah! boom!) cuts (forewarned was forearmed), he concluded his toilette looking like a boxer one wrongly called fight from going to seed. Fresh faced, yes, but, oh!, the puffiness about the eyes, the proboscis disjointed God knows when by God knows who, the cat's claw traces of his clumsy shave. Not having looked at himself thus (in love!) for such a long time, he judged, rather optimistically, that the damage was not irreparable. Further, rather against the grain of events he resolved to —— to —— win her back!

Fairbrother left the hotel room, provided presumably at Garvey's expense, and took a taxi to the bunker, excited by the prospect that Sheril wanted him there. That the summons had been delivered by her improbable new spouse did not dampen his enthusiasm; had she not declined to exercise her veto?

Perplexing the driver, who prided himself on knowing much more than he did, particularly in respect of the knowledge behind the knowledge ("Mini-cab drivers; had one of them in the back of my cab once ——" CENSORED), the passenger disembarked at no. 5, where a funny looking bird table, unoccupied and, in the ever-ready opinion of the cab's nigh omniscient front seat backchatter, unoccupiable, marked the only possible sign of life.

"Are you sure?" barked Fairbrother's conveyor/unshakable escort in a tone which spoke for the knowledge as sure as a cut glass accent speaks for the crystal clear clarity of privilege's self-justification. Condescending to tip the now discomfited boor with more than the average, to make him feel lower, yet less than enough to straighten his face, Fairbrother turned smugly towards the bunker's entrance.

As the taxi executed a one-hundred-and-eighty to cruise in suspicion and curiosity the kerb opposite, Fairbrother realised he was wrong and the driver right: he didn't know how to beggar a response, let alone how to get in.

Some 30 seconds of western B movie tension ensued. Fairbrother, peering myopically at the mail-box, the driver somehow managing to avert his gaze just atop today's super soaraway headline in his stationary conveyance for licensed highway robbery; Fairbrother untying then tying a shoelace, literally imploring that the ground swallow him up, the driver chuckling, almost chucking his chicken and chutney doorstopper into his cheeky, cheery, improvised, yet pre-soiled napkin; Fairbrother snatching left, then right, then left again, as if looking for a taxi, *his* taxi, to admit his mistaken apology for a human being whence he came. The driver moved off slowly, reverse Churchill salute (middle digit aloft somehow too sophisticated? Not brutal enough?) signifying yet another victory for the tyranny of cabbies – motto?: 'never have so many been so rude to even more without come-uppance!'. But Fairbrother hadn't been seeking to hire him again, merely looking to cross the road, the better to identify any obscure methods of entry.

At halfway across the road a perceptible rumble to his rear informed him that entry was about to be his, even if the original intention was merely another's exit. Spinning quickly, he did well to avoid the cab, which appeared to have taken over his driven foe, who screeched in lieu of braking, impervious to the Highway Code, indeed any vaguely gentlemanly code, "fuck" on the approach, "you fuh" in the passing, "king muthaafuuh" in the leaving. Thankfully these demotic Americanisms trailed off into an as yet unstaged sunset. Diving for the cover of the bunker, Fairbrother gained the candled passage, his puffing and panting sufficing to blow out those guiding lights he drew breath closest to as he propped himself against the right-hand wall, looking left for reassurance that the world was once again behind closed doors. Satisfying himself that it was, he travelled the passage unchallenged.

However, realising that the lack of any comings and goings but his probably signified his having been detected and invited in by some piece of Stalag controlled gadgetry (an opening possibly actioned by his ex-wife; still moving the earth for him as remotely as possible, he smiled), he straightened his tie and patted his hair. After all, after last night he wasn't entirely sure as to the nature of this invite.

"I blew out three of your candles," he apologised to Garvey on entering again the bunker's boardroom.

"I know, I saw you, it's OK, they light themselves. Gas, Or as you Brits say, not petrol, right?" Taken aback by two concepts – fake candles and the electronic monitoring thereof – Fairbrother emitted not a peep.

"So, you get home OK?"

Fairbrother nodded, forestalling pedantic quibbles, *videlicet* hotel rooms for the night and long term stay, homely hotel rooms until — until he could work this operation out.

"There'll be no more drinking. At least not in public," directed Garvey. Fairbrother broke silence at this. "Look, I don't know about that —— this. I can't remember last night," he protested and confessed, caught between this and that like a novitiate to an *AA* meeting.

"All will be revealed," smiled his host delphically.

Some fifteen minutes and two pots of black coffee later (served by a delightful looking, frightfully timid Thai girl, no doubt 'rescued' from the pages of one of those magazines from Garvey's loveless, carefree, irreligious prenuptial days), Garvey returned, ordering the hilariously named Suzie (him? her? — there is no wight and wong) to fetch in the menus and usher in the guests.

Dreading food this early after an evening this lingering, Fairbrother prepared polite protestations to the effect of 'busy night, lunch date,' but on receiving said bill of fare saw that it consisted not of comestibles but nigh indigestible homilies, apophthegms, throat lumpeners that could rival 60 a day as a way of living death, set out in the form of an agenda, but resembling more in content an extremely rough draft of a sermon's salient points of light. Heading this curious bill of fare was the heading:

"Agenda of final *Boom Bros/Gloss Bros* meeting, May 1 1992"

Following this revelation were several more in the form of the agenda's items for discussion.

1 Roll call
2 Welcoming back on board of David Fairbrother, late of this parish
3 Prayer for above
4 Re-baptism of entire company
5 Targeting the market
6 Any other business & Thanksgiving Prayer
7 Date of next congregation

Mulling over his agenda, Fairbrother smiled at item 2. Good, that's what he wanted. But the absence of the definite article before 'board' worried him, reducing the item's meaning to the quasi-psychological, nigh religious, meaningless hokum of patio smooth business patois. And item 3. He smiled again, recalling *Great Expectations* and Pip before his parents' headstone. Poignancy took the smile off his face and perplexity wiped its traces. Do they mean me, —— or? Similarly item 4: was that 're' shorthand for in re, or a particularly inauspicious solecism? In contrast, item 5 appeared to be the standard business jargon which, spoonerised to read 'Marketing the Target' would carry the same deliberately vague, non encompassing, non conquering, suggestiveness pervading 'meaning'. And was the curiously dated 'Thanksgiving Prayer' dependent upon the usual method of wrapping up coming up to inspirational scratch? Not a little perturbed at the wording of item 7, Fairbrother awaited enlightenment and the arrival of his fellow worshippers.

Looking more businesslike than even in the early, hungry days, they filed in in suits designed, no, created, as if to undermine a Mormon colporteur's faith in his tailor. Half apologising for his appearance and half pretending its facilitation to be the greatest honour of his life, Fairbrother rose to greet his erstwhile colleagues and spouse. Cal, cooler than ever, wordlessly exchanged handshakes as if passing contraband so hot as to be instantly soluble in the sweat of Fairbrother's palm. Civil, but entirely untrusting, he withdrew, hand and all to his seat as Fairbrother examined his own hand. No spit, just sweat. Mine. Tristan was more effusive, yet didn't quite betray old friendship by shedding the polite, businesslike exterior which, after all, was appropriate to the circumstance. Finding himself ludicrously forgiving Tristan his excessively honed *sang-froid*, Fairbrother turned to greet, to touch his ex's moist hand but, alas, it was not to be offered; she had seated herself opposite. Plainly, a night apart had been no grounds for reconciliation. We'll see, thought at least one of their number.

Saddler took the chair and commenced the meeting, announcing his wish to be referred to as Mr Chairman, adding bafflingly, "just like in the Bible". Glancing around the room's other sets of eyes, Fairbrother detected no sign of anything resembling the tiniest of rolls or yaws and cast his down in sadness and embarrassment towards his already deeply disturbing agenda. After the chair offered an unscripted apology for absences past, more a prayer for the "prolonged absence of our fair brother —", the afore-mentioned (by name or flawed paradigm?) had to issue himself a silent directive to play this whole thing straight.

Item two dealt with, Fairbrother nodded his gratitude at being allowed back 'on board', nutting all but one of the bastards in near revelatory reverie. Well, he wouldn't hit a lady and, yes, that had become a lady since it had ceased to be the wife, he smiled, outwardly ungallant, bowing to Sheril last; inside a Sir Gawain was bursting to declaim "but not least!", but more cunning counsel prevailed.

Item three was, indeed, marry, forsooth, a quaint anachronism incanted on his behalf. Given by Saddler and minuted by Suzie, it read:

"Our Father, hear our thanks for the safe return of a wayward son.

Let his coming to you be nearer completion by this first step;

this first step from misery to happiness, this small step for man, this giant step for mankind.

Bless him and all who set sail with him.

Amen."

Fairbrother's smile appeared beatifically, the glowing faces blessedly sufficient in post solicitous warmth and wattage to excuse his blushes. He particularly liked, um, warmed to the appropriation of 'Armstrong's' words, omission of indefinite article and all (must have been difficult to see the idiot boards) rendering the subjects tautological at best, the whole fathomless. And the banal concern of this whole banal concern! Least said soonest ended, he coughed his laughter away as the room resounded to four occidental 'amen's, one unconsciously risqué oriental 'aah-men!' and an accidental, surprisingly, mercifully unhearkened 'ahem!'

Item four unravelled its threatened mawkishness in a horrendous, unforseeable example of living up to billing, and then some. Minuted verbatim, Garvey proposed its bizarre points thus (no interruptions were recorded, for none were permitted. Thus, the minutes can attempt only to catch a sermonist's blindly faithful view; the perplexed and otherwise, if any, faces are to be imagined, as in a radio play):

"Item four, re-baptism of whole company. In anticipation of queries *re* the exact meaning of this item heading, let me immediately dispel any doubts: just what it says. Further, I would appreciate if all questions were suspended until I sit down. Good. This item deals with the putting to rest of the old companies, *Boom Bros* and *Gloss Bros*, over which we draw a respectful veil, the better to remember them by exercising our fondest thoughts. This motion proposes that they are no more. As chairman and major shareholder in both I put it to a vote of one." (In fact, the companies had become Garvey's playthings, the other two board members reduced to 10% shares each, Garvey – and wife? – having bought them out in a series of shrewd instalments, investments, what you will, predicated on the, ever-increasing, differential between major and minor shareholders. Fairbrother, of course, had nowt but his father's kindly but homely financial goodwill).

"There it is. Oh, I asked the wife. Naturally she approved. There we have it. The new name of the new company is *Money Changers Changed*. David can tell me where to put the apostrophe in later. Further, we are all to be rebaptised in the spirit of this bold new enterprise, each taking a vow of honour in all things, business as in life. Forthwith Cal will be known as Josh Wellbeloved, Tristan as Solomon Fellows, David as Daniel Fairbrother – never change a God given name – my good lady as Mary Mothers, my good self as Jesus Junior Mothers. While these will be our, as it were, stage names, they must also be how we are known in all walks of life. It will not have escaped your keen business brains that the theme of this new company is to be Biblical. To this effect Mary Mothers and I have put together an introductory corporate video. Study its techniques well, for we will be producing many more of these for the delight of an audience, a congregation of many more. Suzie, let there be lights out."

There then followed the showing of the billed video, a pitch for minds set at highest at chest level, which made Vice President elect Gore's subsequent '92 address to the Democratic Convention, that retelling of his young son's dice with death gooily, ghoulishly rehashed as political metaphor, appear as discrimination epitomised. In aptly crude *aperçu*, it proposed the promotion of *Money Changers Changed* as a crusading company of satellite and cable evangelists set on capturing the hearts and purloining the minds of "potential converts", i.e., anyone preconditionally dim-witted enough to take those pernicious triumphs of technology over sense for anything other than association football. Clearly, the promos suggested, here is an audience, sorry, a congregation, tailor-made for the type of brainwashing which produces of once perfectly reasonable, even promising foetuses a teratosis outwardly resembling bank managers, with a darker, mystical, hippyish, masochistic side which 'inspires' them to dispense of their cash as if there were no tomorrow, merely successions of saviour's days. Much play was made of the previous 'immoral' dealings of the believers, religion's hypocritical badge of courage, an ever so slightly boastful confession for the benefit of an ever so prurient Father and a flock who could see a moral a mile off even when there was none to see. On the easily prophesied, much wished cue of 'let there be light, Suzie,' this abominable, selective misreading of greed for creed, this low appeal of infotainment and astrological gibberish pretending to be cosmic truth, this extortionate demand upon those non families desperate to embrace that mythical rhetoric that is the puritanical state of family values, this video nicey, tacky even unto the weather (game show host predicts apocalypse nightly), took its merciful leave. Fairbrother shifted uncomfortably in his seat, as mindful of what not to say as a hibernating squirrel is of the location of its nuts.

"Item five," announced a glowing Garvey, "Targeting the Market. Mary Mothers and I referred to a congregation of 'hopeful sinners'. What do we mean by that?" he paused rhetorically before recommencing his sermon. "People who can be saved, who will be saved, basically decent people in despair at the paucity of good works to be done in this wicked world. Above all, people who want to be saved. I hear what you are saying," he interrupted and, appropriately for one hearing only his own voice, misinterpreted Fairbrother's semi-stifled yawn, "Can't these people salve their consciences by giving to charity? My answer to that, our answer," sickeningly tentacling Sheril's head to his breast, "is no. These people want to do more, to give more, to give of themselves all. *Money Changers Changed* exists to facilitate such noble ambition. Now, gentlemen —— and lady," which of the latter present merited mention as a verbal afterthought wasn't elucidated, "I'd like us all to pray for the success of our new venture, our mission."

Heads down like a series of shamefaced schoolboys — and girl(s), the company listened mutely in to the profoundest thoughts their leader could muster *à propos* the uninspirational cupidity necessary to the fleecing of the no doubt doubting Thomases sure to comprise Joe Public. "Dear Lord, let them that want to give, give to them that want to give. Amen."

Never has the word cryptic seemed so apposite since Charles Manson somehow got his, sorry, His head round *The White Album* and attained from the banal drug-addled musings thereon subliminal directives, aka psychotic drug-addled musings, sufficient unto the masterplan. Cannily, Fairbrother expurgated all thoughts baser than the worrying worship offered Saddler by his co-conspirators to this mystical claptrap. Asked to comment, he mentally filed away a host of objections, to be looked up and used against the seemingly omnipotent host when, come the glorious day!, his manifest destiny would surely rob him of that mad power by stealing up like a thief in the night and spiriting away the preconditional attribute/faculty of ex cathedra comfort. Believing himself to have gained the confidence of all present, including the eminently scrutable Suzie, he emitted the kind of panegyric, dashed with the type of deceptively healthy intrigue (couched in slogan-sized-chunks, rounded off with a joke so feeble as to be fully appreciable only to stage German accountants pigged out at the consummation of a liquid-and-lick-arse-lunch), he imagined the professionally power crazed and their captive acolytes most liked to hear from the potential converts of the willing to be brainwashed laity.

"Good ideas. How to make money morally. Could well be the '90s theme. Lots of profits there. Let's get in before there are lots of prophets, P-R-O-P-H-E-T-S, there." Suddenly the room was filled with the bellowing *dramatis personae* of a *Bierkeller* next door to a *Bundesbank* convention. Fairbrother joined in, laughing at the artifice of his colleagues as surely as an alternative comedian at the contrived conclusions of a house increasingly desperate to be in on the non-existing joke. Then, in a voice for which the phrase 'oozing sincerity' could have been coined, Saddler revealed Fairbrother's role in the masterplan.

"Daniel," he started, startlingly familiar, crudely befitting the forced intimacy of tone, "Daniel is to be our first missionary, the focus of our primary slice of prime time." With a flourish somewhere between Cecil

B. De Mille and the hamstrung hams he terrorised by, well, directing casts of thousands, the leader pictured it.

"Thus. Successful businessman hits rock-bottom. Loses wife, loses career, reputation, loses love of life, the lot. Then, one day abracadabra," shammed the shameless showman/shaman, "he wakes up. *Truly* wakes up. Finds God, forgiveness in his heart, even unto his ex-wife's new *numero uno*," chummy zoom shot, misty eyed lens to a character whose tragic and comedic hysterics fortunately were as indistinguishable as were they undistinguished. Averting his gaze from his subject's either idolatrous approbation or maniacal objection, he continued. "Thus we have a subject who starts out good at greed, falls to all too human failings and is reborn great at redemption. What do you think, Daniel?"

A double take later – one which may have saved his interlocutor's life – Fairbrother served up the expected reply. "Perfect. Honoured to be thought of as emblematic to the cause. When do we start?"

Stunt doubles not belonging to that elite crew of extras preconditional to the telling of a simple moral fable (unless a *deus ex machina* is called for), Fairbrother found himself at times, and against all odds, happily, if awkwardly playing himself. For the sequence documenting his initial rise to fame it was with an eerie sense of period foreboding that he embodied that glad-handing confidence trickster posing with the morning's press (October 13 1983) boldly pronouncing '*Boom Bros* take City by storm'. As the camcorder rolled, or whatever, he stood in its line of fire, stiff as if he were facing a firing squad. Indeed, on the first nine takes, the only sign of life captured was the accidental shake and rustle of the newspaper he was holding, as in on to for dear life. A couple of drinks settled the DTs sufficiently for shooting to conclude successfully, subject imploring audience, as yet as much in buckram as the starch stiff, stark scared star, with messianic eyeball rolling.

"That's a wrap," clapped the director, sure as ever of two things: *1*, that any audience worth its entranced money sees what the performers/creators know they want to see: *2*, that capturing life from behind a camera and torturing it until it begged release on director's/dictator's terms was a lifelong fantasist's dream come true. As Saddler (who else?) announced the end of what he felt, rightly, but for the wrong reasons, to be another turkey shoot – *à la* the Gulf War – Fairbrother snapped out of the frame's transfixing gaze and headed down the pub to do a little preparatory work for the afternoon's shoot, uninspiringly billed as 'From Infamy to the Wilderness Years'. As a combination of plotting and the tyro-director's obsessive dedication to this his new found branch of megalomania would have it, he was able to dine alone with his chosen partner.

"Long time since I've been in a place like this," Fairbrother remarked, as his eyes fixed almost romantically on the tackily tarted up interior, unnoticingly populated by the same tastelessly spendthrift *habitué* of *Yet Another Wine Bar, plc*. "Like *McDonald's* for malnourished grown ups," he remarked wryly as the waitress introduced herself.

"Hi, I'm Jackie. Your command is my wish."

Before this very nascent thespian could louse up the second of her painstakingly rehearsed and painfully rehashed lines, by beggaring the conclusion "What can I do you for?" Fairbrother corrected her, "Your wish is my command," only for his hapless *ingénue* to deliver herself of a rebuke unique to her trade in its well rehearsed combining of vitriol, marketing and banal well-wishing, the whole designed to provide a talking point, a slogan.

"No, they say that at other places. We're better than that. The customer has never been so right as here at *Chez When* —"

Fearing a song and dance routine threatening to be too redolent of this then sweet, now sour first meeting with his ex, and too appalling *per se* (see Saturday night TV, *videlicet* Brucie and the general public, for a flavour of the beast), Fairbrother halted this winsome well-wisher before she introduced a whole cast of waiters and waitresses from the Sammy Davis Jr., Liza with a *zzzz* schhmmaarrmm 'n' schhmmaallltzz school of catering for public taste, and played ball.

"I command you to bring a bottle of your best champagne, from whence came you, wench, while we peruse your frankly overpriced, under-inspired bill of fare rid of the irritating bafflement of your presence." To the fast-fading-back-of-a-smile-wiped-mugwump-skulking-scullery-wards, he added, for the good and gratuitous measure of teaching this gamine graduate of business school bullshit (by '92 waitressing had been elevated to a profession, just like every other 'position' in the land; no student she), that the truth hurts. "And when I do decide what you're for I'll snap my fingers like this," he clicked then cackled.

"You've changed," remarked Tristan.

"For the better?" solicited Fairbrother.

"No, none of us have managed that miracle."

"No," nodded Fairbrother tragi-comically, "that's what I wanted to talk to you about."

Over a meal of less than tender 'Chicken Bits', at prices marginally, the merest standard tip (declined, i.e., not offered) less brutal than a mugging, Tristan enlightened Fairbrother on a few matters. It transpired, as the wine transformed into the passing of water, that Saddler had taken *de iure* control of both *Boom Bros* and *Gloss Bros* almost immediately following Fairbrother's "much lamented" departure. Rendering unto himself what had been Fairbrother's had proved relatively simple – Saddler's work load and all round driven persona determined that the then disgraced shares fall his way. Further control was ceded with an inevitability which, as it grew in hostility, could muster only futile, not hostile bids, each percent of stock handed over with dwindling demur. And so it came to pass. "Now the mad little mother owns us all. He even owns my debts."

"So that's how you became inveigled in this nightmare scheme," sympathised Fairbrother.

"And Cal," confessed Tristan.

"How much do you owe him?"

"A life's work."

"And how do you hope to repay him?"

"Oh, we've thought of something."

This 'something' turned on a sacrilegious plot against their current lord and master. Initially they would play their allotted parts in his *deus ex machina* homiletic treatment of life's dramas, spear carriers all. Then, all going to either plan, two courses would present themselves: *1*, should the homilies not hit home, these would then be presented, returned with interest, with the pleasure of their erstwhile dance-master's head on a platter, knowing they had engineered its fate as surely as had Salome John the Baptist's: *2*, should this implausible madman succeed in his implausible mission, against, lest one forget, increasingly stiff competition, they stood to benefit from the merest proximity to his celebrity, all the while conducting a whispering campaign which would culminate inevitably in the blowing of the whistle on this quixotic Joshua and his tone deaf, misplaced Dulcinea. While the mechanics of his highness's downfall were not yet plotted, the unpopularity of his reign – already spreading amidst his closest apostles like malignancy of the soul – would eventually serve to undermine the wildfire conversions and faith healings to come, as surely as ceremonial keystones are consigned to have their appearances more regularly maintained as their function constantly weakens on being abandoned by the photo-opportunists of celebrity, media and pathetic passers-by. And so were the foundations of the fall of this late 20th century Master Builder laid to a handshake owing its elaborations/embellishments in equal parts to lapsed and laughed off Lodge membership and the equally defunct kitsch, knowing parody from the outset, of hi-5s and hand-jives, apotheosised in the early years of the '80s, that Mammon made man made Mammon made decade.

"Oh, and I want my wife back."

"We thought you might. Can't really help you there," smiled Tristan, "but if prayers count for anything you can pray for your dollars, and let me tell you good, good people, giving thanks is an investment that never ends. Thank you, thank you." And, with that uncanny take off of good God Garvey, we bear witness to yet another deity taking its first perceived bow in public in graven image, as our two merry making souls are moved on by that particular community's policeman, delegated by this particular neighbourhood's watchers to hustle on any hustlers.

Chapter Twenty-three

While evolving a strategy for reclaiming his ex, Fairbrother mused long and hard on the lost property of the past. And not just that of his own, but that of all at *Money Changers Changed*.

Cal and Tristan were the easiest cases to examine dispassionately. Not that there were no bonds between he and they, particularly between he and Tristan, but that they, having been outmanoeuvred by a master manipulator in people's futures, were hell-bent on, and eminently capable of, recouping their losses. What they would do with wealth, power and a *Schadenfreude* perhaps unhealthily concentrated upon a single person, a second time round, one would have to wait and see, but he didn't doubt Saddler's come-uppance in itself offered great excuse for otherwise churlish behaviour. Indelicate as it may seem, all three were out to shaft that sumbitch.

Saddler's past was simple: its spectacular successes were about to be rewritten into an inglorious future. And Sheril? Unfortunately she'd have to suffer some, too. Not primarily for envy's sake, but neither for altogether noble motives. Fairbrother wanted her back and, on achieving that devout wish, would endeavour to treat her with as much respect for her equality and liberty as was ever her right, but first he had to strut that preposterous testosterone loaded pose that would at least frighten off the incumbent deuteragonist for her favours. It would be in the process of putting his rival's successes into something like the proportion their small-minded dynamics deserved, that he would discover if his own true worth were worthy of more than the shop front display so often favoured by courting *coeurs*. En route he would surely rediscover that which had long seemed abandoned to his past; the inverse prostitution of the inathletic years of sloppy bachelordom, those inarguably wasted, all but lost years when, unforced and unbothered, a person has nothing, no feel for anything to sell, least of all oneself: when driven venality takes a taciturn back seat to a poorly sighted, malignly guided fear of future's encroachment which just about passes muster as self-preservation in one divesting oneself of the will to live.

He was slouching towards Saddler's bunker to record the final part in the morality tale which was supposed to so become his public and private lives, when he caught sight of his reflection in a shop front, dilemmas, demons, heavenly bodies and all.

In the warmth of an assured present and presence, three four or so year old children sat upon Santa's knee. In the perversely mirroring backdrop beneath the tenderly cut crude shapes comprising the message 'Welcome to Santa's Grotto', Fairbrother's *Doppelgänger* manifested itself as menacing and evanescent as seemed his genuinely happy childhood at this cold and distant remove. As hidden, bidden hands set the scene, catching and losing his brief recognition as curtly as cruel children enclasping a dreamed of butterfly and clapping a dirty little moth's last, the three little ones were perched not so innocently on an incognito adult's respective knees and left thigh. Oh, they were innocent of that alright, and safe for the time being in full public view, but there was already in their imploring eyes a semblance of the circus dwarf's cupidity on gazing up at the long, heaven-sent legs of the trapeze artist, an awareness that for this, their first advert, they were due some prime payments. My, they start them young these days, he found himself thinking, and in an instant connected this banal observation to the tragedy of not heretofore, no, not recently having known thus; to the real danger of having nothing to sell but a shadow of a former self.

Trudging bunker-wards he cursed the snow, more than ever a cold sleet shower than cotton wool, trailing in his wake the vestigial sludge either fleetingly impressed upon by a large and less than sure-footed child on the run, or an out of ideas man kicking over the traces of an angry notion.

On his entering the bunker Saddler ordered him out again. This was perfect weather for capturing the final chapter in his soon to be commercially available (i.e., available in the ultimate commercial form of a commercial) rehabilitation. Like the simple, at best amoral tales he had hitherto traded in, Saddler had in mind for this simple moral tale the simplest market available; i.e., the in themselves effetely renascent, crassly commercialised communities of the former Eastern Europe, where demonic evangelism was not now a contradictory notion.

On that corner of England's green and not so pleasant land that certainly felt forever Saddler's, filming commenced. In the grand manner of all mega-moneyed *arrivistes*, Saddler aped the director's role with all the tact and skill of an interfering producer. That he had the money to make his vision come true wasn't in doubt (his personal fortune was estimated at £65 million and accumulating). Indeed, that he had a vision was plain to see. It was the nature of that vision which particularly galled Fairbrother.

Peering into his camcorder's sights, seated in the amateur *auteur's* reputedly talismanic director's chair and barking the utterly obeyed, utterly barking command cum wish fulfilment, 'ACTION!', Saddler saw his world in, as it were, his grain of sand. With an inspiration as self-regardingly genuine as it was artistically *ersatz*, he saw, he visioned, in each cinematographically disastrous shot, the world as he wanted it. Thus, Fairbrother, force fed lines most would wish to consign to that area of memory which even the best actors never call, was appealing in his awkwardness, like a sportsman in panto or, better still, the English football manager playing Lear. As Fairbrother balefully incanted his lines on automaton pilot, like a man simultaneously mourning his integrity, Saddler heard these same, his lines sing:

"Then I was reborn. From a meaningless imposition, life miraculously appeared, well, miraculous." And on it went, this folksy, airbrushed, costume warts and all interlocution between, well, an actor and script so talentless they had to be for real (they couldn't be anything else) and an audience waiting for, well, a miracle.

The vision thing done, the visionary commanded his camera to print, and, windswept and interested only in intriguing against this prophet with an f, Fairbrother faked a 'thank *you* for making me a lucky star' parting and headed through October's driven rain, out of this low budget, grossly grossing Utopia to the real world of jealousy, worldly ambition, love and a rendezvous with co-conspirator Tristan. Behind him Sadder and assorted superfluous flunkeys underlined the extravagant filling of the void which only the rich and religious feel free to patronise, clambering into British assembled, Japanese designed golf carts for the gizmo driven haul back the 50 yards down lawn to the comfortably walkable, plushly carpeted corridors. Asked once why he had purchased these, for the non-golfer, at best enigmatic vehicles, Saddler obliged, "They are perfect for the bunker's —— corridors of power." The pause was accompanied by the thought of the sound of running liquid.

As he awaited Tristan in the Hackney dive which all but a semi-reformed alcoholic would be ashamed to call his local – for a tediously bamboozling variety of reasons, unlike the reforming type, the peforming alkie doesn't have locals, certainly not 'a' local –, Fairbrother mused over his pint (no spirits these days: given that there is only so much liquid the body can welcome on board, it is difficult to become an alcoholic on pints). He had never got his ex-wife alone. Still, this reconciliation had to be effected properly; just as divorce had featured the solicitors as grossly remunerated go-betweens, the making up would require the services of lesser salaried, yet no less sullied operatives.

As the person takes on the persona of the business they are in, Tristan entered, gumshoe's report in manila folder, matching (though far from blended) manila raincoat, a walking reminder, fuck it, advert, of dues to be paid.

Disappointed at his messenger's declining of a Singapore Sling, dismayed at his missing the joke, Fairbrother faced the bar for two beers, after battling through the usual belly-laugh of bevviers and less than a bevy of beauties that typically congregate around these serving counters as surely, and somewhat less explicably, as flies round shite.

The gumshoe had done his work. Posing his hirelings as any number of maintenance, installation and fix it men, seemingly taking residence in the bunker, he had, to his client's delight and surprise, succeeded in bugging the joint. The results were more equivocal, however. Having expertly captured the intimacies of the couple, the result was closer to heartbreaking than revealing. Hoping to have stolen damning documentary evidence of financial and/or moral improprieties, the two cohorts listened in to the cassettes on a twin-head-set-Walkman. Looking for all the world that is a saloon bar dangerously like two lovers after a tiff, our voluntary Siamese twins going, getting precisely nowhere, wore faces registering all the emotions, from initial amusement at prayers before bedtime, on Tristan's part to outright dismay on Fairbrother's. There was nothing here they could use to abort Saddler's launch of his satellite and cable TV show. Nothing but a seemingly devout couple utterly devoted to each other. As Sheril took her master's cue and said a prayer for her ex, a disgusted Fairbrother threw off these fiendish instruments of aural torture, sickened less by his voyeuristic intrusions than by the debunking of his motives. "She loves him! And Him!" jangled his brain like a subliminally cruel refrain, and as Tristan squirmed and tittered in the virtual reality of their sweet sweat music, his dubious pleasure was unsatisfactorily climaxed by Fairbrother's unceremoniously yanking his headphones off.

"What the fuck are you laughing at!?" he yelled, in volume and vocabulary once again every bit the experienced Walkman user. The clientele in this natural habitat for seen it all cynicism, every bit the experienced abusers, batted not a collective eyelid.

"I'm sorry, but you must admit it's funny. Prayers before fucking *her* —"

"He *fucked* her!!??" moaned Fairbrother, his change in emphasis, in particular, audible to all and sundry. Still no reaction, though he was running the risk of being made an offer no one round these parts could dare to refuse; an invite to the long past bedtime fuck-ups, kidnapped into the coterie of the after hours lock-in.

"Well, they are married —," reasoned Tristan, unused to, and naturally uncomfortable with, such public breast beating.

"Don't I fucking well know it," lowed his demotically depressed companion.

At this point Fairbrother was mercifully becalmed by an intervention as crude as had been his botched invasion of his ex-wife's privacy. In essence it amounted to "Shut the fuck up, fuck-ups, football's on", at which point, hands across the sea, like joined like, and the two disappointed muckrakers settled for 90 minutes of heaping calumny on the head of Graham Taylor, looking very much like a man expecting any day now to wake up beside a horse's head. That poor bastard's trials and tribulations cheered Tristan up no end, and while Fairbrother revelled rather less in a fellow fuck-up's fuck-ups, he made it through the night with the help of an alcohol intake almost as prodigious as the purging of invective which constantly topped it until, tailing off into incomprehensibility's cussing cups, aphasia and the blessed anonymity of the night air.

Two more weeks' worth of tapes revealed nothing on the discreditable side, and it was with the trepidation of a wage slave that Fairbrother continued attending the bunker to help mastermind the launch of *Money Changers Changed* and re-establish old press contacts for the impending resurrection theme publicity that would accompany the 'true and remarkable', riches to rags to riches, back to life story on the station's first God slot.

Hyped in second coming proportions, *Money Changers Changed* exercised a skilful manipulation of more established media's genuine curiosity in this first weekly godathon to alight upon the UK, and the rather less ingenuous interest in four of their own finding God and still apparently hell-bent on making good.

Corporate policy announced – in that prime advertising space between the ears that is populist curiosity – that, for all its apparent altruism, *Money Changers Changed* was avowedly, if opportunistically, tweely businesslike: 'Making Good With Your Money' was one slogan. That corporate identity would not be best portrayed by sporting hair shirts seemed sound business sense and, better still, displayed the right shade of politics, especially in an age when the C of E was seen as a pinko fellow new age traveller with weirdos and commies.

Intrigued between horror and admiration, the City gave this latest incarnation of *Boom Bros* the golden hello to its money changers that is its blessing, while the government, in nigh daily dire need of some uplift, hitched its falling star to what it saw at the very least as a feel-good distraction from the despair and decay emanating from its seemingly endless succession of dismal foul-ups.

Money Changers Changed first broadcast went out on Tuesday 15th September 1992. Sundays were all booked up till doomsday: old movies, old sitcoms, old chat shows, live sports. Verily, Sunday was a day of rest for all but the superfit and the most dedicated of couch potatoes.

At 8 pm that evening proud owners of the satellite dishes or cable television irreparably eroding the unsustainable hegemony of, *primes inter pares*, the Best Broadcasting Company in the world, with their unbelievable free market, flea market mess of repeats, sports, tabloid news and game shows, were served up yet another unearthly, bound to be earth-shattering treat: their first godathon. Massively hyped, and as such unmissable, this programme, combining Fairbrother's 'resurrection' with tips on how to unburden oneself of guilt by giving the pound in the pocket to an organisation run on avowedly Tory Treasury/bank manager lines (either way, not good timing), drew an audience of 800,000, or, more importantly, 40% of then eligible viewers. As the curtain came down (on a stage before a hired audience) on the showing of the 'film of his life', Fairbrother sat at home alone, reminded uncomfortably of no less, no more than himself, as he gazed, glazed at the commercial breaks which had so unceremoniously removed him from the audience's affections. As owners vouched for the preference and, presumably mastery of language, displayed by their pets (or maybe they new their charades), Fairbrother felt packaged, an idea kicked around by a team with more muscle than skill. Moreover, a team which failed to inspire his allegiance. As a well-oiled rugby team, played by a pack of loud bastards, led by a teetering giant sporting a moose head, embodied and somehow endorsed 'Hi-Alcohol-Lager', Fairbrother reflected that this was his real debut in the selling game. Now he was a product and nothing else, he didn't like it one bit, particularly the *nom emprunté* of Daniel.

The tear-jerker of his story over, a seemingly well-canned audience bore hallelujahed witness to a second half unashamedly upbeat, almost spiritually uplifting. Saddler emceed the proceedings, every inch the seasoned performer able to play to an audience even when actually playing to a house later provided by sound engineers. Grudgingly, Fairbrother conceded that Saddler somehow conveyed an honesty of purpose as he commenced with this appeal:

"Ladies and gentlemen of our audience – here and at home sweet home –, you have just witnessed the, at times, harrowing, but ultimately inspirational story of Daniel Fairbrother, mercifully once again of this parish. Daniel's success out of failure is a lesson to us all never to give up striving for life's rich rewards. A lesson in redemption, nothing less. Yet in this, his, story of one man, do we not see the history of man: namely the fashioning of failure out of success? What drove our fair brother to the three *D*s, Drink, Drugs and Despair, were the three *S*s, Sex, Success and Soullessness: what saved our fair brother were of course the three *R*s, Redemption, Reimbursement and Rebirth. And, dramatic though it seems, is his story any different from yours or yours or yours?" (finger waving over entire 'audience', then turned on self) "Or, indeed, mine?

"Let me tell you a bit about myself, friends. Before becoming Jesus Junior Mothers I went under the name of Garvey Saddler. You may have heard of me, *him*, more likely of our company, *Boom Bros*. Whatever, it is a past I am at once proud and ashamed of. The pride I feel is in my business achievements. I have lived out the American dream in this wonderful, accommodating land of yours. And, too, I would hope I have earned a place in your hearts, if only for all the taxes I have contributed to the Exchequer. Joking aside, my greatest achievement brought my greatest disgrace. After being named 'Young Businessman of the Year' (sic) some ten years ago, and, more importantly, thereafter being joint head of a company with a turnover of more than £25 million in today's money I, perhaps understandably, yet no less unforgivably let success go to my head. Always an indestructible optimist, I set out to puncture the hypocrisy I then detected in this country's attitude to sex by going into erotic publishing. And for a few years all was fine, with the tragic, praise be! redeemable exception of our fair brother. We made even more money. Oh, we had our critics, though their carping was as nothing to the day my conscience was nagged into action and I fell for my wife to be. No pun intended. That day I realised that the rights of free speech, of free expression, in essence the 'rights' I chose to champion in my publishing enterprise, could at times strain the bonds of tact and, indeed, decency. As I fell for my future wife, the future mother of my children, I was seeing the world, and particularly your wonderful country in a new glowing light.

"At 32 I was in love, truly in love, for the first time. Well, we all know that things appear different in that delightful, that delighted, that enlightened state. But it was the delightful and enlightened state I had been inhabiting for 10 years that suddenly revealed itself as truly remarkable. After a decade's residence I belatedly fell for the charms of this sceptred isle. Oh, I had loved her people all along, how could I not!, but I had never fully appreciated the beauty of her constitution (sic): I saw, even as I dreamed of my wife to be in full bridal gown, how her modesty became her, enhancing her beauty in a way that was truly bewitching. I understood then that the much mocked British reserve was in fact a decency that would not be mocked, and that I, chief among her detractors, had better show a little more respect. How I intended doing this was a mystery to me at first, and then it hit this materially rich, morally bankrupt bozo with all the immediacy of a good advertising campaign: how to make money morally? Simple?"

("Fucking right," cursed Fairbrother, drunk but, crucially, not as drunk as evidently he had been that first heady evening of reconciliation and return. Nor as voluble. He listened to Garvey, if only for further points of Recall, Recognition and ultimately Revenge).

"You would have thought so, wouldn't you? But sometimes, in this wicked world, the complexities of day to day existence corrupt our sense of vision so that the beautiful disappears behind a tear-gas smokescreen which leaves us crying without knowing why. Not altogether innocent bystanders to the chaos around us, we weep tears, real tears for the simplest of things: we cry, we are all crying out for a little beauty. 'There is no beauty anymore!' I exclaimed, as I imagined the world I was asking my betrothed and our as yet unborn children, bless 'em, to inhabit. Realising this, this realisation was the hard part, doing something about it suddenly revealed itself as oh so simple. Aptly simple, for I found my definition of beauty to be simplicity itself. Don't you ever hanker after the times when policemen were older, politicians nobler, when the songs meant something, something harmonious, television and movies were less violent, games more fun, more innocent, four letter words enough of a rarity to shock, football rivalries friendly, sportsmen honest? Of course you do, we all do. Even the young, like me, who haven't yet been around long enough, or at the right time, to test fully the truth of those oft, oft lamented qualities of life. Could they be brought back without seeming old-fashioned, reactionary, inapplicable to today's society? I, for one, couldn't see how, until I discovered the Word and accepted the good Lord into my life. Again, that part was easy, what was difficult, even astounding, was that it had taken me so long, here in this most decent and welcoming of lands, to realise just how important a part the good Lord plays in the everyday lives that constitute this great Britain, this world renowned jewel of a nation. I am sure, as sure as faith itself, that were I to take a straw poll of tonight's audience, enquiring after the most devoutly religious of nations, one of the Latin lands, Italy or a South American state, or one of the Islamic dictatorships, Iran or maybe Iraq, would come top. Israel, possibly. Whatever, I am willing to bet that not one of you would think of England. And why not? Because her modesty takes pride of place above her many virtues, her tolerance and restraint serve to censor even her more admirable, most admirable qualities: her things of beauty she will not flaunt. She would fain blush as a new morn maiden to be congratulated on her sheer unadulterated goodness and, while that too is becoming, told she must be. With that observation I set out to sing her praises and, in setting up my new business – *Money Changers Changed* –, make money for the common good. How to square the seeming circle of ambition, which so often sees us losing our way as human beings even as we find the relentless drive necessary to success? Again, simple.

"At first I thought the easy way would be to donate all profits to charity, but then I did some hard business thinking. Can you, the man and the woman in the street, trust in the sound investment of your kind donations? Not to say that charitable organisations are corrupt in themselves, but just how businesslike are their operations? Not having the spare time to devote, nor the power to be a one man audit office on the running of hundreds of well-meaning, perhaps not hard enough headed companies, I naturally decided to keep the operation in-house and applied for charitable status, which application, given my previous track record, was initially treated with understandable incredulity. But, again, your wonderful country came up trumps. Yes, here and only here, even officialdom recognises a genuine repentant, and accordingly I was given the green light to do good works. All of which brings me here to beg your pledges. All the money raised tonight will go direct (sic) to a crack board of top business people with proven track records. And from there it will humbly represent the good intent of you, its beneficent donors, striving towards building a community only just fit to represent this good country and the glory that is God, but one which faithfully embodies all that is good and great in this world. The name of this community? What else but *Little England*?

"*Little England* will be a village based community in England's garden, idyllic in setting, hell to transgress. It will host one prayer multi-complex incorporating places of worship for all denominations, as well as all the other necessities of a village community, saving public houses and tobacconists. Its three feature hotels, the Garden, the St Mary and the Jerusalem, will form a trinity of excellence, tastefully catering for all tastes, additionally hosting all year round religious and cultural seminars, plus exhibitions, again open to all denominations, laity and clergy alike. Each hotel will house its own sports complex, complete with multi-gym: after all, the body is the temple of the soul. The aim of these seminars and exhibitions being to prepare as many as possible for the spreading of the good word, the laity will be made especially welcome. *Little England* will be a haven of family values: there is no need to fear that the little ones will encounter anything untoward within *its* grounds: and as the little ones enjoy the instructive play provided in the village's amusement and assessment park, mum and dad can leave them safely in the care of our fully qualified carers while they themselves attend some of the many services and seminars in praise of familial betterment. And, last but not least, the better to sanctify your home, a furniture and DIY warehouse selling electrical appliances, plugs and batteries included, the lot. All profits going to the running of the village, of course.

"Donors will be invited to buy into our community on a variety of terms. One could, if one wished, live in this sanctuary of the soul, or, alternatively, one could visit on an *ad hoc* or regular basis. Whichever, it depends on one's level of commitment, one's degree of belief in the need for an idealistic haven from this turbulent world. Pledges of £1,000 upwards will be rewarded with a guarantee of a quality time-share arrangement to be, um, arranged with one of our hotels, coupled with a once in a lifetime chance to win, yes!, *win* a historically accurate fully-reconstructed thatched cottage in *Little England*. Pledges of between £500 and £1,000 will be redeemed by free day-trip access for one year. Redeemable, of course. Pledges between £100 and £500 will earn the donor an option on a season ticket for such visits. Other pledges will be rewarded with similar special access, barred to ordinary visitors, as it were, non residents, non shareholders. *Little England* will open in six months time, God and your good selves willing. If the timetable appears miraculous, all the more reason to cock a snook at the sceptics and, by your good works, make it happen, make it happen. *Money Changers Changed plc*, the official developers of this homage to the home sweet home that so characterises this nation, invite you to invest now in this once in this lifetime opportunity to let your money do you good by doing good. We accept all major credit cards ———."

At this invitation, which no self disrespecting squanderer could afford to pass up, Fairbrother switched off, blessedly missing the grand finale, in which Garvey, sorry, Jesus Junior, introduced his wife, "a sinner, if anything more repentant than I".

Thus introduced and traduced, the sinner then proceeded to deliver herself of a rendition of *Stand By Your Man* so smugly faithful and insincerely sensitive as to make the rawest of mawkish, maudlin rednecks puke nuclear. Garvey stood by her side, dutifully taking her confession of love, keeping his mouth shut.

"With great difficulty," mumbled Fairbrother to one couple in particular.

Chapter Twenty-four

Entering *Little England* the casual visitor would be struck by her photogenecy, her surface prettiness as manifest as a vernal landscape seen through the eyes of a little old suburbanite gazing at her reproduction *ersatz* Constable. But casual visitors were never given the chance to chance upon *Little England* 's charms: they were accessible purely by entry fee or subscription, lending this excessively quaint little monument to an arguable past the somewhat strange air of an exhibition centre constructed for those with lifestyles wherein extension was measured by the remote control, and adventure hitherto confined to family Sundays out at the DIY centre. And while the home improvement set would have loved to peek behind *Little England* 's western set style of flattened ambience, they too were barred from its inner sancta, accorded, as they were, the limited privileges of day-trippers (£25 a family, children free, whatever that means. And as the children frolicked happily on bouncy castles 'neath heavenly clouds, their parents, to whom shopping was religion, were falling prey to *Little England*'s charms). A grudging Fairbrother had to hand it to Garvey: the C1s and the C2s – those Thatcherite neophytes, historically recently hijacked from the 'Labour isn't working' classes, now aping the middle-class in an entirely classless manner – were a mark for anything you cared to manoeuvre them into contact with, even anything hitherto unconsidered, or indeed loathed, like religion.

Status conscious and utterly classless, they flocked to *Little England*, ostensibly to offload the kids and get in a few hours shopping. And that part was fine, the kids had a great time, the shopping was competitively priced. Taking away that kind of favourably bland impression, for which it was indeed designed, may only have seen visitors recommending *Little England*'s homely charms to kith and kin, themselves repaying perhaps twice yearly visits. What got them coming back, frequently, and in a significant number of cases, practically residing, was the suggestion, the suspicion, the subliminal entropy that advertising 'inspires' in the small-minded, that their betters – the ones with access to the hotels, for instance – somehow belonged here. Never a truly communal beast, the working class Tory needed something a bit, um, less sophisticated than a few joss-sticks and nostrum mantras to make him part with his hard earned potential home improvements, and *Little*

England was it, in borderers, trimmers and pneumatic, numismatic spades. Enticed in to practise his religion of shopping, he bought the concept, the whole package. He always does. The furniture warehouse, for one, was festooned with curious promotions in lieu of 'Must Go!', 'Last Chance!' and 'Giving it away, missus!' 'Sale!' signs: promotions which cunningly charmed Noachic DIY man by managing to outspiv even those clearly weather-beaten 'Last Day – Judgement Day' sandwich boards discarded many moons since, yet *in flagrante delicto,* outside similarly 'seen better days' 'Last Day – Sale Day' shop fronts by hired frauds in fear of arrest under the Trades Description Act, Bad Busking section. *Little England*'s offers you couldn't refuse offered monthly/yearly memberships in the guise of prize draws, which every purchaser gained ("Free!") entry to. In pure advertising terms this was no more sophisticated than a time-share offer, but it had the following advantages of locale, which saw this promotion reducing a profitable majority of its visitors to, in pure advertisers' terms, time-share takeable: *1*, it was in England: *2*, it was in *Little England*: *3*, 'All *Little England Home From Home plc* goods not made in England are made in other parts of The United Kingdom of Great Britain and Northern Ireland' bored the pompous legend: by which, the company lawyers concluded, the suggestion outweighed the actuality to the extent that *Little England Home From Home* goods applied only to the goods available in the authorised souvenir gift shop, *Ye Olde Gifte Shoppe* . Other emotive notices, like 'Live British, buy *Little England*', served to bolster an illusion not altogether unwelcome or new to the 'Sunday shopping in/wogs out' set (decidedly, tourists while not unwelcome, particularly when well-walleted, were not *Little England*' s stock-in-trade).: *4*, there appeared to be a constant supply of winners (staff, students and rehired frauds): *5*, the people going in and coming out of the hotels seemed particularly well-heeled: *6*, it's in a good cause: *7*, what's there to lose?: *8*, what goes *on behind* those hotel walls?

As disappointed shoppers gazed in wonderment at disappointingly remunerated students aping ecstasy for much more than they were evidently worth, there and then, skipping like a honeymoon couple comprising bride and best man, up the garden path to one of those hotels, the sucker punch was delivered – losers would be entered in the second and third prize draws. Second prize: one night's stay at the hotel/leisure complex of one's choice at 'half-advertised' rate). Third prize, a day at the leisure complex of one's choice, again at 'half the advertised price'. Envious uninitiates all, a highly grossing percentage bought this scam, in spite of the fact that 'advertised' prices were only made available, i.e., only previously *known advertised* to, promulgated among, well, staff and the two or three hundred weekend Moonies who would subscribe sufficiently to take 'advantage' of them. The 'too obvious it's too obvious to see' truth was that 'half-advertised price' was the same as the advertised price, was, repeat, *was* the advertised price: but who was going to know? When intermingling did occur, those visitors captured in the store would rarely volunteer information on their half-price bargain. And if they did? – say £150 a night – this would merely confirm in the minds of the regulars and residents that they too indeed had got half-price, for they too were paying half 'advertised' price of £150 a night, and, what's more, could continue to do so for a yearly donation of upwards of £1,000. Similarly, these and many other similarly discounted benefits were available to the less religiously inclined, less devout members too, for a yearly subscription of upwards of £1,000. Or not. For everything was half-price to everyone, the discount was a miscount. It wouldn't have taken Wittgenstein to calculate that half-price was full-price, and vice versa: that there existed no full-price, nor no half-price, howsoever, he'd care to put it. Alas, he'd have met with greater success persuading these suckers that there was a rhinoceros in the room, so readily convinced were these dupes that they had pulled off *coups du ciel*, each and every one.

Thus *Little England* captured its customers; day-trippers, do-gooders unable to imagine a more productive outlet for their deeds, and the Terry and Tracy set, social Tarzans and Janes, gatecrashing, window crashing the country club. Joining forces (mutually oblivious to the crudely fashioned joins) were the Sunday shopping set and the Lord's Day Observance Society, and never the twain should meet to unpick their stitching up. Be they there for furniture, fulfilment, both, badminton, social climbing, all, they poured in, and, within one month of its 'Grand Opening Spectacular', *Little England* had 4,000 members – 400 'donors', i.e., actual/potential residents, and 3,600 'laity', i.e., those paying donations/subscriptions of less than 1K p.a. All in all not a bad miniature of Garvey's self-proclaimed "world's most religious country".

Chapter Twenty-five

As *Little England* initially went from success to success her considerably bigger namesake took a considerably less rewarding route. For the first year and a half the storms ravaging the wider economy were tolerably weathered; initial interest in this cultural curio kept turnover ticking nicely. Similarly, the satellite and cable God slot – produced and syndicated by *MCC* – had at first met with great public approval, particularly its *vox pop* confessional cum buying peace of mind second half: 'Forgive Yourself – We do!', only for shares in piety to go gradually the way of all flesh when each ass reasons that it is up for grabs, holy invocation or no holy invocation. So it was, within a year and a half of launching these two very expensive projects, that *Money Changers Changed* convened to face straitened circumstances. Gloating together over the *FT* front page 'Money Changers' Shareholders Shortchanged' – "love that apostrophe!" –, Tristan and Fairbrother shared a cab to the bunker. These last few days had not been good, particularly not so for the company's high profile chairman. After announcing interims which saw the previous year's profits more than wiped out and stock subsequently nose dive, Garvey had been inundated, both by shareholders who had suddenly lost the faith, and a speculative, at the best of times, press corps who saw to it that his personal stock that was his fame rose as his company's crashed. The worst agents of the two coincided in the letters pages of the conservative qualities, wherein the great and the good can casually cast the sort of off-colour imprecations which, if uttered at editorial conferences would be understood to be very much off the record and off any future agenda. Never since Maxwell's pension scandal had company finances excited such public comment, never since the Lloyd's Names ignominy, such public *Schadenfreude*; never did either inspire such wrathful, wronged shareholders' opprobrium. And, high profile is as high profile does, the flak was heading Saddler's way, and – as flak does, whether truly aimed, or the shot off the shovel that was Bloom's come as you are rehearsal at ascension, – getting very personal in nature as it honed in like so many (i'faith! Robbed blind!) empty biscuit tins.

"Listen to this," intoned Tristan joyously, "a letter to our leader from a little old lady in Huntingdon."

'Dear Sir

If Garvey Saddler, or Jesus Junior Mothers, or whatever he chooses to style himself as he bids to flee the country (no fond farewells!?), could answer me one question, then I suppose I deserve to have been fleeced by such an unprincipled shaman: was it right to register as a charity, a company which, at the first whiff of trouble rounds on its shareholders in a manner not dissimilar to that once favoured by the late (sic) Iron Lady (sick) and her then cabinet's feebly assenting ranks? I only ask because I, *mens sana in corpore sano* (or so I thought), modestly endorsed his little enterprise; not out of any desire to make a fast buck, but out of what is now cruelly exposed as misplaced admiration for his little venture. Further, precious little money has been raised for charity, a, peradventure, inevitable consequence of the parlous state of the company's finances, as revealed in this week's interims in the full Sensurround calamity and 3D horror of their proportions. Alas and alack, such inept performance does not quite suggest the qualifying adjective 'justifiable' to the homicidal shareholder, but surely I am not alone in wishing a painful end upon a man who has conned tens of millions from bogus registered charity status for his 'professional approach to caring'. The only professional aspect of this company appears to have been the way its chairman has followed the 'best' traditions of big business and gone to ground faster than you can say 'Print It!' at a *Sun* editorial conference on rumours of a Cabinet Minister's peccadilloes. In such supposedly enlightened times is it too much to ask that such religious charlatans be barred from extracting an emotional tithe from those members of the public genuinely devoted to the quiet decencies and, yes, gentle whodunnit spirituality of the best parts of English life?

Yours in faith
Grünhilda Frobisher (Mrs)
The Priory
20 Oswald Place
Huntingdon, Cambridgeshire.'

"I've got one here that tops that," Fairbrother announced, when the laughter had petered out to luxuriously contented sighs. "In the Torygraph." Tristan heaved a hearty, anticipatory inhalation of buoyant spirits.

'Dear Sir

Along with many other thoroughly decent denizens, I actively welcomed the evangelical approach to eroding the moral malaise so recently promulgated by *Money Changers Changed*. In spite of being an old fogey, or perhaps because of not being particularly enamoured of such a growingly disreputable epithet, I was prepared to admit these brash young Little Englanders into the wearying temple of greater England's soul: particularly attractive seemed their willingness at every turn to defend this sceptred isle from the malignant increase in detractors, without and mountebanks within, and, moreover, to champion her virtues in appropriately sacred terms. But, begging His pardon, what in the name of God is this? My money has not only gone to 'doing good better than it has ever had the chance to before' (Prospectus 15:12), it has plunged into an apparently bottomless money pit dug by the 'have a nice day' hell's bitches utterly misappropriating the good name of this holy land. When will we learn that it is get rich quick Johnnies – like this calamitous Yank who has reduced God to a highly unethical marketing pitch – who have robbed the great from England's name?

'If it takes the foreclosure of this supermarket for the soul in order to re-establish the C of E's claim to be the nation's natural dispenser of matters spiritual, all well and good, but one fears the old girl lacks the evangelism (or, if you prefer, marketing strategy), as well as the stomach to combat the cracked libertines on its Politically Correctivist wing. *Money Changers Changed*, for all their belatedly revealed sins, at least showed themselves unafraid to identify the enemy. But, just as the ordination of lady priests appals, so does the casual acceptance of those licensed to preach in Reno, Nevada by those licensed to preach in Reno, Nevada. Unfortunately for them, for we shareholders, for *Little England* and greater England all, a certain overzealous approach to turning a fast buck has demeaned otherwise admirable aims and revealed the philistine side to these supposedly devout souls. Is it any coincidence that their Chairman, Chief Executive, despotic godhead all, is of post-colonial lineage, further that this genuine but injudicious puritan (and, lest we ever forgive, ex-pornographer) emanates from the very nation whose young men infamously were overpaid, oversexed and but grudgingly over here, even when the future of all we still hold dear was, as they would doubtless say, 'up for grabs'? If Mr Saddler sees his

attachment to this country as a penance for the sins of his fathers, even unto the War of Independence, I would respectfully suggest he has got the wrong country and the wrong religion. I fear that, in his self-aggrandisement, he has taken the 'when in Rome' injunction to assimilation too literally.
Yours in good faith.
Colonel Sir H H H Rowbotham-Saville (DSM, Ret'd)
Hilltops
Bournemouth'

"He's getting it from all sides," grinned Tristan. "This one in the Grauniad's a beaut.

'Dear Sir/Madam
(I bet a thousand kisses from my live in lover, Lesley with a 'y', that you expurgate that 'Madam'; We don't care; the term is too derogatory and caught up in pejorative connotations to die for).

'Once again the twin pillars of the phallocracy stand revealed! Just when you though it was safe to come out, straight out of closet 28, sex shun 25, comes another emotionally constipated appeal for the hearts and souls (not to mention tits, c***s and pricks, because you tits, c***s and pricks would never print anything so near to home) of the nation state: *Little England*, a theme park of his story, a monument to the monumental cock-ups that have so characterised life as she is denied in this cuntry (you'll mispell (sic – Ed) my mispelling! (no *we* won't – Ed)).

'What is to become of a country which evangelically denies women's rights, from our own bodies even unto the wholly unlikely Trinity, yet blithely bestows charitable, almost worshipful status on a supposedly repentant ex-pornographer and his cheap trick of a little woman? Are we again about to get it arse-backwards in our, thankfully inimitable, anally retentive 'style'? That is, the message from this little escapade in political incorrectness seems to be, not only is forgiveness a consumer 'good' (as advertised by extremely sorry specimens) purchasable by Dutch auction, whereby cupidity achieves debasement, but that the expediency of women seems to be so valued as such that we seem to wish to say that all these weird, irrational creatures are, *A*, weird, irrational creatures, *B*, potential prostitutes, *C*, potentially 'redeemed' or

'rescued' prostitutes. In these so-called post-liberated days is it the woman's lot only to be acknowledged after she has been 'rescued' by 'her' 'man'? Further, is this nation still prepared to denounce and renounce its multifarious sexualities for the pious innuendo of the *farceur* vicar in 'sitcom' 'scandal' 'scandal'? But, then, what does one expect in a country which alternates equally unworthy patriarchal and matriarchal role models (equal, that is, on a classification system based on primogeniture and crazy 'bout its boys): role models which bear about as much relation to real life as Princess Di (oh, how I wish she would piss off and) ever did to the girl next door; as an inglorious his story of preferment does to a forward looking society?
Yours in sorority and sorrow
Lee Womad
Camden NW1'

The taxi gained the kerb outside the bunker. I've always dared to dream of using the verb 'to gain' in such a context. Actually, it can never, as it were, regain comtemporary relevance, never be, but we've come close here, almost by accident; for the vehicle referred to had mounted the pavement, so disarmed had the, hitherto seen, heard, done, been it all, driver been by the raucous laughter and repugnant 'language!' spewing forth from behind his dramatically, violently shaking head.

"Never heard the fucking like," he responded, to the banter in back, referring perhaps to the abnormality, not the scatology or sexuality, of its subject matter (our driver had nudge, nudged, wink, wanked with the worst of them: alas, the perils of the trade). In truth, the boys were feeling a bit naughty, and preoccupied with their news, had, in ignorance of the taxi-driver's presence (neat U-turn there), contravened his cab's code of behaviour, which code unhappily coincided with the last great unwritten clauses in the as yet unwritten Great British constitution; *videlicet*, they had parted with tradition, they had found humour outside the primed to pop whalebone strictures of the *Carry On, Young Ones* genres, kindred, putrid, mutant spirits all; had ventured far too far off the 'if you can't beat 'em, join 'em track, had escaped from 'any repression mocks expression' to 'any expression mocks repression', from easy laughs at easy targets (so easy you only had to miss to hit). That is, as the back of his head exploded in a shock of guffaws and 'cocksuckers', unmanly screeches and ungentlemany 'cuckolds', howls and 'queer motherfuckers', it was clear his fare had gone too far, was going no further, had got too personal, could have been laughing at him. Cunts. Having given no thought to the matter, they soon easily and happily obliged, dispatched with haste to the, as previously mentioned, gained kerb, robbed of their right to pay, let alone tip, that normally licensed highwayman, who, endorsing timing (and strait-laced, straight-faced ignorance) as the secret of good comedy, had ejected these foul charges all of 30 yards from their intended destination, yelling as he flew past, "I hope the fucking walk fucking kills you!"

Buoyed by the criticisms of their great leader manifestly afoot in the wider world, and by their chauffeur for a day's marvellous unpaid performance, Tristan and Fairbrother prepared to enter the former's inner sanctum with, for once, at last!, smiles on their faces. As the bunker was approached the heavens opened, loosing off an apocalyptic rehearsal. Knowing a thing or two of the efficacy of employing special effects, the two smiled, thanking the real God, the doubtful, sceptical God for trusting in them his account.

On gaining (!) the bunker's innards the two fell into silence. They had discussed this before, necessarily outwith these walls; then they had concluded that any such high profile, publicity crazed personality would have to take him or herself as seriously as did his or her lowest common follower: i.e., see the public face only; therefore, to speculate that celebrity was not by necessity a type of poorly protected species, particularly endangered by self and self-appointed protectors, was a ludicrous notion with which perhaps only the chattering classes sought to amuse themselves. Garvey certainly had the celebrity, and, in the *hubris* that shadowed his standing in that limelight, darker thoughts were at work, slowly, quietly, irrevocably, unseen, creeping up on pride, concentrating obsessively to caricature that noble characteristic as unbearable insolence, finally confronting it unawares one day with a challenge to its sensibility that provoked its redefinition as paranoia: pride was still in place but useless, debased, traduced, now the whole rest of the world ought to be ashamed of itself, or rather, personal does as personal is, themselves, laughing at the monstrous shadow cast by the poor fool who will never see the joke. Ah, how those who burst upon the public stage with an act utterly bereft of sophistication, which announced no more nor less than that here was one famous for being famous, so soon became infamous for being infamous prior to retiring to the ranks of well-earned obscurity; how these queer creatures so soon burst back out of the limelight in a furious blaze of publicity, culminating in the total blackout of a frazzled filament; poor burned up souls, muttering only to a darkened, emptied house their pathetic plea, all the more wretched in its acoustic impressiveness for going completely unheeded, indeed unheard: "will someone put the lights on?", they cry in the dark, knowing little that, in this world of built-in obsolescence, their part in it was an epitome bordering on caricature, and that now was a knee-jerk or so too late to start calling for the marketing of the light-bulb guaranteed good for a lifetime but, alas, no good for the limelight.

As they journeyed down the bunker's bizarrely candlelit corridors, Fairbrother reflected upon Saddler's probable state of mind: soon this man whom he had neither loved nor hated, whose public persona he had merely grown to dislike intensely, soon this celebrity would, with involuntary violence, shed the prophylactic cocoon which protects, contains, insulates and finally stifles and isolates the famous from their adoring, often less than adorable public, and, like an accident waiting to happen, explode all over the public stage, the better for passers-by to stop and stare and mutter their 'told you so's and other irreverent elegies. While, 'serves the bastard right' might accurately encapsulate Fairbrother's words on the occasioning of the impending eventuality, he felt a pang of at most empathy with this precipitous showman; a pang which left in its wake dead cells, a dull sense of loss, of personal ambitions unfulfilled; less 'But for the grace of God there goes David Fairbrother', than a less than wholly logical 'It could have been me'. Of course, this last trusty old saw possibly had more bearing on the young lady whom both antagonists had wed, and Fairbrother fought to, ahem, divorce the two. But he couldn't resist a secreted smirk, as he foresaw how the ruin of Saddler's empire would hasten the fair maiden back to his side. Not that he had proposed any such thing. Yet. Like good comedy – with which it has so much in common – successful wooing is at least as much about timing and staging as balance and logic. As, indeed, is a convincing breakdown.

Saddler was pacing the main conference room floor as his two trusted lieutenants entered. In a jerky, practically involuntary manner, he elicited their handshakes like Dr Strangelove desperately cultivating a dangerous adversary. Commanding them to be seated (only, it came out 'slated'), he was clearly a man with things, some more chemical than biological, on his mind. Avowedly, and very publicly, clean since his conversion, he plainly wasn't now. Some despicable cocktail of amphetamines, hallucinogenics, uppers and downers, had all but conquered his central nervous system, and he came over as a wretch losing sleep precisely because he was afraid of what he might see there, in its harsh, interrogative, lunacy inducing light.

"Ah guess you've seen the presh —— uh, I'm under." It was difficult to tell from this newly acquired redneck slur whether he was referring to the press, or the pressure. The two seemed to merge, and he was under all right.

"And he ought to be under a doctor," suggested itself to Fairbrother, who in turn declined to offer the suggestion to a wider audience.

"Naahhowww," continued Saddler, spitting like a trodden on cat, "whaa whee gawwna doobowditt?", the voice more and more resembling an East Ender's rendering of the bathetic spoken section in Elvis's 'Are you lonesome tonite?'; a parody of a parody of a mawkish text and addled sensibility, all adding up to an hilarious tragedy.

"What do you suggest?" enquired Fairbrother, biting his lower lip, licking it in private and in anticipation, but mostly to efface the smile he felt coming on like a childishly aggitated recrudescence. Sure enough, he bit harder as Saddler moaned the more,

"Noahwhaddyoosssujjezzt?"

"Well, Mr President, sir," offered Tristan, addressing his boss correctly, if with gleeful irony, "it's so long since we've been asked to partake in any decisions around here."

"Oh, so that's your game," retorted Saddler, temporarily recommanding something like his old diction. "Think you can bribe the commander in chief, huh?" Whether he quite realised that he had compounded the joke was debatable: if he had, his stoneface bore testimony to previously unsuspected comedic gifts.

"No, sir," incanted Tristan in the dutifully clipped tones, bordering on fidelity and psychosis, of the human Rottweiler of the parade ground. "It just seems that the attacks appear to be primarily of a personal nature — _"

At this Saddler cried from the wilderness of one assailed alone, "I know! I know! Why me? Why me?"

"Well," continued Tristan, "it was official policy, so to speak, to identify all official policy with your good self — personally — so to speak."

"I know! I know! It wash a mishtake. I ought to have devolved power a bit. You, you two and — where's Whipsnade? — never mind, never mind — I wash going to shack him — the wife — and — never mind, never mind, never you mind — you two can have more responsibility — starting from now? —" he pleaded.

"Why now?" questioned Tristan.

"Well, weerrrinnacryseize," confessed the boss.

"We?" pressed Tristan.

"Oh gawd!" moaned Saddler.

"Cal — and — and — Sheril," stirred the automaton tones of Fairbrother, much in the impersonal, mannered manner of prototype artificial intelligence, slowly getting the hang of it, its function, with the intention of taking over, of getting really personal. "They're not —?" he begged.

"Here, they're not here, that's all I know. Fuck 'em, let 'em fuck each other, we — I've got bigger worries here now. The bizhnesh is chloce to collapshe and, frankly, I'm not far behind. Now, are you going to help me, do my p.a.s for me, face the wolf at the door, shore up the ——? tell them I'm not a fraud, ferrkkrrissakess, tell *them* that!"

"Sure," beamed Tristan, "but you'd better get your lawyer in here right now. I want all this in writing."

"Dave?" begged Saddler, but the called body was many moonlit nights away.

"He's in. Just get your lawyer in pronto," commanded Tristan to a scurrying, to all intents and purposes ex boss and a stock-still shell-shocked colleague.

Chapter Twenty-six

Seated in the bunker's conference room were Messrs Saddler, Fairbrother, Edmond and H A Arbuthnot of *Arbuthnot, Arbuthnot, Bartram & Bartman*, Garvey's personal solicitors. Not actually of particularly advanced years, Mr Arbuthnot had nevertheless been so outmanoeuvred by the onset of ageing – the name and family firm didn't help soothe the ravages of time – that he appeared at least 15 years older than the 39 he had ever creakingly clocked up. When one adds that his clothes seemed even older (as regards the year they were bespoke – as well as to – the fashion) than he, one will apprehend that this pleasantly balding gentleman appeared, if not actually Dickensian at least of a bygone era, of that most uncertain age, ever *epi géraos oudô*, at least a *fin de siècle* out of step with the modern money-go-round most of today's lawyers inhabit. With his quaint fountain pen and fustian phrasing, he struck one as a curio from all our yesterdays, being received all the more trustingly for that. Reeking of gentleman's clubland and much relished privilege, redolent of sportingly relinquished empire, he was just the type of legal representative a reductive, transfixed anglophile like Garvey would hire, and, as he solicited Edmond's and Fairbrother's demands, he afforded even a greatly troubled Saddler a gentlemanly grace, a 'hard luck, old sport' much like that which he, they, the movies, imagined would have greatly consoled the last viceroy as the withdrawal from Empire was grandly gestured.

"One: we want to be joint chief executives," delivered Tristan dispassionately, as if speaking on behalf of a 'we', a they, he neither cared much for or about. But one can't teach a lawyer new trick, if any at all.

"By 'we', one takes it one means Mr Fairbrother and one, Mr Edmond?" begged Arbuthnot.

"We d—. One does. Indubitably," responded Tristan, now enjoying himself immensely, a delighted participant in the whole charade. He could afford to be. He — they — we — held all the aces. Saddler nodded. Tristan reciprocated, in as sad a manner as could be mustered by an ambulance chasing grief-stricken relative giving the go ahead for the disconnection of a life-support machine.

"Two: we take all the decisions. Mr Saddler is given a retainer of, oh, 100K *per annum*, with the proviso that he is a non-executive, non-acknowledged director." Arbuthnot conveyed to his client this coup in as

199

gentlemanly a manner as possible, by means of an avuncular raising of the eyebrows (open, sympathetic, not at all superior or scolding) that spoke eloquently to a fast fading agenda of should have beens. Saddler replied in saddened dumb show, shrugging his shoulders in a negative mimetic response to the efficacy of Arbuthnot's doubts. The fourth partner in this dumb show, Fairbrother, sat aloof, a dumbstruck participant with an autistic's grasp of the plot. By contrast, the recently self-appointed first member of the quorum was making a lot of noise about being a big noise.

"Three: Saddler can do whatever he desires to earn his corn outside his retainer, but never can he utilise the company's name for further commercial gain, nor utter a single syllable on the company's 'behalf'. In short, he's being paid to piss off out of it. In fact, we'd much prefer that he went back to America — whence he came. We can rescue his mess whether he's here, there or anywhere, but let him be in no doubt; we can't, we *won't* save his face sufficiently to have him associated with any future enterprises of ours."

Having briefly indulged his client's whispered response, Arbuthnot relented on his behalf. Saddler, who hitherto had lived by publicity was dying by it, dying for its opposite. With a shrug, Arbuthnot signalled the shunning of an empire.

"My client and I believe this presents him with the ideal opportunity to return to the land of his fathers. He would ask, however, for a retainer of £150K *per annum*, in *perpetuum*, *index-linked* to salaried — to higher executive earnings, payable to him or his estate until the death or bankruptcy of *Money Changers Changed* and its last board member. For this less than princely sum you get his absolute silence, absence and, it goes without saying, non-intervention."

"Dave? Dave? Fuck her! Are you in?"

"On what?"

"We take over the company, debts, ill repute and all. Saddler pisses off back to the States, we pay him 150K *per annum* forever, index-linked, for his silence, for his absence, for keeping out of our faces."

"Dollars or pounds?"

"Pounds."

"Seems worth it. One other thing. He divorces my — his — my wife."

Saddler, at last moved to response, if not eloquence, took up the gauntlet.

"I already have. My man, Marvis Steinlaager, called last night from Reno. It's been annulled." In the absence of Fairbrother's screamingly obvious ability to speak to the matter in hand, Tristan begged the blatant.

"On what grounds?"

"Non-consummation."

"But we have tapes," gasped Fairbrother.

"Don't doubt you have," shrugged Saddler. "Between ourselves – and I figure I can trust you now I've been screwed by you –, the real reason is the cocksucking bitch is screwing that motherfucking Whipsnade. But then, devious as I am, I don't have tapes. Besides which, without me she's nothing — nothing more to screw out of that source."

"And without her you are — ?" invited Fairbrother, intending mockery but achieving empathy.

"Just like you. We're all nothings now," the grimly smiling countenance of Saddler pronounced upon the future.

Chapter Twenty-seven

Busy, busy, busy. As thoughts of Sheril and Whipsnade (who next!?) dragged and drugged his days into night, inconclusive night, Fairbrother was preparing to front *Money Changers Changed's* new peak time cable show, *Fairbrother: In Your Face*. Crudely speaking, the show demanded that his latest persona be a crudely speaking saloon bar bore, who just happened to come replete with the connections and moolah we British so revere in our media mountebanks. The disastrous flirtation with religion denied, an unconvincing deathbed confessional if ever there was one, *Money Changers Changed* had changed tack and dropped the obscure 'making money morally' angle, evangel wangle, reapproaching that, after all, already near universal goal from a blunter, more readily identifiable direction. 'Making money moronically' might have been their new motto, had they felt the need to be so honest. *Little England* was now a theme park, pure and simple, in scale some way smaller than Alton Towers, in 'style' (where baaad means good. God!) some way larger than life, though unsurprisingly somewhat smaller than the larger than life that so characterises the 'attractions' to be found in *Disney* theme parks the world over. With one erstwhile church now a *McDonald's*, another playing host to a ghost train ride, another housing a kinetic waxworks of famous cartoon characters and computer game icons, it was less 'little England' in theme and more a sunset boulevard on the broken dreams and promises of a nation distinctly uneasy with itself. Ninety-five per cent Japanese owned, the emphasis was on the kind of mindless fun technological advances have made possible, no, mandatory. As such, *Little England* was a painfully apposite cameo, a coda to what had so-so become a deeply disappointing century in a deeply disappointed country – two world wars and one world cup aside. And the Little Englanders, with their perverse genius for seeing the good in the execrable (more than matching their self-diagnosed, self-aggrandising nostrum that they always liked to see success fail), lapped it up. Loved it. More comfortable with pomp and circumstance than poignancy and circumspection, the great British public patronised this themeless park, this blatant evidence of their nation's failure (burger bars, not one waxworked British cartoon, a ghost train ride whose avenging hero was *Godzilla*, gadzooks!) with all the misplaced enthusiasm of a prison escapee on the piss and on the rocky road to rearrest.

Tristan, old Etonian, Oxford blue, was the very man to take over the running of this foreign affair between sentimentality for the way we never were and obeisant wonderment at the way of the world out there. In an economy already rivalling Portugal and Greece for low labour costs and minimalist workers' rights (ours surrendered, no, reclaimed, theirs never gained), the profitability of *Little England* was a marvel in itself. In a nation profligately content to implode through 'inward investment', *Little England* stood for all that was great as far as conservative Britain was concerned. Concerning itself only with the smug sanctimony of having survived the 16 boom-bust years of Tory rule, oscillating dangerously between the preposterous and the prosperous, the nation, as electorally at ease with itself in spite of all the evidence to the contrary, like a true solipsist to a man flocked to *Little England*, that nightmare idyll of forest of Arden and virtual reality, thatched cottage and mega software houses, in search of *the* great British tradition; escapism. Under Tristan's nominal stewardship the Japanese elicited from employees and, by extension, customers, oaths of allegiance that would have made the preposterous panjandrums peripheral to our great democracy (and in lieu of a written constitution) cringe: indeed, make them appear to be linchpin functionaries of our democracy, the pussyfoot in mouth pursuivants, Black Rods, the whole Carry on Governing smarm school class of yore. If we are to judge by statistics – and who doesn't these days –, chief among *Little England*'s attractions were the mediaeval jousts, the theme skirmishing (particularly *Taking Port Stanley*: in even the 'serious' stuff, like war games, the con was scripted), royalty lookalike *It's a Knockout* (in which erstwhile members of the public were invited to ridicule themselves twice over by donning wigs, tiaras, the trappings of the nation's number one family, and flail each other to unbelievable heights of merriment and less than convincing audience hilarity, with phallic loofahs over a bathing pool populated by rubber crocodiles which last saw 'action' as animist out-takes from Saturday night variety spoof Tarzan sketches), *Norway nul points*, a virtual reality karaoke arena based upon the *Eurovision Song Contest*: guess who nearly always won?, *Vigilante Alley, Gunfight at the KO Corral, Police & Thieves*, a surreal attraction during which customers paid for the privilege to video actors meting out set-up, but always venial ('contextually provoked,' quoth the guide/met-er out-er in chief) police brutality. Patronised only by the moiety of our denizens clever enough to think keeping the Labour Party out clever enough, *Little England* was again a haven for the C1s and C2s and, with the evangelical connotations excommunicated, popular to an astonishing, even more miraculous degree than before. The 'feel-good' factor, invariably in bad taste, whether peddling its carefree wares via the leisure industries, or the ought to be more careworn arena of politics, was paramount to *Little England*'s success. As Tristan soon worked out, with modifications suggested by the world's most efficient managers, the place, Garvey's concept, practically ran itself, what with staffing problems at such a low anyone could be forgiven for thinking Arthur Scargill had never existed (anyone can be forgiven for wishing to so rewrite history, naturally). Frankly, fronting *Money Changers Changed*'s *Little England* operation for the *Mazakimbo Corporation* was not a full-time occupation, no job for a grown man. The time and effort required to oversee the sub-culture of a sub-culture that was a team of Japanese advertising executives, was merely one of giving limited imagination its head, its limitless possibilities in limited English with a limited grasp of a desperately venal and limited culture. Yes, the place practically ran itself. That is, if we may permit ourselves a lapse into the demotic (and, in the circumstances, permissible that and that alone may be), the Japs did. With Cal and Sheril fronting an amazingly successful, miraculously redeemed C&W cum gospel band (so bad as to give Conway Twitty a good name) on Sunday evening satellite and cable, and Fairbrother limbering up to take on the frankly schizophrenic personae of populist champ/chattering classes' chump as presenter of *Fairbrother: In your Face*, Tristan felt himself at a loose end. And, like all of us he turned to something he knew.

"I'm telling you, Dave, we need someone to pick up the porno threads. If Sheril can't be persuaded, we'll need another floozie. Whaddya say?" Somewhat preoccupied with the imminent pilot of *In Your Face*, an expedient rain check further saved the day.

"Not me, Trist. I'm very busy at the moment. Besides, my awaiting, adoring public may forgive me once for past indiscretions, but further involvement in that area would be begging for trouble."

"When you want to be dishing it out?" Fairbrother shrugged his assent.

"Or is it your no longer waiting, no longer adoring ex-wife you seek forgiveness from?"

"Don't you dare drag her into this. She's given up whoring."

"Unfortunately for you she's taken up with Whipsnade. Lost to a rival is lost to the world, Dave. Let her go."

"I can't. I still love her."

"No you don't. You love the pornography. You only think it's poetry. Only *you* think it's poetry anymore. Take a pal's advice. Forget her. Concentrate on the TV show for a while. It's a challenge and we need them to forget; to remember why we're here. In the meantime I'm going to oversee the second coming of *Gloss Bros.*"

"How about Carrina for editor?"

"No way does a wife of mine go out to work, let alone go down to work. No fucking way. I'll — we'll find someone."

"For my sake, right?" essayed a self-mocking Fairbrother.

"For fuck's sake, live a little, Dave, live a fucking little."

Chapter Twenty-eight

Nestling between bold and brassy adverts which defined rather than nourished him, overshadowed more than showcased him, like a prestigious babe amidst a prodigious wet-nurse, Fairbrother's birth as a TV pundit was never likely to be a less than melodramatic affair. Trading on a notoriety so established as to establish him as the most sung unsung hero still accorded cult status, hyped as a loose cannon on the ship of state, Fairbrother's brief was to get in the nation's face in the doubly de-evolved manner of parliamentary bores aping saloon bar ones, trading in the low oratory of the former and the invariable low blows of the latter. Assembled in what passes for a TV studio these days (a converted assembly hall in a comprehensively shut down school: the burgeoning, no, the budding, no, the forever bidding new TV stations weren't the only aspect of the life of the nation dangerously lacking in production values), Fairbrother's first audience, decidedly sporting more chips on shoulders than silver spoons, was composed of what could only pass for the great and the good in a nation in which the lynch mob represented the pinnacle of political discourse. Not that it is the author's suggestion that the great British nation had sunk to such a parlous low. Suffice it to say, should such a sorry pass becloud future issues of state and, Lord forbid, nature, we will have programmes such as *Fairbrother: In Your Face* to thank for that benighted fall from grace. And the gutter press, and classrooms squandered to TV franchises dedicated to entertain, entertain and entertain: but, lest we forget, lest we should forgive, *Fairbrother: In Your Face* was an ineluctable precursor of some seriously baaad (and this time I don't mean good) TV, some of the most mindlessly cruel sport seen in this nation since bear-baiting went its politically incorrect way some time since.

Dogging the motley multitude into roars of approval, disapproval, vengeance, malicious laughter, Fairbrother worried at his subject matter with an aggression so persistent it served to displace any remaining nagging doubts in his audience's collective mind. Aggressive, cocksure, drunk, I think is the best word, his was a powerful advocacy of, well, whatever he and the *actualité* deigned to deem his subject matter; his to champion, his audience's to cheer. Avowedly, necessarily, populist in tone, *FIYF* was launched with an innate, an *a priori* efficacy; if it hadn't existed someone just as venal, as ill-intentioned would have had to invent it. At once discursive and obsessive (ranting takes little consideration), Fairbrother cajoled, coaxed, connived with his audience to present a disagreeable unanimity to a watching world, in turns too tired, too involved, too implicated to protest otherwise. Championing what passes for the challenging in this post mock-heroic age (irony's full circle is *the* theme of the coming *fin de siècle*: be there or be square), challenging the worthy champions of what 20/20 hindsight and vengeance tell us were dangerously naïve causes and times, *FIYF* came down on the side of the vigilante, down like a ton of bricks on transgressors, sided with the victim, as a professional mourner prepared to kill for some work sides with nature's inevitable victims, swore inevitable revenge on criminals, those who would side with criminals, those who would advocate leniency on those bound to become criminals. On sexual orthodoxy, Fairbrother was orthodox in a manner that made one not merely forget his colourful past in this greyest of great Britannia's areas, as pray for a guest appearance by the Pope to lighten things up, as traducers were cast into the great void of lifelong anonymity, having witnessed their spokespersons' names – and by extension *their* acts – being blackened. On politics, while consistently declaring to be declaring for no party (it was still the law for public broadcasting), his every utterance, gesture, sneer, spit, snarl said Yob Tory, high horse working class Mob Tory; he and his audience were Thatcher's bastards in full battlecry. Tackling the man rather than the issues was the Fairbrother style, and if it took whipping up a frenzy on the terraces then that would be the chosen tactic. And if it never took whipping up a frenzy on the terraces? Wouldn't know, that show is yet to be made, let alone broadcast.

How much Fairbrother believed in this rabble-rousing is anyone's guess (Saddler, I'm sure would smile at his creation). How much he got paid for it was soon a matter of equally envied and approved of public knowledge. If taking on a persona somewhere between a 'Progressive' Ulster Unionist and a conjugally frustrated caveman led Fairbrother into a self-loathing approximate to that which he loosed upon the world he declared to be the enemy, at least the monetary compensation must have eased his pain. And if he believed in this philippic dressed up as a persona? Then he really does deserve our sorrow. Followed by death at our hands, at mercy killers' hands. Judge for yourself. Random, lurid snapshots of the first three shows should provide all the evidence any right thinking people ought to require to make a case against *Fairbrother: In Your Face* as an ill-thought out entertainment, unceremoniously invading the arena of current affairs and, amid much pomp and populism, stealing the show, stealing, it seems, an unrecoverable march on educated opinion.

SHOW ONE: On having invited a till then eminent Euro Federalist Trades Unionist and Frenchman (one man acting as an unwitting springboard for a multitude of fight them for the beaches prejudices: yes, shame he wasn't a Hun, but, then, prejudice knows no shame) to address his assembled audience – billed, without irony, as a 'curious, sometimes furious cross-section of the great British public' – on the whys and wherefores of the British declined Social Chapter of the Maastricht Treaty, Fairbrother saw fit to intercept one minute minute into the poor man's contracted five minute exordium.

"Normally I wouldn't interrupt such clever rhetorical flourishes, but it is my duty to put a growing sense of unease, manifesting itself with this — this — this kind of thing, the, uh, length and breadth of *our* country, and, unless I'm very much mistaken, amongst our audience." *Pour encourager les autres* had always been one of Fairbrother's tried and trusted mottoes and it didn't let him down now. Appreciative whoops and whistles burst forth from the studio floor where, a mere twelve months earlier, children would have suffered untold punishments had they manifested such malevolent high spirits. Struggling to make the point, roughly that the Social Chapter was necessary for Europe, particularly for Britain – 'part of Europe', lest we forget – lest they lapse into the third world, fuck it, the real world, Missyour Pisspoor (hilarious tabloid *nom de guerre* for M Pejpoir), our invited guest, remember?, was increasingly forced to fight like with like, eventually wrapping-up what had promised, threatened, to be a reasoned contribution by rounding on his audience, never forgetting, the country they so blatantly, so crudely (mis)represented, by swearing vengeance ('Promising Plagues of Picketing Frogs' as the front page of a 'mid'-market tabloid had it next day) on those who would undercut those who would honour social, societal, international commitments.

Slyly thanking his guest for "making a muddled issue clearer than even the best English ales", Fairbrother invited contributions from the floor, and, sure enough, out of the woodwork came that dry rot which passes for political debate, all the while critically undermining its very foundation.

"Can Missyour Pisspoor (laughter) ensure the British people that he really believes they can be persuaded to kowtow to the greater judgement of sheep burning farmers, Turk burning Nazis, cowardly and corrupt Ities? If not, I can assure him he has some explaining to do. If so, Missyour Pisspoor can sod orf back to Frogland, toot sweet." Unsurprisingly lost for an answer short of limited nuclear war – target sighted, fallout welcome – twice denied by fiercely patriotic audience self-approbation giving way to, if anything, louder, surer, shriller, more vitriolic catcalls, never at his most comfortable in the English tongue (snap! *touché!*), the doomed commissioner of *entente cordiale* committed the cardinal error of deploying the one French word known to all such English yo! men. For those as yet not yet (un)sophisticated and those hard of hearing, Fairbrother was repeating the misdemeanour like a QC stoking up a jury's disgust to the heights of imagined hitherto unimaginable felony.

"*Merde!* You can't say '*merde!*' on my show —", and, sensing audience participation of the tidal variety, — "on *our* show." And led, who knows, by the same mysteriously canonised being, who had a minute previously threatened the comity of nations by brandishing the brainwashed xenophobia peculiar to those jealous guardians of the collective fools' paradise, wherein misunderstanding punches well above its weight and, *lèse majesté*, wrests the crown of reason, of logic, this crowd, driven by the 'thought' that two wrongs make a right, *videlicet*, 'You're wrong! We're wronged! Our right!', could not not get ugly. Soon *merde!* and its English equivalent would come to describe the more demure, sweeter natured, less foul-mouthed, more open-minded in this midst. The commissioner headed back across the Channel – yes, the Channel – never wishing to be seen again.

SHOW TWO: Richard Lieuton, a 'left-leaning' ('hanging!' 'bent!' 'Dick!!', mused Fairbrother on perusing the CV, the purpose-built-up *mala fides* of the main guest on his second show) TV critic, all-round good egg, had 'fallen', like a lapsed curate, foul of the nation's mood. Sometime stand up comic, many times TV pundit on any topic: from adding a little sparkle to the normally heavy weather of current affairs, a smidgen of fruity wit to the right-on game shows that succeeded alternative comedy and its kind, as surely as their predecessors, featuring representative samples! of the population at large humiliating itself – and the rest! –, followed music hall humour, which in its turn teased titters at the expense of anyone — whatever, if you were a TV producer in a jam, Dick was your man. And if you were a TV viewer, well, Dick was Dick: as hard to loathe as he was to avoid. Whilst holding views which were often anathema to his adoring public, Dick still had them, still held them. Up until now. Because, hitherto he had only really held forth on *those* views in the obscure pages of an arts magazine TV column which, while read by not a few 'offensive' characters, was rarely patronised by the easily offendable. Between those secretive, then unexposéd sheets, he spouted decadent critiques which soon earned him the cult status leading on inexorably to the stand up and TV punditry. Where, in the *Up Yours Culture* TV column, Richard Lieuton could, *ergo would* berate the lowbrow complicity he detected in the nepotistic, inbred relationship between low horizened media and that which their audience, most egregiously C2s, were targeted to term entertainment, the Clever Dick of TV fame was a man whose pet hate had turned out to be his pet subject. From sitcoms idiotically obsessed to revolve around the nuclear family, to game shows exploiting the base desires of same, the Richard Lieuton of *Up Yours Culture*, former cult, now 'cunt!', saw low satire 'wherein beholders do generally discover everybod's face but their own'. Once scathing of the populace from behind the barricades of obscurity somewhat self-consciously erected by all at *Up Yours Culture*, on being made offers of wider fame, Richard Lieuton, cult thorn in the flesh of a sufficiently anaesthetized public, readily took the readies and adopted his alter ego of clever Dick, a man who could be funny about culture and politics, therefore seemingly wise, and culturally, politically right-on about comedy, therefore seemingly even wiser. In the past two years he had risen to the dubious status of the nation's favourite chat show guest, loved by grungies and grannies, a right-on smart aleck who nevertheless took great pains to distance himself from the polemical, which, informed by his own TV criticism, if little else these pell-mell days, well he knew to be his kind of stardom's, that is, showbiz's most likely agent of nemesis. What, then, was this figuratively avuncular 31 year old (favourite sister a dyke, to boot), doing on *Fairbrother: In Your Face*, already established as an avowed shit-stirrer of a show, at first discussing, then being shouted at on the subject of homosexuality? Because, though still beloved of the luvvies and the chattering classes (more so this last traumatic week), clever Dick Lieuton had had a rather calamitous fall from grace recently. As to the question 'did he fall, or was he pushed?', well, the newspaper which did the exposing, followed by the one which did the *exposé*, followed by the one which carried the exclusive, would all prefer to respond to their half of that possible charge in the time-dishonoured rhetorical manner favoured by a fractious Fawlty, his hotel invaded by Germans, himself more mentally unstable than ever, delivering himself of the immortal line 'You started it! You invaded Poland!' Put simply, Richard Lieuton had been outed. Put vindictively, Richard Lieuton had lived a lie, had pretended to laddish, even loutish good blokemanship, had been unfaithful to his quondam adoring public. And, as if the 'sordid' private life wasn't enough, the papers dredged up old *Up Yours Culture* TV criticisms to prove the bugger'd been a political subversive all along. In doing so, in trumpeting the uncovering of an 'underground art mag' in larger, bolder type than that deployed for Ministerial peccadilloes (and 'stories' don't get much bigger 'coverage' than that round these parts), they also proved the paucity of their own culture, even unto calling *Up Yours Culture* pejoratively 'cultured', imaginatively enough. And vindictively was how the opinionated sadists in attendance at *Fairbrother: In Your Face* liked to put it. Not excluding you know who, of course. A cult of the more egregious variety for most of his adult life – wilderness years included, wilderness years especially –, Fairbrother was once again tasting the overnight success granted notoriety's finest. Unsurprisingly cheered 'n jeered to the echo by a congregation comprising 90% homophobes, 10% homosexuals (the show had been billed as 'Fairbrother: Lieuton: Homosexuality: No More Lies'), the two men, bar none, with the highest profiles in the kingdom over the preceding week, were set for a right royal *tête-à-tête*, *sans* privacy, confidentiality, *avec said* melodromanic audience participating wholeheartedly, kit kaboodle 'n' kitchen sink. Buoyed on equally by partisan support and partial thoughts, whose combined malevolence was perhaps understandably misdiagnosed and duly processed into very partial opinions, Fairbrother was bound to dominate this battle, to determine its shape with his lowbrow blows and street fighting vigilantes at his immediate beck and call.

On suffering Lieuton's story – 'I didn't want to come out, but now I have been forced to do so, I'll say it loud, I'm gay and I'm proud' was the gist –, Fairbrother paraded all the sociological skills that charlatan psychology can lay claim to when he greeted this heartfelt and genuinely moving peroration with the challenge,

"No, all that's changed. This week's news is that we know you are a poof. *Then*, only you knew you were a poof. And a few other members of that exclusive club." (Sniggers descending into aggressive catcalls) "I mean, it's not as if you were in politics, not as if you had anything to lose. Or was you ashamed your old mum would be ashamed of what you get up to!? What a lifestyle! Yes, now we know something more. Now we know *then* you were a poof. Weren't so proud then, were we! Why didn't you tell us then, then, *Dick*, then? I mean, I used to like you." At this juncture, Fairbrother, histrion or no, was close to tears, a predicament his audience recognised and respected, suffered with 'one of their own' in silence, i.e., by shutting up, by cutting the inane comments from the floor, the hard man in a hard man's pub challenges.

"Well, you can still like me," moved a desperate interlocutor. In a rage of disgust – not self-disgust, this being a very selective reading of psychobabble –, Fairbrother bellowed *à la* Lady Macbeth *à propos* that damn spot, which 9 out of 10 housewives will tell you would pose not the slightest problem these days,

"No! Never! You betrayed me! Us! You disgust me! Us! And, being forced to come out into the open, being forced being part of what you'd call your nature, I daren't doubt, it seems to me, *us* !, the average blokes and blokesses that loved you, yes, *loved* you!, it seems to us that you disgust yourself. Here, take a card" (hands guest card) "a friend of mine once found useful. Dr Henrik Travolta, trick cyclist, Harley Street, 99 year lease, practically owns the bricks, cures more cures than an Arbroath fishmonger does haddocks. Got a receptionist that could cure any pooftah before the sesh — in place of the session — maybe you just need her phone number —"

"I don't wish to be 'cured', thank you very much," responded a stoic Lieuton, nevertheless stunned mullet fish-eyed at this diatribe. Having assured him that he did, indeed he did, even unto taking a audience poll (roughly 9 to 1 in favour of the motion or, more likely the controversy), Fairbrother sung the praises of the "free press that unearthed this worm" to the cameras. Depending largely upon the geographical location of the reception device, this paranoid peroration moved the heart or moved the bowels, left hardly a dry eye or dry seat in the house (as in the house in attendance). Love him or loathe him, you could say this about Fairbrother:

'Love him or loathe him!' Two further things could be said, one by either camp.

'You love him and I'll pity you.'

'You loathe him and I'll fucking hate you.'

SHOW THREE: The third show 'Making the criminal pay' conveniently honed in on the retribution innate in his audience. In an evangelical monologue (*à la* shady new Shadow Home Secretary to Tory Party Conference immediately following election defeat), which subsequently was to prove but the warm-up routine for the real fire and brimstone to come, a perfervid Fairbrother was, as ever, preaching to the converted. Having, the previous week slain that clever Dick, Fairbrother clearly strived to be taken seriously. Not just 'seriously', as in the actress who aspires to speak diction into a mike after all these years of ululating over a dick in all these unmentionable bit parts; neither the definition of 'seriously' dreamed of by professionally competent politicians whom preferment passeth by due to one more character defect than rival contemporaries (and here, while 'defect' is better defined by one drink-driving offence, one speech impediment, one ugly fizzog, 'character' can just as soon be ascribed to one racist outburst, one sexist comment. For while it is true that there are many non indigenes – *prima* and *secunda facie* – more women, just, than the combined forces of drunk-drivers, lispers, stammerers – whisperers and yammerers are other matters – and self-acknowledged ugly bastards, there are also amongst the 'active' electorate more non non indigenes, more non women). No, Fairbrother aspired to be taken seriously as an alternative comedian aspires to be taken seriously. And as often as not that isn't funny.

Slouching onto the dais with a glazed look most practitioners of the seemingly paradoxical art of delivering morose insights on life to office-workers in party hats would die for (the very look Lenny Bruce died 'perfecting'), Fairbrother was already the practised performer, the world weary, cynical hipster hired to mouth the customers' wilder thoughts. However, whereas Bruce and the like, if such there were, would ultimately aim to liberate – not just berate – the audience, admittedly, often through despairing images and grim reflections on self that, in tone and excess of content, could too often mirror little but narcotic indulgences, Fairbrother, often 'airing' his acolytes' only barely

213

recognisable thoughts, spoke to a very different agenda. Cathartic self-disgust would plainly be wasted on this lot. No, Fairbrother's task was quite, quite simple. Frighteningly so. It was no more than to set the ball rolling, to set the cat amongst the pigeons. Or, more accurately, chickens. Toss this shower the wrong polemic and they'd pass that parcel as if it were a suspect device, shifting uncomfortably from their natural position of *ex cathedra* stand-ins. But toss them a dolly that asked only their opinion and, in full agitprop roar, they would stoke up, then unleash the atrocious controversy that had so usurped, laid waste their thought processes. To vitriolic strains of encouragement more usually heard on football terraces, Fairbrother played their game and, grudgingly, one must admit, the boy done brilliant. Starting shakily, however, he caught them unawares with the relative sophistication of his rhetoric.

"Does crime pay? That is the question." ("No way!" screamed the lynch mob in unison, fantasising in the ugly, thoughtless, desultorily, unvigilant way that would-be vigilantes do.) "I'm afraid the answer is that it does." (Audience becomes a boom of boo-boys, "shame!" shouting shamen). "Should it?" begged Fairbrother, his audience responding 'generously', basically, on cue "No way! Noah waaaayyyy!!!!"

"Glad we're in agreement there." (audience titters, initially uncomfortable at their original misapprehension, finally comfortably, as near to self-deprecatory as they're going to get. And that's not so near, for now we are on familiar territory, now the jokes will be at the expense of others).

"Recent surveys have shown" (rapt silence, the silence of the lambs, of babies transfixed by politicians' kisses, of awe and unfamiliarity, of fingerpointed morals, but above all, of the good listening good to something, anything bigger than themselves) "that eight out of ten of our citizens favour the resurrection, um, reintroduction of capital punishment." (Raucous cheers and parliamentary "hear! hear!"s.) "And yet, and yet, and yet — as with Maastricht, what kind of consultation do we get? No sodding consultation, no referendum," (cries of "shame!", "hang the bastards!", "Irish scum!" and "Missyour Pisspoor!") "Are *we* , the great British public, going to sit back and take this, this criminal lack of consultation as our lot?" (Once the chattering classes' terminology of 'as our lot' had sunk in, the rabble roused themselves to more "No way!"s.) "Are we going to sit back and pass the other way"(?) – author's, not audience's reaction – "while the finest policemen in the world"(!) – ditto – "are being slaughtered by gun-toting, machete wielding drug dealers behaving as if they owned the country, as if they were in their own country?" Plainly 'we' were not. "And what about our children?!" (paternal and maternal "shame!"s) "Our children's children? Our grandparents, our parents, our wives, ourselves, in years to come? Are we going to reap the chaos currently being sown?" (church like hush) "Is there nothing we can do to halt this decline in standards?" ("Hang the bastards! Hang the bastards!", sang the audience, to a jingle popular a few years back quite correctly exhorting the listener to 'Hang the DJ', indeed, commonly misremembered as 'Hang the DJ', it was, in fact eerily titled *Panic*.) "Yes," smiled Fairbrother sleekly, "we can agitate for a referendum but that, as we all know, is very much a catch-22 situation." (A literary reference not beyond their ken! The audience treated itself to an appreciative murmur.) "But what can *we do*?" (Silence) "Maybe we can do something." (Audience lean forward, koppite gobshites all, in anticipation of wilder celebrations.) "How many here are in neighbourhood watch schemes?" (10% of audience raise their hands, arms at an uncomfortably redolent angle. Other 90% caught between envy, shame and admiration, eventually do the right thing and conclude their embarrassed silence in warm applause.) "How many would like to be in a neighbourhood watch scheme?" (Curiously, 100% rally to the cause.) "Enough said." (90% of audience sufficiently sheepish now to be rounded up, resolved to go wherever their dogged, barking mad master bid them.) "Tonight we have two guests, one a leading light in the *National Neighbourhood Awareness League*, the other a criminal, is as polite as I'm prepared to be. Ladies and gentlemen, please welcome Cuthbert Hudson and Wilson Racket." (The aforementioned enter stage left and right, the one to applause, the other to a smattering of applause quickly embarrassed into silence, punctuated by the assorted onomatopoeia of enmity.)

Introducing the two, Fairbrother astonished his audience into a nigh alien mode of reflection. "Cuthbert Hudson, meet Wilson Racket." (He's got it wrong, hum the audience, half in fear, half in hope. Only natural. Third show. People's champ. Suffers no fools.) "Wilson Racket, meet Cuthbert Hudson." (Christ, no! Jesus wept! The spade is Cuthbert Hudson, Cuthbert Hudson is the spade!, went the unaired, miasmatic mantra. Well I never! Takes all sorts! He's the rapist, though. No doubt about it!) Our man wasn't about to let such an anomaly, allow such role reversal go unremarked.

"Maybe you should swap names." How the audience laughed. How the laughter diminished to blushing silence as it became clear that the two antagonists did not or would not see the joke.

"Wilson, you have founded *The National Neighbourhood Awareness League*. Critics call you a vigilante. Does that bother you?"

"No. More grist to the mill. We aim to make neighbourhood awareness more glamorous, do away with the bumbling snooper stereotype that attached itself to neighbourhood watch."

"So, you are prepared to be called a vigilante but not to be called a neighbourhood watcher?"

"Absolutely. Image is all. To have any effect in an increasingly violent and diversified society we need to be seen to be having an effect. Got me?"

"Uh," dunced the host, in a perfect, that is, unknowing and undetected take-off of his audience.

"Let me explain —"

Fair's fair, mused Fairbrother, you invited him. But not to take a rise. Oh no.

"No need," interrupted the discomfited host with a 'that's what *I'm* here for, I used to be in advertising, I've got all my own shark's teeth,' dismissive sweep of the arm.

"High profile, high profits. That is, society profits. Got to be seen to be seen to be seen. Simple really. The more you let people know, the more they desire to know, the more they need to know, it's self-evident, goes without saying, axiomatic, *res ipsa loquitur*," listed the ex-jingle man, unknowingly betraying the tricks of the trade as surely as a cack-handed magician betrays his reflex withdrawal from a demonstrably occupied top-hat with uncharacteristically peckish dove pecked blood on no longer white gloved mitts.

"That's just about it," conceded a reluctant guest, his well rehearsed topic (*viz*, the selling of neighbourhood watch awareness) reduced to a flurry of soundbites, slogan-sized-chunks-nine-out-of-ten-owners of TV sets react best to, no more nor less relevant to his purpose than to shifting secondhand automobiles. Shiftily.

"Citizen's arrest?" queried the host somewhat gnomically.

"Sorry?" apologised the arrested citizen.

"Citizen's arrest? For it, I assume."

"Absolutely. Along with raising public awareness as to the rising crime rate, we wish to create a climate in which the beatability of the transgressor is manifest, in which the victim can best become the victor."

"Valiant," championed the host, subconsciously recalling the glory days, way before his conception, of an Empire secure enough to produce war comics, now merely, as perceived from afar, at least, at tragicomical war with itself.

After more backslapping chit-chat along lines self-righteous enough to grace the most exclusive chambers, Fairbrother deigned to involve the surprisingly well-behaved, still potentially lethal, exotic creature silently stonefacing it through an exchange of views whose orthodoxy were bound to strike him as so extreme as to enjoin of him a concerted counter challenge.

"Cuthbert Hudson," started Fairbrother, turning to audience, to camera, "is an altogether different kettle of fish. Less likely to exhort or inspire his fellow citizens to good deeds, more likely, more *than* likely to do the dirty on them. An 'accomplished' shoplifter at seven, house burglar at eleven, rapist at thirteen, murderer at sixteen, detained at Her Majesty's pleasure, released at twenty-five, yes, having served only *nine* years for but the last listed of those horrid transgressions. As I said, an altogether different proposition. Cuthbert, do you consider you have fully paid for your crimes?" enquired an obviously unbelieving host.

"Sure I paid for them. Paid my debt to society. Uh huh," ventured the ever suspicious guest. "What you insinuating, man?"

"What I insinuating, bad boy," bit back Fairbrother, in charmless parody of hapless, harmless parry "is that life ought to mean life."

"I didn't *get* life. I was detained at Her Majesty's pleasure."

"Only because you were so precocious a villain. No, life ought to mean life. The life of your victim, the life that we, the taxpayers allow you to continue. In fact, bugger 'life should mean life', death should mean death. You take a life, from us, ours, we take a life, yours, from you. Then you'd be nothing. A notorious footnote. A mother's disgrace. A good riddance."

"Man, you don't know the law of the land."

"That's rich coming from you. I might not know the law of the land, like you say, I'm no lawyer, but I do know how to keep it. *We* know how to keep it," as he gestured to the audience they reacted with contempt to this publicity courting, ostensibly reformed (never! give us strength! It's the law of the land that needs reforming, strengthening, not its transgressors!) recidivist, with their 'we don't know art but we know what we don't like', philistine defence mechanism bordering on, no, *taking* the offensive.

"Man, I'm suing you for defa — defa —"

"*Man*, you just provided all the evidence I need against you. Come ahead, loser, sue me. You've got about as much chance as had your victims." To raucous cheering and vicious jeering, Cuthbert Hudson, *citoyen* once denied, subsequently reinstated, was confronted by the arresting presence of Wilson Racket and sundry acolytes. As the fugitive exited (pursued by bears) trailing sluggish invective, which, in other circumstances, with other aims, would have been likely to endear him to the great British public, Fairbrother, begetter in chief of this party political, thrower of this bash, addressed the nation that was his, as if knowing all its addresses as surely as he'd got that bastard's number and mugshot into tomorrow's editions of the great big titted sister medium of print, BIG print.

"Remember, folks, it's up to you. Your community, your country needs you." And so this high kitsch Kitchener had at last gained the kind of fame for which, in truth, he had been ever destined: the sort that only money can buy and publicity increment: that billboard feeling, that cardboard cut out status of celebrity, where two dimensions are plenty, often one too many.

Meanwhile, back in *Little England*, no, somewhere else in little England, Tristan Edmond, Chief Executive in charge of his own eponymous glory, was entertaining the crowds, primarily by patronising minor royalty and major celebrities, all on call, always on call, on photo op location, for the inauguration of the latest attraction to take the theme park by storm. Declaring *Muggers Alley* (sic) open, Tristan retired apace, the better to witness the witless spectacle of those born to the purple and those whose rage, whenever caught out of camera shot, did a fair impersonation, skirmish down a 'metropolitan mean streets' updating of Deadwood, annihilating moronically monodimensional villains with 'don't toy with me' toy *Uzis*. Edmond thought of suicide. And smiled.

Chapter Twenty-nine

In my tiny white hand I held you
And prayed we'd never let go
For size doesn't matter
Our love was born to grow
With the faith of the faithful
You were the one to hear me out
From my sorries and troubles
You eliminated doubt
And to think how you forgave me
And how much you knew
I guess a trouble shared
Is no trouble for two
And from a past that has shamed me
You reclaimed me for myself
So I pledge to you my future
And to nobody else

Oh, the Lord loves a lover
Just like a sister loves a brother
And as our fates we discover
Born to be at one with one and others"

Cal Whipsnade, dobro steel, Stetson crowned, gazed yuckily at Syreenah Whipsnade, Anabaptist *extraordinaire*, as the latter provided the 'perfect' vocal accompaniment to his sub holiday show Hawaiian plunging elevator twang. In a voice deracinated from the soles of her cowgal boots, via Nashville, Tennessee, as rendered in *Faux* Glaswegian karaoke, the better to harmonise with long lost sis, Cheryl, now Winona Knoll, Syreenah Whipsnade lovingly returned her new husband's physiognomic entreaties, improving on them no end, no doubt, but grotesquely mirroring them nonetheless. Billing themselves *Five & Dime Faith Restored*, they were less a musical act, more an hilariously po-faced homage to those sub-musical inexplicables who bafflingly apotheosise the ugly redneck spirit of small-minded small-town folks. As American, and then some, as Americans abroad and at war – not in the same place, not in the same continent, not on your life! – and then some more, the success of *Five & Dime Faith Restored* was – always depending upon where you were, uh, coming from – refreshingly, or depressingly, limited to this side of the big pond. Whether the genuine article would prove to be more jen-yoo-whine than this lot is debatable, but, predictably, the Stateside *cognoscenti* of C&W wore their taste like a Marshal's badge, manifested their much championed community values in the manner of a territorial claim and a vigilant clam: they didn't need to visit these shores, and as for tourist C&Wers from lands afar, they were far less sighted, and far less welcome than invaders from outer space. Musically in that non-noteworthy limbo between the sheer hell that is heavy metal, and C&W so pious as surely to adumbrate its own come-uppance, *Five & Dime Faith Restored* compensated for lack of talent by excess of exposure. Alas, as is so often the way, the more they were promoted, the greater the seeming consequent demotion in the standard of public taste. Hyped as shamelessly as airlines in inflight magazines, *Five & Dime Faith Restored* had a one hour show, *It Can Happen For You,* transmitted three nights a week on what had grown to be the *Little England Satellite & Cable Channel*. A typical *It Can Happen For You* would feature three or four numbers performed by the hosts, a celebrity interview of some ten minutes duration, conducted by the husband and wife team in a manner about as incisive as a marriage guidance counsellor who knows when he's on to a good thing. As anodyne as *Fairbrother: In Your Face* was acerbic, *ICHFY* nevertheless rivalled that more egregious piece of showboating in the satellite and cable ratings. Though transmitted immediately before *FIYF* on Friday evenings, the fact that the shows were recorded kept the two ex-Fairbrothers apart, and, though not engaged upon strikingly similar enterprises their rivalry was now professional, in the way their previous run ins had been personal without their ever getting to really know each other. But, as sure as former mutually consenting/reacting parties to *coups de foudre* never really lose sight of each other's after-image, they were bound to meet again. Fate? No, the guy did it. Always the guy.

Lunching with Tristan at the 'Little England Pancake House', Fairbrother had important matters in mind. Three months into *FIYF* – spectacular beginnings sustained – he was faced with the old dilemma: how to maintain his position, his very self this time. Ostensibly meeting to wet the head of Tristan's fifth child (all irrefutably by him out of Carrina, childhood sweetheart – breeding for gymkhanas with a zeal to match godlikely certain RC's primarily concerned with the demography of democracy – full-time housewife, gainfully employed in charge of nannies, assorted cooks, domestics, gardeners and other factotums), the celebrations soon took on a more serious aspect. Over a meal other tellers of tales could really have made a meal of – until well after the meal was over –, the two friends returned inevitably to business. Toasting mutual success, it was Fairbrother who further proposed the long continuation of their current careers. Surprisingly, Tristan didn't join him in this wish.

"No, Dave, I feel I've got to do something different."

"But you're doing brilliantly — succeeding spectacularly where Saddler failed miserably. Surely that should be enough for any man."

"Yes, but *Schadenfreude*'s no substitute for satisfaction."

"Yes — but? — what are you getting at?"

"I'm not in control at *Little England*. The Japs tolerate me but you can be sure they'll give me the heave as soon as the time is right."

"What do you mean, when the time is right?"

"When the controversy that attaches to them for running the quintessential English company, in Mr Moto toto, can be calculated at less that the cost of having this chinless wonder front for them."

"But surely, as chief executive you have a say."

"Sure, I can say I'm chief executive for as long as that lasts. No, I've got to get out, be my own boss, my own man again. You in?"

"Well, I'm doing pretty good."

"Sure, you're a big bad name. But you're working for them too, remember. Besides, I don't think you're doing so good."

"But the ratings —"

"Sod the brainless and the nameless who watch your show. I've watched it —"

"Sod you then —"

"As a friend —" As they sat silently transfixed in brotherly *zugzwang*, you could have heard a piece-work Hungarian violinist tuning up to effect a reconciliation. Finally, admitting defeat, Fairbrother broke the minute long silence. In words, it was the no pussyfooting, no poofing Fairbrother of *In Your Face*. Indeed, it was nothing of the sort.

"Let me have it —" he conceded *sotto voce*.

"Sorry ——," said Tristan and meant it.

"Let me have it," Fairbrother repeated, with more volume and correspondingly increased resignation.

"No, I heard — you — first —— sorry, I'm sorry — but it's not —"

"—— me out there —?"

"No. Yes. You were never that illiberal. Rich, hell yes, illiberal, never. It's like I said, *Schadenfreude*'s no substitute for satisfaction. Just what's eating you?" Bowing as if to greater judgement, Fairbrother tried feebly to dodge the issue.

"You sound just like Saddler."

"He could always get to you." In silence Fairbrother conceded the point.

"It's still her — whatever she's calling herself — still her, isn't it?"

As if the uttering of her name would prove unendurable, Fairbrother nodded twice, each precipitous bow a seemingly theatrical device charged with steepening the shamefaced decline down which long welling tears now cascaded. The face so often in your face of late was in its hands, shaking in their precarious embrace, like a leaf in the eschatological moment before its always tenuous tendril snapped, precipitating its fall. A waiter with nary a mercenary thought stood sentinel, guarding other diners from the spectacle as much as the spectacle from they, from itself. Himself, for all the diners knew himself, Fairbrother, now in his cups, out of his face. After much entropic convulsion Fairbrother had pulled himself together sufficiently to give voice to his tragedy. Over large brandies delivered and drunk with astonishing haste, Fairbrother poured his heart out, spilled his little hill of beans.

"Bring the bottle, *garçon* - — one each. Where was I? Oh, yes. Sheril. Oh no."

"That's just it!" eureka!-ed Tristan. "I know how you can win her back!" Fairbrother gulped the air, then, realising it alone couldn't sustain him in this moment of crisis, yet more greedily gulped down a goblet of headier brew.

"Go on," he dared, in a croak surprising only in its entirely unintentionally comic aspect.

"We get back into pornography. Me, you and Sheril!"

"No! —— I —— I —— she —— you —— what about the wife?"

"Carrina's ultra-conventional. That is, she's used to money. Born to it. And she'll let her old man do anything, as long as that anything provides her with that something, that *one* thing she needs above all others.

We've discussed it. I laid the figures bare, so to speak. I — we reckon we could cream at least four times as much if we got back into porn."

"But — Sheril?"

"Think of yourself first. Then you can think of her thinking of you."

"But — she's a Christian."

"She's no more a Christian than Carrina's a whore. They're both faking it is all. I can live with Carrie — and you can —"

"You think so?"

"Absolutely. You can't live without her."

"But — me — my reputation —— Christ, pornography again. I'm just finished a show renouncing it."

"Then do one renouncing your renunciation. Better still, walk away from it. Get out of your contract, come back into *Gloss Bros* — me — you —— and Sheril."

"What about Whipsnade?"

"I'll take care of him."

"What about Sheril?"

"I'll get her in."

"No, I was thinking more of her —— her losing another marriage."

"Hey! It's yourself you feel sorry for. One at a time, one at a time. That's all I ask, and I'll cure you both."

Chapter Thirty

Everybody who was anybody was there. Just two years ago the inaugural 'Satellite & Cable TV Awards, Britain and Europe' (Europe here defined as those parts involved in producing/screening S&CTV in, up to and definitely including, thrice removed English), had attracted much ridicule, most notably a glorious put down write-up declaring that everybody who was once anybody was there. How the tables had turned. Even the coiner of said remark had taken the king's shilling, as offered by the fourth estate. Understandably, though his presence was to be as solicitously studied as that of a naughty child at a table. Less subtly, his presence, normally to be cultivated, tonight was to be shunned. Were those in attendance so lacking in confidence, so theatrically superstitious as still to fear this inverse Cassandra in their midst? Not a bit of it: magnanimity was what they lacked in vengeful spades. In the two years that had elapsed since that witticism at their expense, the 'so bad they're good' brigade who substantially peopled the oviparous, practically quarantined world of S&CTV, and nary a home beyond, had burst forth, fully-fledged for flight as the great and the good, no less. Oh, production values were still as miserly as a state pension but, as if in parodic homage to the triumph of technology over intelligent uses that has so undermined the character of this century, the national fibre-optic network saw to it that keeping up with the Joneses and keeping pace with change were, oxymoronically, no less inevitably, identical. Yes, tonight everybody who was anybody was here, the embarrassment that only recently would have overshadowed their vocations, handsomely, extravagantly bought off, if the glittering clothes show ambience that framed their every precious movement was anything to go by. In this top West End hotel the *Satcats* (*Satellite & Cable TV Awards*) were to be dispersed: amidst this convention of ex-BBC and ITV personnel now, alas, with nothing better to do with our time, one spotted a few familiar up-front characters. For some starstruck few from the working side of the camera, or the fast fading end of fame's telescope that was the all but shuttered world of the four channel terrestrial television set, the evening was somewhat of the nature of a school reunion, featuring those we had loved, loathed, *et al*, gone from our lives in a mysteriously inverse, arse-verse, rite of passage. Gone from our lives but not forgotten, indeed returned, were our old favourites: once again cherished by that new old audience out there in tele-revision land, forgiving of lapses in taste though rarely in popularity. There, surrounded by a bevy of bouncy, bubbly blondes he once would have vetoed as the tailpiece to his news broadcasts (no more: 'an attempt on the world's French maids' trampolining record! – for charity!') was Dan 'the loin' Burdock – *nom de théâtre et nom de guerre* – thrice news journalist of the year, twice newscaster of the year, now story of the night, of the year: entertaining was now his exclusive brief, and why not? in this the night of his apotheosis as the first, the formostest broadcaster in the space between the great grey satellite and dish and the likewise void between the ears. There, in the corner, drinking cocktails as if they and he were going out of fashion as fast as out of focus, in a blaze of *paparazzi* fired glory we espy Fairbrother, entrapped in conversation with Mazuo Okhibymi, Chief Executive of *Little England Satellite & Cable Division*. Up for the most hotly contested award of the evening, 'Most Original Contribution to Current Affairs', Fairbrother was variously occupied between maintaining, no, regaining earnest eye contact with his master, desperately seeking Tristan, and dreading the sight of Sheril and Cal. Tristan had confirmed that they would attend. Themselves up for an award ('Most Religiously Original Use of Country & Western': most original in such an unfledged, nascent, would that it were stillborn!, medium, how almost all awards were for most original something or other!), they were always bound to turn up. What Tristan hadn't as yet turned up with was Sheril's acceptance of the proposal that she rejoin *Gloss Bros*. And, tonight, with both bound to win – the competition wasn't just unspeakably bad, it was unspeakably worse – would seem to be the worst time to start anew. For Fairbrother it was the last chance — if she could be persuaded to give it all up — her ludicrous career — he was doing it for — well, *prima facie*, a more ludicrous career — then they could — they could — Tristan, where the fuck are ——?

"Christians, dare they fucka?" chirped the nip.

"Sorry —?" enquired a disorientated Fairbrother.

"That Syreenah, I'm going to ask her to become — how you say — my girl toy —?"

"You — and — Sheril — Syreenah," leapt Fairbrother, his imagination running a drunken riot, arriving, amid much demonic laughter, at the way forward.

"Excuse me, you little sad *sake*," he bowed. The gesture punctiliously reciprocated, he left a sanguine nip convinced that the laughter of his number one current affairs *san* had signalled the male bonding consent so natural back home. The number one current affairs *san* zoomed in on his target, parting the crowd scene, Moses like, or at least like a celebrity mounting a rostrum camera. Mad, bad and dangerous not to know. In this, the movie of his life, he had never achieved higher billing though, blessedly, he was at last aware as the proliferation of camcorder addicts (batteries not included, deluded *auters* attached, hooked) will hideously prove that life the movie rarely lives up to its portentous billing, be it big box-office spectacular or backstreet reminiscence. Fumbling, mumbling his way past the rhubarbative mummers, a face half-remembered here, a face unforgettably beautiful there, unbelievably accompanying 'here', he finally reached Tristan, greeting him to a long-lost brotherish, embarrassing mishmash of effusion and emotion rarely matched even on cod TV reunions (families who haven't met for 40 years should count their blessings; alas, they would then have no 'purpose' on TV).

"Where's your date?" enquired Tristan.

"I thought you were bringing her."

"Her? No, this is Carrina. That's no date, that's the wife. You alright?"

"You know, in all the years I've known you I've never known your wife."

"I trust you mean 'met'. I know, that's why I'm introducing you."

"Me? To who? To *whom*? " added a befuddled Fairbrother, like all drunks, ludicrously pedantic; fighting sense and syntax to the last bell: or, in the more aggressive cases, from the first bell.

"Christ, you're pissed. How do you propose to give a speech when you've lost the power of speech."

"Sssnomattah. Best men do it. Allatime. Wash I you besht man, Trish?"

"Don't you think you might have met the wife if you had been?"

"ZZZpoazz —zzoah. And who, *whom* have I the pleasure of, sweet lady?" slurred Fairbrother, sidling up to Carrina like a furloughed rapist, luckily rendered impotent, quadruple Xed, on Dutch courage.

As if a porno-director talking to an overly amorous horse, his talents to save for his maiden breaking thespian *debut* in an otherwise lesbian scene, Carrina patted the poor dumb beast on the noggin, issuing *le remonstrance juste*, "Down boy," and departed to knots of more interest.

Of course, the Edmond's didn't subscribe to satellite and cable. They didn't *do* that junk. Neither, one suspects did many of the guests, including those who appeared on the mutation, preferring to maintain that even distance from the multitude and view themselves (of course!) through the prophylactic medium of the video cassette. No, Carrina didn't do that junk: hence she has spoken her one and only line. Apologies, but there is no character to develop. Where were we? Ah, yes.

"Where was I?"

"Where were you *when*?" rejoined a perplexed Tristan.

"When you married — where is she?" Fairbrother concluded, baffledly addressing the space to his left, where stood nothing but ambience.

"Fuck Carrie," waived Tristan. "I —,"

"Thanks Trist. Not my type. You know —."

"Thanks Dave. It wasn't an offer. On second thoughts — yes, your type. Aren't they here yet?"

"I wish you'd refrain from referring to them as a couple."

"They *are* married."

"In law only. Besides, *she* won't stay married. She doesn't. Not for long."

"You should know. Are you sure you want her back?"

"No. But I need her. You see —"

"Let's not go through all that again. OK, you need her. She called my office —"

"And — ? And!"

"She sounded interested in teaming up again."

"With me?"

"Ultimately, one hopes. With us, rejoining *Gloss Bros.* "

"And you told her she could do all the, uh, editorial research she, uh, cared for."

"That's the funny thing. She doesn't want to."

"Doesn't want to what?" entreated Fairbrother of a grinning Tristan. "Fuck, what?" moaned Fairbrother.

"That's one way of putting it."

"What? What the fuck! Doesn't fuck anymore?! I'm not having that!"

"Indeed, what would it then be for. No, I doubt it's that extreme. She's monogamous is all. One guy gal."

"I'll believe that when ——"
"You're the guy."
"I'm the guy."
"You're the man."
"I'm the man," Fairbrother incanted as his automaton eyes lit up for the entrance of Sheril Whipsnade, *née* Saddler, *née* Fairbrother, *née* —— whatever was her maiden n — no — never really had one. In name only, when I met her, mused Fairbrother as used, abused, soiled, ever so slightly damaged goods headed this, their, his! way.

In a dress likely to be eschewed by a super model on the grounds of upstaging – not of modesty, never of modesty –, here she came, satin, glitter, glitz, nice tits still, no kids, not yet, not in that dress, hair bigger, better than ever, eyes, nose, lips, bosom, ahem, hips, legs, long heels. MMM looking good, kid, looking baad.

"Sheril," began Fairbrother.
"Yes," she replied.
"Look, let's not fight, I just said 'Sheril'."
"No. Yes. I'll join you. Cal, we're through. You can keep the award. You deserve it. May you continue singing that crap."
"But —— what about us?" moaned Cal, as Fairbrother licked his lips. Where long since there had been but the salty taste of tears he could anticipate her sweet bitch lipstick once again.
"There never was an us, Cal. I've always loved David. I think we all knew that all along."
"You might have given the rest of us a clue, you bitch," spat Cal.
"Fucking right," added Fairbrother, half joking.
"Do you forgive me?"
"Absolutely," bowed Fairbrother.
"Never!" barked Cal, baying at the moon like an old Hank Williams middle eight out-take. Fairbrother laughed at the vanquished sap, suggesting that his forgiveness was given as lightly to himself as to Sheril. As for magnanimity, no way, no fucking way.

As the fanfare sounded and the spotlights zigzagged the room dart eyed dark and light, as in a B&W prison break movie, the man they scanned for in vain spoke warden like from the darkened dais. Eerily disembodied, light headedly tipsy, Fairbrother addressed an agitated crowd. As the murmuring rose to fully-fledged grudging, the house lights at last bathed the stage. Theatricality had failed him again. Yes, it was definitely time to get out of showbiz.

"Ladies and gentlemen," repeated the now visible speaker, hereafter heard in almost complete silence. "I thank you from the pit of my stomach for this award. Cheaply honoured though I am, even I never thought such a hoax hotchpotch of current affairs as *In You Face* would take off to this extent. I thought, one show and they'll get the joke, see the spoof. But, no. Guess we're all stupider than we thought. Well, the joke's on you. This award for, ha ha, 'Most Original Contribution to Current Affairs' is a triumph for bad art. That is, it represents failure: failure to apprehend the difference between current affairs and gossip, between the news and the newsworthy, between the self and citizenship. When we parodied foul-mouthed bigots did people complain? No. Did they get the joke, then? Hell, no, all calls were of *prima facie* congratulation. When we did a show titled 'Political Correctness: Baby Boomers born with no sense of humour', did the viewers register the irony? No, they spumed that they be allowed to call a spade a nigger. No, they, you, we didn't write to redress the redneck idiocies I uttered in the name of all that we perceive to be too good to let go: all that, in reality, was never qualitatively good enough to last, merely goody, good, morally sanctioned by that most curious arbiter, public opinion. Did nobody notice the parody of a public opinion orchestrated by a sociopathic conductor, the diseased surrendering of the thought process involved in dancing knee-jerk attendance to a disharmonious St Vitus, the loss of individuality that becomes the rabble roused to any sophist agenda we proposed? Am I, a mere advertising whiz-kid turned pornographer, turned foul-mouthed bar-room brute, too sophisticated for you? Is culture, like empire, a thing of the past which we re-enact for the tourist paradoxically rooted in our rotting souls? Make no mistake, by casually accepting the lazy future of technological marvel and navel-gazing we commit the same mistake as that perpetrated by misty eyed reminiscence: the mistake of unrealism, the tragedy of pretence, the fallacy of 'ignore it and it'll go away' as well as the grotesque spectacle of celebration justifying itself, of pomp and circumstance lending occasion to manufactured occasions. We commit the unpardonable crime of being strangers to ourselves, bad emotional tourists to our own hearts, visiting, if at all, cheaply, staying uncomfortably, leaving quickly, vowing never to return. In that kind of world who will blame the pornographer? Not a soul, not a soul. Why is it that the people of this country eschew likings for obsessions, loving for hating, prefer the pain of denial to the pleasure of giving? Why is it that I, an Oxbridge boy, can and do make an obscenely remunerated living by money changing, short changing, swindling and cheapening, as opposed to an honest living by more worthwhile means? Why *did* I, we, *Boom Bros* as were, go into the sex industry instead of just industry? Why are we too embarrassed to ask?

"It can hardly be a coincidence that, in this country more than in others, shame so often shadows fame. Set 'em up to knock 'em down. Sure, we do that. The rarely posed supplementary enquiry is 'why?' I believe it is a little to do with politicians who score points off each other in manners more befitting crude sixth-form debating societies than the world's oldest democracy. But, in the world's oldest democracy, style, form is all, the content, to our shame, can not help but fail to live up to the surroundings. So, who in this respect set 'em up?

"Everyone of us who ever hated a foreigner better than they were capable of hating us, or indeed themselves: with that superior disdain of the super-civilised, the last, politest withdrawers from Empire. Everyone who endorsed the short-termism of the great British political system by voting for one of its parties to undo the other lot before doing anything themselves. And where else in the world could government ministers be ruined by sexual peccadilloes so mild as to place them more faithful than the *de facto* norm these days? Do we care more what our politicians get up to in bed than what they get up to in committee? I'm afraid we do, and I'm further afraid we are far from unique in this most disrespectful respect. But I believe a number of common factors play upon the British people, earning them a report card on the 20th Century which, *passim*, reads 'could have done better'. Much better.

"First, the obvious one, sex. We just aren't grown up about it, almost uniquely in the known world we prefer to find it either dirty or funny every time. Sure, it can be both, even both at once. But just once in a while I wish we'd find it sexy. Second, the political system. Would be blue-blooded blinkered self-interest fights red, red rose tinted reminiscing. Where's the vision, the future in that? System'll have to go. Third, celebrity is fucking us all up. From the entertainments industries, to those more entertaining to read about than watch, listen to, laugh with, read, aspire to be, we are in thrall to inflated egos and salaries and consequently in danger of trading in our own personalities for something, anything that looks good on paper. And nothing looks better on paper than a healthy balance sheet; a work of art, of financial legerdemain, its admirers don't want to know the art but they sure know what they like. And an unhealthy balance sheet? So practised are we all at seeing the bottom line, and going for it, that even accountants tend to eschew cost-benefit analysis these days. In the globalised sound bite culture of commerce this country is uniquely advantaged to lend its language to those much in demand sloganised simulacra of commerce, at the very least. Instead, what have we done but bought immediacy lock, stock and barrel, translated the sound bite culture into the shareholders' culture, where those with the remote, indeed unaccountable control are beyond entreaty, themselves perfectly capable of taking a political decision where the politicians have already abandoned the arena. If the market is all, then logically we all owe our democratic duty purely, indivisibly, untranslatably to ourselves. Nothing else. As subsidies die there is only profit making. Our kind politicians want us to have a bit of that, too. Some of us more, infinitely more than others. And finally, what makes this country so disappointing is an event like this. From the universally admired independence of the BBC to this: 40 channels with nothing on: the ultimate party apolitical. Alas, divided by a common language or no, the United States and the United Kingdom marched, in that order, down the road to deregulated tripe in the name of entertainment. Yes, the whole world's been so colonised, but in the guise of economics, too. As quantity usurps quality on satellite & cable, so its corollary hits that supposedly wider world which represents the country as a whole; and which came first, the bad news or its bad portrayal, matters little. As society polarises, so the quantity pocketed by rich shareholders and *laissez aller* government sponsored entrepreneurs undermines the quality of social provisions. Of course, you've heard all this before. But not here, never here. And, yes, I admit, never from me." (Audience at last react, like an aggressive sceptic exiting hypnosis with the grumble 'See, you'll never hypnotise me'.) "So just where do I get off lecturing you thus?" (Sections of audience baying now) "Me! A pornographer! A money changer! An advertising executive! A venal evangelist! A populist hero/thug! I don't. There is nothing I can do to redress these demons in my past, nor is there anything I personally can do to save society, such as it is, from them, from itself. No, all I can do, all I am doing is being honest about them, their highly remunerative relationship to myself, their integral part in all our slipping standards. You takes your choice. That is why tonight I wish to renounce all my past guises bar one. Oh, no money's getting donated to anyone but me and my bank, but I do wish to go on record in defence of but one of my professional indulgences these last few years. Not advertising, no. Not evangelism, hell no. Not even my nascent descent into political dabbling, let alone the figure of the people's thug, for the being of which I am dubiously honoured here tonight. No, I reject this award as a corruption too far, one none of us can afford. Further, I resign from *Fairbrother: In Your Face* and announce the reformation of *Gloss Bros*. Why? Because, in attracting bad press, though typically in this country the wrong kind of bad press, pornography is the only one of my career options likely to get the press it deserves. And I felt it was about time that's just what I got. Ladies and gentlemen, thank you, but no thank you."

   Casting his idiot cards to the multitude, Fairbrother departed the stage to a hushed silence, broken first by a very jolly Edmond's laughter "So that's why he got so pissed!", followed by manic cackling from a female in his company. The audience joined half-heartedly in the merriment. Sheril smiled. There was a lot to laugh about.

Chapter Thirty-one

To a stunned gathering of the media's great and good at a top west-end hotel, David Fairbrother, aka *Fairbrother: In Your Face*, resigned from the top-rated satellite & cable TV show of that name. Declaring himself disgusted with the nature of his fame, the ex-people's champion relinquished his crown, effectively abandoning his faithful supporters. We heard your reasons, Fairbrother – we are where the news is – and, quite frankly, they stink. What was it that made your fortune in the first place? Yes. *Boom Bros*, never a company to deal in the more principled areas of economic activity. Areas which you now inexplicably choose to champion. What then? *Gloss Bros*, whose area of, um, activity, while widely condemned, was stoutly defended by this paper. You were quite right to sell "that stuff" (as the stuffed shirts at the so-called liberal *Guardian* derisively called it) as long as you stayed within the laws of the land. This you did and, indeed, the success of such high-profile, respected and admired entrepreneurs, in an until then covert area, did a great deal in keeping the salivating wolf of Euro-porn from our shores. You and your *Gloss Bros* colleagues – not forgetting your gloss sister; we, like you could never forget *her*! – redressed that hoary old paradox which, like a particularly obsessed stalker, has bedevilled adult entertainment in this country: you made glamour glamorous, took the dirty old mackintosh containing, shrouding the dirty old man out of the picture. We'd like to think we were in the same business!

'And who welcomed you back from the wilderness years with more enthusiasm than us? Your family, maybe, though we have many, many reasons (some as yet unpublished) to doubt that. On the day of your return to the *Gloss Bros* board '(sic)' we said "The Prodigal has returned. Britain is a better place today". And did we report on the more sordid tales that emerged from your years of disappearance? No, we were sympathetic, even *The Times* said we were "uncharacteristically sympathetic" about the whole affair. We didn't put the boot in: that would have been hypocritical of us. After all, who championed the derring-do of *Boom Bros* more than we? No one! Ever champion of your champions, we supported you in your rehabilitation, even in the ill-fated evangelical dabblings. Finally, we rhapsodized over *Fairbrother: In Your Face*. Why did we never leave your side all these years? Why did we never feel the need to criticise you until today? Simply put, with last night's resignation you showed that your championing of the common man was all bluster. So, you say that you were parodying him all along. Fine. Good joke. But hasn't your desire to be the right-on goody two-shoes of the chattering classes come a bit late in life? Do you owe us, your people, nothing for your success? If the answers are no then we have misjudged you: may you rot in hell. But if, as we suspect, you have reason to retract last night's intemperate display of too much champagne and too much socialism, we will be the first to accept your apology and forgive, once again, the indiscretions of one of the great achievers this country can ill-afford to lose. Think again, Fairbrother. Think.'

Fairbrother didn't think. *The Sun* wasn't aware of the irony in such an exhortation. Fairbrother, not the Fairbrother of *Fairbrother: In Your Face*, was. Fairbrother smiled. Sheril laughed. Fairbrother laughed too. *Chez* Fairbrother was coping remarkably well with that morning after feeling. Despite a hangover that threatened traumatically to recall the inglorious days following the split, Fairbrother felt the better for the wear and tear of the night before. And, it has to be said, being lamented in *The Sun* would do any right-thinking man a world of good. Oh, alright, halfway, recently right-thinking. The morning was glad and confident. He was going for it, glad and confident that he appeared to have it within his grasp.

"Sheril, are you going to leave Cal?" She laughed some more. Oh, how she laughed. Most girls with, um, Sheril's history do it like drains, any good humour soon spiralling downwards to the darker sediment of cynicism. Sheril did it with an *ingénue's* giggle, whose main purpose was inevitably closer to teasing than appreciation.

"Turn the page," she said, toning the performance to a sweet, mothering smile.

"You have!" he exclaimed, probably the last *Sun* reader in the country to know (for this glad, confident 'morning' was first espied at 1500 hours), certainly the last attender of the *Satcats* to learn the lie of the land. Though not quite meriting the double-edged honour of a *Sun* editorial, she had made the gossip pages. And how! Informed – by *The Sun*'s gossip columnist – of his ex's exing of her most recent ex, her subsequent retiral from the country scene, her declaration of her imminent return to *Gloss Bros*'s boardroom, her forthcoming marriage ——

"You said all this!? Last night?"

"Aha. You were pretty drunk. Don't you remember any of it?"

"Well, I knew something had occurred, or —"

"I wouldn't be here."

"You wouldn't be here."

"With you."

"With me."

"Forever."

"Woahh!" recalled Fairbrother. "You said we were getting married. In public."

"Well, the last one was so quiet."

"No, you announced. In public. That we. Were getting married. Aren't you forgetting something?"

"Oh. Will you marry me? Is that it?"

"No. You know I will."

"Yes, I know you will."

"You knew?"

"Yes," Sheril blushed becomingly.

"And I knew you knew." Fairbrother didn't.

"So, we're devious. What's to stop us?"

"Well, we've been through it all before."

"So. This time it'll be different. Besides, you said you would."

"When? Last night?" stared Fairbrother blankly, his recall in searchlight mode, alas itself suffering a power cut.

"No, here. Just now. When I said 'will you marry me?' you replied, 'you know I will'."

"Well, yes, but —"

"No buts. Let's do it."

"You kill me, Sheril, you kill me," he shrugged.

"But what a way to go," she giggled, as she jiggled atop his grateful body, his ever grateful body.

"But what a way to go," he complied.

Chapter Thirty-two

Tonight the Fairbrothers would celebrate their first anniversary. Their second first anniversary, in fact. Such are the complications (some would say poetic justice) which hound the rich and famous, to depths and resorts, oh, appreciable to the rest of us, there wouldn't be a lot of celebrating either. In a world more loveless than lovesick, the prognosis for second marriages can't be all that good. Particularly when those, to whom, unbelievably, no legal impediment could be raised, were, celebrities both, David Fairbrother (second marriage) and Sheril Fairbrother (fourth marriage). All in all, the match had lived up to its billing. Like the ceremony, the marriage was conducted too much in public to be a tolerable affair. That was just the problem. What might have made a tolerable affair was turning out to be a hellishly unpromising commitment. In most failed marriages the questions most often begged are 'what went wrong?' and 'did we change?' *Prima facie*, these questions aren't quite as relevant in remarriages. And yet, and yet. Such had been the apparent confidence with which the couple had entered into this solemn contract, that even friends in the know felt, against all odds, that it might just work out. So, what went wrong? Who changed?

Unlike the first time around, it wasn't Fairbrother's jealousy which precipitated the fall from grace. Nor did business rivalry play any significant part in the parting of the ways. Indeed, business had rarely been better, *Gloss Bros* were back in big business, Fairbrother's reputation, particularly as the 'respectable woman's pornographer', was ludicrously elevated. Still, to be shunned, though tacitly admired somewhere between grudgingly and ashamedly, by polite society, was nothing new to Fairbrother. Such snobbish snubbing was more than adequately compensated for by his being patronised by the plebs and feted in their versions of newsprint as, well, the type of businessman the plebs liked to do business with. No, this time the troubles emanated from Sheril's almost devout reluctance to ignite the spark of jealousy in her husband. So, she had changed then, certainly. For the better, the purists would attest. Alas, Fairbrother had gone through a far greater, a far uglier mutation, quite certainly not for the better.

At first Sheril's refusal to adopt her previously well-studied supine role was tolerated by Fairbrother as a reluctance easily to be surmounted. Money would see to that. Incredibly, however, his blandishments were declined; Sheril accepted a lesser salary in exchange for her previously worthless honour. Once surrendered as readily as a pervert's desire, it had, taken on a characteristic unfathomable to the surface fixated Gloss Brother. Call it mystery, call it depth, call it retrospective innocence, call it what you will, all the poets in the world could not have inspired appreciation of it in Fairbrother. To his horror it dawned on him that what he really loved about Sheril was —— Was? Nothing, really nothing at all in particular to her. Not only did other women excite him more than his now monogamous – and reluctant at that! –, almost dowdy wife, other women's, erm, accoutrements were what really turned him on. Stripped of the lipgloss, the 'fuck me' pose, fuck it, the 'fuck me' 'pose', the leather, the never windswept, ever sculpted, always big hair, the appurtenances, nails, spike heels, the dirty, doing the dirty, *filthy* look, Sheril stood revealed as —— just another chick, really. And one who plainly wasn't trying her considerable, much considered best. Appreciating the effort that women make as much as the next man (albeit, yes albe *it* the next man in the queue at the porno-emporium), Fairbrother's lurid afflatus, his heavy breathing, if you will, disappeared into thinly aired sighs as his love doll turned out to be flat, unattractive stripped of artifice of role playing. Even in the sack she performed with about as much expertise, passion, gusto, acting ability, sexuality as a fat old frumpy nudist volleyballer in one of those decidedly unsexy, ugly Super 8 films in vogue before filth was finally liberated. And by whom?! Fuck it, man, she owes me *it*. Everything, she owes me everything, would grunt a limp and disenchanted Fairbrother as sex again climaxed unsatisfactorily, instinctively, sadly, favours once granted, now withheld. Deliberately! Bitch! For the first time in their ill-starred trysts, Fairbrother took for himself a 'significant other'.

Suzi Uzi was discovered in the Readers' Wives section of *Jiggle & Bonk*, a product of a rival publishing house of illrepute. 'Discovered' is probably the wrong word. Uncovered, unmasked (unlike so many others) and nakedly unmarried. Plainly she was always bound to be discovered, uncovered, what you will, what you will. Resembling, for all her spectacularly animated life, a younger, more contemporary, filthier Sheril, this girl clearly had potential. Fairbrother first met her, where else but in *Jiggle & Bonk*. Perusing this rival product more out of matrimonial frustration than any self-vindicating professional duty, Fairbrother stumbled upon this unlooked for, no, groped for pleasure and knew he had to have it. Her. It. We've all seen these movies, where the stargazer fixes fate full in the face with a combination that is a once steely and misty eyed and recites, 'I have to have her'. And, while the line is delivered with all the apparent sincerity and fluency of a Tarzanogram in a foreign tongue, you just know this transfixed automaton means it. Between then and the inevitable happy ending, however, heave the vicissitudes which lend the tale the drama, not to mention the story itself. This wasn't one of those cases. Sure, Fairbrother's eyes were as doubleglazed as his hermetically sealed environment, replete with a translucent, juicy Suzi Uzi lapping him up like he was a naughty child betraying a *tableau vivant*; but when he indeed chanted the immortal line to his no longer inanimate inamorata, you knew she had to be had. Money talks. End of story. This wasn't the movies, and Suzi, starlet though destiny would have her, was about to be offered a far simpler script than even Hollywood could dream up. And to be fair to Fairbrother, she couldn't have handled any other kind. Further, to be fair to Suzi Uzi, she wasn't to know this; her ignorance presented the severest limitations as the greatest possibilities.

All the while Fairbrother's gaze strayed, Sheril kept her eye firmly on the prize. Not to mention Fairbrother. Disgusted by his disgust at her refusal to appear in suggestive and provocative poses, Sheril set about completing her sexual education on the editorial pages of *Girls' Talk*, an all sex text adult magazine written 'entirely by women' (Sheril, again in various guises), 'entirely for women' (Sheril now, not then). *Girls' Talk* took an editorial line which infuriated feminists and puritans alike. While refusing to appear in, or publish suggestive poses, Sheril's editorials cried out for hardcore porn as a liberating force 'Time this country fucked right' was one Op-Ed banner. Roughly speaking, its line was that pornography could only be said to exploit women in its soft-core guise, in its peculiarly British guise. In this version the innuendo that is so crucial to male bondaging, from public school to the City and the Houses of Parliament, from no-way-out education to dead-end-life, was amply mirrored in the voluminous smut spoken by the pictures of the pre-volcanic slut. Ever available, taken in photographs but never by men, this version of female flesh represented a voyeur's delight, invited a lonely hand's caress. Such sexing by proxy was only fully, unquestioningly achievable in the genre of soft-core. The hardcore, the *echt* stuff, as available to consenting, if disappointing, adults in most other civilised nations, didn't invite such cold eyed, glazehearted detachment. Indeed, as *Girls' Talk* was never too coy to point out, thirty per cent of the hardcore videos rented in the USA were taken out by women, as much of the remainder being hired by couples as by men only. Supposedly. Only by focusing the consumer's gaze on sex in all its glorious, glamorous, spurious availability, i.e., its unavailablity, as symptomised by soft-porn, did we, milk the dirty mac, dirty jack-it market, foster the idea that sex achieved its apotheosis through the at arm's length individual. And, argued *Girls' Talk*, video, in all its writhing, graphic representation was a more honest medium than was the stills photograph: for, for all its inartistic depictions of male dominance, the non-simulated sexual act, while inaccurately directed, could never quite depict the female as pure victim, as merely submissive in waiting. 'Wake up Britain' cried *Girls' Talk*, sex is enjoyable, here to stay, not something to frighten the horses with. With a circulation matching its notoriety, *Girls' Talk* was at once an unwilling *cause célèbre* for pornographers and the *bête noire* of that 69er of an ethical alliance, perversely formed by the more radical feminists and the more reactionary puritans. Fairbrother's response to his wife's, um, outstripping of his fame was typical of a man with his track record; that is, it bordered on misogynistic psychosis. That her various, spectaculr career moves, from seemingly willing victim to successful businesswoman, to faithful banshee, to faithless sexpert had been better executed than his own rankled also. Naturally. No, it wasn't women he hated, it was Sheril —— and —— and —— her — type.

Declaring his wife a dyke (strictly not true), he sought her reincarnation in the unobtainable dreamscape of Technicolor simulacrum. So, tonight, on their first anniversary, Sheril was celebrating the estrangement with new found friends, while Fairbrother was seeking solace with a new found stranger. Recognising his wife as finally irretrievable, that is undesirable, Fairbrother this night asked for Suzi's hand in marriage.

"But what will your wife say?" shot back baby doll, displaying all her customary cognizance. Fairbrother was charmed.

"She'll probably say she is a legal impediment, but bugger her, Suze. As soon as we're divorced we'll get married."

"You mean quicker than last time?"

"Sorry?"

"You're going to divorce me to remarry me! Wow, two dowries! Gee, David, I'm the luckiest girl in the world."

"Then, will you marry me?" shrugged Fairbrother, accepting his fate as the luckiest guy in his pathetic little world.

"As many times as you like," she simpered.

And so it was, Fairbrother jettisoned the liberal declarations of principles he had announced in his 'in your face' resignation speech, just as soon as he realised they meant nothing in relation to Sheril, to 'her type', really his type of woman.

Chapter Thirty-three

Whither venture those with whom herein we have made acquaintance, if not found common cause? As our story is bowed back into life so our characters must be unleashed back upon the no longer watching world to set themselves free, navel-gazing or resenting the earth that bounds them from flight, older, yes, wiser, who can tell, who can tell?

Cal Whipsnade now fronts, yes, that is the verb, as an implausible consumer endurable, the satellite and cable shopping channel, *For Your Leisure*. Overseeing a global networking franchise of bogus sales, hocus-pocus salesmen and women, he is aptly as convincing, tasteful and truthful as the catch-'em-hook-line-'n'-sinker-phrase 'Reduced to Go!'. Sumpsimus tells us that the phrase is a common misreading of 'Pay! Sucker!' but sumpsimus isn't much in evidence these days. Unlike Cal. Married, one kid (i.e., the wife: 'ex' game show hostess; how does one leave behind a life that wasn't?), he presides over a perpetual hawkathon, crossing the credibility gap into hearth and home through the electronic legerdemain of an unappetising dish on the wall, of a verminous tunnelling of fibre-optic vermicelli, delivering slender means to slender ends, carrying light, yet delivering darkness to the gentiles. He's happy, they're happy, everyone and every one's a winner, bargains galore: even the poor, benighted bastards, whose only affordable purchase from so aptly named disposable income is that tartar emitting electronic Tantalus in the corner, promising little, delivering little, tempting, diverting a lot: well, it's better than nothing. Cal? Happy? With one notable exception.

Tristan Edmond works day and night, night and day under the height of the *Mazakimbo Corporation*. As *Little England*'s 'Director of home team operations' he is charged with overseeing the dwindling aspects of that dwindled representation which still bother to refer to its eponymous land. Rumour has it that *Little England*, already 70% Japanese owned, 30% US owned, will soon lose even the minuscule nominal dignity it has remaining, hasn't yet remaindered, and masquerade anew under the name of *Pacific Basin Street*, combining Mardi Gras with virtual reality in a manner that makes Rio's street carnival seem real, seem everyday. In spite of his reduced functions, Tristan, too, is happy enough. Always the least ambitious of our characters, he has done remarkably well for himself. That he had once done remarkably better troubles him less than it would (it does, it does!) the others. For that, for Tristan's semblance of humanity at large, may we be grateful eternally. Ah, men!

Garvey Saddler, always the most ambitious of our characters, is now preparing his presidential candidacy as leader of the *You!* party (their exclamation, my italics) in the land of his forefathers. First he must celebrate his 35th birthday to qualify for the race. The human race, one hopes, may continue to deny him membership for a few more years yet. But, my, how he's bounced back! Well, no, not exactly. At the last count the *You!* party had 'support pledges' from but some 2% of the American electorate. All things to all men, the *You!* party is that rarity amidst political parties: one that tells no lies. No truths neither, granted, but no lies. With no immediate prospect of election, no policy hostages to fortune, the *You!* party says simply *You!* That the most important members of the political process, the electorate, haven't yet bought this post-colonial ennobling, this 'have yourself a muthafuckin' nice day at others' expense' which has so disingenuously usurped the creepy-crawly 'Sir' of our own *ancienne noblesse,* isn't down to their sudden embracing of principle. Oh no, no, no, the *You!* party is in the doldrums because, in this kingdom among, *above* kingdoms of the blind the cock-eyed and blinkered faith is invested in *We! The People!* (10%), the *National Rifle Administration* (8%), *Power to he People – Black Section* (11%), *Power to the People – Hispanic Division* (6%) and the *Moderate Confederates* (6%). *The Democrats* (26%) and the *Republicans* (29%) still set the pace but no longer the agenda. Garvey is currently bunkered down in Arkansas with former Capitol Hill hotshots and Madison Avenue whiz-kids planning on a *You!* party relaunch, with no more emphasis on what *You!* stands for (still nothing) but much, much more on what it stands against. His day may yet come.

And me? Happily married to Suzi —— ah, it's time, long since time to come clean. Okay, who guessed it? Congratulations, suspicion's a healthy quality these days. Oh, there's enough, a plague of it about alright but, well, not of the right kind. You've got me at last, at last you've got me. Sheril, that's me. Well! —— so what's it all about —? —— a new slant — more *roman à clef* than memoir, in fact, if that latter still passes muster as a valid expression. Why did I, I whodunnit, do it? These people, these times were times when dreamers and dreams came true, when the darker corollary dawned. Yes, that's oxymoronic, but these were idiotic times. Yes, it was black and white, good and evil but, then, I believe, or rather I disbelieve anything than that such heavens andsuch hells are the crippling products of man's fevered imaginings. Our characters, though nominally incorrect, are substantially —— insubstantial. Their inventiveness, surrendered, fightless, to the profit motive, has, alas, proved contagious. Yes, come clean, I am now a *bona fide* publisher, my own *inter alios*, this book is written under a *nom de plume*, only a shameless self-publicist could compose a sentence such as this, *quod erat demonstrandum!* In this book, then, I set out to biographize the *Boom Bros* boys – names changed to protect the innocent. My part in the story? Well, I'm a woman. All woman. All women. That's my part.

Ah, the *Boom Bros* boys, the applied scientists of commerce, their lives are journeys, such as they are, from the unknown to the known, such as it is. And up to now mine, my life, too, has been in the same direction, though differentiated by being conducted as purer science, if you like. Both bogus, of course, both, all of us characterized by ideas, by epiphanies above our stations, speculation masquerading as progress, as earth-shattering unearthings — as gropingly we discover — that — that the true heroes and heroines of this book are the fathers, the mothers dishonoured by offspring; of this, my life, the heroine is my beloved Cheryl, my sister, hers, the artistic, is a voyage true and brave in its discovery — from the known to the unknown ———— clear-sighted and dreamy at one and the same time, she discovered, bless her, *we* discovered that —— that —— than one instinctively knows that —— one knew all along.

I know, I know, how did I get mixed-up with this miasmatic mishmash of ne'er-do-wells made the great and the good, the sickening smellers of sweet success, how specifically did I, how *could* I, a smart bitch and make no mistake, deal with the dirty little devil that is man's pornographic image of woman, that sinister synecdoche misrepresenting the sisterhood, all woman, all women? Someone, anyone, everyone! would have done it. Not anyone else. I mean *to* me, eventually to me in every particular, to my sex in general. Nothing peculiar in that, not much more peculiar in me than in any of you. As I said, I'm you. And then some. No, to me the real scandal is the scandal of sex as scandal, that adapted from the 'good' book by the missionary positioned father figure invoking the hired hostess to come clean! come clean!, fucking her up, mucking her up. No, there is no hypocrisy in doing such deals with such dirty little devils (except perhaps in the juxtaposition of accruing heavenly rewards for taking up such lowly positions). One knows one's part, one has learned one's lines and — when the director's out to lunch dreaming, scheming of casting yours truly couchant — one adds a little of one's own. And how does the director get to learn of these departures from the script? He doesn't, he doesn't. Listen, he doesn't listen. Not his job, but then I'm not his part, no longer his accessory to the crime, disposable on successful conclusion, that is his tale told with his roving eye of his obsessions detailed — detailed to remain in his eye, the public eye for as long as he, it! cares to dwell. No, I won't be typecast. Won't be cast. Won't be cast away.

So, I'm a hypocrite. We all are to a greater or lesser degree, but even I know in my heart of hearts that the tabloid media is the true pornography, the abiding lust affair, the thirst for vengeance that so becomes the pissed stained whore that has so unbecome this nation, this stand offish notion, so disappointingly transmutating into being substantially peopled by its insubstantial people, cruder stereotypes, so in danger of being crudely stereotyped by its people. Double standards? You want double standards: there is no cant in skin magazines. Bad art, yes!, granted; twisted visions, certainly; hypocrisy, no: pornography, massage parlours, prostitution, the hypocrisy comes with the denial. Slash the shrink wrap, even like Norman Bates did the shower curtain, and you will unveil, unleash less deceptive exploitation, less vested interest to depict stupid people as even stupider than they are, less charismatic evangelism inviting gross audience participation than in many other 'respectable' tabloidized media. Now *that's* pornography. And which, oh which!, of our characters are 'guilty' of indulging in these certainly venal, probably venial, certainly sins? All. Some more than others, that's all. You be the judge of them, that's your job in this whole affair. And of me? I need you to be the judge of me, too. Your verdict notwithstanding, what's left the likes of us? Me and Cheryl, Cheryl and I are presently establishing a post-feminist publisher called *Manbaiter Publications*. Got in, got our money, *earned* our money, got out. Been there, done this and that. Hated it, hated myself for it but, then, who hasn't been in a compromising position? And, while we're at it, was it entirely coincidental that *Boom Bros* went eyes agog and gloss when I, um, came on the scene? Our first book, my first book, this book, hold that 'Author! Author!' in just a bit, is out soon. The title, *Memoirs & Mememormees*. Mememormee?: Anna Livia Plurabelle as she prepares to meet her sea, the beautiful parting shot we all have in us, that combination of memories and 'remember me's. 'Till thousendsthee'. As Bill Hicks said, ' —— we've all got this fucking poem in us.' Memoirs?: that tacky genre beloved of magniloquent oiks whose monodimensional, dissembled at that, monomaniacal private lives are paraded as a manifesto for public morality that would shame a Tory whip (that, alack, we all imitate, but hallelujah!, badly, half-heartedly, as we poorly peddle our public personas), now suddenly revealed, publicised! (by their own hand!: conclusive proof that the pen is mightier than the sword!), oh!, horror of horrors!, as two trick ponies (fame and the avoidance of capture, that the notorious somehow manage as they part us with our hard earned), ghostwritten, ghost-ridden by the four horsemen of the apocalypse contorting themselves arse over backwards, bent double for our delectation (rallying cry: take us 'seriously or we're all going to die!' – laughing presumably), po-faced celebrity reveals hidden depths, scoop!, that money-for-old-rope-ladder-to-the-stars-which-we'd-dangle-to-the-rich-and-famous-were-we-up-there-and-they-down-here. Most of our lives get better, get done better by omission, by unwritten resipiscence, by not doing that which has previously offended: can our celebrities, our politicians say the same, or do they represent that state of unreality that wants, with but a hey! and a presto!, the world to be a better place? What may here appear as a memoir is nothing of the sort. Mememormee!, that's all, mememormee!

The follow up, based on the story of Cheryl and I, will be called *Joined up thinking and the importance of hair*. Joined up thinking? Well, wasn't a certain status conferred on one in one's schooldays, in one's innocence, on achieving joined up writing? Well then, writing is just joined up thinking; the title aims also to evoke a return to childhood, to innocence, to times before our public personas, our lifestyles, our jobs, for Christ's sake only our jobs, conspired to consume us faster than we could consume all the crap from all the other little crappers-out. (And, yes, I know I was unfair to David in allowing him no childhood, but then he never betrayed signs of a life previous, outside his adult self, his business self.)

Ah, the '80s: the decade in which all these jobsworth johnnies lucky enough to hold down important positions, 'unlucky' enough not to have lives, were ludicrously apotheosized while the rest were held down, shamefully damned. Yes, I know, I more than anyone know, every day, each and every day we all must fall between solipsism and the presentation of a plausible persona: vacuous status, empty celebrity being but the former writ LARGE!!! as the latter, in which self-awareness becomes a grotesque that can't tell a hawk from a handout. Nothing wrong with that, but — nothing right either. Nothing worth championing, not like the '80s wherein the cocooning husk of symbolic status and the empty shell of cracked celebrity ruled the roost, too pleased with theirselves by half, when we knew we were hatching a teratoid void, when we knew we would know what —— what? —— what we know now.

And what do we know now? We did it, Christ, we did it! A terrible realisation, but a realisation nonetheless. The travesty that was, *pace tanti viri* the Chingford Skinhead and gang that n to the nth rate decade misrepresented the multitude as a baying mob. But still they bawl!! — still they queue for tickets to their own undermining, these underlings cum hirelings of the media *Übermenschen* of the *Kulturkampf* to end all *Kulturkämpfe*. It's a terrible racket all round. Murdoch, Perot, Berlusconi, Saddler —— ah!, at last we name the guiltiest placemen — sorry, no, butlers — mere megalomaniacs peddling Utopia to democrats, with astonishing success — the pygmy darts in the body politic — and as we twitch with the remote control, the sad truth is that only the right-wing, the vindictive tendency striking out on its own from the family of man, can peddle Utopia to democrats — in the words of Barry McKenzie, 'You wouldn't read about it' — ah, will we never learn? — do we ever want to? — or do we just surrender the baton to these vigilante orchestrators of deregulated cacophony and sit back while they drum up the acoustic and logistic nonsense that is fascist chants over train station announcers' barely recognisable apologies for the unavoidable lateness of the much touted, the blind faith in the second coming of the never was; shall we dance to the tune of these jobsworth commandants, baton wielding at their orchestra of second fiddlers, or shall we fashion a little discord, a little dissent from within the ranks? At the risk of finger-pointing the moral, tragedy befalls belittled lives because they, their inhabitants, their tenants, don't face up to its inevitability. One would like to think that in such vainglorious, such narcissistic times we would have at least stumbled upon more recognizable images of self. *O tempora! O mores!* , oh boys! oh girls!, *O imitatores, servum pecus!* it doesn't have to be this way!

So! Farewell to all our fair brothers and sisters and, yes!, to one in particular, one I, accorded by some devious counterplot, one I, yes!, loved, damn it, loved! Not during nor before the first marriage – I told you I was mercenary – no, he was just a little boy with bags more money than sense then. But, during the second, having lost his mother, he needed me — and for a while I was compelled to return the compliment — he'd changed for the better — indeed, continued to grow, never, as so many men can, rejuvenesced for the worse — but — but, having made my pile, having more money and sense than I for one had ever had, I needed to take myself seriously, to be contemplated no more in rectilinear rectitude, in one-track, one-dimensional obsession.

Ah, farewell fair brother, you knew me when I was a nobody, a nobody. I trust my saving grace will be that so did I. And you? Oh, you were always a somebody, a somebody in my life, you or your like. Can you say that you knew who you were when you were a nobody, a nobody? Can you say who is nothing without who? Could you ever? Did you ever!